M.A. Avery

The Rebel General's Loyal Bride

A true picture of scenes in the late civil war

M.A. Avery

The Rebel General's Loyal Bride
A true picture of scenes in the late civil war

ISBN/EAN: 9783337412630

Printed in Europe, USA, Canada, Australia, Japan

Cover: Foto ©Andreas Hilbeck / pixelio.de

More available books at **www.hansebooks.com**

THE

REBEL GENERAL'S LOYAL BRIDE

A TRUE PICTURE OF

SCENES IN THE LATE CIVIL WAR.

By M. A. AVERY.

———•———

SPRINGFIELD, MASS.:

W. J. HOLLAND AND COMPANY.

1873.

CONTENTS.

I. — The Wedding at Hunter Hills 5

II. — Scheming. — Broken Bonds 24

III. — Family Jars. — The Elopement 44

IV. — The Rebel General. — The Proposal 62

V. — Bull Run. — The Overseer 81

VI. — The Guerillas. — Death of Major Hunter 99

VII. — Going to Camp. — The Brother's Danger 122

VIII. — The Brother's Escape. — Old Acquaintances . . . 141

IX. — Marriage of the Rebel General. — The Noble Work . 164

X. — Philip Atherton. — The General's Return . . . 182

XI. — The Abduction. — Catharine's Illness 196

XII. — An Old Admirer. — Riding in State 213

XIII. — The Overturn. — Early Love too Late 230

XIV. — Catharine in Libby Prison. — Released 254

XV. — No Home. — Again in Bonds 274

XVI. — Escaping. — The Field of Battle 294

XVII. — Theodore. — The Memorable Seven Days 315

XVIII. — The Rebel General. — Home at Last 326

XIX. — The Child's Rescue. — The General's Danger . . . 344

XX. — The Rivals. — Death of Philip Atherton 369

XXI. — Catharine's Mission. — The Rebel General's Death . 385

XXII. — Going Home. — The First Love at Last 398

3

THE
REBEL GENERAL'S LOYAL BRIDE.

CHAPTER I.

THE WEDDING AT HUNTER HILLS.

UPON the brow of one of the lower range of the Hunter Hills, in the Old Dominion, once stood a handsome stone mansion, that was noted for its large size and admirable proportions, and was the pride and glory of the surrounding country.

This grand old mansion, with its quaint turrets, gables, and cornices, was built in the old Colonial days, and baronial style, by a younger son of a prominent English nobleman, who came over to America at that time to seek that fame and fortune the laws of primogeniture denied him at home.

From its commanding position, this mansion overlooked a large extent of territory, and probably for that reason had been occupied as a fort in Revolutionary times, and the still earlier wars with the Indians.

The house had never passed out of the hands of the descendants of the family who reared it. And Major

Hunter, its representative and possessor in the year 1860, was quite as proud of "Hunter House" as he would have been of Windsor Castle or the palace at Versailles, had they belonged to him. It had spacious halls, parlors, and drawing-rooms, abundance of long galleries, kitchens, closets, pantries, and sleeping-rooms, with a great, roomy library. This was filled with choice books, costly pictures, beautiful statuary, and rich and rare carvings in black walnut and English oak, with antique furniture of the grandest description.

The treasured relics of past generations were in fact gathered at Hunter House; nor would their owner submit to the desire of his comparatively young and fashionable wife to have them replaced by modern improvements and inventions.

The house had fine out-buildings, handsome gardens and shrubberies, spacious orchards, and a long line of whitewashed slave-cabins in the rear; while thousands of acres of rich plantation and grazing lands, belonging to the same princely estate, surrounded it in every direction. A road crossed the grounds from east to west; though the house itself was more than a mile from either of the great northern and southern thoroughfares that crossed the country.

But, though Hunter House was somewhat isolated, the scenery around it was very beautiful, with its background of rocks and hills and magnificent forests, and its foreground of cultivated fields and (in their season) abundant harvests.

And so evidently thought the gay cavalcade of visitors who rode up towards the old mansion one fine afternoon during the Christmas holidays of 1860; talking of the ancient glories of the race who occupied it, and gazing upon the magnificent scenery. It was a gala-day at Hunter House, — one long to be remembered in the annals of the family; for sweet Lucy Hunter, the major's eldest, and indeed only daughter by a former marriage, was that day to become a bride.

Preparations commensurate with the wealth and cultivated taste of the family had been made in every department of the household for the pleasure and entertainment of a large number of guests, some of whom were to remain several days. The rooms were adorned with flowers and evergreens, the tables with the old family plate and china, as well as with every delicacy that could please the eye or gratify the taste. And the long lines of servants standing at every angle, ready to do the bidding of the guests, were evidently partaking of the general joy of the household. Major Hunter, a tall, portly, white-haired old gentleman of seventy, with keen gray eyes, a florid complexion, and decided Roman features, appeared to excellent advantage as a host that day; while his lady, a handsome, black-eyed woman of forty, was the very perfection of a hostess. Her friends, the Athertons, were all there; and, conspicuous among them, her brother, Col. Atherton, who had just returned from a two-years' residence in Europe. He, with his son and daughter, and Judge Tremont and his two daughters, the uncle and cousins of the bride, had fortunately been recalled from their European tour just in time to be present at the marriage. And most of the distinguished families in the county were there, as well as a good many from Richmond, and still more distant localities out of the State.

The hour fixed upon for the ceremony arrived at last: the chandeliers were lighted, and the guests were arranged to their satisfaction in the great drawing-room.

Mr. Harlowe, the aged clergyman, took his place, and all was eager expectation; when the band in the anteroom struck up a grand march, the drawing-room doors were opened with an extra flourish by Uncle Nick, a favorite slave, and the bridal party entered the room. They immediately took their places; and the solemn ceremony was performed that made James Hamilton and Lucy Hunter husband and wife.

They were not by any means a youthful pair: but, though more than thirty, the bride looked good and lovable in her white satin, orange-blossoms, and costly bridal veil; and the bridegroom, who evidently thought so, was one of the finest-looking men in the room.

The bridesmaids, too, in their ethereal white robes, with coronets of white roses, came in for their share of admiration.

But there was none among them all who excited greater attention than the lady who leaned upon the arm of Lloyd Hunter, the brother of the bride, who seemed to be a stranger to most of the company.

"What a splendid girl!"

"Who is she?"

"Which do you mean?"

"Why, the first bridesmaid of course," was echoed presently from lip to lip in a distant corner.

"I can tell you," said Mrs. Clyde, a proud, aristocratic-looking lady, with a scornfully-curling lip: "it is the governess! *Only* Mrs. Hunter's *Yankee governess.*"

"Why, Philip, as sure as the world, it is Catharine!" exclaimed Grace, the eldest of Judge Tremont's daughters, to Philip, her present cavalier, and the son of Col. Atherton.

"I believe you are right," he returned. "But where *did* she come from? I do wonder how she comes to be a favored guest in Aunt Jane's drawing-room!"

"And I wonder your aunt will permit such an exhibition of democracy, or that Lloyd Hunter will consent to exhibit himself in *such* a way at *such* a time!" echoed Mrs. Clyde. "I assure you, Mr. Atherton, that neither *my daughters* nor *I* have taken much pains to cultivate that girl's acquaintance."

"Of course not," said Philip dryly. "Yet I assure you, Mrs. Clyde, that we all used to do it when we were at school up in New England, — Lloyd among the number. He and Grace and Nell and I boarded two whole years in her mother's family."

"*That*, then, explains it, — an old flame of his, I suppose."

"Yes: but one we thought burnt out long ago," echoed Nell, the sister of Philip Atherton.

"Don't be ungenerous, Nell. Catharine Hale was a noble girl; and I, for one, shall be delighted to see her," said Grace Tremont.

"Ay! but wasn't her brother Theodore nobler, and wouldn't you be glad to see him?" Nell returned sarcastically.

"I certainly should be glad to see the whole family," said Grace with a conscious flush. "But come, they are congratulating: let's go and see Kate too."

"*You* can go, if you like," said Nell. "I am in no hurry to look up the Yankee governess, or any of her plebeian relations."

"Why, Nell! Have you forgotten, that, but for The-

odore, Harry, and Jim Hooker, we should once all have
been drowned ? that, but for Theodore, *I* should have
gone over the cliff, and been dashed upon the rocks
below ? Whatever misconstructions came afterwards, I,
for one, can never forget what I owe to Mrs. Hale's
family. You can scorn her if you like ; but *I* shall do
no such thing ! " and she tossed her bright golden curls
defiantly at both.

Philip laughed, yet not very joyously ; for he was
now a suitor for the hand of Grace Tremont, with the
full knowledge that she had once, when they were all at
a celebrated Northern classical school together, six years
ago, cared much more for Theodore Hale than himself ;
and he also knew how much he had then thought of
Catharine, the fair Yankee governess. As he had said,
for two years they had lived under the same roof, and
eaten at the same table. They had studied in the same
classes at school, been rivals for its honors, and not
always generous ones. They had played the same
games, sung the same glorious harmonies, and rode
and walked and rambled over the New-England hills
and valleys together, in search of nuts and berries and
fish and game.

And this intimate acquaintance, overcoming strong
prejudice, culminated in strong attachments, but ended,
through some mysterious means, in doubt, misconstruction, and disappointment. They were mere school boys
and girls together then, full of youth's bright hopes
and dreams, crude fancies and unformed plans, — living
in the present, and comparatively careless of the future.
Now they were men and women, meeting for the first
time upon a new arena ; where, though they knew it not,
they were about to become actors in some of the

grandest yet most terrible scenes of a nation's history.

The meeting between Grace and Catharine was indeed a joyful one, for they had loved each other fondly
and truly; and later in the evening, when the elegant
supper was over, they had a long and to them deeply-
interesting conversation. It was interrupted by Lloyd
Hunter at last, who said, as he and Philip came up to
where they were standing, —

"Ah, Catharine! I have been looking for you everywhere. They are getting ready for dancing; and I
believe you promised me the first set."

"Yes," she replied; "and I am ready, if Grace will
excuse me." She did of course.

Lloyd took her hand, and marched away with a step
as light as air, his hopes were so buoyant, and with a
glance at his fair companion that spoke volumes of love
and trust and admiration.

"Do you see that, Philip?" said Grace familiarly,
after watching them a moment.

"Of course I do. And Kate has improved wonderfully; hasn't she? She is really beautiful; and Lloyd
evidently thinks so. You know he always had a fancy
that way. Can it be, that, in spite of his pride, he is
really going to marry her?"

"I hope so, for I always liked her; and I don't know
her superior anywhere. But won't Nell fume?"

"Why?"

"Do you need to be told, you stupid fellow, that Nell,
in spite of her shabby treatment of him in Paris, has
come home determined to win him back to his allegiance?"

"I suspect she has thought of it. But she was a fool

to break off with him in the first place. Lloyd is a
noble fellow, and worth all the Count Larois in the
universe."

"So I think. But Nell deserves to lose him for
playing such a double game."

"She always plays a double game; didn't you know
it? But what matters that, if it is only the winning
one?"

"I don't know: I like an open, honest deal far
better."

"Then, why will you not give me one, dear Grace,
and make me supremely happy by setting an early day
for our marriage?"

"Because I want my freedom a little longer," said
Grace, laughing and blushing.

"But won't you be just as free as my wife? There'll
be no crusty *old people* to look after you *then*."

"But there would be a young one, who might be more
tyrannical."

"You know me too well to believe that, Grace. You
have kept me waiting for years, but do have some pity
upon my lonely condition now," said he pleadingly.

"I think you, as well as myself, have been quite satisfied with your freedom till now. And, if you could have
suited yourself better, you know you have always had the
privilege."

"Well, I will own that our conditional engagement
has hitherto suited me far better than to have felt myself tied hand and foot. But now that we have seen a
little of the world, and our travels are over, we ought
to marry, and settle down at home, contented and happy
for the rest of our lives."

"Contented, with every thing and everybody in a

turmoil! Don't you see that every thing is getting into
a whirlpool here? and don't I know that *you* have come
home on purpose to put your foot in it? Don't talk to
me about marrying, Philip, till we can see what it's all
coming to."

"Then you may have to wait till doomsday," said
Philip angrily. "These troublesome elements of which
you speak have been boiling over for years; and there
is little prospect of their resting very soon.

"There, the music has struck up; and it's time for
us to go. We will talk over this subject another time."

Grace was half angry, and had a great mind to refuse; but, seeing Major Hunter and Col. Atherton coming towards them, she took Philip's arm, and walked
away without more ado.

"You are an elegant dancer, Atherton: why don't
you look you up a partner, and join them?" said the
major suggestively to his friend.

"I am in no hurry: I may do so by and by," was
the reply.

"Come, then: we will go and look on a while."

So they went out into the hall, where the sets were
forming, stationed themselves in a retired window-seat,
and began their observations. The dancing commenced
very soon; and for a time both gentlemen silently watched
the performances.

"You have seen, and taken part in, a great deal of
this kind of amusement in Europe, I suppose, colonel,"
said the major at last.

"Yes: especially in Paris, where it is cultivated to
perfection. Our young people took lessons there, you
remember. You can see now whether they profited by
them," returned the colonel.

2

"Ah! they do dance beautifully, and especially Nell. She glides over the floor like a sylph. She always did do every thing that she undertook ingeniously; and she is really beautiful."

"Yes: but she made one awkward blunder when she broke off her engagement with Lloyd. I wanted to express to you my deep regret for that occurrence, which, I am quite sure, she is heartily ashamed of and sorry for. She thought she was playing off a harmless piece of coquetry, as silly girls too often do, and did not dream of serious consequences, — consequences that might, I think, have been prevented, had I known the truth previous to his departure from Paris."

"You cannot regret them more than I did at first, Atherton; nor could I believe it until assured by Lloyd of the truth. He blamed her, of course; but you know, better than I, whether the blame ought equally to rest upon him."

"No: I do not blame him; and yet I can but wish that he had had a little more patience with her folly."

"Well, after all, colonel, there seems to be a kind of fate or fore-ordination about these things. It seems in vain for us to try to have them all our own way. Nor is it best perhaps that we should. As an instance of this, there, now, is Lucy, who looks so proud and happy to-night, and at least ten years younger than she did six months ago. Sixteen years ago I refused her hand to that noble-looking man, — whom I am now proud to acknowledge as my son-in-law, — for no other reason than that he was unable to support her in the style to which she had been accustomed. He went off to Kentucky to seek his fortune, and wear away his disappointment; while she pined and faded at home, like a lily

with a broken stem. She would marry no one else, as I
wished, because of the old Hunter blood in her veins,
which, you know, when pure, is constant, and true as
steel. Last summer we took her to the Springs; and
there, to her surprise and our own, we found Hamilton,
now a noble and successful man, on his way to see her
once more. The *dénoûment* you can see for yourself;
and I shall bear it in my mind as a lesson for evermore."

"Well, I suppose we do look too much at hereditary
and mercenary distinctions here in Virginia. Our descent from the old chevaliers and English nobles leads
us to that. And the gold we need to keep up our aristocratic dignity leads some of us to make unhappy marriages, as you well know."

"Yes, indeed. But to return to my own family.
There, now, is Lloyd : he don't look much like a disappointed invalid ; does he ? Well, we all, I suppose, considered him and Nell as good as married when they
went off to Europe. But they get to Paris, that high
school for all kinds of deviltry, — get mad and jealous,
have a little tiff, and off he flies to Germany. He gets
ill, either from disappointment or eating their abomi-
nable Dutch cookery ; and home he comes, sick, hopeless, desponding, and, I suspect, hypochondriacal, —
thinking he had come home to die. His letters had
miscarried, so we knew nothing of his coming ; and,
when he arrived, we were away at the Springs. But
we had left the children at home with Miss Hale, our
admirable governess; so, in our places, he found, to
his surprise and her own, the very girl he had loved
in their earlier days, when they roamed over the New-
England hills together. They had parted in doubt
and misconstruction, it seems; and for a time they

avoided each other: but the old magnetic attraction brought them together at last; and the old love has triumphed."

"Indeed!" and Col. Atherton's countenance betrayed his surprise and disappointment. He knew now that his own labor was lost in trying to pave the way to Lloyd's reconciliation with Nell.

"Yes," continued the major; "and, strangely enough, Jane and I — blind instruments in the hands of a higher power perhaps — had brought it all about ourselves. Our governess left us about the time you went to Europe. We wanted another; and, hearing of this Miss Hale, — of her remarkable talent for teaching, and that she had finished her engagement with the Masons, who were about to leave the country, — we took a ride of twenty miles to intercept her journey home. By tempting offers, we succeeded in securing her services, and at once brought her home with us. By her correct deportment and many endearing qualities, she won our regard as no governess had ever done before. Afterwards, when we all came down with the fever, and the servants were frightened half out of their senses, and the neighbors dared not come near us, I have no doubt but that she saved all our lives, by her calm courage in the hour of danger, her firmness in managing the servants, and that tender, protecting care, that surrounded us day and night with all a sister's or daughter's watchful solicitude. Could we be otherwise than grateful? She took the disease from us, and came near forfeiting her life to her philanthropy. But she has a good constitution, and recovered very soon. She has ever since seemed like one of our own family, — as dear almost as Lucy herself. What, then, could I say, when we came

home last summer, found Lloyd here, and was told by
him, that, in spite of his affair with Nell, he had loved
Catharine always; that their estrangement had cast a
dark shadow over his life; and, now that it was dissipated, he wanted my consent to make her his wife?
What indeed could I say, but that we all loved her, owed
her a deep debt of gratitude, and, if she cared for him, I
would not be the one to stand in his way? I think my
experience with Lucy made me a little more lenient than
I otherwise should have been. Yet, after all my condescension, he had hard work to get her consent, she was so
strongly opposed to slavery; and it took me — proud old
aristocrat as they call me — to convince a poor Yankee
governess that she could do more good by becoming my
son's wife, and the lenient mistress of hundreds of
slaves, than in any other way; so she yielded the point
at last."

"But do you know any thing of her family?"

"Oh, yes! Lucy, who, you know, was educated in New
England before the others went there, also boarded in
her mother's family. Though not rich, she says they are
highly respectable, and that Mrs. Hale, who is a widow,
is a sensible, noble-souled Christian woman, who was
then making the most energetic and persevering efforts
to educate and bring up her family respectably. There
were four of the children: Theodore, who was about the
age of Lloyd and Philip, won the valedictory, both in
school and college, and is now studying law; while
Harry, the younger brother, is in the engineering service.
We see for ourselves what Catharine is; and Lucy, who
loved her as a child, is quite ready to receive her as a
sister. She says, too, that Jessie, the pet of the flock,
who is about to marry a young Dr. Morven, was the

2*

sweetest and loveliest child she ever saw. But, if all the
rest of us are well enough suited, Jane is not; and,
though she says little, I can see that she thinks Lloyd
is making a sad *mésalliance*. She says Lloyd is
blinded, and that I am old and childish, or I would
never have given my consent. Perhaps I am; but
somehow, of late, true love seems more precious to
me than gold, or all merely worldly distinctions. I
value personal qualifications, too, a great deal higher
than I did; and I think there are few to be compared
with our Catharine in mind or person. She is going
home in June; and in the autumn Lloyd intends to
bring her back as his bride. I tell you all this in confidence, colonel; for as yet no one knows it out of our
family: and I prefer it should not be known. I would
like to have you become acquainted with her, so as to
see if your opinion will not justify Lloyd's choice."

"It does already, so far as the eyesight is concerned,"
said the colonel, smiling at the old gentleman's confi-
dences, yet not with the satisfaction he would have felt,
had that choice been a different one. " She is certainly
beautiful. She has a splendid form; and no lady on
this floor queens it with quite so royal a grace," he
continued.

"Ay! Queen Elizabeth, Victoria, or even the fair
Eugenia herself, ain't a touch to her, in my opinion; and
I'm a pretty good judge of women. If I was forty
years younger, and a single man, I think the lucky dog
would have a rival, and a persevering one too;" and
the old major laughed merrily over the idea. "What say
you, colonel? Shall I introduce you when this dance
is over, and secure her for your first partner?"

"As you please. She is probably engaged;" and his

eyes followed her admiringly, as Lloyd led her to a seat.

"Come, then; we will see;" and, advancing at once, the major presented his friend and brother, Col. Atherton.

Of course Catharine was pleased to receive such thoughtful attention from the father of her affianced husband; but, when she looked up to meet the gaze of Col. Atherton's dark, magnetic eyes, she felt a tremor of the nerves for which she could not account, and received the introduction with unusual embarrassment. She had never seen Col. Atherton before; and, though somewhat prejudiced against him, as the father of Nell and Philip, whom she had long ago had reason for distrusting, was particularly, and not unfavorably, impressed by his appearance.

He was tall and commanding in person, courteous and gentlemanly in manners, easy and polished in his address, and with a peculiar tact in conversation that set Catharine at her ease when he once began to address her.

He asked her hand for the dance; and, though much surprised, she accorded it, and continued conversing with him, upon different topics, until they were ready to begin.

She rather liked him, upon the whole, and was not sorry she had accepted him for a partner when Philip, too, came to ask her; and she was rather amused than otherwise at Philip's suspicious glance at him when he left them together.

In music and dancing and song, and games of various kinds, the evening passed delightfully away. The elderly ladies discussed fashions, etiquette, their children, servants, and domestic matters generally; while the gentlemen talked of foreign affairs, as well as dogs and horses, negroes and crops; but, more than all, of *Secession*, which was beginning, just then, to agitate the heart, and unsettle the brain, of Old Virginia.

It was known throughout the house that South Carolina had seceded from the Union but a few days previous. Before the evening was over, a note was brought to Major Hunter, from Gov. Letcher, excusing his non-attendance, on the plea of urgent business; and saying, informally, that he was about to call a convention relative to joining the proposed Southern Confederacy, and taking Virginia out of the Union.

"Take Virginia out of the Union!" exclaimed the major indignantly, as he read it. "Why, it is rank treason to talk of it, much more to act upon it. I advise you all to have nothing to do with it, gentlemen. I have fought too long under the glorious old banner of the stars to consent to see it trailing in the dust."

"Better trample upon a soiled old banner than the brave hearts of our Southern people. They have borne *that* from the cowardly North long enough, in my estimation," said a bystander.

"When, where, and how?" demanded the major with flashing eyes and excited tones.

"In Congress and out of it; at home and abroad; in city and country; at hotels, and in steamboats and rail-cars, — everywhere, in fact, where Northern and Southern people come together, we have to hear their eternal abolition howling."

"Would it be less, were we, like a rotten branch, severed from the glorious old Union tree?"

"Yes: for then we would have nothing to do with them."

"Ah! but, if we had nothing to do with them, who would manufacture our clothing? and where would be the market for our cotton, tobacco, and cane?"

."In Europe, where we could find perfection in manufactures, equals for associates, and friends who would be true to us."

"And where they despise our peculiar institutions much more than they do in New England," said the major excitedly; "where they consider slavery the most horrible crime on earth, and a slave-breeder worthy of the hottest berth in hell."

"Father! father! this is not the place for *such* discussions," whispered Lucy anxiously at that moment. "Pray remember what is due to our guests!"

"Yes, yes: all in good time, my daughter," said he impatiently. "I am an old man, of full threescore and ten. I have seen a great deal of the world. I may not live long. And there may never come a better time for me to tell these gentlemen, that, if they touch this red-hot pitch of secession, they will get their fingers burned. I know that the spirit of it is burning in their hearts: I see it flashing from their eyes. It needs but a spark to kindle it into a flame. Once kindled, all the water in the Potomac could not quench it. Water! It must be blood! Rivers of that will flow, if Virginia joins in this hot-headed conspiracy against the government."

"Little fear of that, major, — little fear of that," said his opponent. "The Yankees will boast and brag and cheat and bluster; but, when it comes to *blows*, they are all cowards, and will stuff their lying mouths with cotton, and run like a pack of whipped hounds."

"I know you all think so," returned the major; "but you'll find yourselves mistaken; for I have fought beside Northern troops long enough to know what stuff they're made of. Though not quite as ready as we are to rush into a fray, their courage is quite equal to, and their endurance far greater than our own. Toughened, many of them, by hard labor, they have nerves like steel; while we of the better class are, some of us, enervated by a life of luxury. You may frown, gentlemen; but you know that it is the truth: and you deceive yourselves when you think such men will not fight till their last breath to prevent the downfall of this republic, and the dissolution of the Union."

"Let 'em fight, then," said his opponent doggedly. "If it comes to blows, we'll whip 'em within an inch of their lives, and string that renegade Southerner, Lincoln, up on a gallows higher than Haman's, in a fortnight."

"Don't you believe that," said the old man solemnly. "Those bloody-minded seceding States at the South of us, thinking just as you do, are but waiting for the countenance of old Virginia to commence the strife, and march on to the Capitol; considering its treasures and rich spoils an easy prey. But remember what I tell you, gentlemen: if Virginia does this thing, it is at a fearful price, — the price of blood, — the blood of her best, her bravest, and her noblest sons, — and the desolation of her fairest fields, forests, and homesteads. For here would they all congregate, — from east and west, north and south, — because it is a central point, and near to the Capitol; and here would be some of the bloodiest battle-grounds of the Union. Here brother would meet, and war with brother, and father against son; destroying every human and fraternal tie that binds us to our nation and our race: and bitterly would

we rue the day when we joined in so unholy an alli-
ance!"

As he uttered these words, which, though few there
believed them then, have since proved so prophetic,
the white-haired, noble old man's face grew pale with
emotion ; his wide-open eyes fixed themselves on vacancy, with a deep, far-reaching expression, as if he
were looking off into the distant future, and, with a
solemn prescience, beholding the bloody scenes since
recorded upon history's pages, — in one of which he
was destined to become a victim.

So different did he seem from the jovial, garrulous,
and somewhat childish old man of the past few hours,
that many were particularly struck by the change; and
though still disbelieving his opinions, and sure of the
truth of their own convictions, they thought it best to
let the subject drop.

As it was getting late, most of the guests soon afterwards bade adieu to their entertainers and the bridal
party, and the company dispersed.

CHAPTER II

SCHEMING. — BROKEN BONDS.

MONG the guests who were invited to spend the week at Hunter House were the Athertons and Tremonts, who, as we have already said, were near connections of the Hunter family.

Having been separated so long, by the absence of the two former families in Europe, they of course had a great many things to talk over; though the Athertons were as yet a little careful about displaying their strong secession proclivities. For Grace Tremont and Helen, her half-sister, and Lloyd Hunter and his sister Lucy, had inherited large fortunes from an uncle of theirs, who was the judge's only brother, as Lloyd's mother had been his only sister. And knowing all this, and knowing, too, the loyalty of the two families, the Athertons had thought it advisable to secure this wealth, if possible, before fully and finally and openly announcing their determination to join the secession party.

So Miss Nellie Atherton, who knew of his engagement, from her aunt, did her best, in the succeeding days, to excuse her conduct in Paris, and win Lloyd Hunter back to his allegiance. And Philip took this last opportunity for daily intercourse to urge Grace

24

Tremont to fulfil a partial and long-standing engagement by an immediate marriage. He pleaded, urged, reasoned, and entreated, but all in vain; and at last he got so angry, that he would not speak to her for several days. Then he was all attention to Catharine, Nettie Clyde, and Bess Hamilton; and, being remarkably handsome, polished, and captivating, made his attentions to the two latter very acceptable. But Catharine distrusted, and was shy of him. By a mutual understanding, she and Lloyd, though sufficiently polite, avoided each other, not caring just yet to publish their engagement; yet, because they were engaged, careful about encouraging the attentions of others. Yet Catharine appeared to great advantage in the days following the bridal; winning golden opinions by her rare musical and mental gifts, and disarming by her unobtrusiveness some who were inclined to be intolerant.

Miss Atherton, however, took pains to make it pretty evident that *she* considered her beneath her notice, and especially after trying in vain to win Lloyd back. It maddened her to see the eager flush come over his cheek, and the love-light in his eyes, when Catharine came near him, and compare it with the indifference with which he evidently regarded her. She flirted desperately with Harry Clyde and Hugh Carrol, old admirers of hers; while Philip did the same with Bess and Nettie: but it was all of no use, so far as winning Lloyd back was concerned, or driving Grace from her defensive position.

But, notwithstanding these and a good many other little by-plays, every thing seemed to go on merrily; and every effort was made by the generous and truly hospitable family to amuse and entertain their guests.

3

The weather had been fine for the last of December; and there had been innumerable walks and drives to view the varied and beautiful scenery around the Hunter Hills, with athletic games, and shooting excursions out of doors, and gentler sports within, such as music, dancing, amateur theatricals, and tableaux.

The gentlemen had discussed farming, politics, law, theology, and secession; and the ladies domestic affairs until they were tired, and it was decided unanimously that their own required them at home. The evening before their departure, and the breaking-up of the party, Lloyd Hunter went down to the slave-cabins for something, and was returning to the mansion, when he came across Philip Atherton going the same way as himself.

There had been a great friendship between these young men in days past and gone, even though they were opposites in character. But since their return from Europe, and Lloyd's engagement to Catharine, a coldness and distance had grown up between them, that it was no easy matter to get over. During the last day or two, however, they had had considerable debate upon the all-absorbing topic of secession; and now it was renewed again. They entered the garden by a little wicket, to shorten the distance to the mansion, and walked up towards the fountain. Becoming earnest and excited in their discussion, they sat down upon a garden-seat, deeply shadowed by evergreens, and at once went into the subject as they had never done before.

For, angry with Grace and her father, and tired of concealment, Philip had resolved to throw off the mask, and, if he could, win Lloyd over to the ranks of secession.

In spite of his father's contrary opinions, Lloyd believed, like multitudes of other young Southerners, in
the right of a State to secede, and have an independent
government, and that it was the duty of every good
citizen to uphold her in that right, if a majority of her
people so decided.   But he did not think it politic or
wise to do so at that time ; that any of the States had
as yet any just cause for doing so ; or that they could at
all sustain themselves if they did.

Philip, however, thought secession not only just and
right, but that Lincoln's election, which had shorn the
South of her power, and of course endangered slavery,
had made it absolutely necessary for her to throw off the
galling chain that had bound her too long to a Union
that oppressed her, and had no sympathy for her peculiar
institutions.   He believed, too, that, united in one, the
South could abundantly sustain herself against all the
power that could be brought to bear upon her by the
Federal government.

As the sun went down in a flood of golden glory, and
the soft, wintry twilight fell around them, the two young
men eagerly continued their discussion, each bringing
his best arguments to bear upon the case, to convince, if
possible, his sturdy opponent.

Suddenly they were startled by the sound of low,
sweet-toned female voices, apparently quite as eager in
debate as their own ; and then a couple of female figures
came sauntering slowly down towards the fountain, near
which they were stationed.   With an exclamation of
impatience, Philip paused in the middle of a sentence ;
and both were silent in the hope that the intruders
would pass on.   Instead of this, however, they stepped
up to the fountain, and, turning their faces to the light,

Lloyd saw that it was Miss Nellie Atherton and her pretty quadroon attendant, Jett, who had been her waiting-maid during her stay in Europe, and also when she was at school years before in New England.

The fountain was covered in frost-work and glittering icicles; and, as their animated discussion went on, Nell began whipping them off with a willow twig she held in her white, jewelled hand.

"I say, miss, you'll be sorry if you don't," said the slave-girl eagerly.

"I expect to be," Nell returned; "yet I can't bring myself to the point of doing what a sense of right and truth and justice demands."

"Or let me do it?"

"Or let you do it, for that would be just the same as doing it myself."

"But Jett thinks it too bad to let sich a grand family as the Hunters — your own aunt's family too — be so awfully imposed upon by that good-for-nothing Yankee trollop. And Massa Lloyd sich a fine, handsome young gentleman, too, and the biggest match in all the country."

Lloyd, out of politeness, had risen from his seat, and was just about stepping forward to make his presence known, when these words smote upon his ear with the force of a blow. It levelled him at once, in his descent unconsciously grasping Philip's arm, and holding him like a vise, when he was apparently trying to rise and rush forward.

"I know it's too bad," echoed Miss Nellie; "but what can I do? I commanded you to be silent when we discovered her shameful intrigues and midnight meetings with Dr. Morven, more than six years ago. And, when I knew that Philip found it out, I swore him to secrecy.

He was very ready to do this, because he was so bewitched about that silly little flirt, Jessie. For her sake
he wished to save the honor of the family. Philip
thought Lloyd had discovered the intrigue himself, and
that the discovery was the reason he left her as he did,
after paying her so much attention. But, if so, I can't
imagine by what *hocus pocus* she has got round him at
last. I wouldn't let you tell of it when we got home,
because I didn't want people to know that we had associated so long with so vile a creature."

"Jett knows all that; and, if the girl stay to home,
where she belongs, nobody care. She good nuff for them
abolishum fellers. But, when she cum down here to
trap fine Virginny gentlemans, she think it alter the case,
and miss orter tell."

"O Jett! you know well enough why I cannot; if I
had not myself loved Lloyd Hunter; if I had not been
engaged to him; if I had not lost him by my own
thoughtless folly, sacrificing the whole happiness of my
life for the pleasure of flirting with one I despised and
scorned," she passionately exclaimed, — "then Lloyd
Hunter should know the truth; and " —

"Hold! Stop, Nell, for God's sake!" gasped Philip,
as if just recovering from a trance of surprise, and
seized with a sudden fear of Nell's exposing to Lloyd
Hunter the hidden secrets of her heart.

And Nell, with a little shriek of wounded delicacy,
turned towards them for an instant, and then, followed
by her sable attendant, ran swiftly towards the mansion.

It was indeed a well-acted performance. And who,
in Lloyd's place, would have dreamed that it had all been
rehearsed, not an hour before, in Miss Nellie Atherton's
chamber. ,

3*

To describe the feelings of Lloyd Hunter, as, with a face turning to a deadly white, he listened to those damning words, would be impossible. Nor did he know, till the treacherous Philip cried out with pain, how tightly he was grasping him.

For several minutes after Nell was gone, Lloyd sat still as death: then, turning fiercely to Philip, he said, —

"Philip Atherton, was that — that the truth?"

"I fear so," returned Philip in a deprecating tone.

"But did you know it to be a fact?"

"Did you not know it *yourself*, Lloyd Hunter?"

"Alas! yes, — at least by circumstantial evidence."

"And that was the reason you left her, without an explanation or one kindly word, more than six years ago?"

"Yes: that is the truth," groaned Lloyd. "I found a note, addressed to *him*, and signed by *her name*, appointing a midnight meeting; and, at the hour named, I saw some one wrapped in her shawl go to the summerhouse, and there meet a man who came in from the adjoining grounds."

"Well, what more do you want? And how did you get over *that?*"

"Oh! she looked so innocent, and acted so nobly, and I loved her so well, that I was ready to believe her assertion that it was all a vile plot and forgery, got up by some enemy to ruin her in my esteem."

"And now that you know others saw it too, night after night?"

"Oh! I must renounce her, if it breaks my heart."

"Ah! hearts are not so easily broken. I thought mine would break, when I found, years ago, that sweet little Jessie was no better than she should be; but it didn't: and I guess you will survive, if you do step out of the siren's snare. I believe we were all bewitched in those days, and saw every thing through magnifying-glasses, — Grace as well as the rest of us. She seems perfectly fascinated by Kate still, and is thinking of Theo, I fancy. But she had better look out how she plays high games with me now; for I will not bear them."

The two young men continued to converse for some time upon the same old subjects, — Philip fully substantiating every vile assertion regarding poor Catharine by numerous facts that had come to his own private knowledge at the time of their occurrence, and bringing such a weight of corroborative evidence to prove them, that Lloyd could doubt no longer.

To believe, brought with it the keen agony of separation, the bitter necessity of renouncing one who had become dear as his life to him ; and, with such a multitude of facts staring him in the face, how could he disbelieve ?

It maddened him, too, to think what a dupe he had been ; and Nell's confession of love for him, and forbearing nobleness, in comparison with Catharine's falsehood and deception, raised her at once far higher in his esteem than she had ever been before.

The suspicion that there was any plot or complicity between Nell and Philip, though it occurred to him, seemed disproved by all the attending circumstances; for he had overtaken Philip a long way from the mansion, and going towards it ; while the others were coming directly from it.

Silly fellow! As if Philip had not been sent out on purpose to be waylaid, so as to bring his victim into the toils, and, when it was all over, returned triumphant to report his complete success.

For having been born of, and reared by, a proud, scheming, irreligious mother, — to say nothing of the father, — intrigue was the breath of life to both Nell and Philip Atherton; and, to the few who knew it, it was a sad drawback to the beauty, graces, talents, and accomplishments every one allowed them to possess in a very high degree.

Catharine noticed during the evening that Lloyd watched her furtively, but never once came near or spoke to her; and she felt that something had gone wrong. But her true heart did not take the alarm until she heard the announcement, that he had decided to leave next day with the party who were going to Richmond, — including the Tremonts and Athertons. He had said never a word to her of such a plan; so the news came over her like a shock. She felt instinctively that something had happened to alienate him, and that it was to avoid her that he was leaving his home at this time.

She had feared some such thing from the hour of Nellie Atherton's arrival, and persevering attempts to ignore and put her down as far as she could. She had felt, years ago, as if the mystery of Lloyd's alienation pointed to Nell, more than any one else, for its solution. And the almost certain knowledge, that, in the school-rivalries of other days, Nell had procured and destroyed a fine composition of hers, upon which a handsome prize depended, assured her that she would do almost any thing to carry out her plans. She had herself, by chance, found the remains of the burned composition behind the fire-board in Nell's room; secretly and indignantly rewritten it at the last moment; and, most unexpectedly to Nell, won the first prize. And for this she felt as if that young lady had never forgiven her, even though no one knew it but themselves.

That was a sleepless night to both Lloyd and Catharine; and both looked pale and wretched enough at the breakfast-table next morning.

When the meal was over, as had been previously arranged, the carriages were ordered, and amid smiles and tears, kisses and fond embraces, the farewells were spoken, the bride bade adieu to her early home, and the bridal party broke up.

Amid the general bustle, no one but herself noticed that Lloyd said never a word to his betrothed, and that his only farewell was a cold parting clasp of a hand that left within her own his letter of renunciation. She took it, with a pale cheek, quivering lip, foreboding heart, and questioning glance, that had in it a world of appealing tenderness; and, with trembling fingers, she transferred it to her pocket, and turned away to hide the gathering storm of tears until the guests had departed.

Once alone in her room, the restraints were thrown off, and she wept long and bitterly, with such a feeling of loneliness and desolation as had never come to her before.

She had forgotten to lock her door; and, in the midst of her trouble, a dark form glided in, and a hand that seemed just like her mother's was laid upon her bowed head, and began smoothing her soft, shining auburn hair.

She raised her tear-stained face, and seeing that it was Aunt Dinah, the kind old slave-nurse and housekeeper, exclaimed almost angrily, "Why are you here?" for she was ashamed to have even a slave witness her weakness and humiliation. "Don't, don't!" said Dinah deprecatingly and pityingly. "Dinah see an' hear it all, goin' up an' down; an' she sorry, dreful sorry. She know it all wrong somewhere."

"Pray don't speak of it, Dinah," Catharine implored.

"Neber you fear. Mebbe it all come right bimeby. Any way, ole Dinah know, dat, if Miss Kate mean right and act right herself, de good Fader can cure de pain; an' he on'y can. He know all about it. He can make it come right if Miss Kate on'y ask him."

"Thank you, Dinah. I, a professing Christian, ought to know it too. Now go, please," she sobbed.

Dinah silently left the room; and Catharine, awed, reproved, and yet doubting God's goodness, knelt down, and offered up a fervent prayer for help and guidance. And she did rise up comforted, and strengthened for whatever trials were before her, and gathered courage to open Lloyd's letter, the purport of which she had already guessed : —

"O wretched girl!" it began, "was it not enough that you had darkened six of the best years of my life with bitter memories, that you must come here to my own home to renew your enchantments, deceive me to my ruin, and wreck my peace of mind forever? Oh! must I believe that fair face is but a decoy to the innocent and the unwary; that graceful form but a whited sepulchre, — a tomb of lost innocence; those eyes, through which I thought a pure soul looked forth, but lures to entrap ignorant dupes to their undoing? You thought, no doubt, that no one here would ever find out your true character; but, in spite of all your precautions, the truth has followed, — proofs of your infamy that it is impossible to disbelieve. As a consequence, *here* and *now* I renounce all claim to your hand.

"If you are mercenary enough to want pay for our broken engagement, the law would perhaps give it you. But I, without that intervention, will give you any reasonable sum you may demand, rather than link my fortunes with those of one whom every principle of honor teaches me to despise and scorn.

"I have not informed my family of what has transpired, and cannot do it at present. As I am going to Richmond, you can do as you like about leaving, or spreading reports that would only disgrace yourself while you remain in the Southern country.

"But for the shame to us all in proclaiming the truth, I would not have my young brother and sisters under your care another day. But, just now, I can't bear to have my best friends know how shamefully I have been imposed upon. I beg that you will remember that God will require an account of your stewardship, and that you will do them no harm. May you repent of your misdeeds! and oh, may you never know the bitter agony that wrings my heart in bidding you an eternal farewell

"L. H."

Catharine's tears blinded her as she read this outpouring of a noble heart, that she knew felt itself cruelly deceived and wronged.

But, though his accusations wrung her own soul quite as cruelly, she could not blame him as she would have done, had she not believed some enemy was at the bottom of the whole affair.

But, sustained by her own conscious innocence, and

the hope of help from on high, her mind at last became tranquillized. She would not leave her position, or fly from the country like the guilty thing he thought her, unless obliged to do so, she told Lloyd Hunter in her reply; and that she would be glad to stand face to face with her accusers. They had undoubtedly some strong motive that would appear in the end for defaming one who was utterly incapable of lowering herself to any thing that was immoral or infamous. God, who knew all hearts, would, no doubt, make the truth manifest, and support her through the bitter trial, she added.

She neither expected nor received any reply to this letter; so, burying proudly the memory of her wrong in her own bosom, she began once more her usual round of duties.

Long before the wedding at Hunter Hills, the monotonous mutterings of secession and discontent had been heard throughout our land, like the roll of distant thunder. Soon afterwards, like the play of forked lightnings, could be seen the fitful flashes of a strife that was soon to be hot and deadly; threatening the disruption of all ties of interest and affection, as well as those more enduring ones that bind the States together in one nation.

Yet few of us at that time realized the imminent danger. Scarcely any one dreamed that this was but the prelude to an earthquake shock that was to upheave existing institutions, convulse a continent, disturb the commercial and financial relations of a world, and bring distress and ruin, not only to multitudes of our own people, but also to many in distant regions of the globe. But, after the time of which we have spoken, began a new phase, not only in the history of those old Virginia families, but also of the State and the whole nation.

The feeling for and against secession every day grew stronger and stronger. As the people began to take sides, many who were near relations, or had been dear and tried friends, found themselves in opposite ranks; and very soon, by the mere force of circumstances, they became mortal enemies, — ready to appeal to arms to establish their rights and opinions, and imbrue their hands in each other's blood.

It was late in December when South Carolina reck-lessly put herself out of the pale of the Union. Before January was over, five or six other States had joined her, and openly avowed their secession principles There is no doubt that Virginia, the mother of presi-dents, and queen State of the South, was, by her emis-saries, in league with them from the first; though she was kept in check by the large number of her loyal people. So she waited until the Confederacy was de-clared, Fort Sumter taken, and other public property along the Southern border purloined or destroyed, and the new President had called for a large army to put down the rebellion, before she ventured to come out openly, and join in a strife that was, as Major Hunter had said, to immolate thousands of her noblest sons, and drench her fair fields in the most precious blood of the nation. The leading secessionists in Virginia had only waited for the excuse that their rights were about to be invaded by the Federal power to justify them in the eyes of the world.

The longing for the power they had wielded for fifty years, but lost, as they thought, by the election of the new President, and the fear that, through him, their

4

right to enslave, and enlarge the bounds of slavery would be interfered with, undoubtedly provoked the whole South to rebellion at that time. Yet their ambitious leaders had been looking forward, and preparing for some such movement for years. During the previous administration, wherever they could, they had been draining the public treasury, getting the best arms into their power, and sending every available government vessel to distant regions of the globe, so as to weaken the hands of the incoming party, and place it at the mercy of the leaders in the intended rebellion.

Soon after the wedding at Hunter Hills, and while the family were preparing to go to Richmond to spend the winter, Major Hunter was attacked by a fit of the gout, which rendered him for the time perfectly helpless. While thus confined at home, a patriotic, noble-souled, yet exceedingly troublesome invalid, the Montgomery Convention met, and chose Jefferson Davis as their leader; while the Peace Convention, which met in Washington about the same time, failed to do any thing to satisfy the clamors of the Southern people.

The major fumed and fretted and chafed, and sometimes swore, when he heard the news, — Catharine was generally employed to read to him; and he cursed the disorder that kept him an invalid, and prevented his taking an active part in the stirring scenes that were being enacted all around him. His lady, however, gave him little consolation. Much younger than himself, with few feelings in common, she had little sympathy for the ailments that kept her at home when she was longing for the gayeties of Richmond. And, more than all, being connected with many distinguished rebel families in the South, her sympathies were all with the

rebellion. Having been a belle and beauty in her
younger days, though comparatively poor, she was still
vain enough to wish to keep up her popularity in society. This made it peculiarly irksome for her to stay at
home with the aged and invalid husband she had married for his wealth and position, and who, in his age
and helplessness, when she herself had unexpectedly
inherited a fortune, she would sometimes gladly have
seen laid beneath the sod. Her three children, in whom
she worshipped her own beauty, as well as some of their
father's noblest attributes, were all that reconciled her
to her present mode of life at all; and in watching
their improvement under Catharine's guidance, and in
witnessing their wild frolics, she managed to exist until
this great trial was over.

Yet, so far as she could, Mrs. Hunter threw the care
of nursing and entertaining her invalid husband upon
Catharine and her children and servants. And to the
former, with her mind burdened, not only by her own
private griefs, but the woes and distresses of her country, it was perhaps a benefit, by occupying her mind,
and keeping her from dwelling too much upon the darkened personal and political horizon.

Major Hunter had been in the army in his youthful
days, and had afterwards travelled extensively. He
was possessed of vast stores of information, and general
knowledge of the world, and liked to talk over his past
experiences. This was irksome to his wife, but afforded
pleasure to Catharine in her present mood. Moreover,
Major Hunter continually admired her judgment and dis-
criminating taste, as well as the ingenuity and fruitful-
ness of a mind that could relieve the *ennui* and wretchedness of his wife's restless soul.

He had himself been educated at the North, from whence he had brought a good many ideas regarding human freedom that would never have disturbed the serenity of his soul had he remained at home. With these liberal ideas, he had acted in such a way as to give offence to some of his slaveholding neighbors, who, believing that *slavery* and the *lash* were made to work together, were constantly reproached for their cruelty by his uniform kindness to his slaves. He had inherited them, and believed he could not get along without them : yet he hated slavery in the abstract ; and at his death designed setting those of them he thought able to care for themselves free.

Though she dared not oppose him openly, his wife thwarted his views and liberal measures whenever she could. Of course, in such a household, Catharine had little opportunity of seeing much of the horror and dark side of slavery. And seeing the slaves so generally happy there, was what, more than aught else, reconciled her to the thought of becoming a slaveholder's bride. She could not bear to add to the affliction of this family by telling them that her character was suspected, her engagement broken off, and her peace of mind wrecked. So, conscious of her own integrity, and believing she was in the path of duty, she kept steadily on her way, wondering how soon the truth would be made manifest.

Lloyd wrote frequently to his father, always enclosing notes for the children, telling of the distinguished men convened in Richmond; of the measures and opinions they were adopting ; of the doings of the war and peace conventions ; of the mustering and marching of troops, and the many exciting reports in circulation ; but never a word about Catharine or his broken engagement.

As she, too, had Richmond letters, no one seemed to suspect any thing; though hers were from Grace Tremont, who, in the bustle and whirl of city life, found time to keep Catharine posted regarding her own affairs, and those of their mutual acquaintances. By midwinter the major was a great deal better; though the news arriving by every mail kept him in a continual fever of excitement.

, At last a letter came from Lloyd, saying that he was about convinced that the South was right, and justified in quitting a Union that oppressed and trampled upon her most sacred rights; that he was tired of waiting for the slow but sure voice of Old Virginia, and, at the earnest solicitation of some of her leaders, he had concluded to go South to confer with the ruling spirits there. Then, if the government really attempted to coerce them into submission, he might conclude to join them, and take office under the new confederacy; and believing, that, under such circumstances, a marriage with a Northern lady would be unadvisable, he had concluded for that, and other reasons she would understand, to cancel his late engagement with Miss Hale, and fulfil another made long ago, as they all knew, with Miss Nellie Atherton. They were to be married in church the next Tuesday; and he hoped his father and all the family would be able to be present, as they were to start, immediately after the ceremony, for Charleston, South Carolina.

Thus far the poor old major got, reading this letter to his wife, Catharine, and Dr. Stearnes, who had brought it from the office, when his voice began to falter, his hand to tremble, and his face to blanch to a sudden whiteness, as he stood by the parlor-window: then he

4*

put out his hands, clutched at the empty air, and fell heavily to the floor.

The knowledge that his first-born son, the pride and hope of his declining years, was about to turn traitor to his country and his betrothed bride, was too much for the poor invalid to bear, and almost broke his heart.

By the application of strong stimulants, he was revived, but could not be reconciled to the unlooked-for dispensation.

Catharine had known, from Grace's letters, that Nell was trying her best to win Lloyd back; and yet, perhaps unconsciously, she had treasured a hope of his return to her, and that all would in some way be satisfactorily explained.

The sudden overthrow of this hope came like a blow to her; and for a moment her senses reeled, her head swam, and she sat down dizzily in the nearest chair, pale as marble, and almost glad that something, she scarcely knew what, took the attention of those present from herself. Every one pitied her, and admired the fortitude with which she bore up under her disappointment; though it must be confessed that Mrs. Hunter's pity was mingled with joy at her niece's success in winning Lloyd from a *mésalliance*. She liked Catharine in her place; she felt as if she could hardly live without her a day; she had always treated her with kindness. Yet the feeling was very strongly impressed upon her mind, that she belonged to a lower caste than the Hunters and the Athertons, who were some of the oldest families in Virginia.

The major had had something of this feeling at first, until a knowledge of Catharine's goodness, virtue, and amiability had won a daughter's place in his heart.

And now he seemed to feel for her, in her desertion and disappointment, quite as much as if she were a daughter of his own ; and all the more, in that his own son was the cause of her trouble.

CHAPTER III.

CONTRARY to all expectation, the major was up betimes the next morning, and announced his determination to go immediately to Richmond.

His lady feebly remonstrated, saying that he was certainly not well enough; yet fearing only, that, in his present state of mind, he would say or do something to break up the match, or disgrace the family. She had a great many preparations to make before leaving, and the wardrobe of herself and family to prepare for the great occasion; and all they wanted was to get there the evening before the bridal, she said. So, in one way and another, she contrived to delay him until the sabbath was over; and then they made the journey to Richmond.

Catharine did not want to go to Richmond at all, and had a great mind to go home at once. She did not want to see Lloyd Hunter. To be near him, when she knew he was falsifying his vows to her, and solemnly plighting them to another, would be very trying to her feelings. But neither the major nor his lady would consent to her going home when the children needed her so much; and it was so difficult for them to get any one at all competent to fill her place.

44

So, after a confidential interview, it was decided that she should remain at Hunter Hills until Friday, when Uncle Nick was coming back to look after the rest of the baggage, and servants, and then, return with them. Before the end of February, they were all comfortably installed in their elegant town mansion; and Mrs. Hunter was once more in her glory. She had always been noted for her hospitality; and now she kept an open house, and spent most of her time in going, and receiving company.

The major bore his journey very well, but his moods and state of health were variable.

Sometimes he would see and talk with every one; dealing out his denunciations against secession and treason with an unsparing hand and tongue. Then again he would be confined to his room, unable to sit up, and yet chafing and worrying continually about the state of the country generally, and the doings of the Convention, then in session, of which he was a nominal member. When he was able, he attended its sittings, and did all he could, by voice and vote, and by public and private influence, to prevent the State from going out of the Union.

But his wife's influence — and, in one way and another, it was fully equal to his — was all the other way; and she did all she could to prevent him from influencing the minds of her friends and acquaintance. And later still, when the inauguration they had hoped to prevent was consummated, and Sumter was bombarded, and the new President had called for an army to support his tottering power, and she knew from her friends that the final vote of the Convention was about to be taken, this woman secretly gave her husband an opiate, that caused him to sleep through the terrible crisis that gave Virginia over to the horror and devastation of a bloody civil war.

When the old man woke to a knowledge that all was over, and that no effort of his could now prevent that dire calamity, his anguish and despair, though not stormy, were terrible.

Suspecting the truth, and disgusted with the meanness and chicanery that he knew had produced such lamentable results, he resolved at once to retire to his estates, leaving his giddy wife and family to enjoy town life as long as they pleased. So he left the next day, with Nick, his faithful servant, greatly to the pleasure of his lady. From that hour she made her house the home of all the rebel leaders in the city, and especially of her brother, Col. Atherton, and Philip, his son, who had previously boarded at a hotel.

And thus it was that Catherine, though disliking it much, was brought into close communion with the Athertons, and had a chance to see, and make the acquaintance of, those who were afterwards leaders in the rebel armies.

She knew that both Nell and Lloyd were gone; yet, strangely enough, no one, not even Major Hunter, had told her how or where. This was partly out of regard to her feelings, but much more from the mortification of their own at the way things had turned out. The truth was, that, after every arrangement had been made for the bridal, which was to be attended with great splendor, Count Laroi, Nell's Parisian lover, arrived in Richmond. Having come over from Europe on purpose to secure the great Virginia beauty and heiress, he took measures accordingly.

Finding how matters stood, he procured a private interview; and, after ascertaining that Nell still fancied him, he proposed a private marriage, and elopement. Wishing to gratify her fancy, shame Lloyd, punish him for his attentions to Catharine, and at the same time make a romantic sensation, Nell concluded an elopement with a live count would be just the thing. She knew very well that Count Laroi had been a suspected character in Paris, and that neither father nor brother would consent to their union; so she resolved to take the responsibility into her own hands, and do as she liked, in defiance of everybody. So she gathered up all she could secure of her own private property, was secretly married to Count Laroi the evening before that appointed for her marriage with Lloyd Hunter, and immediately set sail for New Orleans.

She was determined to be a rich countess, in spite of them all, she told her friends in her farewell letter. Her father and Philip were terribly shamed and offended. But Lloyd, though mortified by the publicity of the affair, really felt relieved, because he had, by this time, begun to suspect the duplicity of her character. And it was because all the connections were so chagrined, and had forbidden the children and servants to speak of it before Catharine, that she failed to learn the truth.

Mrs. Hunter knew that Catherine was invaluable to her in her present position; and now that Lloyd was gone, and there was no one of the family to be deluded by her charms, she was very glad to bring them into notice.

That an Atherton, with her own blood and pride in his veins, could think of her seriously, was something of which she did not dream.

She knew that she could trust her to look after her

children and servants, and have every thing managed to perfection, because they all esteemed and loved her. And she fully appreciated the rare personal and mental charms, that she knew helped to make her house so attractive to the rebel officers. Her musical and conversational gifts were constantly called into play, in assisting Mrs. Hunter in the entertainment of her company; and, if she was ill or absent, Catharine must receive her guests, and make her excuses. Catharine disliked the publicity of the part she was desired to act at first, and the notice she received from the Confederate officers. But, forced into it by circumstances over which she had little control, she learned at last to appreciate and enjoy their society. Knowing her Yankee proclivities, some of them loved to draw her out upon the political questions of the day, even though she sometimes wound them up and worsted them in the argument. But she was generally shy of expressing her opinions, knowing it could do no good.

Among the rebel officers whom Catharine particularly attracted at this time, was, strangely enough, Col. Atherton, the father of Nell and Philip, and brother of Mrs. Hunter. He had been a widower for years; and, from his age, position, great wealth, and unbounded family pride, no one who knew the man would have suspected him of such a weakness. He had avoided rather than sought her society at Hunter Hills, after he knew of her engagement; but, now that was broken off by the intrigues of his own family, he seemed anxious to cultivate her acquaintance, and win her confidence. Distrusting both the son and the father, because she thought they had had something to do with Lloyd's desertion, she treated them at first with uncommon coolness and reserve.

When they became domesticated in the family, she found it more impossible to do this without attracting special attention. So, by degrees, as the colonel won upon her esteem, her reserve and haughtiness wore away; though she could never quite forget certain suspicions of Philip's conduct in their earlier years.

Both the Colonel and Philip had daily military duties to attend to, yet managed to spend some part of each day or evening at home ; and, though neither suspected the other of ulterior motives, they generally managed, not only to avoid each other, but also Mrs. Hunter, whose hours for her *siesta*, dressing, and calls were the ones selected for being at home with Catharine and the children, who were, of course, always uncertain companions.

Catharine noticed this, but never dreamed that she had aroused in both some of the strongest passions of the soul. She knew something of the lofty pride of the Atherton family, and sometimes wondered why they would condescend to talk to a Yankee governess, and labor so hard as they did to convert her to their own views and opinions.

Both admired her beauty, though every one did not call her beautiful. But there was something in her pure and elevated sentiments, in her lofty patriotism, in the clear, decided, yet musical tones of her voice; besides the nameless charm always thrown around a cultivated intellect and polished manners, that singularly fascinated both, even though they could not respond to her sentiments, or feel that national patriotism which inspired her true and loyal heart.

Philip had admired Catharine more than any one else in early life, and was provoked by her preference of

5

Lloyd to himself; yet he had no serious intentions regarding her then.   His greatest ambition then was to
win Grace Tremont and her large fortune; but Grace
had rejected him before her departure from the city, for
his avowed secession sentiments.   This rebuff rankled
deeply in his vengeful heart; though it left him more
at liberty to follow out his own impulses than he had
been for years.

But Philip worshipped wealth and position; and
Catharine's want of both made him hesitate how to act.
He knew in his own heart that he was unworthy of
her; yet he felt as if he would be a better man if he
could marry her, and make up as well as he could for
the wrong he had done her.

That he had schemed and lied her out of one husband,
did not worry him much, however, so long as she did
not know or suspect the truth.   But it did trouble him
that she should always express such decidedly religious,
moral, and thoroughly loyal sentiments; that she met
every attempt at freedom or familiarity with a dignity
befitting an empress; and that she had never, by word,
look, or tone, seemed to be seeking his favor, or given
him the least shadow of encouragement.   Yet he could
not believe that she, a portionless Northern girl, would
refuse, if he once brought his pride down enough to ask
her, to marry him, — which as yet he did not intend to
do.

Catharine knew that there was great excitement
among the Southern people.   She knew that large
bodies of troops were gathering near Richmond, and all
through the Southern country.   She heard a great deal
said against the Federal government and Northern people
that irritated and pained her; and she sometimes freely

expressed her own opinions. Yet, like almost every one else, she believed those deluded, hot-headed Southerners were but blowing off steam, like a locomotive, to frighten the North to terms, and that the rebellion would not amount to much after all. And there is little doubt that most of the leaders in the movement were of about the same opinion, and little dreamed of the storm of woe and blood they were evoking when they raised their rebellious hands against the government.

Believing thus, and not at all alarmed for her own safety, Catharine resolved to finish her engagement, in spite of the threatening elements around her, and then set out for home.

The bombardment of Fort Sumter, the investiture of Pickens, and the President's call for a large army, roused her a little from her dream of security. But somehow the boasting tone of the public prints, and conversation of those around her, tended to allay, rather than to excite, her fears, and induced her to wait until the coast was blockaded, and the country filled with troops in every direction.

June came at last. She had promised to stay no longer than this; so, in spite of the children's tears, Mrs. Hunter's urgent entreaties, and the distracted state of the country, she decided to go home at once.

It was hard to part with those who loved her, and were so kind to her; but she had come to believe that the strife might be a long and bloody one. Duty to her immediate friends, her country, and her own loyal opinions urged her to leave the ranks of her country's mortal foes before it was too late.

The day before her intended departure, while Mrs. Hunter was out for a call, Catharine was surprised by the arrival of Mr. Garland, a near neighbor of Major Hunter, whom she had known and highly esteemed at Hunter Hills.

He had come to inform them that the major had taken a heavy cold on his way home, which had produced a fever and inflammation of the lungs, and that he had now a racking cough, and every symptom of a quick consumption. He had no one but slaves to attend him; believed it was his last illness, and was very anxious to see his wife and children before his departure. If his wife refused to come, as he feared she might, he begged Catharine, whom he regarded as a daughter, to come to him with his younger children.

Catharine was deeply affected by this news, for she loved the desolate old man as a father. As it was but a dozen miles out of her way, she readily promised to accompany Mr. Garland the next morning.

When Mrs. Hunter arrived, Catharine left the room; but she knew afterwards that she and Mr. Garland had a very exciting interview. She was wilful and unreasonable: she would not believe in the reports of her husband's danger. She knew that he had sent for them to get her away from Richmond, and prevent her using her wealth and influence, as she designed, in the cause of the rebellion.

And for that reason she utterly refused to return to Hunter Hills, or let her children go with Catharine, with whom she was vexed because she was going to leave her. Mr. Garland tried to reason the case; but, finding it only angered her, he desisted, and left the house.

But there was, unfortunately, a listener to this interview, who was deeply affected by it, and who made his presence known by his bitter sobs as soon as it was over. This was Walter, Mrs. Hunter's little son, who happened to be sitting in a window-seat, and thus became an unnoticed observer of all that transpired.

This boy, who was ten years old, and the youngest and pet of the flock, almost worshipped his old father. He had wondered, and questioned and worried his mother continually regarding his absence, and was now wounded in his tenderest feelings to have the truth made known to him in such a way.

"My father ill, — dying! and the mother I love so bitter against him for such a cause!" he exclaimed, as he threw himself at her feet, and besought her to take him to his poor father.

Not without reason, Mrs. Hunter was extremely proud of Jennie and Fannie, her beautiful and amiable daughters; but this boy she almost worshipped, he was so spirited, handsome, and talented, her youngest-born, and her only son. But she was angry and unreasonable at that moment; so she rebuked him sharply for his eavesdropping, and sent him from the room without listening to his exonerating explanations.

Alas! she little dreamed of all the consequences to him, to herself, to Catharine, and all with whom she was connected, that would result from that thoughtless act.

Col. Atherton had been away from home for a week, and of course knew nothing of Catharine's early departure. But Philip did know of it; and he grew more restless, moody, and taciturn every day. Just before sunset the last evening of her stay, he drove up in an open buggy; and, as the family were just about getting into the carriage for a drive, he asked Catharine to ride with him.

5*

From one excuse and another, she had always refused before; but now, encouraged by Mrs. Hunter, as it was her last day with them, she accepted the invitation.

It was a delicious June evening, and the streets were thronged with people, — on foot, on horseback, and in carriages; many of them richly dressed, or in glittering uniforms, — so suggestive of coming events, — seemingly so far off, and yet, alas, how near!

Philip, too, was in the stylish uniform of a staff-officer; and he looked so handsome and manly, with his fine form, jetty hair and eyes, and clear-cut features, that Catharine could not help admiring him, as he sat beside her, even though she doubted his principles, suspected his past conduct, and felt as if it were wrong for her to have any thing to do with him.

The sun went down in a sea of golden glory, tingeing the church-spires, and tops of the loftiest buildings, with a glittering halo; and the sweetest perfumes were wafted upon every breeze, from the thousands of beautiful flowers that were blooming all around them. And the bands, playing martial airs in the distance, contributed, with all other pleasing sights and sounds, to lull the senses into a happy forgetfulness of the past, and a serene enjoyment of the beauty and harmony all around them. They rode on for some time in perfect silence, — she looking and listening, yet never dreaming of the struggle going on in his bosom; he oblivious of outward objects, yet keenly sensitive to the strife within, and trying in vain to make up his mind how to act.

He had never fully realized, till they were about to part, how dear Catharine had become to him, how necessary she was to his happiness. But, though passion clamored, pride still held him in chains; and he could not make up his mind to speak the words that, he believed, would make her his own forever. That she would refuse to wed one of his high birth, manly beauty, and large fortune, he could not believe. But could he, with all those advantages, — he, who knew he could choose from some of the greatest beauties and fortunes in the realm, — wed a portionless Northern bride, who mocked at slavery, despised his opinions, and, more than all, loved another better than himself? No: he could not bow down his pride to that, or wed one whom he thought Nell and his proud father would despise.

And yet how he loved her! How could he bear to part with her. He drove out among the green fields, lowing kine, and fine country residences, where every thing breathed of peace; and for some time Catharine did not observe his unusual taciturnity.

"Catharine," he said at last in a tone not unmingled with emotion, "why will you leave us? Will no Southern heart or home content you longer?"

"I have no claim upon any of them; and it is time the weary, wandering bird should seek its parent-nest," said she, smiling.

"You have long been weaned from that, Catharine, and, if you will only stay with us, may one day have a warm nest of your own;" and he flashed upon her a glance of peculiar meaning.

"I do not want one. I feel myself more of an alien among your people every day. Our thoughts and views and feelings are of a different color; and among you I should never feel perfectly at home."

"You did not tell Lloyd Hunter so," said he sourly.

"How know you what I told Lloyd Hunter?" and the telltale blood surged over Catharine's face.

"I have heard that you were engaged to him at one time."

"Perhaps you know how I was disengaged?"

"No: I do not. But I would really like to know."

"When you see him, you can ask."

"I would not ask him now for a kingdom; nor do I care, if you will only forget him, and think of me."

"I shall never forget him or the lesson I have learned through him. I shall treasure it as a warning through life."

"Throw it to the winds. He is a moody, critical, cold-hearted fellow, who is never of the same mind long at a time. Whoever has him is to be pitied."

"I do not think so," said Catharine mournfully. "I still believe him to be one of God's and Nature's noblemen, — high-principled, pure, and true, yet not above being deceived and wronged."

"How can you think so highly of one who proved himself to be so inconstant and changeable?" he said with a guilty, conscious flush.

"I would be just to others whether they are so to me or not, especially when I believe they mean to be. That higher Power who shapes our destinies probably sees that it is not best for me to stay here, with all my Northern prejudices, through a bloody war; so he orders it otherwise."

"I do not believe that; yet I do think you will be in great danger to go to the North alone and unprotected at the present time. For the country between here and Washington is already alive with armed men, some of them villains of the deepest dye, gathered from among the uncivilized borderers of the frontiers, who are ready to stop trains, waylay travellers, or commit any other lawless deed for the sake of plunder."

"Then the sooner I get out of it the better."

"No, Catharine: you had better stay in Richmond, where there are those who will guard you from all danger, — those who love you well enough to lay down their lives for you."

"That is all moonshine, Philip; though, as regards the danger, there may be truth in what you say."

"Believe me, it is not all moonshine, Catharine. You do not realize your power over human hearts."

"You and I have heard a great many thrilling tales of deathless affection, Philip; but I, at least, have got past believing them," said Catharine, with a scornful curve to her expressive lip.

"Don't you believe that *I* love you thus, dear Catharine ? "

"No," she quickly responded, blushing, and drawing herself up with a haughty dignity.

"But I do most truly and fervently," he said, almost in spite of himself; "and I would do almost any thing to win a return ! "   His every look and tone testified to his sincerity.

"You surprise and pain me by such doubtful professions, Philip. Must I believe they are such as you make to every lady of your acquaintance ? "

"No, indeed! But why should you doubt ? " he asked, with an angry flush, and keen, questioning glance.

"Because I had supposed you all this time engaged to my friend, Grace Tremont."

"Grace Tremont indeed ! " and Philip's face grew dark with rage at the thought of the indignity of her refusal. "I was once engaged to Grace Tremont: I am not now. I would not marry her now, if she had the wealth of the Indies at her disposal, and knelt to me for the favor."

"You surprise me : I thought you were the best of friends."

"We were once : now we are bitter enemies. But, Catharine, I solemnly swear to you, that I never, never loved Grace Tremont as I now love you. I admired you more than all others in our earlier years; and, had you favored me, I believe I should have loved and been more worthy of you than I am to-day. But, such as I am, I feel for you now a stronger love and a wilder worship. And if, for my sake, you would stay in the Old Dominion, forget the past, and love me as well as you could, I would be everlastingly grateful, and allow you to mould me into your highest ideas of perfection and virtue."

"Could I make of you a good Christian, and a patriotic Union man ? " said Catharine, who had little faith in his rhapsodies, and could not help putting a little sarcasm into her tones and words.

"I don't know but your love might Christianize me, Catharine. I believe myself as patriotic as any man in the nation. I would lay down my life for Old Virginia, God bless her ! And no one is more strongly in favor of Union, — a union with *you*, dear Catharine, than myself," said he, smiling.

"You know that is not what I mean, Philip," said she seriously, "as well as you know that you are solemnly pledged to do all in your power to divide this glorious Union, and give the death-blow to our national life."

"I do not deny it. Yet did I not hear you say this afternoon, that difference of political opinion ought never to divide true friends ? "

"Nor had it, when, like your uncle and aunt, to whom I referred, they have sworn before God to love and to cherish each other till death.   This we have not done; nor would I now, under any circumstances I can think of, to any man, love him as I might, whom I believed to be an enemy to my country."

"And you regard me as one: do you?" he eagerly questioned.

"I regard every man as one who takes up arms against our lawful government, and schemes and plots to overthrow it."

"You say this deliberately, when you know that I acknowledge no allegiance, except to my native State, and shall do all I can to uphold her in her right of sovereignty."

"I do, Philip.   And yet I would give all I have to be able to convince you, and all other misguided Southerners, of the fallacy of a doctrine that is about to plunge this country into a horrid civil war, which, if it does come, will drench the land in blood.   It may be yours — or Theodore's."

"Don't talk of that: it makes me shiver.   Let us hope it will not come to so deadly an issue."

"God grant it!   But it must be getting late.   How far are we from the city?"

"Some six or eight miles perhaps."

"Six or eight miles!   Why, it will be ten o'clock before we get home!   What will Mrs. Hunter say?"

"I don't care.   But, Catharine, do you know how strongly I am tempted to run away with you, and hide you somewhere, to prevent your going home?" he said, as he wheeled around in the homeward direction.

"You would not do so mean a thing as that."

"I don't know but I would: the thought of parting with you is not a pleasant one. Why won't you show me some present favor, or at least give me a promise to come back to Richmond, after making the major a visit?"

"No promise between a secessionist and a Yankee will be good for any thing, if this war goes on."

"Just make me one, and see."

"No, Philip. It is too serious a subject to trifle with. I am grateful for your good opinion, and the pleasure your society has afforded me; though I did not dream you had any serious object in seeking mine."

"Nor had I, till you bewitched my senses, and wiled my heart away from me."

"Pretty Bess Hamilton can wile it back again."

"Bess Hamilton is a pretty coquette, but less than nothing to me."

"As I shall be, after a week's absence."

"Catharine, why is it that you trifle with my affection, and have so little regard for my deepest and tenderest feelings?" he passionately exclaimed.

"Forgive me if I have wronged you, Philip, or undervalued your affection. I do not mean to trifle with any man's feelings. I was simply trying to do right."

"How, pray, and wherefore?"

"Philip," she said, blushing, hesitating, and smiling, "do you not know that you are a very handsome, polished, and fascinating young gentleman; and that, if one had no previous prepossessions, it would be just the easiest thing in the world to love you?"

"Why don't you then?" said he eagerly.

"You do not need to be told, Philip. There are some who can never love but one. But would you be satisfied

to have a poor, dependent, but ambitious girl pretend
to an affection she did not feel, for the sake of winning
your name, position, and large fortune ? "

"Certainly not."

"Say no more then.   Do not add to my temptations,
but let us part in friendship."

He took the hand she offered, pressed it passionately
to his lips, then threw it from him ; and little more was
said during the remainder of the ride.   They got home
at last ; but, as soon as they entered the house, a new
trouble presented itself.

Little Walter was gone, — no one knew what had become of him ; and Mrs. Hunter had been in paroxysms
of fear, lest some evil had befallen her beautiful boy.
A little note was found at last upon her dressing-table,
printed with a pen, telling her that he had taken the
money given him for a Christmas present to buy a
ticket, and was going on the cars to see his dear father.
He hoped she would forgive, and take no trouble about
him, and come with the girls very soon.

When this note was found, Mrs. Hunter's fear turned
to anger ; and she told Catharine to "send the little rascal home just as soon as she got to Hunter Hills."

There were a good many last things to do, a good
many last words to be spoken ; and it was very late before they retired to rest.

Catharine's mind was so troubled about her affair with
Philip, Walter's curious escapade, and the dread prescience of coming events, that she did not sleep at all
this last night of her stay in Richmond.

6

CHAPTER IV.

MR. GARLAND called for Catharine quite early the next morning, as he had promised; but it was only to bring his excuses.

He had found it necessary to remain a few days longer in town. If she did not like to wait, he would take her to the cars, and place her under the care of a good and true friend of his, who was going out to Hunter Hills to make the major a visit.

Catharine was all ready, and dressed for the journey. She was deeply anxious to go home as soon as possible, and did not like to wait longer. So, tearfully kissing and bidding the family and servants "Good-by," she entered the carriage, and was driven to the depot.

They were just in time. Mr. Garland procured her a ticket, and checks for her baggage, found her a convenient seat; and she was just thanking him for all his kindness when the whistle sounded. He turned around quickly, presented his friend, Col. Atherton, who came smilingly up at that moment, bade her "Good-morning," and immediately left the train.

Catharine was confounded. She had not dreamed of her escort being any one she knew, — least of all the father of Philip Atherton, who, though she knew it not,

62

had contrived business to detain Mr. Garland in Richmond, that he might have the pleasure of her company to Hunter Hills.

He was going out, it was true, to make one more effort to win over the old major to the secession cause ; though but for his meeting with Mr. Garland, and knowledge of her proposed journey, he would have waited a few days longer. He did not suffer this to be seen, however; and she had not the least suspicion of his object, when, with a polite bow and " By your leave," he took the vacant seat beside her.

Of course there could be no refusal of the companionship of one of whose escort any lady in Richmond would have been proud. So she blushed, bowed a silent acquiescence, and rather unquietly settled down beside him. Though he had a son of twenty-five, Col. Atherton was at this time, four years less than fifty. Though not a handsome man, he was yet so distinguished in his personal appearance, that you would instantly have selected him, out of a hundred promiscuously-gathered men, as the superior in ability to nearly every one. He was full six feet high, with a form of perfect symmetry, dark, unsilvered hair, a high, broad brow, prominent Roman nose, and an eye at once black, penetrating, and magnetic. His features were marked, decided, and stern in repose; yet when he smiled, as he did rarely, they lighted up with a most genial and magical glow. Educated, talented, and accomplished in all the arts and habits of good society, he was in fact as fine a specimen of a polished Southern gentleman as one would often find.

He had been quite distinguished as a successful and courageous officer in the war with Mexico. Wise in council, and brave in the field, he was one who was well calculated to be a leader of men.   And, though you may not find his *name* in the list of Confederate officers, you may be sure that the *man was there.*   He was indeed a man whose will was generally the law to those around him, and one, too, who might at times be unscrupulous as to the means to make that will a law, though this did not often appear upon the surface of his character.

From the first hour of their acquaintance, Catharine had been conscious of a strange species of fascination in this man's society, — far more indeed than in that of his polished and handsome son.   She felt and acknowledged his superior ability, dignity, and strength of character.   His voice was singularly deep-toned yet melodious. He was specious, eloquent, and highly gifted in conversation.   She had often found herself listening spell-bound to his descriptions of thrilling scenes in the Mexican war, as well as of distinguished persons and places in foreign lands.   And when he had talked to her of slavery and secession, and the rights and wrongs of the South, with the justice of her demands upon the nation, and of the grasping, over-reaching spirit of our Northern people, he would succeed so well in making "the worse appear the better reason," that she would be almost convinced of the truth of his side of the argument, and ready, in spirit, to yield to all the South demanded.   In his presence, her spirit bowed to his superior will, and strength of intellect.   His deep, melodious tones enchained her attention in a room where the sound of many voices mingled.   His eye held and attracted hers by a species of magnetism, which she felt, but for which she could give no reason.   Did she love him then, this stern, domineering, unscrupulous man of more than twice her own age? Far from it. She was uneasy in his presence, and though conscious of a strong attraction towards him, yet felt a stronger and more irresistible one to get out of the danger as soon as possible. And now, when he sat down beside her, — nearer than he had ever been in her life before, — a strange thrill that was almost a shudder crept through her frame; and a sudden but intangible fear, like a warning shadow, swept across her mental sky. It was dispelled the next moment, however, by the sound of his voice, as he said, with one of his rarest smiles and most winning tones, —

"I hardly know whether you accepted or rejected my escort, Miss Hale, the cars started so suddenly."

"Oh! I would like it, if it is not too much trouble to you, sir," she returned with a bright blush and a slight tremor in her tones; "though I am not afraid to go alone."

"It is no trouble, but really a positive pleasure to me to have such society as yours to beguile the monotony of the ride to Hunter Hills."

"To judge by what I see around me, you might have that which would far better suit your taste," said Catharine; for she began to observe that the train was crowded to its utmost capacity by soldiers, and officers in full uniform, some of whom she knew, and that there were very few ladies on the train.

"A thing is precious just in proportion to its scarcity," said the colonel, smiling as he read her thought. "I presume there are few gentlemen present who do not envy me the pleasure that no temptation would induce me to resign to them."

"Gallant speeches are a part of a soldier's tactics, I

6

believe," said she, smiling; "and ladies are wise who do not attach too much meaning to them."

"Soldiers have eyes and ears and hearts, too, Miss Hale. And sometimes — as in the present instance — they mean more than their words imply," he said with a look so admiring and significant as to startle and set her to thinking.

Could it be possible that this stern man, old enough to be her father, could have a serious thought of her, a poor Yankee governess, and abolitionist at that? Or could it be that Philip had told him of his partiality, and begged his intercession with her in his behalf. He would not get it if he had : she felt sure of that. And she was glad that no love for Philip bowed her own honest pride down to the feet of so haughty a race. If Col. Atherton knew any thing about her affair with Philip, he was glad, no doubt, to assist in getting her out of the country.

While she sat thinking thus, with her eyes cast down, the colonel was seriously regarding her, but with very different feelings from what she had imagined. He knew nothing of Philip's passion, and had enough to do to master his own conflicting emotions. She instinctively shrank from the strange light in his eyes when she raised hers to ask why so many of the soldiery were on board that day.

"I don't know that there are more than there has been every day for weeks," he replied. "You must know that large bodies of troops from North and South are massing upon the line of the Potomac; that collisions are of daily occurrence; and that we are probably on the eve of a bloody civil war," he continued in a low, solemn tone.

"I read and hear so, but have hardly begun to realize it yet. It does not seem possible that our people can be so mad as to imbrue their hands in each other's blood. Oh! why will you not accept such terms as the government can honorably offer, and cease this strife about slavery?"

"Because slavery is the strength, the vitality, the life-blood of the South, and we should be slaves ourselves were we to yield up the right to extend it as we please. But we have discussed this subject before; and this is not the place for it, if we had not," he said in a lower tone, as he saw the attention of the people around began to be attracted by their conversation.

Little more was said of special importance during the remainder of the ride; though Col. Atherton sought, by many little attentions, to establish an interest, and secure a confidential intercourse, with his fair companion.

When at last, sometime in the afternoon, they reached the station nearest to Hunter Hills, they found, as they expected, Mr. Garland's carriage awaiting them. After partaking of some refreshments, they entered the carriage for a drive of twelve miles. Once on board, seated side by side and alone, as the driver was on the outside, Col. Atherton's manner changed very perceptibly.

"I have been greatly concerned to hear that you are about to leave Virginia, Miss Hale," he said in deeply-earnest tones.

"And glad to get rid of even a female representative of the 'Yankee abolition nation,' I presume;" and Catharine tried to laugh off the uneasiness she began to feel by using an expression she had often heard at the South.

"No," he exclaimed with sudden energy, and a look that thrilled her. "You should never go home if I could help it."

"Why, surely, surely, you do not suspect me of tampering with the slaves?"

"No: but rather with their masters, whom you are robbing of their best treasures," he replied, smiling at her frightened look.

"You are pleased to joke, sir. But really I am beginning to fear that I have tarried here too long, and that my journey home will be a serious if not a dangerous undertaking."

"That is perfectly true. If you had gone home, instead of coming to Richmond, last winter, you could have done so in perfect safety, and saved more than one from a heartache. As it is, I think you had better remain here. And indeed we cannot allow you to leave us."

"But I must. I fear I am unsafe here even now."

"There is a way in which you can easily become safe."

"How is that?" she eagerly asked.

"By casting your prejudices to the winds, and becoming one of us," he said with a keen, searching glance.

"That is impossible: they are ingrained in my whole being. And besides, you Southern aristocrats with whom I have associated as an inferior would never consider a poor Yankee governess your equal. At home I am as good as anybody; and I can never feel, and I will not acknowledge, my inferiority to the best of you, or allow myself to sink to a lower level."

"I do not ask it, or wish to lower you from your loftiest standard," he said, smiling at her spirited words, and proud, queenly manner. "We have prejudices, I must admit, and strong ones, against your people as a class; and perhaps we do them some injustice: but we have none whatever against yourself; you have overcome them all. You are better and nobler than the race whence you sprung. We admire your beauty and talents. We acknowledge your superior powers, and would gladly exalt them to the high station you are so well fitted to adorn."

Catharine, even now, had no suspicion of the colonel's object in addressing her thus; so she indignantly answered, "I will not suffer you, Col. Atherton, to flatter me at the expense of my race and ancestry. There are thousands of Northern girls who are my equal, and even my superior, in every quality that can ennoble and exalt the sex. And you wrong and undervalue our men when you place them so low as you do in the scale of courage, ability, generosity of soul, and all human excellence. You will find this out to your cost, if this dreadful war goes on; though God grant that it may not come to a fearful issue!"

"That issue has already come, Miss Hale, — from which there is now no honorable mode of retreat."

"Oh, there is, — there must be! And let me entreat of you, Col. Atherton, to use your great influence towards the peace and harmony of the nation."

"Your abolition President inaugurated war when he re-enforced forts and fortresses, and set State rights at defiance. The war must come."

"Must! Oh, I believe I could lay down my life to prevent a strife in which thousands of other lives must be sacrificed!"

"I think you overestimate the danger. Your people had rather work and traffic than fight; so it will soon be over. And you can do better with your life than to sacrifice it, even in thought, to a chimera."

"Perhaps not. Life is but a series of troubles and disappointments; and death is sometimes welcome."

"But not to one like you, whose life would be the most precious thing of earth to him whose home your love would make a paradise."

"That home and that him, I think, will never be found by me," smiled Catharine. "The only home upon which I have a claim seems a great way off just now, with rivers of trouble rolling between it and me."

"There is a· home and a him on this side of that river, — a home of beauty and wealth, comfort and luxury, awaiting your acceptance; whose owner would endeavor to make it a paradise, if you would become its mistress. Won't you, fair Catharine ? " and he eagerly grasped her hand, and looked searchingly into her deep blue, downcast eyes for his reply.

"Whose, — whose do you mean ? " she asked tremulously.

"Mine ! mine alone ! "

"Then Philip has not " —

"Philip has had nothing to do with it, and dare not interfere with my wishes. It is I, Edward Atherton, who ask you to become my wife, the sharer of my destiny, and to make a hitherto joyless home a happy one," he said in a tone of deep emotion. "Will you do so ? "

She was really frightened now; and her hand trembled like a leaf in his strong clasp. He felt it; and her rapidly-changing color and continued silence alarmed him at once.

"Is there indeed no hope for me?" he eagerly questioned. "Do I seem old and repulsive to you, Catharine?"

"No, no! But this is so sudden, so wholly unexpected!" she gasped.

"But Philip, — you mentioned his name. Has he indeed dared to rival me?" he exclaimed with a darkening frown.

"Col. Atherton, there must be no question of rivalry between you two. If there were, I might prefer the elder to the younger. But I think now of other and more insuperable objections, — one of the strongest of which is, that I have loved another too well ever, ever to love you, or any other man, as a wife ought to love her husband," she murmured blushingly.

"Oh! I know, and deeply regret, all that; yet I would heal the wounds another has made in your heart by his inconstancy. I believe there is a strong chord of sympathy between our souls, and that I can teach you to love *me* better than you ever did *him*. I *know* you could not resist the power of the deep, strong passion I feel for you, if you were once my wife!" and his eager, ardent looks and eloquent tones testified at least to his truth and sincerity.

"Possibly it might be so, Col. Atherton. I know you are strongly attractive: it may be that I might learn to love you. And yet, if I did, our home could never be a happy one; for, aside from those strong political prejudices, that would be sure to breed strife, *I know* that your children would hate me as they would a viper, and surely make my life wretched; while your other friends would look down upon me."

"Must I, then, be beholden to children and friends

for the happiness or misery of my whole future life?"
said he passionately. "I yielded all once to their solici-
tations. I married one older than myself, whom I did
not love, to please her and them by securing her fortune. Knowing well that she had bought me, body and
soul, she was ever inclined to treat me as a slave, until
the inheritance of wealth greater than her own made
me in her eyes her equal. There could be no happiness
in such a union; and, when it was broken by death, I
resolved never to form another. It had defrauded my
youth of love, the sole creator and diffuser of happiness; and I had grown to be a disbeliever in its existence until I met with you. I had then been a widower for years, and had seen hundreds of beautiful and
talented ladies, who might perhaps have been won,
without a wish to make them mine. But you took
my heart by storm before we had exchanged a word.
You were betrothed, and unapproachable to me then;
but fate ordained that we should meet again under other
circumstances. And our familiar intercourse in Richmond has served to strengthen the bond by which you
lead me, until it has brought me here, an humble suppliant for your favor. O Catharine! must my loveless
youth, my defrauded manhood, my unbounded love, plead
in vain to you for affection and sympathy?"

Her heart was softened by his eloquent appeal. Lloyd
Hunter had deserted her; and she was sure she never
would find another who would love her so fondly: so there
were tears in her eyes as she said, —

"I do sympathize with you, Col. Atherton. I am
deeply grateful for your preference; and if you were
alone in the world, and engaged in what I considered a
holier cause, I could almost find it in my heart to respond

as you wish. As it is, I do not dream of it. Your
family have demands upon you that cannot be silenced
or ignored. And more than all, and above all minor
considerations, we stand, in a national point of view, in
the light of mortal enemies. You are, if I mistake not,
a leading conspirator against what I consider our lawful
government, and all too soon probably will be in arms
against my country and my own kindred. I hear nothing from them of late; but I know their patriotic spirit
too well to believe my brothers will hesitate one moment
in offering their lives and services to their country.
Without doubt, they are already upon the banks of the
Potomac, awaiting the terrible onset; and God's curse
would fall on me, were I to send a husband in all the
panoply of arms against them. So, if there were no
other reasons in the universe for declining your suit, Col.
Atherton, this alone would compel me to do it."

"Must, then, my devotion to what I consider a just
cause prevent and blast the happiness of my whole future
life? Oh! it is a fearful price to pay for a mere difference
of opinion."

"Col. Atherton, if this war goes on, you will have to
pay a far greater price than that. For what is one man's
happiness or misery to the devastation by fire and sword
of all this beautiful land, the bloody sacrifice of thousands of her best and noblest sons, and the utter ruin
of numberless happy families? Oh! I beseech you, by all
you hold dear on earth, to give up this wild scheme of
separation from the Union, to return to your allegiance,
and to use your eloquent tongue and noblest powers in
persuading others to give up this mad plan of secession."

"No, Catharine, I cannot do it, even though your
love, the most precious treasure of earth, were to repay

7

me; for I have had too much to do with planning and forwarding this grand scheme of secession to retreat from it now ingloriously, without covering my name with infamy and dishonor. I believe with my whole soul that the North and South' have such different interests, tastes, and feelings, that they can never live and work together harmoniously. They must separate. And it may as well be now as ever. I have thoroughly studied the principles of human governments. 'I know that republics are but the resource of small communities: they are never adopted by mature nations, who have passed the period of pupilage. We have outgrown that; and are now impatient of a system founded on past necessities.' We of the old noble Cavalier descent, too, are impatient of the domination of the descendants of the old Puritan exiles of New England, who come from a far lower grade in society."

"Why, then, do you desire to ally yourself with one of their humble descendants?" said Catharine with spirit.

"Because you have talents of the highest order, and a spirit as soaring and aspiring as my own. You must know that I am a proud, ambitious man, Miss Hale; and, if I judge you aright, you have enough of those feelings to understand mine, when I tell you, that all my hopes and ambitions for the future are centred in this scheme, which is to found one of the grandest empires on the globe. I have already a general's commission offered me; but that is nothing to the positions of honor to which I may attain if our plans succeed. O Catharine! listen for once to the councils of wisdom and prudence. Renounce your cold-hearted Northern people; become my bride, the idol of my heart and home; and I will raise you to a position in which your beauty and talents would

command the homage of a nation.   And is it not better
to share such honors; to have wealth at your disposal
for purposes of benevolence; to be able to surround
yourself with luxury and splendor; to have every thing
that can please the eye and gratify the taste, — than to
condemn yourself to a menial station for life, and doom
yourself to poverty, toil, and a thousand privations, until
death puts an end to your misery?"

"It may be so, Col. Atherton.   And to an ambitious
girl, as you rightly judge that I am, the temptations of
wealth and a high social position are almost irresistible.
And yet, to my mind, there are worse things in the
world than poverty, toil, and an humble position in life."

"What, I would like to know?"

"The continued upbraidings of a guilty conscience,
which would be mine, were I to sacrifice principle, home,
friends, and the most sacred national and individual ties,
to a vain and paltry ambition ; and for that alone to consent, by my example and influence, to fasten upon the
necks of millions the yoke of a more enduring bondage.   Ah, Col. Atherton, do not try to tempt me further :
it can do no good to yourself or me.   The prejudices of
my Puritan education are too strong to be broken by
your fallacious reasoning.   And no fear of poverty, toil,
or an humble position, shall induce me to renounce principle, and do human nature so foul a wrong."

"You promised to wed one slaveholder.   In what am
I worse than he?"

"There was not then this fearful issue to contemplate,
— no empire founded on slavery talked of; and I hoped
to ameliorate the condition of two hundred human
beings."

"I have five times that number, — here and in Georgia.
Can you not as well do good to them?"

"I am wiser now than I was then, Col. Atherton. I realize more what slavery is, and is to be."

"What is it to be?" he questioned.

"A bone of contention between North and South, until a mightier hand than ours sweeps it from the face of the continent."

"There you are grandly mistaken. I believe it is to increase and prosper, until, like a giant tree, it overshadows the whole country. But here we are at Hunter House; and I have not time to convince you, as I believe I could, if I had the opportunity, that your positions are false, and that we are in the right. Of that I must convince you before we part, for I cannot give you up so. If, as you say, you have no personal objections to me, I shall not take this as your final decision. I want you to think of it well before you positively reject one who loves you as his life, and would gladly surround you with every blessing."

"Col. Atherton, though I respect, esteem, and even like you personally, I believe that every hour at this time but adds to the weight of my objections."

"Let us hope not," said he gloomily. "I cannot bear to part with you, Catharine. Oh! if you were my wife, I would be the happiest man in the universe. For your sake I could resign the hope of fame, broad lands, or the most precious earthly treasure; but not for your love must I consign the honored name that has come down through many generations to shame and infamy."

"If you were ready to do so, I would not accept the sacrifice, Col. Atherton. I can see very plainly that it is better for us both to part as we are; and you will see it hereafter. You will see, that, in wedding a poor Yankee governess, you would have yoked yourself most unequally, in every way, and filled your life with bitter regrets. I have neither wealth nor fame nor power; yet, as a child of the same loving Father, I feel myself your equal. But with the inborn pride, — child of that noble birth of which you boast, — and the prejudices created by a life-long training, I know that you would not think me your equal long, even though love may blind you now."

"Do not believe it. I am no changeling; and I feel that I love you too truly and fervently ever to undervalue you in the least. But we will talk of this further before we part," he said, as he helped her out of the carriage.

Though it was growing dusk, Walter at this moment discovered, and came running out to meet them. He was delighted to see Catharine and his uncle; but his eyes filled with tears when he told them how very ill he had found his father. He had found no difficulty in getting a man at the dépôt, to bring him home; and he had a warm welcome at the end of his journey.

Catharine was surrounded, welcomed, and disrobed by the delighted servants, as soon as she entered the house. They were all eager to hear the news, wondering why mistress did not come home, and anxious to tell all the particulars of master's illness.

The moment he heard of their arrival, Major Hunter sent for them to come to his room. His face was pale and cadaverous, his cheeks hollow, his eyes sunken and glittering, and his form thin and attenuated, as he lay upon the bed, with Uncle Nick's anxious black face bending over him. They saw at once that he was indeed sadly changed, and felt that his days were numbered. He shook Col. Atherton warmly by the hand, and said that he was glad to see him, but drew Catharine down to him, and kissed her tenderly.

7*

"O Catharine!" he exclaimed in a faint, feeble tone, "you don't know how I have longed for your presence, and that of my family; how much I have suffered from pain and loneliness. If you had, I believe you at least would have come to me."

"I certainly should, my dear friend," she returned. "I came at the earliest possible moment after I knew the truth; though Walter, it seems, got the start of me."

"Yes: poor boy! he has braved his mother's anger, of which she will repent some day. God bless you for coming! and grant that it may not lead you into danger in these troublous times." Then, turning to the colonel, he said, "Well, colonel, — or perhaps I ought to say general, — secession begins to work bravely; don't it? — you will be getting out a patent for the article. You see I am beginning to reap some of its benefits. You will be getting them by and by. Catharine, dear, you look tired and nervous. Pray, go and get you some tea, and then retire to your room, and sleep off your fatigue; while the colonel and I will take ours together here, and have a quiet chat."

She did as he desired, and knew little of their eager, exciting interview, except that it exhausted the major's strength, and was thoroughly unsatisfactory to both."

The colonel left soon after breakfast next morning, but not before he had sought and obtained an interview with Catharine, and used every argument in his power to induce her to retract her decision. But she was still firm in her refusal; and, though not unmoved by his eloquent appeals, felt it impossible to accede to his wishes. She had heard a great deal from the servants since her arrival about the troubled state of the country around the Hunter Hills. Bands of soldiery and guerillas were plundering plantations, burning houses, murdering unoffending inhabitants, and committing all sorts of lawless depredations. All this tended to excite her fears, and would have hurried her home, if she could have found it in her heart to leave her helpless old friend, who clung to her like a little child, begging her to stay with him, and whose life she thought was nearly ended. Col. Atherton was sure of this, and thought he might die at any time; so he encouraged Catharine and little Walter to remain with him to soothe his last hours on earth, and smooth his passage to the tomb. He promised to make the boy's peace with his mother; persuade her to come to them, if possible; and, when all was over, to give Catharine a safe-conduct out of the country. They parted in a friendly manner; for, although his last interview with her had been even more unsatisfactory than the first, he had not yet given up all hope regarding her. Major Hunter had been so ill as to be unable to sit up a moment, worn out by a racking cough, night-sweats, and bloody expectorations; but, cheered by the bright presence, careful nursing, and tender attentions of Catharine and little Walter, he soon began to mend. His cough grew easier; his dangerous symptoms vanished; his strength and appetite gradually returned; and very soon he was able to sit up, and at last ride out every day. They had saved his life by coming, the doctor said; and there was now a fair prospect of his recovery. What he lived for, when hope had almost ceased, and death would have been a blessing, will be seen presently.

Col. Atherton wrote to Catharine as any other friend might have done, saying, that he could not persuade Mrs. Hunter to return to her husband; though she was willing that Walter should stay, under Catharine's super-vision.   He begged her to write, and tell them how the major was ; and whether she had concluded to go, or re-main with him.

She replied, that the major was much better, but so very anxious for her stay, that she could not find it in her heart to leave him at present; and that Walter, though lonely, could not be induced to leave his dear father.

CHAPTER V.

THINGS had worn a very serious aspect in Virginia for a long time previous to this. The people had thought and talked and argued upon the subject of secession; and, though there were many strong Unionists, there were more who had played a double game, — mystifying both parties, so as to be able to join the strongest by and by.

Now, however, when large bodies of troops from the more Southern States — the hot-bed of the rebellion — were daily arriving, to bully and overawe all who were unfavorable to their views, these were obliged to show their colors, and act. As the rebellion gained strength, the bitterness and hostility between the opposing parties grew so hot and deadly as almost to surpass belief. Pillage, murder, and every other known crime, was committed without a scruple of conscience. The whole country was in a state of turmoil and contention. Hundreds of escaping slaves, and bands of desperadoes, roving in every direction, made it unsafe to travel without a military escort, or even to remain at home.

The tocsin of war, and rebellion against the government, very naturally sounded like the trump of freedom in the ears of the poor slaves : it suggested very strongly to them the idea of rebellion against their legal masters. So as soon as hostilities really commenced, and they felt as if there was a friendly arm somewhere to protect them, they began to escape in large numbers. And, even when driven back at the point of the bayonet by some of our misjudging proslavery officers, they continued to brave death in every form to regain freedom, — "that dearest gift of God to man." This, of course, added a thousand-fold to the turmoil, wretchedness, and strife of the people in the border States, and fed the fires of passion, until the whole country was in a blaze, and the white people were ready to pour out their blood to regain what was indeed, in most cases, lost to them forever.

But time sped on, with quite as hurried a march of events as was ever known in the world's history. By the last of June, a hundred thousand patriotic Northern men, fired by the insults offered to their national flag at Sumter, were gathered upon the line of the Potomac to protect the Capitol, — that fancied bulwark of freedom. More than a hundred thousand, well-armed and better equipped, with arms surreptitiously obtained from the national armories, faced them upon the opposite shore. Both parties were eager for the contest that was to decide their supremacy; but neither as yet dreamed of the length and breadth and deadliness of the conflict in which they were about to be engaged, or the wonderful events they were preparing to record upon the pages of a world's history.

Already battles had been fought at Big Bethel, in Missouri, and in Western Virginia, in which our Northern troops were for the most part victorious, when the defeat — nay, total rout — of our army in the advance upon Bull Run cast a shadow upon our national arms, and a pall of deep gloom over the hearts of all who were true and loyal to their country. It is not our purpose to describe that battle, or dwell upon that terrible disappointment of individual and national hope. We will only say, that it was fought within a few short miles of Hunter Hills, where the sulphurous smoke could be distinctly seen, and the thunderous roar could be heard and felt.

To describe the feelings of Major Hunter, Catharine, and indeed all who listened to those dread and ominous sounds, during those two dreadful days, would be impossible. It seemed as if that sweet July sabbath that dawned so brightly and beautifully over the land, would never, never come to an end. This battle had taken them by surprise. They knew the Confederates were massing their troops at Manassas Junction, but nothing of the advance of our lines, until the murderous roar saluted their ears. Immediately after this battle, more than ever before, small detachments of troops and bands of guerillas, flushed with victory, and lusting for rapine and plunder, began scouring the country in all directions.

Though more than a mile from either of the great thoroughfares, the plantation had already been visited several times by foraging and patrolling parties, to whose demands Major Hunter had been obliged to yield an unwilling assent. Still he would not believe there was really any danger to be apprehended there from opposing factions of his own countrymen. Catharine wished him to go North with her as soon as he was able to travel, or else back to Richmond.

The first was too dangerous, and was indeed impracticable then, he said; and, as for the last, he never would go back, and force himself into his wife's presence, after she had refused to come to him in his need.   No: a man's house was his castle; and he had plenty of arms, and two hundred able defenders, who would fight till their last breath for him.   He would stay there, in spite of every thing; yielding only his substance because his country, however wrongly, demanded it, and had the power to enforce her demands.

Catharine, as may well be supposed, was uneasy enough under the circumstances, but, seeing no present mode of escape, tried to content herself, and make the best of it.   As it was, she would not have cared so much, had not a new source of annoyance presented itself.

The old overseer, under whose judicious management the major's affairs had thrived for twenty years, had resigned and gone to the West three years before; and a new one, a Yankee by birth, had taken his place upon the plantation.   This man, whose name was Sweep, was at heart a scheming, unprincipled, time-serving rascal, but had contrived thus far to deceive the major by his speciousness.   He was heartily disliked by the slaves, but soon subdued them to his will; so that they dared make no complaints to the master.   Sweep was there when Catharine entered the family; and as he had none of his own, and frequently took his meals with them, she had a chance to see him almost every day for months.   From reasons she could not have explained, she took a dislike to him from the first, though one of her own New-England people, and avoided him when she could.   She could not do this as well in the absence of Mrs. Hunter after her return, as he had contrived to make himself very necessary to the major, and was forever around him when he had the opportunity. So she unavoidably saw a great deal of him, and very soon, to her great annoyance, received from him an offer of marriage, which she politely declined. To Catharine and the major, this man professed Union sentiments; but, from some things she had heard whispered among the slaves, she suspected him of underhanded dealings with the Confederates, and of instigating the raids upon the major's property.

One evening, a few days after the battle, it was very warm; and the family at Hunter House were gathered upon the broad piazza, watching the going down of the sun, and the gathering of the evening shadows over the landscape. They were talking of the details of the battle, and the blighting effects of the war upon the country. The major had been sadder and far more depressed that day than usual. Catharine's music and conversation, and his son's glad voice, seemed to have lost their power to cheer him. And now, as he sat there in his easy-chair, with her on one side of him, and Walter on the other, with one arm thrown lovingly around his father's neck, and the other hand playing with the tassels of his rich velvet dressing-gown, the old man's head was bent down, and rested on his hand; and his whole manner betokened the deepest dejection.

"Catharine," he said at last, raising his head, "I have loved you, I believe, as well as if you were my own child; and you have done that for me which gold can never repay. Yet I begin to fear I have done you a great wrong in selfishly keeping you here, when you ought to have gone home. Perhaps, too, I was unwise in refusing to go with you and Walter to Richmond. But you know

8

my reasons. Surrounded by so many strong hands and
loving hearts, I felt safe, or I would never have asked
you to stay, or kept Walter, whom I might have sent
back with his uncle. Yes: I felt safe enough here; but,
strangely enough, last night my sense of safety vanished
before a dream. I was told that Hunter House was in
ruins; that the strong arms upon which I leaned were
broken reeds that would pierce my heart, and warned to
flee at once from some great danger. Now, I never believed in dreams, and I always considered it a mark of
weakness to place the least reliance upon them. Yet
this one has affected me singularly; and I cannot get it
out of my mind. If it hadn't looked so silly, I don't
know but I should have acted upon it to-day by taking
you and Walter to Richmond. Perhaps you had better
go to-morrow, if you think it safer there than here; for I
would not have you harmed for the world."

"Oh, do go, papa, and let us all be happy together
once more!" said little Walter with a homesick sob.

"We may live together; but we never can be as happy
as of yore, my son. I hope you and Catharine may be;
for you are both young, and may live to see the end of
these troublous times."

"And you too, my friend," said Catharine fervently.
"May the dark clouds in your political and domestic horizon soon pass over, leaving you to a serene and happy
old age!"

"I do not hope for it: I know but too well that these
troubles are long, while my span of life is short. I have
been hoping all along for a peaceful solution to our national difficulties; but now that blood has been shed, and
a victory won, our people will consider themselves invin-
cible. No amount of coaxing can win them back; until

rivers of blood have rolled over the land. Our people
are rash and impetuous; and political fanatics have been
kindling the flames of discord among them for years.
But still, if the North had been actuated by a conciliat-
ing spirit, and yielded what they might without the
sacrifice of one particle of honor, this war would never
have been. But those old, stiff, puritanical principles
that actuate your people would not allow them to do
this. They knew that slavery was wrong, and that they
were in the right; so they would not concede one jot to
Southern prejudices; and we must abide by the consequences."

"If our countrymen had known each other better, —
known that there were souls as pure and as true, hearts
as brave and as tender, and feelings as warm and kind
and sensitive, at the South as at the North, — at the
East as at the West, — it might never have been," said
Catharine with a sigh. "I am sure a more thorough
knowledge of each other would have dissipated many of
our strongest prejudices."

"That is true; and yet slavery would have remained
a festering sore, a blight and a blot to any nation, and,
most of all, to one professing to be free. Yet, if our
people had treated their slaves as they ought, there
would never have been such a hue and cry about the
Fugitive Slave Law, which, first and last, has created more
than half the trouble: indeed, there would never have been
a Fugitive Slave Law at all. You know how my slaves
are treated; and never, until after Sweep came here, has
a single one left my service. He means well, and is a
grand hand to get a great deal of work out of a gang;
but I can see that they do not like him as they did Grover.
Now, however, the whole band will be scattered. I have

already been obliged to fill a large requisition to work on the defences at Manassas Junction; and I can see that the time is at hand when this land is to be overrun with hostile armies, — the one battling for slavery, the other strong in the cause of freedom; yet both devastating the country, and sounding the trump of freedom in the ears of these very slaves for whose possession the South are fighting so madly. They cannot resist that bugle-call. They will rise against their masters. And if, when that time comes, your people are true to the principles they profess, and improve their opportunities, the bond that holds them will not be worth a straw. I told Atherton so when he was here; but he, like all the rest of the leaders in this rebellion, is thinking more of founding a glorious empire, of which slavery is to be the chief corner-stone, and they the rulers and nobility, than of the interests of humanity, or best good of the nation."

"Yes: he mentioned some such thing to me."

"Ah, he avows it then? Atherton is not a bad man by any means; but he is madly ambitious, and as well fitted for a leader in an unjust cause as his daughter was to entice and mislead my apostate son. O my God! that he upon whom I had hoped to lean in my old age, should turn traitor to his country, and that my wife and my other children should be joined to their idols, and leave me to die uncared for and alone! Walter, my youngest-born and dearest child of my old age, sole scion of my house that is left to me, promise me, that, whatever happens, you will ever be true to your God, your whole country, and the noble principles I have taught you;" and he laid his hand tenderly upon his son's head.

"I swear it," said the noble boy, reverently holding up his hand as he had seen others do.

"It is enough," said the old man solemnly. "I have felt to-day more than ever before, that my life is almost ended. I shall not live to see the close of this war. But when I go, Walter, I shall now have the satisfaction of knowing that I leave one to bear up the name who will never disgrace his noble lineage. I wish he could go to our dear Lucy and her noble husband, who are true and stanch and loyal; or else home with you, Catharine, for I know you would make of him a good and noble man. But I ought not to ask it; for you have already had trouble enough to wear the bloom from your cheek. God forgive those who have caused it!"

"Don't speak of it," said Catharine tearfully. "It was all for the best, I am sure. As to our dear little Walter, I would take him if I could;" and she looked tenderly and pityingly into his great, dark, loving eyes.

"Well, I suppose that is impossible just now. His mother no doubt will claim him; and I believe you must take him to Richmond to-morrow. Though the city is wedded to secession, it must be safer there than here, where lawless bands, belonging to no party but Satan's, are roving in every direction. I fear now we are too isolated here to be safe; so you and Walter had better go. Then, if you still wish to go home, you can call on Atherton for the pass he promised to give you."

"But you are not going to remain here, alone and in danger?"

"Yes, Catharine. My wife refused to come to me, even when they thought me dying; so, whatever comes of it, I will not force myself into her presence now. I truly pity and forgive her for what must ever be a

8*

weight upon her conscience. I know my darlings, Jennie and Fannie, would have come to me if they had had a choice; and I want you to give them my blessing."

As she looked and listened, Catharine's heart began to thrill with a strange feeling of dread. The old gentleman seemed quite as well as usual; yet his pathetic words, solemn tones, and deeply-impressive manner seemed so much like those of a dying old patriarch, that she began to feel as if she was in the presence of death.

"Major Hunter," she said at last, "you have been very, very kind to me; and I cannot think of leaving you in danger and alone. If there is a safer place, you must go to it with us to-morrow. We can go to a hotel, or a friend's house, if you dislike going home."

"No, Catharine: that would be just publishing our disgrace to the world,—nothing more. But there comes Sweep. I wonder what news he brings to-night."

The news he did bring was a great many soul-stirring and heart-rending particulars of the late battle; of the terrible rout of the Union army, which was represented four times as large as it really was; of the large number of prisoners and wounded who were being carried by every train to Richmond; of the great strength of the fortifications at Manassas, and the arrival of large re-enforcements from the South; and, finally, that the whole country was full of roving bands, who were stripping and devastating the plantations.

"It is a horrible state of things," said the major, "but no worse than I have anticipated for months. I have prepared for it as well as I could. Since my return here, sick as I was, I have forwarded, by a trusty hand, most of my money, plate, and most precious papers to

Washington, intending to go there myself just as soon
as I was able. That is now impossible. But if it
should happen, Catharine, that you or any of my family
are in want, go or send to my old friend, John Brandon,
in Washington; and he has my orders to supply you
with whatever funds you need."

"To Washington! Every thing sent to Washington,
and I know nothing about it!." exclaimed the overseer,
in a sharp, surprised, interrogative tone.

"There was no necessity for any one's knowing that
my friend Randolph took more away in his trunks than
he brought here," said the major coldly.

"Randolph!" echoed Sweep. "Strange that I
never suspected!"

The major looked at Sweep in surprise and displeasure, if not suspicion, until he adroitly changed the subject. "It is getting late for you to be out, major:
hadn't you better retire?" he suggested.

"Perhaps so; but I would like to wait and see the
moon rise: I am not sleepy in the least."

"But you are still feeble; and it might be dangerous," said Catharine.

"I know; but the house is stifling. I am too strangely
excited and nervous to sleep. I could not be more so
were I going up in a balloon — as I wish I were — to
the clouds, and above them, where the woes of old
Virginia would never afflict me more."

"Those dreadful details have been too much for you,
my friend," said she anxiously, putting her arm around
him caressingly. "Pray let Walter and me persuade
you to retire."

"You know you can always coax me, darling; don't
you?" said he, smiling, as he rose to his feet. "There,

give me a good-night kiss; and may Heaven bless you for all your kindness, my child, and soon restore you to peace and happiness!"

Catharine kissed him tenderly, receiving as warm a return. Sweep came forward officiously with Nick, his favorite servant; and the major, taking Walter's little hand in his, bade Catharine good-night, and left the piazza.

For some time she paced back and forth, anxiously musing upon the major's strange manner, and thrilling with horror at the thought of those dreadful battle-scenes. Dreading lest some dear friend of her own was among them, she longed for invisible wings, that she might go at once, and see and succor and save. "Who knows, after all," she mentally murmured, "that my stay here may not be providential? Can I not contrive to see and care for my suffering countrymen in Richmond as I could never have done at home?" While musing thus, she sat down in the major's easy-chair, watching the glimmering beams of the rising moon, and the rapid fading of the lights in the slave-cabins; inhaling the fragrance of the flowers that were blooming all around her; and listening to the croaking of frogs, and the incessant chirp of crickets, katydids, tree-toads, and multitudes of insects. All at once she became conscious that she was not alone.

"Plaguy fine evenin'; ain't it, Miss Catharine," echoed the squeaking, disagreeable voice of the overseer.

"Yes," she replied rather curtly, hoping to get rid of him.

"I thought you'd be lonesome out here by yourself."

"Not at all: I generally enjoy my own thoughts about as well as anybody's."

"Well, I see you wanted to get the old man an' boy off; but I didn't know but you'd want to talk to somebody."

"I was about to retire, Mr. Sweep," said she, rising; "so I wish you a pleasant night's rest."

"Don't be in sich a hurry, Miss Kate. Pray be seated, an' listen to a feller once in yer life. You'll be sorry to the day of your death if you don't hear what I've got to tell ye this night; for, as sure as you live, it's the crisis and turnin'-pint in yer destiny."

Awed a little by his manner, she dropped again into the seat, and looked up at him inquiringly, though the looks of the man were not encouraging. He was a tall, gaunt, broad-shouldered, yellow-skinned, weazen-faced individual, with a low, narrow forehead, little twinkling gray eyes, a long nose, thin, cadaverous features, sandy hair, and a smirking, deprecating manner. In age he was probably about forty. Catharine inwardly shrank from him, as he came and placed his arm familiarly over the back of her chair.

"These are terrible ticklish times; ain't they?" he began. "It's my opinion that we Yankees would be a plaguy sight safer t'other side of the Potomac; don't you think so, Miss Catharine?"

"Of course I do. But to get there is out of the question just now, as they grant no passes to Northern people."

"No, 'tain't out of the question, by ginger! for I can get there 'most any time, for all the rebel pickets, and be as safe as a thief in a mill."

"Why don't you then, if such is the fact?"

"'Cause I'm waitin' for somebody to get willin' to go with me," he returned with a smirking laugh. "You see, Miss Kate, we never half·done that talk we had t'other day; and I wanted to finish up the argyment before I left Old Secesh for good.   I forgot to tell ye, strangely enough, how I'd been down South here, one place and another, this dozen year or more, and have got together over twenty thousand dollars, all safe an' sound up in New England, besides four or five thousand more with me here in Virginia.   Now it stands to nater that a gal of sense like·you would have a feller that's got the rhino a leetle quicker than a poor scalawag who might let her starve.   Now, I took a shine to you, Miss Kate, the minit I set eyes on ye; and I felt like wringin' Master Lloyd's neck when I see him shinnin' round ye.   He was a rich gentleman; and you wa'n't to blame, in course, for tryin' to du as well as you could. I was darned glad, though, when he quit; and I won't be at all stomachful about it, if you'll only come round, and have me."

"I have told you already, Mr. Sweep, that I could not do that," said Catharine almost angrily.   "So, if there is nothing else" —

"But there is something else.   Now, I happen to know that you ain't at all safe in these diggin's, unless you want to be toted off some dark night by a young Confederate officer I see down to the village inquiring after ye."

"Who, pray?"

"Oh! a tall feller, with a handsome face, midnight hair, big black eyes, and a small scar on the left check."

Catharine was a little startled.   The description just fitted Philip Atherton; but she would not show interest enough in the subject to ask if it were he.

"I guess you know well enough who it was," he con

tinued. "But say, now, hadn't you rayther get spliced to a feller that means honestly by ye than to run the resk of bein' toted off by one of them proud devils? They can talk moonshine by the hour; but they would no 'more marry a poor Yankee governess, than they would be hanged."

"Do you mean this for an insult, Mr. Sweep?" said she indignantly. "We are going to Richmond to-morrow, where there are those who will protect us; and I am not afraid of your Confederate officer."

"To Richmond! Ay! But hadn't you rayther go back with me, now, to old New England, where, with my money and yourn put together, we could cut as big a swell as the best on 'em?"

"No!" said she decidedly. "You and I, Mr. Sweep, could never become congenial companions."

"But why? Ain't I good enough for ye?"

"You may be too good, for aught I know; but our ideas, opinions, ways of thinking, and past associations have been wholly dissimilar; and we never could be mutually happy in each other's society."

"In what do we differ, I should like to know, except some little notions about niggers?"

"Well, that is enough, if there were nothing else. A Southern man, with a Southern education and prejudices, inheriting slaves, to many of whom he is strongly attached, has some excuse for retaining and ruling them. But a Northern one, born and reared in the land of the free, and then coming down here to be a slave-driver for the sake of gain, has none at all, in my estimation."

"So that's the talk, is it? I guess, though, if he was as rich, his gold would tempt you jest as quick as Lloyd Hunter's or Philip Atherton's."

"Never! I abhor slavery; and no amount of gold would tempt me now to wed either a slave-owner or a slave-driver."

"What's a poor Yankee governess better than a rich Yankee slave-driver, I'd like to know? It strikes me that the condescension, if there is any, is all on his side, ma'am." And his thin lips curled with scorn, and his gray eyes glittered and flashed in the bright moonbeams, and his low brow contracted into a dark frown, as he said it.

Catharine was angry and excited, or she would not have said what she did; and, when she saw his ominous looks, she began to feel as if this fawning, sycophantic man was neither silly nor trifling, and that she was making of him a dangerous enemy.

"Yes, yes," he continued bitterly: "you were very ready once to wed a slave-owner, but not a slave-driver, forsooth. You had sense enough to see the difference. But what is one better than the other?"

"Perhaps not any. Both commit the sin for the sake of gain, but it is none the less a sin; and I shall respect myself more to have nothing more to do with it."

"Or me."

"Yes, Mr. Sweep. I wish you well, and am sorry for your disappointment, if it is any; but conscience compels me to decline the honor of your hand."

"Very well. You may wish it didn't, though: for, mark my words, I am not used to bein' thwarted; and this is not the end of the matter."

"It is of no use to carry it further. Good-night, sir," said she coldly, as she rose and entered the mansion. She felt troubled not a little by his covert threats and sinister manner.

"That man is a villain! I always felt it instinctively. For gold he would sell his own soul, his father's bones, or his sister's honor. Whoever trusts him does it at his peril. How I blush that my own State should suffer the disgrace of rearing so degenerate a son! Thank God! there are few like him," were Catharine's mental comments, as she laid her head on her pillow. But she was too much excited to sleep. The clock struck ten, eleven, twelve; and still she was tossing upon her pillow, or sitting up watching the moonbeams, thinking of all that had transpired, or listening to noises in the major's chamber, which was next to her own. She knew, from various sounds, that he was waking, and two or three times, when she had almost gained the land of dreams, a smothered groan would thrill her nerves like an electric shock; and in an instant she would be sitting up, wide awake again.

"Any ting de matter, massa?" she would hear Nick say.

"No, Nick. But speak lower, or you will wake little Walter. Poor fellow! he has sobbed himself to sleep. He's an early student in the school of sorrow," was the reply to such questionings.

Since his arrival, Walter had insisted on sleeping there: so a bed was made for him in one corner; while Nick, as usual, slept on his mat near the door. After the clock struck twelve, Catharine, tired out with watching, sunk into a deep slumber.

From this she was awakened by a dream of horror; and, starting up with a shriek, she found her room brightly illumined, and her bed surrounded by a band of black, fierce-looking men. Terror froze the wild cry upon her lips; and, though for a moment it seemed but

9

the continuation of the fantasy of her dream, the
reality soon enough forced itself upon her startled
senses. There was no mistaking those fierce, malignant, blackened faces for any her imagination had con-
jured up; and she knew very soon that she was in the
presence of a band of desperadoes.

CHAPTER VI.

THE GUERILLAS. — DEATH OF MAJOR HUNTER.

"STAND back, comrades, or you'll scare the gal like thunder!" exclaimed a tall, bony, grizzly-bearded villain, who appeared to be the leader of the band. "And you, miss," he continued, "jest put on your clothes, and pack up your duds, and get ready for a little journey to-night."

Catharine did not faint; but she sat there, dumb and stupefied with terror, like one bereft of her senses. Her eyes were wild and distended, her cheek and lips pale as marble; and her shining auburn hair rippled in heavy, tangled curls, over her white shoulders, as she gazed upon the villanous faces around her. Secure in their villany, the men soon began searching for valuables, and at last opened Jenny the slave-girl's door.

"Hallo, Blondel! here's a likely wench, half-white, and worth six hundred any day," said one of the gang. "There! get up, you black beauty, and help your mistress dress;" and he gave her a kick with the toe of his boot that roused her pretty effectually.

"Who are you? and what is the meaning of all this?" exclaimed Catharine tremblingly, as soon as she could command her voice.

"You'll find out soon enough, I reckon. All you've got to du is to submit, and do as I tell ye."

"And if I refuse!" she exclaimed with flushed cheek and flashing eyes.

"This!" and he drew a glittering bowie from its sheath, and flashed it up before her eyes.

She recoiled instinctively; and her lips grew white with the fear that now assailed her.

"Is the argyment convincin'?" said the wretch with a loud laugh, in which he was joined by the others.

"If so, dress yourselves, — you an' that gal, — tie up what things you want in bundles, and march down stairs with this man : for we've other work to do;" and, at a sign from the leader, all left the room but one, — a dark, low-browed villain — the cruelest-looking of the gang. He had previously been rifling trunks, drawers, and closets of the most valuable things, comprising nearly the whole of Catharine's wardrobe and jewelry.

Seeing there was no way of escape but death, she roused the terrified girl, who was crouching beside her bed, and proceeded tremblingly to do as he required. Luckily she put on her best travelling-dress, which she had taken out the night before, in anticipation of her journey to Richmond; and in the waist of this had been stitched most of her ready money, which, with the watch under her pillow, that she managed to secrete, and a few of her commonest garments, was all she succeeded in saving. The poor girl saved a few articles, the man all the time watching them grimly, and, as soon as they were ready, ordered them to march.

Just as they emerged into the upper hall, they were met by a volley of oaths, and angry voices : the major's door was burst open; and the white-haired old man, undressed as they found him, and madly struggling with his captors, was dragged out and down the staircase.

He was followed by Nick, and poor little shrieking half-naked Walter, who was striking right and left with his puny fists, yet pleading in piteous tones for mercy.

"Stop yer bawlin', or I'll give yer a settler, you young lion's whelp!" exclaimed Blondel fiercely. "I'll teach ye what it costs to despise and tyrannize over us poor white folks, Mister Major."

"We have never wronged you, sir, in word or deed, that I know of; and why do you outrage us in this way?" said the poor old major tremulously.

"Aha! you never wronged *me*, — did ye? — and, through me, my whole class! As if I didn't get an honest livin' tradin' with the niggers till you come to the estate, an' broke it all up by your tarnal Yankee inventions."

"So — so — you are Blondel; are you? I thought you were in" —

"States prison, — out with it. No thanks to you, I wa'n't in for life. Wonderful 'fraid you was of havin' yer nigs cheated, and encouraged to steal, and trade for knick-knacks an' whiskey: so you must furnish 'em every thing to home, an' spile my trade, an' blege me to rob housen to get a livin'; an', instead of whippin' on 'em, as they desarved, payin' the devilish nigs premiums for their smartness an' sassiness: an' preachin' an' prayin' till ye shamed all the planters round. But we'll teach ye what it costs to fly in the face of the good old fashions, and honester men than you. We'll larn ye Yankee reforms with a vengeance. So come along, you old rebel!".

"My God! what are you going to do with me? Hallo,

Sweep! Nick! Jerry! Tom! Dinah!—where are you all?" shrieked the wretched old man, struggling at every step, and clutching at the balusters in frantic eagerness.

"Here, here, massa! We'd help ye if we could!" shouted Nick, as he pressed forward eagerly. But his efforts were cut short by a dozen eager hands clasping his struggling limbs, and, in spite of all his efforts, pitching him down stairs, over the head of his unfortunate master, and landing him, stunned and apparently lifeless, upon the marble floor of the hall.

Catharine and the slave-girl, with their escort, waited until the way was cleared, and then descended. Notwithstanding their terror, the sight that met their gaze as they emerged from the house filled them with curiosity and wonder.

In front of the mansion a large fire was burning, that cast ruddy gleams upon the windows, the lofty trees that shadowed it, and the weird figures of some thirty or forty villanous-looking men who surrounded it; while drawn up on the spacious lawn before the door were some half-dozen of the major's best mule-teams, already loaded with valuable plunder. Upon the tops of these teams, as drivers, were seated some of the smartest negroes belonging to the plantation. Beside each wagon sat an outlaw upon one of the major's best horses, revolver in hand, ready to fire upon the least symptom of disobedience. At a little distance the poor old major was bound to a tree, with a halter around his neck; while poor little Walter was clasping his knees, and sobbing piteously.

"All ready?" shouted the leader to the guards beside the teams.

"Ay, ay, sir!" was the ready response.

" Move on, tnen, as if the Devil was arter ye, as I s'pose
he is; and don't let the grass grow under yer hosses' feet.
Turn off from the road where I bade ye, and be sure you're
out of the way of pursuers when we have the illumination by and by."

The teams moved off at a rapid pace, amid the cheers
of the motley crew, just as Sweep, followed by Dinah,
Lulu, Dell, and the rest of the house-servants, rushed out
wildly from the mansion.

" Good God! What is the meaning of all this ? " he
exclaimed.

" That's a good one ! I guess you know about,as well
as anybody, you long-legged Yankee snipe ! " said the
leader with a shout of laughter.

" What should I know, pray, — just roused from sleep
as I am by your hellish noises ? " and he rubbed his
eyes vigorously, as if to prove his assertion.

" Jest hear him, you old skeleton," echoed Blondel.
" He wants to make b'lieve he's innocent as a lamb. But
you'll find out, the minit you get to t'other world, you've
been harborin' a jackal. Tell old Beelzebub he's comin'
fast as time can carry him."

" Good heavens! You here, major, — and in that condition ? And you too, Miss Kate ? " turning to her,
pretending not to hear what Blondel said. " Wretches !
what are you about to do to that white-haired old man ?
Unbind him instantly ! Here, Tom, Nick, Harry, run
to the quarters, — rouse the niggers and dogs. We'll
see who is master here ! " he eagerly exclaimed, as he
opened his jack-knife, and ran towards the major as if to
release him. But a hand was laid on his arm, in which
a knife glittered, and a voice hissed in his ear, —

" Look out, or you'll go too far, you lyin' scoundrel. We

come to du our part of the work, jest as we 'greed; but you ain't done your'n. You've hid the gold an' silver, an' then come out to us with a lie in yer mouth, pretendin' 'twas all sent off to Washinton. Then you dodge back inter the house to cut up some prank, an' come out with a mouthful of lies to deceive an' cheat the poor old fool who's harbored an' b'lieved in ye so long. But I don't b'lieve in one lie more than in t'other; and if you don't bring forrard the proofs, man, you, tu, shall swing at the end of a rope."

The overseer turned pale as death. Once or twice he opened his lips to speak to prevent Blondel from exposing him, but could utter no sound. For the first time he began to realize that he had been playing with edged tools to work out his dishonest purposes, that were now to be turned against himself, and that his hypocrisy would avail him nothing. "I did tell ye the truth," he said at last tremblingly; "and you solemnly promised not to have me known in the affair. You ain't done as you agreed."

"I should, if the gold had been forthcoming; and I'd divided it fair. You might lied yourself out of it as much as you pleased. Bring that forrard, an' I still hold to my side of the bargain. If not, the gals and nigs are our'n, with all the plunder; the house burns, an' you swing at the little end of nothin'."

"I can't bring it forrard: I ain't got it!" screamed the frightened wretch, with his teeth chattering with terror. "I didn't know as 'twas gone till to-night: the major and Miss Kate will tell ye so tu."

"Is that true?" said Blondel, turning to the major. He received no reply; for the wretched old man, overcome with weakness and terror, had fainted, with his head fallen forward upon his bosom.

" He's got a fit, captin ! " exclaimed one of the merci-less crew.

" No, no : he's on'y shammin'. Jest give him the licks, Blondel; and you'll bring him to his senses," echoed another.

" Well thought of, Cooper. Pass along the cat, Ring : we'll wake up the old scoundrel."

Poor little Walter heard the cruel words as he lay there upon the ground sobbing; and, rising with a wild shriek, he encircled his dear old father with his feeble arms.

" Aha, my fine young game-cock ! You've got too much flash in your eye to stan' there an' take the licks when ye begin to feel 'em. But ye can du as ye like about it."

The blow that descended upon the poor child's bare and defenceless shoulders also drew blood and groans from the wretched father. But the barbarian was right: there was too much flash in the boy's eye, and spirit in his soul, to bear such indignity unavenged. Springing with the agility of a squirrel and the fierceness of a young lion, with his face aflame and his eyes flashing, he caught a knife from the villain's belt, and would have sheathed it in his heart, had he not seen and caught the blow with his left hand.

" So, so, you little devil ! You have got the snap in ye; ain't ye ? " he exclaimed with a frightful oath. " Here, some on ye bind up this ugly cut with my han'kercher, and hold this young tiger-cub till I can finish that busi-ness. I'd whip the devil out of him, tu, if I had the time."

When all was ready, the villain again took the cat, and was preparing to strike, when the wretched and writhing old man began in piteous tones pleading for mercy.

"What is it you want?" he groaned. "Take all I have, but do not, I entreat of you, treat me with such indignity."

"Did you never have a white man or a nigger treated so, you old tyrant? I mean you shall feel what I have felt more than once, through your means, before I swing you off. But tell me, first, what has become of your plate, jewels, and money."

"If I am to die, you shall never know from my lips," said the major firmly.

"For God's sake, du tell, major, or they'll kill me tu," snivelled Sweep in pleading tones. "They won't b'lieve *me;* and it's tu bad to have to die for other folks' duin's."

"Hannibal Sweep, do you deserve to live? My senses deceive me, or you have been plotting to betray *me*, and all I have, to those bloodthirsty men."

"No, no, major: I never meant to betray you. It all comes from a little misunderstandin'. So pray du tell 'em what they want to know."

"And I say, *yes!*" echoed Blondel. "True, he didn't bargain for my private vengeance; but he did for the plunder and the nigs and the gal, if she scorned him. And he it was who shut up the mouths of yer yelpin' curs, dosed all yer nigs with drugged whiskey, — on'y them we wanted, — left all yer doors ajar, stole yer gold, an' silver, an' then came out with a lie in his mouth, — for which he, tu, has got to swing. Here, fix a rope round his neck, boys, an' tie him to that tree for a preparatory lecture; for, as sure as fate, we'll send a pair of the pretty birds to glory."

"Help! help! murder!" screamed the frightened wretch, struggling madly with his captors as they proceeded to fix the fatal noose. "Oh, I can't die! I ain't fit to die! Major Hunter! Miss Kate! O Miss Catharine! for God's sake, pity and save me!" he shrieked.

Little reason as she had to pity and save, Catharine could not resist this wild appeal. So, stepping forward, trembling in every limb, she exclaimed, "It is the truth he tells; and this very night I heard it from the major's own lips."

"Yes, yes," echoed the major at length. "The rascal deserves no mercy at my hands; but let him live — to repent. I did send all my treasures to Washington to save them from such rapacious wretches as you. But spare us all, and you shall have the whole of them."

"And be cheated of my vengeance! No, no : that is dearer than gold to me. You can have all the plunder, boys. My part shall be a sweet revenge. Now, some of you go and set fire to that old rookery; while you, Cooper, give that snivelling scamp a dozen for his knavishness, and then untie, and kick him out of my presence."

In spite of Sweep's shrieks, both orders were instantly obeyed.

"And now," he said, turning back to Major Hunter, "prepare to take what you have deserved this many a year!" and, drawing the sharp, cutting thongs of rawhide through his fingers, he glared upon his doomed victim with the ferocity of a fiend.

Brave as a lion in battle in his younger days, and ready, even now, to fight till his last breath, if his hands were free, the poor old man's heart sunk within him at the thought of such an ignominious end.

"Oh! is there nothing I can say or do to prevent this horrible outrage?" he groaned.

"Aha!" laughed the villain. "An outrage, is it, upon your boasted chivalry! An outrage upon your rich aristocracy! But none at all upon me, a man as white as yourself, who was whipped within an inch of my life through your means, and then sent to the chains and stripes and ignominy of the State's prison!" and, with a face fairly fiendish with evil passions, he raised his vengeful arm; and the blows descended until Catharine, forgetful of her own danger, rushed frantically forward in a vain attempt to save the major's life. There was a flash, a loud report, and a rifle-ball whizzed through her bonnet and raised left hand, cutting the veins upon her temple, and stunning her so that she fell forward to the earth nearly senseless.

"What did you do that for, Sharpe?" exclaimed Blondel, turning to him fiercely. "The gal's mine."

"I jest obeyed orders, that's all."

"Ah! I remember. Take her away, some on ye;" and again the blows descended.

But we sicken of the horrible details of a scene that was but one out of hundreds that were being enacted through the South at that time. We will only say in conclusion, that, when the poor old man was insensible to pain and indignity, he was strung up by the neck until life was ended; and that poor Walter screamed and struggled and implored until he wore out the patience of his keeper, who then struck him down senseless with a heavy club, and left him, supposing him dead. Catharine, meantime, dragged out from under foot, revived, and, her wounds bound up by the pitying slaves, was standing at a little distance, trying to avert her horrified gaze, and shut out the awful sights and sounds from her keenly-aroused senses. Every groan,

and every stroke of the whip, cut to her heart like a
knife, until she was glad when the poor victim's sufferings were over. By this time a cloud of dark, frightened faces began to gather upon the outskirts of the
scene, roused by the thunderous din: but the true
hearts and strong arms upon which the master had re-
lied were palsied and stupefied with drugged liquor;
while many of their comrades were still dead-drunk in
the cabins. The overseer had indeed done his work
well, — much better, in fact, than he anticipated. Knowing there were some disaffected spirits in the slave-
gang, he had for some time been tampering with them,
and promising them freedom; so they proved willing
tools in his hands to work out his own dishonest purposes. But, though Sweep was villain enough to plan,
assist, and share in this raid and robbery of the major's
property, he had never dreamed of their burning his
buildings, outraging his person, or taking his life.
He had thought to share a large sum for the night's
work, get Catharine into his power, if she otherwise refused him, and still retain his place at a large salary,
until such time as he could make off in safety with his
plunder. As to Catharine's destiny, he had not yet
fully decided. For, accustomed all his life to rate every
thing at a money value, her refusal, after hearing of
his wealth, had so surprised and angered him, that a
desire for revenge now ruled him quite as much as
any fancy he had ever felt for her. But, in thinking
and doing all this, he had wrought a just retribution
on himself. For all his papers, clothing, and money —
the hoarded gains of the past three years — were in
the burning dwelling. The feelings of such a man may
be imagined, as he looked back, smarting with pain, and

10

burning with anger and shame, after gaining a secure hiding-place. To see the flames beginning to pour from the lower windows, and know that his gold, more than half of which had been surreptitiously obtained, was to be sacrificed to his dishonest rapacity, was more than his avaricious nature could bear. Gold was the idol of his worship: he could not endure the thought of losing it; so, in spite of the double danger, he resolved to make one effort to secure it. The band of outlaws were in front of the house, busy with their nefarious work; while he had got round in the rear of the long line of slave-cabins at the left. By crossing the large orchard and kitchen-garden, he thought he could gain the rear entrance unperceived. There seemed to be no fire there as yet; so he thought he could go up the back staircase to his room, and regain his treasure with little danger. All this he stealthily accomplished to his perfect satisfaction. He gained his room, secured his valuables, and was upon the landing with his best suit thrown over his arm, when, to his horror, his egress was cut off by an unexpected obstacle.

But sly and stealthy as had been his approach, it had not been wholly unperceived; for Uncle Nick, the major's valet, though stunned, was not killed by his fall over the balusters, but subsequently revived, and crawled out, bruised and bleeding, to be a vengeful witness of deeds that set his blood aflame with the fires of vengeance. His clear intellect at once comprehended the facts. He knew, from what he had gathered from the slaves as well as their dying master, that they had been betrayed by the wily overseer, whom they all hated. Nick would almost have laid down his life for his master; but what could he and the few sober slaves

do, unarmed, against thirty or forty bloodthirsty desperadoes armed to the teeth? As he could not look on
coolly and see his master and darling little Walter murdered, he crawled off to the slave-cabins, roused a few
old men and women, and armed them with clubs and
pitchforks. They were just coming up to the rear of
the house, undecided as to what they could do, when
they saw Sweep stealthily enter it.

"Dere, dere he go, de ole Satan dat make all de
mischief!" he exclaimed. "He goin' to get de gold an'
tings: dat's what he arter. Now, boys, we got 'im in a
trap," he whispered in clear, sharp tones. "You gals sly
in, an' brung out all ye can o' mistress's tings, dat de
rogues dun left to burn up; while we boys fotch de fag-
its, an' smoke out de ole coon."

The order was instantly obeyed: those who dared
rushed in, and, in defiance of the stifling smoke, saved a
great many useful articles of furniture; while Nick and
the men seized great bundles of fagots and shavings,
piled them in the stairway, and, when they thought
Sweep was about to descend, with burning brands set
fire to them in a dozen places. Dry as tinder, the fire
caught them with devouring fury, and roared up the
narrow staircase in a fierce column of seething flame,
instantly cutting off all egress in that direction.

Met by the stifling smoke and roaring flames, Sweep
knew at once that he had enemies in the rear as well as
in front of him. But, knowing that the one within was
more to be dreaded than either, he rushed back through
the upper hall, breathless, gasping, and despairing, to
find the magnificent front staircase one mass of smouldering ruins, into which, blinded by the smoke and
stifling heat, he came very near plunging headlong. He

knew there was but one other mode of egress ; so, rushing back to his room, with his hat gone, his hair singed
off, his clothes smouldering, he opened a window, and
looked down upon the depths below.   It was the end of
the building, and no one was there.   There was no
alternative but to leap from the window with a bare possibility of escape, or to meet sure and certain death by
the flames.   Fanned by the draught from the window,
the fire was fast approaching : yet, cautious to the last,
he waited to tear his bedclothes into strips, tie them together and to the bed-post ; and then, with his frail
rope, he attempted to descend.

But alas for the miserable man ! just as he got
cleverly out of the window, and was hanging by the sill,
the outlaws discovered him.   For having finished their
work of destruction, and fearing the light of the fire
would bring some government patrolling party upon
them, they hunted up Catharine, and a few of the best-
looking female slaves, placed them in a baggage-wagon
that was in waiting, got in themselves, or mounted their
horses, and were driving swiftly away.   But Blondel, the
leader of the gang, who sat on the back seat beside
Catharine, happening to look back, discovered poor
Sweep just in the act of descending.

"Aha, Cooper, stop a minute ! Just look there !" he
exclaimed.   "I'll bet you a hundred dollars that it's that
scoundrelly overseer.   He couldn't quit with a whole
skin, but went back after the plunder.   By Jove ! I'll
give him one parting salute ; and, raising his rifle at a
venture, just over Catharine's head, he fired.

The mules jumped and ran, coming very near upsetting the wagon ; while Blondel dropped into his seat
with a loud laugh, exclaiming, "There, if that don't
finish him, the cuss is hard to kill."

Catharine, meantime, had made one attempt to escape since she fully recovered consciousness, but was discovered, brought back, and a guard set over her by Blondel, until he finished his fiendish work; and then, forced into the wagon at the point of the knife, with the poor unresisting slave-girls, she felt as if it were in vain to try to escape, even though her hands, in consideration of her wounds, unlike the others, were tied in front instead of behind her. This was some relief; but the thongs cut into her tender flesh, as it swelled rapidly; and her wounds pained her very severely.

The road that crossed the great Hunter plantation was not a public one; but it intersected the great Northern pike a mile or more from the mansion. This it was necessary for the outlaws to reach, and follow for a while, before dispersing into the by-paths that led to their mountain *rendezvous*. Some had come on horseback, and some on foot; but all were now well mounted upon the major's fine stud. Elated by the generous liquors they had found in the cellar, and by the success of their enterprise, they cantered off with buffaloes and blankets for saddles, and in the highest possible spirits. It was after four o'clock in the morning as they debouched upon the main thoroughfare. A beautiful summer day was dawning in the east. The birds were singing in the tree-tops, and the flowers were blooming all around them, filling the pure morning air with sweet perfumes; while every thing in nature looked as lovely as if no deeds of horror were ever enacted; yet afar upon the hill-top the flames still towered up grandly to the sky, tingeing the passing clouds with ruddy and golden tints, and gloriously lighting up the magnificent landscape.

10*

"Now, boys, ride for your lives!" exclaimed Blondel, as they emerged from the fine arched gateway.

"We are two hours later than we ought to be upon this piece of road : we shall be safer from the patrols if we separate.   You, Cooper and Baker, Hines and Mc-Caffrey, stay with me to guard the prisoners; and the rest on ye ride like the deuce."

The order was instantly obeyed; and very soon a great cloud of dust was all that could be seen of the party of horsemen. The guards fell back behind the heavy mule-wagon, in which were seated the four captives, with the driver and Blondel, both heavily armed and keenly watchful.

As soon as it was light enough, Catharine knew that Blondel, who was an ugly-looking, grizzly, low-browed villain, was closely scanning her looks and appearance. She shrank instinctively from the peculiarly-repulsive and snaky glitter of his eyes, as she met them furtively, and shivered with dread, as he turned and said to the driver, "That rascally overseer had devilish good taste; hadn't he?   It won't hurt my conscience a bit to step inter his shews. What say ye, gal?" and he turned to Catharine: "hadn't you ruther clean my cabin, cook my grub, and dance to my music, than du the like for that lyin' rascal, Sweep?"

A shudder and repressed sob were his only reply.

"You see," he continued quite confidentially, "that my old woman scattered the young ones, and went off with another feller, while I was up there to work for Old Virginia; and somehow it's never come handy to get another. Now, by Jupiter! one's come right inter my hands that I like the looks on;" and he gave her a sly wink of his wicked gray eye. "You sha'n't be sorry for't,

nuther. I'll dress you up as fine as a peacock. Come,
what du you say? Will it suit ye?" and he put his
brawny arm around her very lovingly.

A shudder of horror and repulsion shook her; but she
was saved the trouble of angering him by a reply; for
at that moment the sharp click of steel-clad hoofs, and
the sound of voices in the distance, struck upon the ears
of the guard; and "The patrols! The patrols! a
host of them!" was echoed from every lip.

"The devil they are!" exclaimed Blondel. "But
where are all our men?"

"Don't you see? They've got safe round the turn,
with the woods in their rear."

"Thank fortin for that! But how in hell are we to
get out of sight? It can't be did; so we've got to face
the music. Here, you wimin! you're my runaway
slaves, you remember. An' if you say one word agin it,
I put this knife through your hearts;" and he flourished
the glittering weapon up before their terrified eyes.

"Now, boys, keep behind; and, if you can't du any
better, you're goin' up to camp to enlist. But mind, and
all tell the same story. In any case, we don't belong to
the same gang."

"By thunder! I'll not resk it," exclaimed Cooper.
"You forget that we're all as black as the ace of spades,
and no chance to wash it off. We must take to the woods;
and let you who's not mounted du the best you can."
And, suiting the action to the word, he leaped the low
fence that skirted the road, followed by his companions;
and they were soon lost to sight in the woods.

After a moment's hesitation, Blondel took up the skirt
of his dingy coat, and, holding down his face, gave it a
thorough scrubbing; polishing off by a dirty handker-

chief wet from his brandy-flask, until it resembled a huge pickled beet. His hasty toilet was completed not a minute too soon.

"Now, hurry up, Hoffman," he said, "and show 'em we ain't afraid to meet 'em. And remember, you're my nigger-driver, and must swear to the truth of every word I say."

"Ay, ay, captin : I understand; and it's neck or nothing this time, I'll be bound to say. But you know I'm up to all the dodges; and we'll get off if we possibly can."

The words were hardly out of his mouth before they met the advance-guard of the on-coming train. They proved to be an officer's guard in front, followed by their superiors, with a long train of baggage and foraging wagons in the rear.

"Hallo, there! Halt! Who are you?" was the polite salutation.

"Peaceable citizens, taking home a gang of runaway slaves," returned Blondel, in a brusk, assured tone. "Turn out there Jake, and let the troops go by."

"So, so! But what ails that one beside you with the white skin, and the bloody rag round her head?"

"Brought her down with a crack of the bull-dogs, jest as she was makin' off: she's the sassiest of the whole lot, as white wenches always be."

Catharine's heart beat as if it would burst her bodice. Must she sit there passive, and see her last chance for escape go by? She raised her eyes and bloody, manacled hands, and impulsively opened her lips to speak. But a warning gesture and glance from the blazing eyes of Blondel, who was nervously playing with the hilt of his bowie, froze the half-formed words upon her lips, and prevented their utterance.

"Drive on now, Jake," he said, — "a little furder to the right. The troop can go by now, if they want tu."

"No: halt! What's the meaning of that fire off there upon the hills yonder?"

"Dunno. We've bin watchin' on't this long time, and spect it's some house burnin'. We see a gang of fellers come from that way, and go off there into the woods, that we reckoned might know somethin' 'bout it;" and he pointed in the direction his troop had not taken to divert pursuit.

"What do you think of the old chap's story?" said the sergeant, turning to the officers. "Shall we let him pass on?"

"It may all be true, but I have my doubts," said a voice that made Catharine start. "That is certainly Hunter House burning off there upon the hills; and these may be some of the Hunter slaves they're running off in the *mêlée*."

The officers and guard now drew up beside the road, a little way in front of Blondel; and the baggage and foraging wagons passed on.

Blondel uttered a frightful oath below his breath. "Don't you see we're in a trap, Hoffman?" he whispered. "How I long to put this knife through that rascal's heart!"

"Yes, yes: but play spooney as long as you can. It's our only chance."

The officers now rode up beside the wagon, when Blondel cunningly leaned forward, and spread himself all he could, to shield Catharine from their observation. But this movement, as it proved, defeated itself, as, in doing so, he partially turned his back to her.

Quick as thought, she raised her manacled hands, removed her torn and bloody veil, and pushed the bandage up from her eyes, resolving to dare death now, rather than lose this opportunity for escape: for it was Col. Atherton's voice she had heard; and, though he was not the one she would have chosen for a protector, she felt as if he would not see her wronged.

"So you have runaway slaves; have you, my man?" said the colonel in his quick, decided way. "Where did you take them, sir?"

"Oh! down here, thirty miles or so. A friend of mine knew and nabbed 'em, and sent me word."

"And where do you belong, sir?"

"Oh! up here a piece, — a few miles above."

"Up above and down below: that's definite, at any rate. But is it the truth, girl?" he said to the one nearest him. She answered only by a sob, so strong was the fear of the glittering knife at her back.

"Why d'ye ask her, yer honor? You know they'll all lie sooner than speak the truth. Pray let us drive on: it's gettin' hot, and we've a long road to travel."

"Well, your gang seem to have gone the wrong way for runaways: they generally go due north."

"The fools got their heads turned, that's all," said Blondel with a laugh; in which he was joined by Hoffman.

"Any way, we have no more time for parley," said Col. Atherton anxiously; "for I am bound to know the meaning of that fire up yonder. I have friends at Hunter House I would not see harmed for worlds. I designed calling on my return; but, as it is, I think I will do so now. You may pass on, sir."

Catharine's heart sunk like lead in her bosom: her face grew pale as marble at the thought of death or the far worse fate that wretch had in store for her; but she made her choice. Rising noiselessly to her feet, she looked up at Col. Atherton, then down at Blondel; shook her head ominously, and then sank back into her seat again without his knowing she had risen at all.

The effect was electrical. Had an apparition appeared before the eyes of the officers, they could not have been more startled or surprised. For Catharine's manacled and bloody hands raised in mute supplication, her wild, imploring eyes, her bandaged head, and pallid yet beautiful face, down which the blood was trickling, touched every chord of human sympathy in their bosoms.

In spite of her horrid appearance, and the blood and dirt, and disorder of her apparel, Col. Atherton knew her at once. Whispering an order to an attendant, he dashed round upon the opposite side of the wagon, and exclaimed, as he tenderly took her wounded hands in his, —

" My God, Catharine! what is the meaning of this?"

" This!" echoed Blondel fiercely, as he pointed and attempted to fire his revolver at Col. Atherton. But his arm was knocked up just in time by Major Mulford; the piece was discharged in the air; the dancing mules were caught by the bits by firm hands; and five minutes later Blondel and his accomplice lay swearing and writhing upon the ground, bound with the very thongs taken from the hands of their captives. The revulsion of feeling was so great that Catharine came very near fainting. When sufficiently recovered, she explained the whole affair to the officers, who were very ready to return with her to the plantation. The awful scene that there presented itself too well attested her story. The body of the poor old major had already been cut down by the faithful slaves,

who had tried in vain to resuscitate it. They were now
gathered around it, weeping and wailing, and uttering
long, mournful howls of lamentation for the dear master
who had always been kind to them, with threats of vengeance against his murderers. As yet, they seemed
wholly indifferent to either a prospect of freedom or
change of masters.

The shell of the grand old mansion was still standing,
for it was of solid stone of great thickness; but the
inside work, which was mostly of wood, was a mass of
glowing coals, and burning beams, and brands, with the
lurid flames still towering up fitfully towards the sky.

Poor little Walter, for whom they first inquired, was
found in the nearest slave-cabin, still insensible and sorely
wounded, yet tenderly cared for by the kind slave-mothers
of the plantation.   Sweep, who was wounded through
the cheek by Blondel's shot, and had fallen upon the hard
paving-stones below, still lay near the burning dwelling,
where he had succeeded in crawling with his last remaining strength.   He was out of danger, except from flying
sparks, and possibly falling walls, yet stifling with the
heat, parched with thirst, and apparently in a dying condition.   He appeared to have no bones broken, which
was a wonder, and had evidently bound up his wound
as well as he could with his handkerchief before relaps-
ing into insensibility.

Catharine's heart ached for both the dead and dying,
the deserving and the undeserving: and at her desire
Sweep was removed to one of the out-houses that was
spared, where it was cooler; and there, with her own hands,
she poured water into his parched mouth until he partially revived, and looked gratefully up to her.

" Why do you do that ?   The wretch is unfit to live,"

said Col. Atherton, after watching her proceedings a few moments.

"He is unfit to die, Col. Atherton," she replied: "let him live to repent, atone, and prepare for death, if he can. If he dies, may God have mercy on his soul!"

By this time Mr. Garland and some of the nearer neighbors had arrived upon the scene; and it was judged best by all to place the remains of Major Hunter in the family vault near by, where the Hunters had reposed for several generations, and dispense with all unnecessary funeral ceremonies. While the preparations were in progress, the officers dashed off upon the business they had in hand, but returned in time for the burial, which was conducted by the parish clergyman with unusual solemnity. This unseemly haste was judged necessary, because otherwise Col. Atherton could not be present; and it was very doubtful whether his wife would come with her other children, if sent for. It was also very warm. Doctors could not be obtained short of the camp or in Richmond, and hardly there, so many wounded and dying needed attention. Walter's and Catharine's wounds required immediate care, which it was thought they could get in the camp sooner than anywhere else. But many poor wounded Union soldiers still lay in the barracks, and even on the field of battle, untended, uncared for, and dying a thousand deaths in one; while the birds of prey, and more hideous robbers of the dead, pursued their hellish work, unmindful of their piteous prayers for help or their dying agonies.

Catharine would have preferred to go back to Richmond; but as it was thought best to take little Walter to the camp, which was much nearer, she could not find it in her heart to desert him under the circumstances.

11

CHAPTER VII.

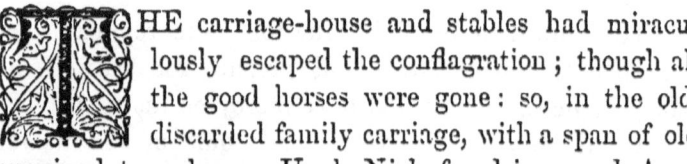HE carriage-house and stables had miraculously escaped the conflagration; though all the good horses were gone: so, in the old, discarded family carriage, with a span of old spavined team-horses, Uncle Nick for driver, and Aunt Dinah for attendant, Catharine and poor little Walter made the journey to head-quarters. It was a ride of sixteen miles; and they were obliged to go very slowly: so it was dark long before their arrival.

Sending some of the officers forward, the colonel patiently attended them the whole distance, striving by his presence and words of encouragement to beguile the journey of its tediousness and anxieties, and assuring them of safety from the outlaws by the armed guard by which he was attended.

Worn out by excitement, fatigue, and the pain of her wounds, Catharine's head ached so she could scarcely see before her arrival; so she was obliged to resign the care of little Walter to other hands, and lie down at once. In spite of all her pain and anxieties, as well as the new and strange camp noises, she slept that night the dreamless sleep of utter exhaustion. Gen. Atherton — he bore that title now — had a tent prepared for their accommo-

122

dation, and did every thing that was in his power to make them as comfortable as possible. He also sought out the most distinguished surgeons; and, as soon as they could attend the next morning, he was in waiting. Walter was still speechless and nearly insensible; which was a mercy, as his skull was broken by the blow he had received, and the operation of trepanning was considered necessary by the experienced surgeons. Catharine's wounds were considered slight in comparison with his: but they were very painful; and if the one on the temple had varied the twentieth part of an inch, the doctors said, she would never have seen daylight again. They were now dressed scientifically; and, feeling much better, she was thankful to escape with her life. "With the best of care, Walter might live," they said; but it was very uncertain; and it would be at the risk of his life to remove him to Richmond, as she had hoped to do. As it was, she consoled herself with the idea, that Mrs. Hunter and her daughters would return with the messenger Gen. Atherton had sent to them with the news of the dreadful tragedy and Walter's extreme danger. But in this hope Catharine was doomed to disappointment; for the messenger brought back word, that, upon the receipt of the terrible tidings, which he communicated as gently as possible, Mrs. Hunter had fainted, and gone from one paroxysm into another, until her reason, if not her life, was despaired of. Under these circumstances, her daughters could not leave her, and begged Catharine piteously, in a letter so blotted with tears that she could hardly decipher it, to remain and take what care she could of little Walter. They thanked her for all she had done for their dear murdered father, and concluded by sending her some apparel, which she greatly needed: so there was no alternative; stay in the rebel camp she must for some weeks to come, surrounded by a hundred thousand rebel soldiery. There were other women there, it is true, — some of them ladies of rank, attending upon sick and wounded relatives, too ill to be removed. But, confining herself mostly to her own quarters, she saw little of these, and felt, so far as her own sex and color were concerned, as if she were alone. But Dinah was a great comfort to her, — Dinah, whose love and good-will she had won long ago, when they had the fever; who still considered her in the light of a daughter of the house, and who was ready to take every possible burden from her shoulders. But Dinah and Uncle Nick both had treacherous memories, and could not read writing; so the real care came upon Catharine. She very soon found out a way to make them eminently useful, however, in the care of the poor wounded Union soldiers, who were sadly neglected by their exasperated enemies, and would have suffered more but for the kind and pitiful negroes.

She visited them herself as often as she could; and many were the prayers that went up for her future happiness. This experience alone made her feel as if her coming there was providential, and not altogether in vain. Gen. Atherton was unremitting in his attentions, and, when off duty, spent all his leisure time with them. And never for one moment did he suffer her to forget that he passionately loved her; was a suppliant, though not an humble one, for her favor; and would be repulsed by no common considerations. Not often in words indeed did he indicate this: but every look and tone revealed it to her; and his manner, at once respectful, devoted, and protecting, announced a feeling of determined ownership that was very difficult to resist or gainsay. She tried to avoid him, — to plead fatigue, and resign her charge to others when she knew he was coming; but it was of no use: he always inquired for her, and was so close in his questionings when they met, that she could not disguise the truth.

"Why is it you avoid me as you do?" he said to her one day. "You have said that my personal presence and society were not distasteful to you; that you were willing to be convinced, if wrong in your opinions; and that you could respect any man who was sincere in the avowal of opposite ones. Why, then, if that is the truth, will you not allow me the privilege of free social intercourse, that I may, if such a thing is possible, win the regard I so ardently covet?"

"Because I consider it wrong to encourage in any human bosom hope that I mean to disappoint," said Catharine, blushing.

"So you mean to disappoint mine?" he eagerly questioned.

"You know what I told you in the beginning, Gen. Atherton, — that every obligation that binds me to my kindred, my country, and my home forbids my forming any closer ties with one of that country's avowed enemies. I am under infinite obligations to you for releasing me from a band of ruffians, — possibly a fate worse than death, — and very many kind attentions since. I assure you that I am deeply grateful; but, knowing I could not make the return you wished, I have felt as if it would be better, for your sake, that we should see less of each other, and for me to go home at the earliest possible opportunity: you would then forget me very soon."

"Never, Catharine! Whatever the event, I shall

11*

never forget you. But tell me, now: are there not other
reasons, besides those you have named, why you cannot
make the return I wish ? "

"Yes : a great many.   Northern principle and prejudice, clothed in poverty, is no suitable match for Virginia pride.   That always arouses in my heart a spirit
of rebellion and antagonism."

"Catharine, I don't believe you ever loved Lloyd
Hunter; but you do love some one else, — some accursed
Yankee in the Union army perhaps, — whose life is
more precious to you than all I have to offer."

"No, Gen. Atherton : I have no knowledge of any
one in the Union army, though I may have many
friends there; and, aside from my kindred, I love no one
in the wide world who cares for me."

"Then you must be mine, dear Catharine, whether
our people are friends or foes : for I care for you, and
would shield you with my life from every danger; and
no man can love as ardently as I love you, without, in
some sort, compelling a return of his fervent passion.
Oh, think of it as a foregone conclusion that you are to
be my bride ! " he passionately exclaimed.

"If I were, your friends would not respect me. Lloyd
Hunter doubted, and was made to believe me unworthy
his regard, — as you would be, were it known that you
sought me for a wife."

"No, Catharine : I could not look into your innocent,
truthful eyes, and believe you guilty of wrong. I was
told of Lloyd Hunter's suspicions by one who should
have scorned to repeat them; but they made no difference in my feelings. I can read human nature better
than he; and so far from doubting am I, that I would
stake my life upon your innocence, purity, and truth."

"Gen. Atherton, I am deeply grateful for your just and generous appreciation, which so few under the circumstances would have accorded me; and I solemnly assure you that your judgment of me was right, and his wrong : but that cannot alter our relations to each other. Your people, and you yourself at times, scorn and despise ours; and I can be no true Southern wife while my blood leaps so with indignation, as it did when I went out to-day, at the unmerited insults heaped upon us as a people."

"Ah, Catharine! what would I not give had you been born south of Mason and Dixon's line! From somewhere you have got the old chivalrous blood in your veins, that is just now flushing your check with crimson, and flashing in true courageous fire from your eyes," he exclaimed admiringly.

"I have the blood of honest and loyal New-England farmers and mechanics in my veins," said she ; "and of that I am as proud as if it came from a kingly line."

"Perhaps it did, far back of the days of the stern old Puritans, who subjected the rugged New-England rocks and hills to their dominion. But of one thing I am sure. — that, if you were a man, you would at least lead a brave Northern brigade against us, that would never retreat as ingloriously as some of them did the other day at Bull Run. As a woman, you will leave such a glorious name behind you as we can ill spare from the records of old Virginia ; " and, with a triumphant yet admiring glance and smile, he rose and bade her "Good-evening."

Catharine felt vexed and indignant, both at him and herself. Yet what better could she have done with such a bold, presuming lover as Gen. Atherton? She felt thankful enough that Walter was improving, and would, the doctor said, be able to be removed very soon ; for she could not help feeling annoyed by the general's persevering pursuit, and that her reputation would be endangered by remaining much longer in such a place, and under such circumstances. That he took every precaution to prevent this, she well knew, because he sought to make her his wife. But she did not know that he had used his influence with Dr. De Homergeau to prolong the excitement of her presence.

The next morning, observing an unusual stir and bustle about the camp, Catharine learned, upon inquiry, that a spy from the Union army had been caught the night before within the Confederate lines. Some of the troops were clamorous for his immediate execution ; but the officers said he must have a fair trial, and gave little heed to their complaints.

Somehow, Catharine's heart beat a note of fear when she heard this news; and all day she kept thinking of it, until the general came in for his evening call. She greeted him with cool politeness.

He, on his part, inquired tenderly about little Walter, who was asleep, but otherwise, though he watched her narrowly, seemed unusually silent and depressed. At last she remembered to ask, —

"What is this I hear, general, about a Union spy? Is his fate decided?"

"Yes : he dies at sunrise," was the reply.

"Heaven help him !" she exclaimed with a sinking heart. "But do you think him guilty, general?"

"No : I believe him an innocent man."

"But were you not one of the court-martial who condemned him to die?" she questioned.

"Yes : but I was in the minority, and could not save him."

"What is his name? Poor fellow!"

The general hesitated, looking at her pitifully. "Catharine, have you a brother in the service?" he said at last. "The young man gave his name as Hale; and, from his resemblance to you, I feared"—

"My God! It is my wild, adventurous brother Harry! I have felt and feared it all the time," she exclaimed in agonized tones.

"His name was indeed Harry Hale. But it is a common name enough; and it may not be your brother, after all," said the general in sympathetic tones.

"Oh, it is, it is! I feel it here;" and she laid her hand on her heart. "And for him to die in such a way,—so young, so brave, so talented, so much beloved! O Gen. Atherton! is there no reprieve, no appeal from this wicked decision?" and she got up and walked the floor, wringing her hands in tearless agony.

"I fear not: the whole army will demand his execution."

"But you are all-powerful! You can save him, if you will only use your influence."

"No, Catharine: I failed to do so at the trial; and nothing that I can say or do will avail aught with the powers above me."

"But is there no way, no escape from a fate so ignominious, so terrible? O Harry! generous, noble-hearted brother! What is there I would not do to save thee? Do you think I can see him, general?"

"Certainly; at least I will try and pave the way for you immediately. But pray sit down! You are exhausting yourself by these emotions, when you will need all your strength to bear you up in this sad interview;" and he led her gently to a seat, called Dinah, and went out immediately. He returned presently with the written order from the proper authorities for Catharine's admittance to the prison.

But for a shrewd after-thought, the general would have attended her himself. As it was, she went with a proper escort, and Dinah for an attendant; while Uncle Nick remained with Walter, and he went out among his brother-officers. She found poor Harry confined, and doubly guarded, in an old, strong, yet somewhat dilapidated building, that was used as a prison, but so changed in appearance, that, had she not been expecting to find him there, she would not have known him. His form was thin and attenuated, his cheeks pale and hollow; dark circles were around his once laughing, but now sad and mournful eyes; his mouth was compressed as if with acute bodily and mental suffering; and his whole appearance, as he sat there upon a dirty pile of straw, leaning his head upon his hand, betokened the deepest dejection and despair.

"A lady to see you, sir," announced the grim jailer, as he opened the door; "but what she wants of a cussed Yankee spy is more than I can tell," he muttered in a lower tone as he reluctantly closed the door.

Catharine advanced a few paces, followed by Dinah, and then stopped, overcome by emotion. Poor Harry, for it was indeed he, slowly raised his head, blinded for a moment by the brilliant sunset rays that came pouring in through the open door. The moment his eyes rested on Catharine, he sprang to his feet, and, with a cry of joy, held out his manacled hands to her, and was soon sobbing like a child upon her bosom.

"O Harry, dear brother! It breaks my heart to find you thus, — so changed, so wretched, and in such frightful peril!" sobbed Catharine.

"And mine to be in this horrid condition," said he gloomily.

"But how came you to be in it, dear Harry? Were you indeed a spy?"

"No, Catharine: God knows I was far enough from that. I was wounded, and left for dead, in that terrible battle of Bull Run. The night after the battle I revived, and crawled away into the bushes. After suffering every thing but death from pain, thirst, and starvation, I was found by a friendly negro, who took me to his hut, and nursed me back to life and comparative health. And it was in trying to make my way through the rebel lines to our own, that I was caught by the rebel pickets, who of course would not believe my story. Tried by a court-martial, I am condemned to die a felon's death; to which some of my friends long ago consigned me, you remember," he said with a miserable attempt at a smile.

"I know; but, O Harry! I feel as if I cannot have it so. Is there nothing I can say or do to help or save you? They tell me there is no hope of a reprieve, but I will not believe it."

"You must. Like tigers they are thirsting for blood; and they will not let me go."

"Then you can only look up to God for help and mercy, and meet death as bravely as you can," she said in a voice quivering with emotion.

"O Catharine!" he passionately exclaimed, "better a thousand times that I had died upon the battle-field than live to suffer untold agonies, and die at last by the hangman's rope;" and there was a pitiable note of fear in his tones, that made Catharine's heart ache. "You may think me a coward," he continued; "yet I fought manfully to the last, and stood up before the cannon's mouth without blenching. And when I lay dying, as I thought, upon the battle-field, though I longed to live, I felt as if I could trust in God's mercy, and was resigned to die for my country. But now, with feeble health, shattered nerves, and a heart sick with vain longings for home and friends, the thought of a felon's death strikes me with a nameless terror. I try to combat it: I strive to think of it calmly; but it is of no use. Oh, I shall die a very coward in the face of our enemies!"

"But, dear Harry, it is really no worse than any other mode," began Catharine.

"Yet the flash of the sword or the whir of a bullet I believe I could bear bravely; but the scaffold — the hangman's rope — O God! Catharine, I cannot — oh, I cannot bear the thought!" and again he laid his face on her bosom, and wept like a grieved child.

She pressed him to her heart, and mingled her tears with his; but what could she do or say to console him? — what to comfort herself?

"O Harry!" she sobbed at last, "God knows I would save you if I could. I will go to Beauregard or Jefferson Davis himself, and plead for your life, or do any thing in the world else you think would be of any avail."

"It would be all in vain, Catharine, — worse than useless; for they thirst for the blood of every Northern man, and would not spare me."

"But you do not know that, Harry; so just let me try. Gen. Atherton, I know, believes you innocent, and will help me to gain an audience, and perhaps I can persuade others to the same opinions."

"No, Catharine: not for me shall you kneel at the feet of these arch-rebels, to be spurned, and spit upon, if nothing worse. But how, in the name of wonder, did you get here any way? I thought you had gone home long ago."

In a few brief words she explained her position and past experiences.

"What! Staying here in the rebel camp!" he exclaimed in astonishment. "Oh! I tremble for your safety. Pray get out of it, and go home as soon as you can!"

"That is my intention; though I have had nothing but honorable treatment thus far, and may have saved precious lives by coming here. But how are they all at home?"

"Well, when last heard from; and Theodore, who was with me in the battle, is a captain in the Union army. Whether he lived or died, I cannot tell."

"Time's up! Only five minutes more!" sung out the jailer.

"Oh, must we part thus, and forever!" sobbed Catharine. "O Harry! is there nothing I can say to reconcile you to this terrible destiny?"

"Nothing, dear sister, — nothing but pray that I may have courage given me to die like a man. But, oh!"— and again the tears burst forth, — "to think that there is but a night, a span long, between me and eternity! To think of the gaping crowd, — the choking breath, — the dying agonies, — the dread hereafter."

"O Harry! try and not think of the pain of death, for it will be short; or, if you must, remember, that, in dying thus, you just as much sacrifice your life for your country as if you laid it down on the battle-field, or in the hospital. It all seems unnecessary, and horribly wicked to me; and God knows we pay a fearful price for our national crimes! But we cannot help this. You have done what you considered your duty to your

12

country : you are to die a martyr to the cause of truth, justice, and liberty ; and now all that remains is for you to make your peace with God. Oh, come to the Saviour now, dear brother, if never before ; and he will bear you safely over the dark river of death !" she exclaimed with a convulsive sob.

"Oh, I cannot prepare, Catharine ! I feel as if it were impossible under present circumstances. Once the future life looked bright and glorious to me ; now all is doubt and darkness, gloom and despair. I can see no help or hope for me, here or hereafter. I ought not to tell you this to add to the bitterness of your grief ; and, for God's sake, do not tell my dear mother. Give my best love to them all at home, and tell them I shall think of you all to the last moment. Bid Theodore fight for us both, if he is still living, — not to revenge my death upon these poor, deluded people, but to uphold the banner of freedom, set the oppressed and enslaved millions free, and support the best government the sun ever shone upon."

"Time's up, — not a minit more !" exclaimed a gruff voice, as the guard opened the door.

There was of course no alternative ; so, amid sobs and tears, the farewell words were spoken. Catharine tore herself away, and, blinded by tears, was led by old Aunt Dinah from the grim prison-house.

The walk home somewhat calmed her ; but still her heart was bursting with grief at the thought of her brother's sad fate, — a thousand times more terrible for his agonizing terror and grim despair: and she was sitting with her head bowed upon her hands, — racking her brains for some expedient by which to save him, when Gen. Atherton entered the room.

Knowing, from Dinah, something of what had passed, he came up beside her; and, laying his hand gently upon her bowed head, he said in a tone of deep commiseration, —

"Catharine, may I sympathize with you in this deep affliction?   God knows I would lighten it if I could."

"Oh, you can, — you can!" she exclaimed eagerly, as she raised her tearful eyes to his: "you can procure me an interview with the commanding general, and help me plead the cause of an innocent man."

"It could do no good, Catharine: I know his opinion of this case too well to believe we could influence him in the least; and, even if he were made to believe in your brother's innocence, he dare not pardon if he would.   As to our President, he is in Richmond, and could not be reached, and a messenger return, until all is over."

"Oh! is there, then, no help, no hope, no ray of light to illumine his sad fate, — no possible change to be hoped for in the mode of that death he dreads so much?"

"Is he then, a soldier, so much afraid of death?"

"Not of death, for he has walked bravely up to the cannon's mouth, and would again; but he shudders with horror at the thought of a felon's death.   Can you understand such feelings?"

"Yes, yes: they are but natural to a noble soul."

"And he has one, — too pure and noble for a fate like that, too precious to be so ignobly sacrificed.   Oh! I would almost lay down my own life to procure his acquittal or escape."

"Catharine, do you realize what you are saying?" said the general suddenly, after a pause, during which his face flamed up with a rapidly-formed resolution; and his eyes and hands eagerly sought her own.

"I think I do;" and she raised her tearful eyes to his face.

"And would you give less than life, yet what is quite as precious as mine, to him who would secretly procure your brother's escape, and safe transmission through our lines?" he continued in a low, thrilling tone.

"Why do you ask? and what is it I could give?" she questioned; while her face blanched to a deadly white, as a keen perception of his meaning flashed over her.

"I asked, because the devotion of a life, and the re-quital you could give, would tempt one who loves you to run a great risk, — to set free an innocent man for your sake."

"And without that requital, — for the sake of right and justice and humanity," she tremblingly urged.

"Those are certainly good and sufficient reasons, but too far off and intangible for a nature as earthly as mine. Ah, Catharine! nothing in this world but the gift of yourself could tempt me to run a risk, that, in case of discovery, would involve me in disgrace and ruin, if not death. But all this risk will I run for the sake of the love you perseveringly withhold from me."

"Gen. Atherton, I have already told you that I re-spect and esteem, but do not love you; and, as regards that, we cannot command our own feelings."

"I would also take that risk," said he eagerly; "for I know that no one can love as ardently as I love you, without winning a return at last. Become my wife, dear Catharine, the sharer of my destiny; and I know you would learn to love me."

"Oh! I cannot, Gen. Atherton, — I dare not, with my present feelings: it would be a wrong before high Heaven, both to you and myself; and you would wrong yourself too, — however urgent my need, — to involve yourself, and run such a risk for my sake."

"That is my affair. I would do it gladly to win the reward that it is in your power to bestow. Allow my chaplain to unite us this night; and I will do all that is in the power of man to do to save your brother from death. To-morrow it will be too late, — both for him and for me. I am ordered to join the army of the south-west immediately, and cannot even take you with me in my hasty journey, if you become my wife, much as I might wish it. Yet that need not prevent your becoming so now, and giving me the right to become your future guardian and protector through life. Oh, will you not do this, dear Catharine?" he pleaded in most persuasive tones, as he sat down beside her, and put his arm lovingly around her.

"Oh, do not — do not urge me now," she sobbed: "it seems so like a mockery, with his precious life trembling in the balance. And, oh! it is revolting to every feeling of delicacy in a maiden's heart to sell one's self to save another's soul, — to traffic a life for a wife. Oh, be noble, be generous, — be your own true self, dear general! Save him if you can; and gratitude hereafter may win for you what a persistence in immediate returns might lose you forever."

"Ah, but to be my own true self, I must be selfish enough to insist upon my own rights. I was neither born nor educated to self-abnegation; and for no trifling scruples of delicacy can I resign the dearest and sweetest hope of my life. I think I know and can understand your feelings under the circumstances. For poor Harry's sake, you are willing to waive all the political scruples that have divided us. But the suddenness of my pro-

12*

posal, and thoughts of its future consequences, shock and frighten, and fill your heart with a dread of me that future experience will not justify. But I am no ogre, that you need to fear me, Catharine. Give me but a husband's claim to you hereafter, and I will prove to you that I can love fondly, cherish tenderly, and wait patiently for the return of the fond affection you have inspired in my bosom."

He saw that she wavered; that his strong will and earnest determination were overbearing the frail barriers she had raised to oppose them; and, lowering his voice to a tenderer tone, he continued, —

"Cannot you trust me, dear Catharine? Do you fear to place your happiness in my keeping? If it suits you better, we will wait for the solemn ceremony that is to make us one until you know that the scaffold has lost its victim. And then, when you are mine for all time, all your scruples of delicacy shall be regarded. Much as it will cost me, I will resign all present claim to your society if you will promise to join me when I come or send for you hereafter. Oh! will you not do this?"

Catharine could only sob: her heart was too full for words. She saw nothing clearly, but poor Harry's agonized face, and sad, pleading eyes, as he told her of his terror at thought of a felon's death, his dread of the dark, unknown future. And she, by a great sacrifice of feeling, could save him. Would she not, before God, be guilty of his murder if she refused to do so? was a question she asked herself, — that struck such terror to her heart that she dared refuse no longer.

Gen. Atherton looked eagerly into her eyes, as these things were revolving in her mind, and he seemed almost by intuition to read her very soul.

"O Catharine! is not your brother's life worth a purchase like this?" he questioned tenderly.

"Yes, yes, — a thousand times yes! Oh! save him, Gen. Atherton, and I promise to be your wife," she exclaimed with a shuddering sob.

"Mine, — mine at last!" he said with deep feeling, as he pressed the hand he had clasped to his lips. "O Catharine! if I live, you shall never, never repent of this decision. And don't, pray, look forward to this consummation with fear and dread. You shall have no reason to do so. You shall always be treated kindly and respectfully, cared for tenderly, and have abundant means at your disposal to do all the good you wish. And certainly, if this war goes on, you will not lack for opportunities you never would have found at home. But time is flying. If I would win this precious guerdon, I must be up and doing. I will see you again ere I sleep."

He was gone at last; and Catharine sat there with bowed head, just as he found her. But what a change had come over the spirit of her dreams! Was it true that that short interview had decided her destiny? It would seem so; and yet she could only realize a dull, aching pain in her head and heart, a shivering dread of the unknown future, a horrible fear lest she should sacrifice herself in vain, and poor Harry be murdered. Could she ever love this man to whom she had sold herself? Could she ever forgive him for taking such an ungenerous advantage of her in her dire extremity, when he might, if he would, have proved himself so noble, and worthy of her regard? Overcome as she was by the thought of Harry's danger, she would hardly have consented, but for his promise to leave her as soon as the ceremony was over, and the undefined hope that something, she knew not what, might make that separation eternal.

That night, when he called again, he told her that every thing was in train for Harry's escape. And then it was arranged that the marriage was to be a private one, with no one present but Aunt Dinah, the chaplain, and two of the general's friends; all of whom had promised to keep the secret until his return from the Southwest. Immediately after the ceremony, they were to set out for Richmond, where he was obliged to go for orders previous to setting out upon his Southern journey. But for the fact of his projecting Harry's escape, and it being known to some that she was of the same name, and had visited him in prison, Gen. Atherton would gladly have claimed and proclaimed her publicly as his bride. As it was, it was judged more prudent not to do so, through fear that some suspicion might fall on them, when it became known that the prisoner had escaped. His friends, Major Darwin and Col. Mulford, had suspected his attachment from the first, but admired her too much themselves to wonder at his securing her, if he could, before his departure for distant battlefields.

CHAPTER VIII.

THE BROTHER'S ESCAPE. — OLD ACQUAINTANCES.

THAT night, when all was still in the rebel camp, save the voices of the sentinels as they paced their weary rounds, the groans of the wounded, or the low, sad tones of tired watchers by the couches of the sick and dying, poor Harry Hale lay writhing upon his bed of straw. He was sleepless, inexpressibly wretched, and not a whit more resigned to his fate than he was when Catharine left him. He had been visited by some of the rebel chaplains, who came to prepare him for the sad change awaiting him : but, though he conversed with and listened to them respectfully, their prayers were not blessed by his late repentance, conversion, or even resignation to his sad destiny; for, though not what might be called a hardened, impenitent sinner, poor Harry was, as yet, essentially earthly in all his thoughts and feelings, and had no bright hopes of a better world to wean him from the pleasures and joys of this. Still he had pride enough to prevent him from exposing his weakness to the rebels, as he had done to Catharine ; and, if he had really died by the hangman's rope, that pride would probably have supported him to the end.

The rough hut in which he was confined had been

141

built by Irish laborers at the time of the construction of the railroad. It had but one room, aside from the attic, and the small one in which the prisoner was confined. The larger room was now occupied by the guards, some of whom were stationed on the outside of the building. This hut still belonged to an Irishman, named Mike Flannegan, — a jolly, good-natured, warm-hearted, whiskey-loving genius, always full of his gibes and jokes, and ready to do a good turn to whoever was the best paymaster. He now worked by the day upon the fortifications; slept at night in his attic; and everywhere and always was a great favorite with the soldiery. As there was supposed to be no mode of egress from Harry's room but by the door, and one small and strongly-barred window, and the room was found to be full of filth and vermin, — the companions of its late occupant, — Mike Flannegan's pig, — they concluded it was unnecessary to remain in the room with him. So, locking the door, and posting a guard outside, they thought him perfectly safe. But a good many had been in, during the day and evening, to gratify their curiosity by looking through a certain knot-hole in the prisoner's door, some one of whom had *forgotten* a basket of cakes and cheese, garnished by a bottle of uncommonly soporific whiskey. No guard could be expected to withstand a temptation like that, when it was once discovered. The consequence was, that they all got — not exactly drunk, but quiet, and slightly oblivious of surrounding objects. But poor Harry knew nothing of all this: he only knew, as the unmarked hours glided by in the darkness, that his life was fast fleeting away; and he watched the faint ray from the knot-hole, expecting soon to see it exchanged for the light of his last earthly morning.

Though he knew nothing of the time, it was past midnight; and the camp, as well as his guard, had long been comparatively still; when, all at once, he thought he heard a faint knocking beneath him. He lifted his head, and eagerly listened. It was repeated, — this time a little louder.

"What can it be?" he murmured wonderingly.

"Whist, for yer life, if ye want to escape!" whispered a voice directly beneath him.

"Who's there?" he whispered in return, his voice trembling with the nervous eagerness of a renewed hope flashing out of the blackness of dark despair.

"Don't ask, but get up, and softly pull away the straw from the corner, — far as ye can," was the reply.

Harry managed to do this with his feet and manacled hands, when, to his astonishment, the floor began to rise, disclosing a trap-door — over which he had lain securely — and the faintest possible ray of light beneath. Immediately afterwards, an honest, sympathizing Irish face appeared at the opening; and its owner crept stealthily up into the room.

"Whist, for yer life!" he repeated in Harry's ear. He then produced keys, and proceeded to unlock his shackles, and rub his benumbed limbs to get the blood in circulation once more.

"Now follow me!" whispered his good genius kindly.

Harry could not believe the evidence of his senses, and kept thinking it was all a dream, though ready enough to follow his conductor. Blinded, dizzy, and benumbed as he was, he would have fallen through the trap but for the assistance of his warm-hearted friend.

"Now, me darlint," he said, when he had got him safely down the rude ladder, "you must slip out of this toggery," — pointing to his Federal uniform, — "and jest step into another sarpent's skin, if ye want to give 'em the slip ; " and, by the dim light of a dark lantern, he produced a suit of common citizen's garments, that Harry readily exchanged for his own, which the man hid in a sly corner.

"Now, honey," he whispered, "pluck up yer courage, put on a stiff upper lip, and don't make a noise louder'n a misketer; for we've got a narrer chance to run.   Here, take a drink of the swate crater, and then foller me."

Harry obeyed in both particulars; for he sadly needed something to recruit his exhausted energies, and give him the strength and courage he needed for an adventure so highly dangerous.   Without further questioning, he then stooped, and followed his guide through a narrow passage, leading into a ruined cow-shed behind the hut. This passage had been cut by former occupants for the convenience of their pigs and poultry, which had been in the habit of wintering in the rude cellar of the little mansion.

"Now, me honey, on thy belly shalt thou crawl, and dust shalt thou eat for a while, — like any other sarpent," whispered his guide with a low, merry laugh, as he lay down upon the ground, and began to crawl in the direction of the outposts.   It was dark and cloudy ; but, as the guide knew every inch of the ground, this was a favorable circumstance.   So, by crawling around sentinels, walking in the deepest shadows, and creeping around opposing obstacles where it was more exposed, taking paths that were very circuitous, he succeeded in piloting Harry safely out of the rebel encampment.

"Now, me darlint, we'll stop and rest a bit," said the unknown guide, when he thought they were at a safe dis-

tance from camp; "and p'ra'ps a bit and a sup wouldn't
come amiss wid ye now."

"No, indeed!" said Harry, who, having eaten
scarcely any thing since his capture, now began to feel
the keen demands of hunger after his tiresome exertions. He ate a piece of dirty corn-bread and a slice of
cold ham with the keenest relish; nor did he disdain to
wash it down with some of the contents of his guide's
"pocket pistol," though he was a strong temperance
man at home.

"Now, my friend," he said, "that you have fortified
the inner man, and set the outer one at liberty, will you
be kind enough to tell me to whom I am indebted for
all these favors, and why you take interest enough in
me to run such a frightful risk for my sake?"

"Spake lower, honey, if ye don't want a twist in yer
gullet. As to the first, I'm Mike Flannegan, at yer sar-
vice; and for the rest, I wish I could tell ye it was
for the love of yerself, and not the yaller boys, I did it.
Truth it is, though, that I'd risk me neck in this way
for none but an innocent man like yerself, now."

"Thank you for that. But, if not to you, to whom,
then, am I indebted, my friend?"

"There's the rub, darlint. I swore by the holy poker
not to divulge the jintleman's name. I'll whisper in
yer left ear, however, that he wore stars on his shoulder-
straps; and this child suspicioned that he did it for the
love of the bright eyes that looked inter yer prison anon.
Any way, ye are to write her a little billet that yer safe
and sound, for me to take back to her;" and he produced
a pencil and memorandum-book, on a stray leaf of which
Harry scribbled, —

13

"DEAR C. — I am safe beyond the inner lines of the enemy. God grant that I may get safely beyond the outer ones; and you, too, dear C.

"H."

"Strange," he mused, "that Catharine should know of my intended escape, and probably helped to plan it. — But what am I to do now, Mr. Flannegan? As soon as the alarm is given, they will scour the whole country in search of me; and lucky shall I be to keep out of their cruel hands."

"Ah! the jintleman has pervided for all that. There, I hear the click of steel-clad hoofs."

Harry started up in alarm, thinking the patrols were after him.

"Whist! I spects it's the old nigger with the hosses. Jist step behind them bushes, and I'll see."

He returned presently, exclaiming, "Bless yer lucky stars! it's Old Nick, sure enough; and he knows all the roads from Dan to Barsheba. He'll get ye safe through, if anybody can. But hurry up: there's not a minit to lose."

Harry needed no urging. They soon reached the road; and he mounted as fine a horse as could be found in the country, while his new guide was mounted upon another. Both were well supplied with all necessary military equipments, as well as food for the journey.

"Good-by, my friend!" said Harry, warmly grasping the Irishman's hand, as they were about to part. "I owe you more than words can express. I hope no harm may come to you from this night's adventure, and that I may live to repay you at some future day."

"Divil a bit of pay do I want, more than the jintleman gave me; and, as to the harrum, I guess I can fix it. So good-by, and good luck to ye both; and may the divil break the necks of all who pursue ye!"

"Thank you, and good-by," said Harry. The next minute he and his dark guide were, as slowly and noiselessly as possible at first, but at a two-forty pace afterwards, dashing down the road, soon leaving the Confederate camp far in the rear.

It is needless to say that the rebels were terribly exasperated, when they found, at daylight next morning, that their prisoner had escaped. The guards were all found at their posts guarding the empty cage; but the bird had flown. And yet there was no mystery about it when the place was examined by the light of day. There were the pigs' nest hustled to one side, the trapdoor plainly visible, and the underground path to the cow-shed easily traced. The mystery was, how the prisoner could have got his irons off, or got away without discovery; and no one believed he could have done it without assistance. But "Who was the traitor?" was the question asked, and "Why was the prisoner put in such a place without a more thorough examination?"

The guards were arrested on suspicion; but, as nothing could be proved against them, they were soon set at liberty. No one mistrusted Mike Flannegan, who, they all said, was helped up the ladder in the guard-room, half-drunk, the previous night; and there in his attic he was found snoring in the morning, with an empty whiskey-bottle beside him. Of course he did not tell them of the knotted rope by which he had descended and ascended: he disclaimed all knowledge of the trap.

"Faith, and what should I know about thraps," he said, "when the pigs had always, since the memory of man, had their nest in that corner.   I have never bothered myself to find out what there was under 'em besides fleas.   Only an infarnal Yankee nose could have scented out so strange a thing, in my opinion."

Every spot about the camp was searched, and the country scoured in every direction; yet they could obtain no trace of the fugitives.   When it was found that Uncle Nick had also disappeared, it was supposed that he had helped the prisoner to escape.   But the general had been too cautious in his plans to be suspected himself, or cast a shadow of blame on Catharine.   Harry, meantime, with his unknown guide, was scouring over the country with the speed of the wind, — not, however, in the shortest and most direct road to Washington, but in an entirely different direction.   They followed this break-neck speed for some time, and not until the horses began to show unmistakable signs of fatigue was their pace moderated in the least.   Day was now dawning in the east; and Harry found that they were entering a wild, wooded, broken country, very different from any he had previously seen in Virginia, and that the road was growing rougher and evidently more untravelled at every mile.   They came at last to a high hill that overlooked a large extent of territory, on the top of which the guide suddenly halted.

"I am glad you have found a stopping-place at last, my friend," said Harry; "for I began to think I was following the wild huntsman."

"Had ye rudder staid, an' tried de strength of de rope?" queried his good genius.

"No, no!" he exclaimed shudderingly, just as the

thunderous roar of an alarm-gun in the direction of the camp announced the escape of the prisoner. Soon afterwards they saw the clouds breaking away in the east, and the sun rising in his splendor, — a gorgeous sight to behold, yet ever after, to Harry Hale, fraught with fearful memories of that eventful night, and the glorious morning that came so near to being his last on earth.

"No," he continued, after a long pause, and silent yet heartfelt thanksgiving. "Thanks be to God, and you, my friend, that I am not at this moment swinging from the end of a rope in the rebel camp."

"You come mighty near to it, dat's sartin. You'll be luckier dan my poor dear massa, if you get off wid a whole skin."

"Who was your master, my good man? Seems to me your voice sounds mighty familiar;" and he turned to look more closely at his sable companion.

"Ole Major Hunter of Hunter Hills *was* my master, — the best and kindest one dat eber breaved," said the man with a sigh.

"Indeed! Why, he was Lloyd's father, of whose sad fate Catharine told me in the prison. And you — why, as sure as the world, you are my old friend Nick!" and Harry eagerly held out his hand, which the other grasped quite as warmly.

"Yes: it's ole Nick, sure enuff, Massa Harry; an' he no forgit de little feller dat help Grace, an' save black Jett an' de proud Suveners from drownin'. He no forgit Massa Tedo nuther, or leetle Jessie. An', more'n all de rest, he no forgit Miss Kate, who nussed us in de fever, an' resk her life tryin' to save massa an' little

13*

Walter. An' it's for her sweet sake, I'm quittin' ole Virginny dis day."

"It's to her, then, I owe my escape; is it?"

"Not zactly. Nick t'ink somebody help for her sake; but he promise not to tell. Here is de puss he send to Massa Harry;" and he presented a plethoric one.

"Strange, that my benefactor should so shroud himself in mystery!"

"Not a bit. D'ye t'ink a big high ossifer want he neck stretched for lettin' prisoner go? No, no: Nick know better'n dat."

"But why he should do it at all is what puzzles me."

"Ay! but it no puzzle Nick. He say, 'Poor feller! he no spy: he innocent as a lamb! Nick want to help git him off, — cheat de gallows, an' git he own freedom massa promised?' Dis he say wid he lips, but de eyes tell Nick he care noffin' for poor prisoner, but t'ink all de worl' of Miss Kate; an' p'r'aps, if he let brudder go, she 'sent to be his wife."

"Well, I can't imagine who it is, but I suppose it is of no use to pump you; yet I fear poor Kate is going to involve herself in some way for my sake. It would be just like her: she is always so ready to do, and to sacrifice herself, for the sake of others."

"Dat's a fact. Nick allers know it. She tu good for dis world, — tu good for dat man, or anybody on dis arth. De angels git her bimeby."

All this time the eyes of the slave had been roving over the varied landscape in search of pursuers; but, seeing none, they dismounted to rest themselves and their horses, and take a lunch.

"It seems to me, Uncle Nick, that we've been going the wrong way all the time," said Harry.

"Dat's a fact," Nick returned. "Yet it's de right way, arter all. Dey look eberywhere else for us, 'fore dey t'ink to look here; an' bimeby we'll come round inter de right way to go home."

After this they went on a little more leisurely, until the burning August sun made it extremely uncomfortable for man and beast. Then they turned into a piece of woods, in a green, grassy glade of which, beside a spring, they picketed the horses, and, one at a time, lay down to rest beneath the shadows of the trees. Here they remained nearly the whole day.

Nick knew very well that he was not a great distance back of the Hunter Hills, where he had often been with his master. He also knew something of the character of the inhabitants, so contrived to avoid passing the dwellings of those who were inimical by daylight. Towards night, with themselves and their horses refreshed, they set out again, turning their course to the northward; and, before morning, they had passed over quite a long stretch of mountainous country.

By this time Harry had got the history of the late military and other operations at the South, as Nick understood them, as well as particulars of Catharine's late experiences, that were new to him; for Nick was unusually intelligent for one of his class in life. Having lived two years at the North, and boarded with Harry's mother when the young people were at school in Gleneden, Nick was of course an old acquaintance and warm friend of the family. This residence at the North, even though it was as a servant and general waiter for Lloyd and Grace, Philip and Nell, had served to enlighten Nick on a good many subjects, and fit him, more than slaves are usually fitted, for the freedom that his master

had promised. But Major Hunter's death had been so
sudden, that Nick was doubtful whether his will was
completed, or would be allowed to be legal by the rebel
authorities. He had a shrewd suspicion, too, that he
was to be pressed into government service to work on
the fortifications, — a most unendurable bondage. So
he embraced Gen. Atherton's proposition, as much on
his own account as on Harry's; though he felt many
regrets at leaving poor little Walter, and indeed the
whole Hunter family. He loved them all, and his life,
thus far, had been an easy one; yet freedom was dearer
than every thing else to him.

Upon the morning of the second day, they had a very
narrow escape from a party of rebel cavalry, whom they
evaded only by leaping their horses over a high fence,
and hiding behind a great pile of rocks near the roadside.
Soon afterwards they entered a fine, fertile tract of
country, that seemed more thickly populated than any
they had previously traversed, as Harry remarked.

"Ah! Nick know him well enough," was the reply.
"Before long we come to Massa Tremont's plantation."

"Tremont? Not some of Grace Tremont's relations?"

"Sartin, Massa Harry. It's nobody but Miss Grace's
own fader; an' Nick spects de sweet little critter's herself up dere."

"Indeed! How glad I should be to see her! But do
you suppose she would know me, Nick, after seven long
years of separation?"

"Nick spects Massa Harry's own mudder not know
'im jes' now. He forgit dat when he took up de sword
he lay down de razor, an' dat he now look like one poor
long-faced he-goat. Miss Grace 'member on'y Massa

Harry's smooth face, full of fun, wid rosy cheeks, dimple chin, an' curly head."

"Oh!" and Harry put his hand up to his face despairingly, "I forgot that I hadn't seen a razor for weeks, and that I must look altogether Jewish, dirty, and unpresentable. So I think we must give Miss Grace, who used to be an unmerciful hector, a pretty wide berth as we go by."

"Nick no t'ink so. Leetle Grace lub fun, but de heart's in de right place; an' no doubt she dreful glad to see Massa Harry. Massa Tremont good friend tu, — good Linkum man; hate rebellion. Nick t'ink it good place to stop till de fury's ober. Dey no care if Massa Harry look like one big buffalo, if he good Linkum man."

"Do you think so? But how is it? I thought Grace was an orphan cousin of Lloyd's when they were at school." •

"So she war. Her mudder, Massa Hunter's sister, die when she leetle baby; an' Lloyd an' Miss Lucy's mudder took her home to Hunter House, where we all brung her up till she went off North to school. But, when she cum back, Massa Tremont's nuther wife die; so he took her home to stay wid her little half-sister, Helen, who must be a big gal by dis time. But what's dat?" he exclaimed, reining up his horse suddenly, as a succession of shrill, sharp shrieks, and the sound of rapidly-rolling wheels, rang out upon the clear morning breezes.

They were just descending to a large stream, spanned by a high, uncovered, arched bridge, with but a slight railing at the sides for the protection of passengers. On the other side of this stream rose a steep, thickly-wooded hill, up which the road wound circuitously, and from which the unusual sounds seemed to come. Before there was time for a thought of escape, if escape had been necessary or possible, a close carriage, drawn by a span of fiery horses, but driverless, and with the reins dangling about the horses' heels, came thundering down the hill towards the bridge. Our two horsemen, who had just passed it when they saw the carriage, instinctively gave them the road. But Harry, who saw at a glance that there were ladies within, and the danger to which they were exposed, turned like a flash, and, dashing after them, was lucky enough to seize the near horse by the bit, just as they were rushing obliquely across the bridge to inevitable destruction below. As it was, it would have been impossible for him to have stopped their wild career, but for the rise in the centre of the bridge, or to have held them a moment but for Nick's opportune arrival, commanding "Whoa!" and strong grasp upon the other frightened animal, so mad were their struggles to get free. But they were saved, and led panting and trembling across the shaky old bridge, and up the hill to a safe distance, before Nick, who guided them, ventured to stop to relieve the anxiety of the wretched inmates.

"But who are the inmates? And how do we know but what they are our bitter foes?" thought Harry, as he took the horses by the bits, with his cheek pale with excitement, and his heart beating strangely, as Nick proceeded to open the carriage-door.

Nick knew very well what he was about, however; for he had seen a pale face at the window, and knew the horses and the old Tremont family carriage very well: so he was not surprised to find Grace and Helen within, pale as marble, and half fainting with terror, while their black servant-girl lay in strong convulsions upon the carriage-floor.

At the sight of Uncle Nick's black, honest face at the door, joy and surprise created a sudden revulsion in Grace's feelings; and, overcome by her emotions, she leaned forward, as she had done a hundred times in childhood, laid her head on his shoulder, and gave way to a passionate burst of tears. In that moment of joyous recognition and deliverance, the prejudices of caste and color were forgotten. The affection engendered in infancy displayed itself to Harry's astonished gaze, in defiance of all the strict rules of propriety, that had for years been instilled into the proud little maiden's heart. Nor did he think it surprising when he came to know that she thought they had fallen into the hands of rebels or guerillas, instead of those of tried and trusty friends. Uncle Nick, too, seemed quite as much overcome with emotion as herself.

"T'ank God! T'ank God!" he kept repeating; "dat leetle missy saved;" and the big tears rolled down his dark cheeks like rain.

"I do — I do thank him, and you, too, my dear. old friend!" sobbed Grace; while Helen, too, grasped his hand, and poured out her fervent thanksgiving. Both were so bewildered, and overcome with emotion, that they did not see Harry, until Nick turned to him and said, —

"I guess Nick have to divide de t'anks with he young friend here; for, if he no turn quicker'n litenin', de hosses got off de bridge for all Nick."

"Then he has our thanks, our fervent gratitude," said Grace, crimsoning as she looked up to find his eyes fixed searchingly upon her face, yet failing to recognize in the pale, careworn, bearded young man her smooth-faced, merry, boyish friend of other days. But Harry knew Grace at once, as she had changed far less than he; and he was slightly amused by her evident attempt at recognition.

It did not take long to explain the position of the young ladies : they were in great trouble at home. The judge, their father, had been arrested by the rebel authorities, and put in prison, for denouncing their usurpations, and declaring his loyalty to the Union. The slaves, their master gone, were escaping in gangs every day from the plantation. And, to crown the whole, the guerillas were roaming over the country, murdering and devastating the property of all Unionists, and some who were not, their crimes too evidently winked at by the rebel authorities. In this state of things, the young ladies, expecting nightly an attack from the desperadoes, had decided to flee from the neighborhood, and seek shelter, as their father had advised them to do, with their dear old uncle at Hunter Hills. And they had set out that morning early, with the coachman and two armed outriders as an escort, intending to sleep that night at the house of a friend, and reach Hunter House the next evening.

They had come but a few miles, however, before shots were fired, very near to them ; but whether at them or not, they could not tell. Any way, they had frightened the horses, who started so suddenly as to throw the driver off the box. Then they ran down the long hill, as if pursued by the evil one; while the cowardly outriders, it was presumed, sought safety in flight.

"And now," continued Grace, "you can't think how glad I am to meet you, Uncle Nick. I know God sent you for our deliverance, and to pilot us to our dear uncle's arms."

Nick and Harry exchanged meaning glances.

Oh! how could they tell them that the home to which they were flying, and the friend in whom they were trusting, had passed forever from the earth?

"I tell you what I t'ink," said Nick, swallowing his emotion. "We come right off from Hunter Hills, an' de hosses drefful tired an' hungry, an' you gals drefful scairt, an' rumfled up; so 'twill be best to go back home a leetle spell an' git rested, an' talk ober matters."

"Well, just as you think best, my friend. But first, how are they all at Hunter Hills?"

"Not bery well, Miss Grace," said Nick, wincing at the question. "Nobody dere now but niggers. Dey all gone to Richmond."

"To Richmond! Is it possible! What, uncle and all?"

"All gone, little missus," said he solemnly.

"Why, I thought they always spent the summer in the country, or at the watering-places."

"Ah! dey used to did. But times drefful bad. Country drefful dangerous jes' now."

"It is here, I know, — so near the lines; but we hoped it was better there. And uncle is such a kind, good, influential man, that we felt as if he could protect us; and so did father. But what can we do now? Do you want to go to Richmond, Helen, that nest of secession and treason?"

"No, indeed! And I am sure father would much prefer that we should go to Washington," she returned in clear, sweet, yet decided tones.

"So am I. But I can't bear to go, leaving him in captivity. Perhaps we had better risk it to remain at home."

"Where is your father?" asked Harry pityingly.

14

"He was taken first to the county jail, where we visited him. But he has since been removed: they will not tell us where, but most likely to Staunton or Richmond."

"You see, there were people here, whom his sense of justice in his legal capacity had offended, who were only too glad of an opportunity to be revenged upon him, and get him out of the way," said Helen sadly. "I fear uncle, too, will be unsafe, with his plain speech and known loyalty. He will surely be caught up by the rebel authorities, if aunt's friends do not interfere to save him; and then where would be our safety if we were with him?"

"I do not think you would be unsafe in Richmond, ladies, at present. The greatest danger would be in getting there. And you must have friends there aside from your aunt's family, — even among the rebel authorities."

"I don't know who, I am sure," said Grace.

"Are not your old friends, the Athertons, in the rebel service? Why not claim their protection?"

"No," said Grace quickly, while her cheek crimsoned: "I could not do that. We have mortally offended them. And that may be one reason of our father's arrest."

"Indeed! Why, I thought Philip was an old friend of yours," said Harry with a questioning glance.

"He may have been: he is not now. I have none I value in the ranks of rebellion. But what do you think, Uncle Nick?" she continued. "Is it safe for us, or for uncle, in Richmond?"

"Ah! Massa good man, good Christian: he safe whereber he go. Young pretty Linkum gals no bery safe anywhere in Virginny, jest now."

"Nick," Grace exclaimed, after looking at him searchingly a moment, "you are in trouble. Something is the matter at Hunter House: I see it in your eyes; I hear it in the trémulous tones of your voice; I feel it here;" and she put her hand to her heart. "Why did I not see it before?" Then, after a pause, "Tell me, is dear uncle, too, arrested?" and the tones were low, husky, and tremulous.

"Dere, Nick neber could keep noting from leetle Grace: she allers find him out. He hab got bad news. Dear old Hunter House cotch fire, an' burn all to pieces."

"Merciful heavens! But the family"—

"Dey gone to Richmond."

"Dear old uncle too? O Nick! there is something you are trying to keep from me," she said in a tone of alarm.

Nick turned appealingly to Harry. Knowing how tenderly she loved her uncle, he could not bear to tell her of his death. Harry, understanding the mute appeal, came forward pityingly.

"We have indeed a sad story to tell," he said. "This dreadful war fills almost every home with sorrow and woe. Your dear uncle has been dead for weeks. He was murdered by the guerillas, who burned the mansion, and carried away every thing of value they could lay their hands on."

Grace was white and dumb with grief and terror, so long that they were glad when the sobs burst forth. Helen was pale, and awestruck; but, knowing less of her uncle, she did not feel it so acutely. When Grace grew calmer, the rest of the sad story was told, as well as that of their deliverer, whose identity with her old friend, Harry Hale, she had more than suspected.

Just as they were preparing to turn the carriage about,

and return to the mansion, poor coachy came limping over the bridge and up the road, swearing at the cowardice of his late armed companions. He had seen the hunter who fired the shots; and thus put to flight all present fear of the guerillas. His ankle was badly sprained by his fall; but otherwise he seemed to be uninjured. Helping him up to his place, they were soon on the way to Tremont Hall.

It was a large, handsome wooden structure; and, with its towers, balconies, out-buildings, and shadowy trees, presented quite an imposing appearance. As they drove up the broad carriage-sweep, and entered the gate, a ludicrous scene presented itself to their view.

Perched upon the top of the front balcony sat the two cowardly runaways, gun in hand, watching for the enemy; while, within the mansion, a scene presented itself that beggars description. They had spread the greatest consternation among the slaves upon their return, by the report that they were attacked by the outlaws, and the young ladies carried off by them, and that they had barely escaped with their lives. They had heard the shots; and, frightened half out of their senses, fear and cowardice had filled up the picture. At sight of the carriage, returning with its new attendants, they slipped down from the balcony, cowed and crestfallen, and very considerately disappeared.

As soon as they alighted, the young ladies ushered Harry and Uncle Nick into the mansion, expecting to find every thing in order, as they had left it a few hours before.

What, then, was their surprise, to find every thing in confusion, and the house-servants all packing up their treasures, in anticipation of an attack, and a sudden flight from the premises. The halls and alleys were lined by an indiscriminate collection of frightened servants, sacks of clothing, baskets of provisions, boxes of trinkets, bundles of bedding, squalling children, weeping mothers, barking curs, mewing cats, and frisking kittens; all contributing to make it a very pandemonium. Here sat Phillis, upon the top of a big bundle, weeping bitterly; while Tull, with his effects strapped upon his back, was trying to afford her Christian consolation. Chloe, more resolute in spirit, was brandishing a frying-pan over the head of an obstreperous youngster, and threatening death to all the outlaws in Christendom who should harm him. Betty, the housekeeper, more intent upon the interests of the family, was packing a big basket with her young mistresses' best bonnets and dresses, interspersed with various cakes and condiments, jars and bottles of her own, that altogether would have made a heavy burden for any mule on the plantation. The fat old cook, too, had her budgets surmounted by a good-sized nest of pots, tin kettles, and sauce-pans. But the crowning glory of the whole troop was the big bundle of Nett, upon the top of which was strapped the great tin oven; inside of which, nearly smothered with pillows, was snuggled her cute little black baby, with a loaf of bread and a roast of meat still warm from its late slight exposure to the kitchen fire. The little youngster was kicking and crowing, and clutching at the bright new tin; and seemed delighted with his fine quarters. A more laughable or mirth-provoking scene could scarcely be imagined. And, in spite of their grief and trouble, the new-comers did laugh uproariously.

"What in the world is the meaning of all this?" Grace exclaimed, as soon as she could find her voice.

11*

"O missis! Little missy! Good gracious!" they all exclaimed in a breath. "Lordy massy! We tought de grillers got ye bofe sure; an' comin' arter us ebery minit!" and they all crowded around the young ladies, testifying their joy at their return in every look and tone.

"So those cowardly rascals came back and frightened you all out of your senses; did they? But calm your fears. There's not an outlaw within a hundred miles of us, I'll venture to say. Some poor loafer fired two or three shots at a squirrel, so near that it frightened our horses; and they threw poor coachy off the box, and ran away with us. They came very near dashing us off the Old Murder Run Bridge, and but for Uncle Nick and this young gentleman, who were coming from Hunter Hills, we should have been killed. But poor Jack got his ankle sprained; and I want you, Aunt Betty, to doctor it up, and take care of dear Uncle Nick; while the rest of you clear away this wreck as soon as possible." Saying which, Grace led the way into the parlor, to entertain her new and welcome guest.

Grace was delighted to see Harry once more, and had a hundred questions to ask concerning the friends and scenes of other days, as well as the weightier and more embarrassing ones of the present time. Regarding these, Uncle Nick was at last called in for a consultation.

Ignorant of the fate of their father, knowing that their secession neighbors were inimical, and spies upon all their actions, and considering the terrible state of the country, the young ladies were afraid to remain in their present quarters. So it was decided at last that they should set out that very night, on horseback, with Uncle Nick and Harry, for the Union lines. As spies were

said to be in almost every household, they took no one
into their confidence but the overseer and Aunt Betty,
whom they thought they could trust; and their preparations were made very quietly.   They knew it would be
a dangerous adventure ; but both ladies were at home in
the saddle, of good courage, and ready, as they said, to
fight or run, as the case might be.

So that night, when the lights had gone out in the
slave-cabins, and vanished from the neighbors' dwellings,
they set out on their dangerous journey, taking with
them their money, jewels, and their father's most valua-
able papers, through fear that they would fall into the
hands of the enemy.   They were obliged to leave the
family portraits, however, and a hundred other precious
things that gold could not buy, — never more expecting
to behold them.   It was, indeed, a sad farewell to the
old home.

CHAPTER IX.

MARRIAGE OF THE REBEL GENERAL. — THE NOBLE WORK.

E will now return to poor Catharine, who had never in her life passed a more wretched night than that which preceded her bridal morning. It was the night of Harry's escape; and she had but just got into a doze, when the morning dawned, and she was wakened by the alarm given for the escape of the prisoner. She had believed that he would find it impossible to escape, that he would be executed, in spite of Gen. Atherton's promises; and not until thus assured that he had done so, and she received his farewell billet, did she fully realize that now her part of the contract must be fulfilled.

How little, alas! did Harry dream, as he dashed over the Virginia hills and valleys that sweet summer morning, with a heart filled with thankfulness for his unexpected deliverance from bonds and a fearful death, what an exorbitant price his sister was to pay for his liberty and life! It was a price beyond all computation in her estimation, — a bondage to which that of slavery, in her eyes, was far preferable.

Did she, then, regret her promise, mean to evade the penalty, or refuse to fulfil her bargain?

No, not for a moment. Harry's life was more precious than aught else to her then. She believed he would have done as much for her under similar circumstances; and she had too much principle to falsify her word, even though it might save her from a fate to which she looked forward with fear and loathing. Yet, as she arrayed herself that morning in her plain gray travelling-dress, — her only bridal robe, — she felt as if she were preparing for sacrifice; and the tears would fall, and the idea keep returning, that poor Harry would be caught and executed, and thus render her sacrifice a vain one.

Gen. Atherton came at last, flushed, and eager for the ceremony that was to make them one, yet evidently fearful lest some untoward event should rob him of his coveted treasure, or reveal to the world his treason.

"What! in tears, my dear Catharine!" he exclaimed, as he came forward and greeted her with a kiss. "This should not be. I shall teach you to look back with joy to this hour that gives you to my keeping. Your brother is undoubtedly safe by this time; and what is there to fear in becoming the bride of one who loves you so fondly and truly?"

"Every thing," she sobbed. "Every thought and feeling of my heart unfits me to become a rebel general's bride."

"Banish your fears, my Catharine; for I have none. We differ at present in our political views, it is true; but I think I know you well enough to believe, that, once my wife, bound by the most solemn vows, you would never be one to betray your husband's secrets or his honor, even to your dearest friends. Have I not judged you truly?" he eagerly questioned.

"I hope so. I should despise myself were it otherwise. Yet that does not fit me for the prominent yet false position I should have to occupy as your wife."

"I have no fears for the result, Catharine. You have sense and intelligence far beyond most of your sex. In dignity and queenliness, few can compare with you. Your manners are faultless, so far as I have observed them. In beauty, there are none to compare with you in my eyes. I shall be only too proud to present you to the world as my wife. So pray repress your sobs, and try and look forward more hopefully to a future I shall endeavor to make bright and happy for you. My friends will soon be here; and I cannot bear to have them think I wed an unwilling bride. It might excite suspicions, too, that neither you nor I would care to arouse; so I beg, I entreat, of you, for your own sake, and that of the name you are soon to bear, to dry your tears, and, by your own quiet dignity, justify to them my choice of a wife."

There was something in those words and tones of passionate entreaty, — a compelling power in the stern, serious, yet admiring eyes to which she could not help raising her own, — that hushed the rising tempest of sobs, and made Catharine say, "I will try and do as you wish," even though she felt as if her heart were bursting with its burden of grief and fear; and she had been upon the point of kneeling to implore him to spare her the fulfilment of a promise made under a species of compulsion, and bitterly repugnant to all the finer feelings of her heart.

He read it all in the look of eager, passionate entreaty, and in the fitful color that faded into sudden pallor, as she said with a great effort, "I will try." And it cost him a keen heart-pang to know that she regarded him

The ceremony was performed that made Catherine "The Rebel General's Loyal Bride." Page 167.

with such deep feelings of repulsion and loathing. The
thought, too, crossed his mind, that, by generously re-
signing her, he might inspire gratitude that would ripen
into love, and in the end more surely gain all his fond
heart coveted.

"But no," reason whispered. "If he did that, she
would go at once beyond the reach of his influence."
So his only hope was in securing her now while he had
the power, trusting that kind and generous treatment
afterwards would win for him the heart and fond affection he coveted. He drew her down beside him at last,
and, by soothing words, drew from her a reluctant
promise that she would join him, wherever he might be,
just as soon as circumstances would warrant her comfort and safety, and try to be to him a good and loving
wife. And, more than this, that she would not leave
the Confederacy, unless compelled to do so, without con-
sulting him regarding its propriety. He knew Catharine well enough to believe she would endeavor to keep
her promises when once made; and, having won these,
he did not despair of the full measure of bliss he
coveted.

The chaplain and chosen witnesses soon made their
appearance; Dinah was summoned; and the ceremony was
performed that made Catharine "*The Rebel General's
Loyal Bride.*" She neither wept nor fainted as she took
those solemn vows upon her lips; but she was as pale as
marble, and her heart felt numbed by the icy chill of
despair. But the color came back to her cheek as the
general warmly pressed her hand at the close of the
ceremony, and made her look into his eyes as he
murmured, "Mine! mine at last, — now and forever!"

The chaplain and Major Darwin speedily offered their

congratulations, and were duly thanked; but Col. Mulford said in a half-serious, half-laughing tone, —

"I suppose I ought to follow the example of our friends here, general; but I assure you I cannot do it with so good a grace, for I must own that I do not like it at all that you should so cunningly steal a march upon us before your departure. You knew very well that some of us, in your absence, would be striving for the prize you have won, and, such being the fact, that your chance would be remarkably small, if you did not secure it at once."

"That is true enough," laughed the general. "I knew its intrinsic value too well to leave it to the chances of surprise and capture by another. But don't be disheartened, Mulford. You know the old adage, — 'That there are as good fish in the sea,' &c."

"Ay: but you don't believe in it, or I either. Yet I must try and be resigned. I really hope, Mrs. Atherton, that you will have as kind and obedient a husband as I would have been, with every blessing earth or heaven can bestow."

"Thank you, for your good wishes, and all your flattering intentions besides," said Catharine, laughing, in spite of herself, at his odd humor, yet knowing very well that he was really more than half in earnest in all he said.

The gentlemen bade them adieu soon afterwards; and Aunt Dinah, who had been a good deal put out and mystified by the whole proceeding, went back to Walter, muttering to herself, —

"Dinah know noffin 'bout it. Can't understan' it nohow. He big, gran' gemman; look like king: but den he so old, he so stern. Dinah know Miss Kate 'fraid:

she scairt inter it somehow.   If 'twere on'y Massa Lloyd
now!   He plaguy fool to go off in dat way!   He neber
find anuder Miss Kate."

As soon as they were alone, Catharine sat down, pale
and trembling.   The thought that her destiny for life
had been sealed by the solemn vows she had spoken
took away all the fictitious strength called up for the occasion.   And oh, how she wanted to be alone, and give
way to her feelings unobserved!   He went and sat down
beside her, put his arm around her, and pressed his lips
to hers as he said, —

"Catharine, you performed your part nobly.   You
don't know how proud I am of the wife I have won.
And I know you would forgive my seeming selfishness, if
you knew how strong, how mighty, was my temptation ;
how fondly and passionately I love ; how impossible it
seemed to live without you, and how fearful I was lest
another in my absence should win what I valued most in
life.   Oh, say, Catharine, that you will forgive, and try to
love me !"

How could she, with all the secret chambers of her
soul still occupied by the old love, which she had tried
so vainly to cast out? or while her rebellious heart
rose up so bitterly against the ungenerous course he had
adopted to gain his own selfish ends?   He had saved
Harry's life, it is true; but for this she could not be so
grateful as she would have been, had he done it from
more noble and honorable motives.   But, whatever his
motives, Catharine knew that she herself had made the
election, and really chosen her destiny.   She knew that
this man, however unscrupulous, was now her husband
and life-long companion, and that from henceforth it
would be sin to think fondly of another.   She had con-

trolled her emotions by a strong effort of will during the ceremony; but the sobs kept rising in her throat all the time. Now, when she thought of the irrevocableness of what she had done, and he pressed so earnestly for a reply, they burst forth in a passionate gush of tears.

Naturally refined and sensitive, though his mind had been warped all his life by untoward circumstances, he intuitively understood her feelings, and sighed deeply, as he thought of the bitter repugnance she might feel towards the man who had won her in so questionable a way. Tenderly he drew her up to him, and tried to soothe her as he would a grieved child.

"Pray don't, Catharine! It goes to my heart to see you grieve thus," he said. "I understand your feelings, and these tears are a bitter reproach to my selfishness. It was wrong, I confess, to take advantage of your necessity as I have done; but oh! I will try and make amends for it in the future. And, if the most unbounded love and devotion can win a return, we will be happy in that untried future to which you look forward with so much dread."

From this tempest of grief he won her at last; and, when she became calmer, he told her, as he had never done before, all his plans for the future, both for her and himself. He wished her to remain at Mrs. Hunter's during his absence; and when he returned, or sent for her, he thought would be the best time to announce their marriage to the world.

Every arrangement having been made for their comfort when the time of departure drew near, poor little Walter was carefully removed to the cars in his uncle's strong arms; and lying there, with his head most of the time in Catharine's lap, he was carried back to Richmond.

His pallid face and pitiable condition won a great deal
of sympathy from the passengers; but Gen. Atherton's
protecting care made all other attentions needless.

They arrived in Richmond at last; and sadly and silently
they bore him into his mother's desolate home, — a wreck
of the brave and beautiful boy who had left it so bright
and blooming with health but a few short weeks before.

Nor was the home, or the mother to whom they had
brought him, less changed than the boy himself, as they
saw at a glance when admitted to her presence. For the
most poignant regret for her treatment of her husband,
horror of his awful death, and thoughts of the danger of
her boy, had nearly driven her distracted, and made
of her a pale, nervous wreck of her former self. She
knew they were coming, and thought she was prepared
for it; but the sight of her orphaned boy, with his bandaged head, sunken features, and great, dark, mournful
eyes, affected her so much, that she nearly fainted, and
had to be removed to her room; while his sisters were
overcome with grief.

Gen. Atherton left very soon to attend to the business
that called him to Richmond, but came back for a parting interview. Catharine, as she had promised, awaited
him in the parlor, when he came down from his sister's
chamber; and glad enough was she that there was little
time for leave-taking. He looked grave and solemn as
he came up to where she was standing by the window,
and seemed deeply agitated as he took her hand.

"Catharine, my dear wife," he said tenderly, "if circumstances will not permit your wearing my name at
present, it is fitting that you should be provided with the
means of locomotion and independence;" and he placed
a well-filled purse in her hand.

"Indeed, Gen. Atherton, I do not need it. I have enough for all present necessities," she said, as she tried to return it.

"Nay, Catharine, you must keep it, — if only as a recognition of the tie that binds us in one, and your rightful claim to all I possess. Your wardrobe was nearly all burned; and I want you to fit up another, suitable for the position you will occupy as my wife, and the journey you may be called upon to take by and by. Do not hesitate to spend the money, or ask for more if you need it, at any time. Write to me by every mail, if you can, as I shall be deeply anxious to hear from you, and my friends here, until we meet again. Ah, Catharine! what would I not give to be able to take you with me, or to remain with you myself! If you knew all the anxieties I have in leaving you thus, the bride of a day, you would pity me, and wish to go too. But I must: it is time for me to go. Won't you give me one kiss of love or forgiveness to repay me for all I resign?" and he drew her up to him in a close embrace, and passionately pressed his lips to hers. "God bless and keep you!" he said, "and turn your heart to me in my absence, even as mine is ever turned to you, and filled with your image always. Farewell."

With a face flushed and deeply agitated, he turned and left the room; while Catharine, scarcely less so, sat down dizzily, to think over her singular position. But she was not one to spend much time in sighs and tears and vain regrets for what could not be helped. There was too much for her to do in the world for that. A great many women in her position would have felt justified in breaking vows extorted under such circumstances; but she did not. They were sacred in her eyes, when once made; and, however repugnant to her feelings, she resolved faithfully to fulfil them. She realized, too, that her marriage to one in his position, when known, would put much greater power in her hands, for good or evil, than she could ever have hoped to wield in an humbler calling. And if she gained this power, and could exert it in the cause of liberty and humanity, she felt, even in that bitter hour of retrospection, as if her sacrifice would not be all in vain.

Mrs. Hunter was overjoyed at Catharine's return; and so were her two young daughters, for they all felt acutely the need of a strong, brave spirit to rely upon. They begged her to resume not exactly her old place, but that of a dear sister and friend, with whom they could at times intrust the care of the household. The servants, too, were all delighted to get Catharine and young Massa Walter home again; and he, poor fellow, could hardly contain his joy at being once more among his friends, though he still clung to Dinah and Catharine more than all the rest. Of his father's death he could never hear or speak without a shudder of horror; and no one was allowed to mention it in his presence. He was gentle and patient, and liked to have the family around him; yet his brain was still weak. He disliked noise and confusion; and perfect rest and quiet, the surgeon said, was the best medicine that could be given him.

Catharine found that little Jennie and Fannie had grown very old, womanly, and careworn during her absence; and that their mother, in the habit of relying upon her, and full of her own private griefs, had neglected every thing, thus devolving upon her young daughters the care of the household. The children had

15*

all loved their father dearly: they could not speak of him without tears; and his death had cast the first dark shadow over their young lives.

After the first shock and excitement of their meeting was over, Mrs. Hunter relapsed into her old nervous lethargy, leaving every thing to the care of others. She would shut herself up in her chamber for hours, brooding over the troubles she had brought upon herself, and growing more strange and taciturn every day. She would come into little Walter's room every morning, look mournfully upon him a few moments, ask how he was, press a kiss upon his pale brow, and then leave the room until evening, when she generally went through the same ceremony; seeming to do it as a sort of penance, and not from her old motives of fond affection. One morning, as she was leaving the room, Walter turned to Catharine with his eyes full of tears, and said, —

"Why is it that my mother never stays with me now, — never talks to me, — does not love me any more?"

"Oh, she does, darling!" Catharine replied. "But she is not well herself: and she can't bear to see you so ill, sad, and suffering; it makes her worse."

"But it would be such a comfort to me, dear Miss Catharine, to have her here, and sometimes lay my head on her bosom, as I do on yours. And then you could go out, and take the air, or do what I know you are longing to do, and I want you to do, so much."

"What is that, dear?"

"Why, to help take care of the sick and dying Union soldiers, whom I heard Dinah telling you were treated so cruelly, one day, when you thought I was asleep. Oh! I want you to go to them; and I want mother to go and help them; and I guess I can pick lint to dress their wounds pretty soon myself. I can hardly sleep for thinking of those prisons and hospitals, full of sick and wounded and dying men; so near to me, yet so very much worse off, — with nobody to give them nice food or drink, or care for them in any way; while I have every thing, and everybody is so good to me, — but my mother;" and the repressed sobs burst forth with a violence that was quite alarming.

"Don't! pray don't take it so to heart, dear! Your mother does love you: we all love you very dearly. And, as soon as you are well enough, we will all do what you desire, and what you guessed truly I was longing to do. Yet I am sorry you heard what Dinah said."

"I am not sorry," he sobbed: "I wanted to know the truth, which nobody would tell me. Now I shall not rest until something is done."

"But you do not realize, my dear child, all the difficulties in the way of my doing what I could wish. You are hardly old enough to understand the jealousy and bitterness of feeling engendered by this unholy strife, which would at once cause a Northern lady to be suspected, if she attempted to do any thing for the comfort of her own people. Joined by some Southern lady of distinction, and known Southern feelings, we might perhaps arouse holier and more enlarged sympathies in the hearts of the people of Richmond, that would lead them to see a man and a brother, for whom Christ died, even in the enemies he commanded them to love."

She was interrupted at this moment by a bitter sob, and, turning, saw Mrs. Hunter, pale and agitated, coming towards them. She had stopped for something near the door, that happened to be ajar, and heard it all. She advanced tremblingly to the bed, and exclaimed, as she put her arms round Walter's neck, —

"Oh! forgive your wretched mother, my darling, in that she so sorely sinned against you and your poor father. Oh! she does love you as her life, but has felt as if you did and must hate her. If you don't — if you love her still " —

"Hate my mother! Oh, never, never!" sobbed the poor boy, as he laid his weary, aching head, for the first time since his return, upon her bosom. "I know you did not mean to do it, mother; and I love you all the same. But you will help dear Miss Catharine, won't you, mother, in all that I want her to do?"

"Gladly, my dear, so far as I am able. But then there is very little two poor, feeble women like us can do. Our dear Catharine is already worn out with doing and suffering for us all, while I was neglecting the duties that ought to have devolved upon me, and giving up to my own selfish sorrow. But it shall be so no longer. Reproved, and brought to my senses, by what I have just heard, I will henceforth take the place beside my child God and nature assigned me. And Catharine shall rest, and get the roses back into her pale cheek once more."

" But the poor soldiers, dear mother?" said he eagerly. "Our Catharine cannot rest while they are sick and suffering all around her. She couldn't in the camp, it made her heart ache so."

"Is that so, Catharine?" said Mrs. Hunter, taking her hand. "Cannot you forget others long enough to take a little care of yourself?"

"Ah, Mrs. Hunter! if you had ever beheld such dreadful and never-to-be-forgotten scenes as I have witnessed within the last two months, you would not ask; and I know your kind heart too well to believe you would re-

fuse to do all in your power to mitigate the suffering
caused by this cruel war.   We both seem doomed to suffer by it in various ways.   Our warmest sympathies are
with different parties and opposing squadrons.   If we
were men, no doubt, we should be in arms against each
other. But as we are not men, and belong to that sex
on whom devolves a heavenly ministry, may we not join
our hands, and devote our best energies to that mission
that has made Florence Nightingale, and a host of
other noble women, immortal?   You know that I am
strongly loyal in my sentiments; yet, if I know myself,
I can so far sink the partisan in the philanthropist, as to
see a common humanity in both friends and foes, and
perform the same kind offices for both.   And, O Mrs.
Hunter! is there not Christianity enough among the
ladies of Richmond to lead some of them to this noble
work?"

"No doubt there is, Catharine, if they could be aroused
to a sense of their duty.   But then, with all my cares
and troubles, what can I do?" she said in the old hopeless, nervous tone.

"Mrs. Hunter," said Catharine earnestly, "you are
just the one to arouse them to a sense of their duty to
God and man.   Have you forgotten the power you
wielded, and the generals and statesmen who surrounded
you, but a few short months ago?   Surely no lady in
Richmond, not even the wife of the President, could
exert such a wide and ennobling influence as yourself, if
you chose to do so.   I should know my work, and should
not hesitate a moment regarding it, were I on the other
side of the Potomac.   But here I can do nothing without your patronage, or that of some other person equally
influential, who is not afraid to set a noble and magnani-

mous example to Richmond and the world of Christian love and forbearance and gentle kindness towards those even who are regarded as enemies."

Catharine had touched the responsive chord in Mrs. Hunter's bosom at last, — the ambition for pre-eminence and distinction, the desire to be first in a good work that would win the applause of the world, the wish to set a noble example for all inferior people to imitate. And even the real danger of arousing a suspicion of disloyalty, and consequent persecution, in the existing state of public feeling in Richmond, had a subtle charm to such a troubled, repressed, but naturally ambitious and active spirit as Mrs. Hunter's.

We will do her the justice to say, however, that she was really a kind-hearted woman, though not one who would be likely, unprompted, to adopt a course like this. And, if Catharine had done no other good by coming back to Richmond than arousing Mrs. Hunter to a sense of her duty, its value to the cause of humanity could not be counted in gold. For, absorbed and half crazed by her own private troubles since her husband's death, she had secluded herself from society, and, shut up in her own rooms, had known very little of what was going on around her. Now she took the opposite course. And, being of an enthusiastic temperament, she went into every thing, as she had done into the secession movement, with her whole heart. She had receptions almost every evening. Her nights were spent with her darling boy, and her days associated with Catharine, and a few choice spirits whom her influence and enthusiasm raised up around her, in visiting prisons and hospitals, — to which her influence with men in official position gave her easy access, — and in relieving the distresses of their inmates by every means that lay in their power. Enough other ladies were extending such benefits to Southern soldiers at that time in Richmond, leaving those of the Union who were prisoners in their hands to die untended and uncared for. So it remained for Mrs. Hunter and her associates to take broader and more philanthropic views of Christian duty, and set a noble example of generous kindness to those they considered enemies, even at the risk of sacrificing themselves to the fury of popular prejudice.

Mrs. Hunter had from childhood been a fashionable church-member, and read the responses in church with the most devotional unction; but out of it she was quite as gay and worldly as the dictates of fashion demanded. The change in her seemed all the more striking from these circumstances, though indeed a perfectly legitimate and natural one. She merely sought distinction at first in a new field; one that pointed her out to the world as a nobler and better woman than she really was. And so conspicuous had she been in aiding the rebellion, that no one thought of attributing to her, it seems, any but the most generous and philanthropic motives.

As she advanced in it, and familiarized herself with the details of her work, however, all the tender and womanly sympathies of her nature were aroused. Her mind and heart enlarged in view of its great magnitude. Her own selfish ambition was lost, in a measure, in pity for the woes and sorrows and keen agonies she daily witnessed. Her house was open every evening for the reception of distinguished visitors. Her kitchen became a cook-shop, where Catharine, who thoroughly understood all such mysteries, with Aunt Dinah, manufactured every day large quantities of gruel, broths, jellies, and other dainties, for the sick and sorely wounded. Things like these they could not get through the medium of the authorities, whose policy dictated starvation or the poorest fare as the surest way of getting rid of the Union prisoners. Mrs. Hunter's drawing-room, too, became a perfect workshop for the manufacture of lint, bandages, and necessary clothing; in the preparation of which, the precious stores of old linen were brought out. Every member of the family, down to little Walter, was actively engaged in this work during every leisure hour of the day, that was not employed in visiting the wretched but deeply-grateful pensioners of their bounty.

Mrs. Hunter had still great influence with the rebel leaders, and could frequently bend them to her views regarding the amelioration of the condition of the sick and wounded of both parties. And those views, though she was unconscious of it herself, were suggested, moulded, or corrected by Catharine in their daily confidential intercourse at home. For good and wise reasons, Catharine did not deem it prudent to make herself too conspicuous in the work. Though she was Mrs. Hunter's head, heart, and right hand, she appeared to others to be only her executor and handmaiden. Her heart bled for the suffering of her people; and she strove by every means in her power to alleviate them by calling Mrs. Hunter's attention to them. But even Mrs. Hunter could not always secure the attention of the leaders to frightful cruelties, and abuses of power, neglect of duty, or official prejudice, so fierce and vengeful were the passions aroused by this terrible civil war. Yet, though little was done in comparison with the great and urgent need, those few

noble women performed a good and glorious work. They
were the means of saving hundreds of precious lives;
and their names are now a praise and a blessing at
many Northern as well as Southern firesides.

16

CHAPTER X.

GENERAL ATHERTON, meantime, had found himself placed in such circumstances as precluded the idea of his joining Catharine in Richmond, or sending for her to meet him in the South-west, for several months. Battles had been lost and won; and the whole Southern country was in arms, and convulsed as by an earthquake. Travelling had become so dangerous that he dared not risk a long journey for her unattended; and, besides all this, his unacknowledged marriage stood in the way of his sending for her through government channels, or giving her an unsuspected position at the end of the journey. He wrote very often, however, telling her what he was doing, and always deploring their separation.

Catharine, as she had promised, always replied, — detailing their present mode of life, and all their small plans for alleviating the terrible suffering he, as she told him, was doing his best to inflict and perpetuate on a thousand times larger scale. If she must be his wife, and in that way be joined to a ministry of evil and wrong, she determined, from the first, to tell him the truth, and do all that was in her power to neutralize the

182

evil, and alleviate the suffering. She secretly rejoiced that he could not come to claim her, and kept hoping something would intervene to save her from a destiny she dreaded more and more as the time of his expected arrival drew near.

To increase her anxieties, in the mean time Philip had returned to Richmond, temporarily taken up his residence with his aunt, and was again perseveringly suing for her favor. He had come back quite a hero in his own estimation, and that of some of his friends. He had been sent, just after Harry's escape, with a company of soldiers, to search Tremont Hall for the treasure and treasonable correspondence of the judge, its late occupant, in the hope of finding proof that would condemn him for treason. On the way they had captured Harry and Uncle Nick, with Grace and Helen, who were on the way to the Union lines, and taken them back to the Hall. While there, searching the house, and his men carousing over the judge's fine wines and liquors, they were discovered, and in their turn captured, by Theodore, Catharine's elder brother, who, with his company of picked men, had been making a reconnoissance within the enemy's lines.

Philip and his men were taken as prisoners to the Union camp, with the glad and rejoicing Harry, who was welcomed as one risen from the dead. Uncle Nick and the young ladies were also rejoiced to escape the dangers that had surrounded them, and be able to take up their residence with their aunt in Washington.

Philip had managed to escape from the Union lines, and took great credit to himself for what, if they had known the truth, he needed to be ashamed. But he had seen and captured Harry, and been captured himself by

Theodore; and, by magnifying and exaggerating all the circumstances, made capital of this with Catharine, who was so anxious to hear of their welfare at home that she gladly listened. But when Philip came back to his old ground, and began to plead his love for her, she told him, that she could not now listen to such words from him or any other man; and that something as insuperable as death must forever divide them. He thought, of course, she meant their political differences: but he would not for them give over his pursuit of her; for he had come back to Richmond on purpose to win, and even wed, her, if he could get her consent to do so. He hated Grace Tremont now with his whole heart, and had indeed accepted the mission to Tremont House out of revenge; but Catharine he loved with all the fervency of an impassioned and selfish nature that was ready to gratify itself at the expense of honor and truth. He pleaded his cause most fervently the very first opportunity he could get, but of course all in vain. From that time Catharine avoided him all she could; for to be the wife of the father, without daring to tell the truth to the son, who persecuted her continually with lover-like attentions, placed her in a very unpleasant predicament. Angered at last by her determined avoidance, Philip began to revolve dark schemes in his head. In the fervency of his passion, he had offered marriage to one he thought far beneath him in the social scale; and his pride was exceedingly galled by her refusal. When his mind was in just this state of turmoil and irritation, Catharine received a letter from his father that filled her heart with renewed fears and apprehensions for the future. The letter read as follows:—

My dearest Catharine, — I am coming at last to claim my beloved and beauteous bride. You cannot imagine with what impatience I look forward to the hour which is to make you really mine for all time and for eternity. Oh, if you only felt as I do, what joy would be in the thought of clasping a loving as well as beloved bride to my heart! Yet no man can love as fervently as I love you, without inspiring, in some degree, a kindred passion in the object of his affection, I still believe and fondly hope. I shall be with you by the day after to-morrow, at furthest, and there will be time enough then to announce our relations and future plans without troubling yourself about it at present. I think, however, that your dread of the announcement to Philip and my sister is needless; for they both appreciate you too highly to offer any serious objections. Jane herself says that she knows no lady who can compare with you; nor can she ever repay the deep debt of gratitude she owes you for all you have done, and are still doing, for her family. In any case, I have a right to choose my own wife and my own destiny; nor will she be indebted to them for wealth or social position. So do not worry the roses off your cheeks for any of them, but keep them all for me when I come.

Yours ever,
EDWARD ATHERTON.

Catharine was waiting on the veranda for Mrs. Hunter and the carriage when this letter was presented to her by a servant who had been to the office. Seeing no one near, she opened and read it, with her cheek paling and flushing, and with every evidence of strong emotion.

Philip meantime, unknown to her, had been watching

16*

her from the parlor windows. He knew she had received letters before ; and he had been extremely jealous
of her unknown correspondent. He had questioned his
aunt, but without eliciting the desired information.

"She has a good many acquaintances among the officers; and I think she corresponds with some of them, —
your father among the rest," was her reply.

The carriage rolled up to the door, and Mrs. Hunter
came down stairs almost as soon as she had perused her
letter. Covering it with her handkerchief, and thrust-
ing it into her pocket, was the natural impulse upon
which she acted. Philip saw it all; and, more than
this, his eagle eye noted the fact, that, in slipping the
handkerchief in so hastily, the letter fell out of it and
over the railing down into a clump of twining roses,
without her perceiving its loss. His first and honest impulse was to go out, restore the letter to its owner, and help
the ladies into the carriage; his next, upon which of
course he acted, was to stay where he was until the carriage rolled away towards the hospital, then go out, get
the letter, take it up to his room, and at once greedily
devour the contents. How little did he dream of the
terrible surprise awaiting him in that coveted epistle!
and, when read, he could hardly believe the evidence of
his senses. For a time he was fairly stunned by the blow.

What! Catharine, whom he loved as his life, marry
his father! — his own father! — a man of more than
twice her age, — of whose love for him even his father
seemed to doubt; when he, young, handsome, rich, and
accomplished, wooed her in vain for his bride! What
could it mean? This, then, was the reason "as insuperable as death" that was to deprive him of the only
woman he had ever really loved.

That his proud, aristocratic father should condescend to wed a poor Yankee governess was not the least of his wonders. In a young, ardent man like himself, such a *mésalliance* would be much more excusable; though he was very sure his father would never have excused it in him. Men of mature age, he felt sure from what he saw around him, were much more ready to gratify their taste in the choice of poor but young and lovely wives than to accord their sons and daughters the same privilege. But Philip could not endure the thought of having Catharine for his mother, — the wife of his father; and he walked the room for a long time in a state of excitement that defies description.

It must not be! He must do something to prevent it. His father was an old man, and he could not love Catharine as he loved her; nor could she ever love him. In mercy to her, in mercy to himself, he *must* do something to prevent the sacrifice. But where had they met? How could he have obtained her promise to become his bride? It came to him at last, — her stay under his protection in the rebel camp at Manassas Junction; and he cursed the day that ever sent her back to Hunter Hills. But all this time Philip was laboring under a misconstruction. His father's letter was, unfortunately, so ambiguous that he did not dream of their being already married, or he might not have done what he did.

It so happened that Mrs. Hunter forgot to read her letter, that came with Catharine's, until after her return from their round of calls; so, when they all met at dinner, she turned to Philip, and said, —

"Oh! I have such good news, — your father is coming home in a day or two, — safe and well!"

"Is he ?" said Philip musingly.

" Yes : and he says, too, that he has a very pleasant surprise in store for us when he does return. What do you suppose it is ?"

"I am sure I cannot tell. Perhaps Catharine can assist you, — Yankees are so proverbially good at guessing," he said with a feigned laugh, and keen, searching look into her expressive face.

Catharine had looked pale and anxious ever since her return, and as if she could hardly repress her tears. But that was nothing strange, coming from such sad scenes as she had witnessed that day. Now, however, the rich color flashed over cheek and brow, as she said in a cold, forced tone, —

"I am fast forgetting my Yankee proclivities, Philip. I can fathom no mysteries, except those where I am myself concerned. Among all the changes going on around us, I fear I shall not know myself much longer."

Mrs. Hunter rather wondered at her flash of color and singular reply; but Philip, who had the key to it, read a deeper meaning in it than appeared on the surface. And he also read in Catharine's averted eyes a deep-seated feeling of pain, and dread of her approaching fate, that he wished the face of no bride of his to wear. He watched her closely, yet without seeming to do so, and became very sure that the heart had nothing to do with the sacrifice of youth and beauty and strong loyal feeling she was about to make. Either she was doing it from ambitious motives, — a desire for wealth and position, — or else there was some compelling power, urging her on to the sacrifice. He cared little for his father's feelings; for he had no business, at his age, to have any thing but a fatherly regard for any woman as young and fair as Catharine, he thought. And new claimants to the Atherton estates, unless they were of his own raising, were inadmissible in his calculations. Philip had a short journey to make that same afternoon, and did not return until the next morning. At dinner that day, he seemed in better spirits than usual, and chatted quite gayly upon passing events.

He should be obliged to rejoin his regiment, he said, in two or three days; and he was rejoiced to know that his father was coming home, so that he could see him before his departure from Richmond. Contrary to his usual custom, he spent the afternoon at home, with Walter and his sisters; while Mrs. Hunter and Catharine, with their usual supplies, went their usual round.

Ever since her return to Richmond, Catharine had been deeply interested in the fortunes of a young couple, whose wedding she had attended a short time before her departure. The young husband had been sorely wounded at the battle of Bull Run, and had lain in a very critical condition ever since. The young wife, who had been one of Catharine's best friends in Richmond before marriage, frequently sent for her now, when unusually alarmed about her husband.

Just after dusk that same evening, as they were all sitting in the parlor, talking over the events of the day, a servant came in with a note for Miss Hale.

"O Mrs. Hunter!" she exclaimed, after looking it over, "Mr. Gordon is a great deal worse; and Emma is very anxious for me to come and spend the night with her."

"Well, I am very sorry for them both. But you are tired and half sick yourself; and hadn't you better send your excuses to-night, my dear;" and she took the note, and glanced over it herself.

"It would be cruel to refuse in a case like this," said Catharine. "You see, she thinks he will not live till morning. One can see by the handwriting alone that she was hardly like herself when she wrote it."

"Perhaps it would be cruel to refuse under the circumstances; but pray take care of yourself as well as you can."

"Why cannot I take your place, Catharine?" said Philip anxiously. "I will do so with pleasure to save you trouble."

"Oh! that would never do. There are men enough there, no doubt. It is because she craves a woman's presence and sympathy, that she sends for me."

"Let me go with you then, and see you safe there."

"Thank you, Philip; but it is altogether unnecessary. I shall be perfectly safe with Mrs. Gordon's coachman."

Philip did not urge the matter; but, when Catharine was ready, he attended her to the carriage, helped her in, said "Good-night!" then bidding the coachman drive carefully, it was so dark and cloudy, he returned to the parlor, and spent the evening with the family.

The next day, upon the earliest train from the Southwest, true to his announcement, came Gen. Atherton, strong in the hope of meeting and claiming his fair young bride.

The time spent in delivering his despatches, and reporting the progress of military affairs in the South, to President Davis and his councillors, seemed intolerably tedious to the expectant bridegroom. It was over at last; and then he was driven with all speed to Mrs. Hunter's, where a joyful reception awaited him.

He was at heart quite as much surprised as pleased

to find Philip there. He had heard nothing before of his capture and escape, and supposed him still with the Army of the Potomac. He was glad enough to see him, —glad to know that he was safe and well; yet somehow it dampened his spirits to meet him in the place of his lovely bride. It was not the fond meeting and greeting he had anticipated so long. It made the announcement of his secret marriage much more difficult than to Mrs. Hunter's family alone. To him he had intended to make it by letter, which he felt would be far less embarrassing to both.

He inquired after Catharine at last, after Walter and every other member of the family had had their share of attention, and was told the circumstances of her absence at Mr. Gordon's.

"Pray send for her at once; won't you?" he said to Mrs. Hunter. "I want to see the whole family together once more."

"I have already sent John to make inquiries," she replied. "I think he must be here soon. But what is it about that pleasant surprise, brother? I hope it is yet in store for us."

"We will see presently," he returned, smiling, and looking out eagerly, as the carriage rolled past the windows, and on towards the stables.

"What is this? Why, John has not brought Catharine! James Gordon must be dead or dying. Tell John to report himself at once," said Mrs. Hunter to a servant in waiting.

John, an old servant of the family, who, like all the rest was very much attached to Catharine, soon presented himself, but looking particularly dismal, and a good deal frightened withal.

"Well, what is it, John?" said his mistress eagerly.
"Is Mr. Gordon dead or dying?"

"He be no dead, but bery much better, mistress."

"Then why did not Miss Catharine come home?"

"She no bin dere at all, mistress.   Dey no send for her
last night at all."

"Good heavens! What can have become of her,
then?" exclaimed Gen. Atherton in alarm.

"I am sure I cannot tell," said Mrs. Hunter. "We
all know some one came for her; and I saw the note
they sent in myself. Catharine remarked some singu-
larity in Mrs. Gordon's writing, but evidently thought it
was owing to strong nervous excitement. That note
must have been a forgery."

"But there was no collusion! She evidently believed
in its genuineness; did she?" said the general, half in
doubt.

"Certainly. None of us doubted it, I am sure."

"Any more than we did that she was worn out with
watching and caring for others, and would have preferred remaining at home," put in Philip eagerly.

"Then there must have been some plot to entice her
away for some infamous purpose; and I tremble for the
consequences!" exclaimed the general with a sudden
revulsion of feeling, that made him dizzy and strengthless as a child. He sat down by the table, leaned his
head upon his hand, and turned his face away to hide
the strong emotions that no one but Philip keenly
observed. Could it be that Catharine had planned and
gone off in this way to avoid him, and the fulfilment of
her marriage-vows? He could hardly believe it. Such
plots and intrigues seemed wholly discordant with all he
had seen of her open, truthful character. Yet it was

just possible that her dislike and dread of him had become so strong, that she could not feel justified in pretending to fulfil vows against which every feeling of her heart rebelled; and so she had gone off in this mysterious way. That thought gave him bitter pain; but he did not harbor it long before another, much more startling, presented itself. The city was full of troops, — many of them lawless borderers, who would hesitate at no crime; and Catharine, so young and unprotected, and mingling among them so much in going and coming from the prisons and hospitals, might have attracted the attention of some ruffian or ruffians, who had in this way secured her for a victim. In either case, it was best, he thought, for her connection with him to remain a secret, seeing it had been so thus far; for its announcement under present circumstances would attract more attention and remark in both public and private circles than he cared to be the subject of in his present state of cruel anxiety and disappointment.

"Oh, dear! what shall we do?" exclaimed Mrs. Hunter hopelessly. "I'm sure I cannot live in such suspense about the dear girl, or hardly live without her a day. You cannot imagine, brother, what an angel of hope and blessing, what a help, support, and reliance, she has been; not only to us, but to scores of the sick, wounded, and dying in Richmond, since your departure. They hailed her coming with eager joy, and looked upon her face with as much admiring reverence as if it had been the face of an angel. Oh, how they and we all shall miss her, if she never comes back to us!"

"Well, we will sift the affair to the bottom, and find her if we possibly can," said the general, starting to his feet energetically. "The city is under martial law, and

17

it cannot be that a lady can be abducted in this manner without somebody's knowing something about it."

"But it was very dark and misty last evening, father; and they might on that account have escaped the vigilance of the sentinels," said Philip.

"Or bribed them, more likely. Such things are oftener done by men of high than low degree. And we know that Catharine has been a shining mark for the admiration of more than one in positions of honor and trust."

"I know very well," said Mrs. Hunter, "that she has refused offers of marriage from men you would never have dreamed would have condescended to wed a poor Yankee governess. I have often wondered at her seeming indifference to the advantages of fortune, her blindness to her own worldly interests, as well as her evident feeling of equality with the proudest of her suitors. I do believe she loved Lloyd, though; and I feel sorry now that her affair with him turned out as it did."

"She was certainly a very remarkable girl," said the general; "and in beauty, grace, or intellect, few could compare with her."

"We are ready to concede her every perfection," said Philip rather sarcastically; "and I am ready, my dear father, to join you in any search for her you may think proper to institute to-day. To-morrow I shall be obliged to return to my regiment."

"Then we will commence at once, my son. Too much time has already been lost, I fear, for her honor or safety."

They did commence the search at once; and every seeming avenue of information was traced up to its fountain-head, without eliciting the least clew to her mysterious disappearance. Both the civil and military arms of power were tried in vain; and large rewards were at last offered to obtain some knowledge of a fate that seemed shrouded in mystery and gloom.

The general and others at last settled down upon the conclusion that some of Catharine's Yankee friends had been playing a cute trick upon them in thus spiriting away a Northern lady, who rumor said was about to marry a distinguished rebel officer, — nobody knew whom.

The whole Hunter family soon came to regard Catharine as dead, or lost to them forever; and never was a friend more sincerely mourned or missed. Poor little Walter could hardly be comforted. Mrs. Hunter missed her every hour; and, if brother or nephew could have brought her back as his wife, perhaps she would not have objected to the terms.

Never was a man more suddenly cut down or keenly disappointed than Gen. Atherton; and it was as much as he could do to keep from displaying it to all around him. After a thorough search and a mature deliberation, he came to the conclusion that Catharine had, most likely, found some unexpected chance to return to the North, and had gone off in this mysterious way to deceive Mrs. Hunter, and evade her duties to him. Possibly she had gone with some favored lover, who might be equally cheated with himself, regarding her secret marriage. He had believed in the duplicity of all women before he met Catharine; and now he rapidly drifted back to the same opinions, and inwardly cursed the hour that made her his wife. He sought active service now, and became a much more zealous and active partisan than he would have been with Catharine for a companion.

CHAPTER XI

THE ABDUCTION. — CATHARINE'S ILLNESS.

BUT where all this time was Catharine?

When she entered what she supposed to be Mr. Gordon's close carriage, she was a little surprised to find that it already contained what appeared to be a female occupant.

"Missus t'ink Miss Kate no want to come 'lone, so she send 'long Thetis," said the unexpected attendant.

"She was very kind. But how long is it since your master began to grow worse, Thetis?"

"Eber sense Miss Hale come away dis mornin'. Thetis t'ink he die dis time."

It was so dark in the carriage that Catharine could only see the dim outline of a black figure. She knew Mrs. Gordon's maids well; and that was the name of one of them. But somehow the voice seemed unfamiliar. Yet it was true that she had been there in the morning, as she had said. Still she felt no suspicions until she began to wonder they did not arrive at Mr. Gordon's.

"We seem to be a long time in getting there," she said at last. "The coachman must have lost his way in the fog. But there was no need of it here, where there are street-lamps all the — Why, there are none here, as sure as the world!"

196

At this moment Catharine became conscious of an overpowering smell; and a minute afterwards a strong arm was thrown around her, and a handkerchief was pressed to her nose, that must have been strongly saturated with chloroform. She struggled and resisted with all her might, and tried to scream; but a hand was laid upon her mouth, her breath came thick and gasping, her limbs relaxed, and she knew nothing more until gradually aroused from a long gap of unconsciousness. Then she found herself riding along a country road, in a heavy military wagon, reclining on the arm of a tall and powerful man, in the undress costume of an officer in the Confederate service.

Though clouded and hazy at first, her senses soon returned, enough for her to remember her last stifling sensations; and then she became terribly alarmed to think, not only of her present position, but also of what might have been done in her state of insensibility. As soon as she began to move, the man spoke; and there was something in the tones of his voice that re-assured her, and in some measure allayed her fears.

"Do not be alarmed," he said: "you are perfectly safe, and going to the house of a friend."

"What friend?" she eagerly asked. "I have none in this country out of Richmond."

"You will know in time, but not now."

"But why this — this outrage? Why have I been drugged, and brought here against my will?"

"To save you from a worse fate, — one to which you were looking forward with dread and loathing. Can you understand that?"

"Perhaps I do. But why take these extraordinary measures?"

17*

"Pray be content with what you know. I am not permitted to say more. I am here only to oblige a friend, to whom I am under infinite obligations." And more he would not say; though she tried more than once to elicit something regarding her destination. She soon became deadly sick, as people usually are who have taken chloroform; and he was again obliged to surround her with his arm to keep her from falling out of the wagon. He persuaded her at last to take something that tasted very strongly of brandy, that he carried in his pocket, and the draught seemed to do her good. They rode on until nearly daylight; and she thought they must have gone at least twenty miles. Turning off, then, from the turnpike, they came to a broad, shadowy lane that led them up to a handsome country residence. It was built of stone, and surrounded by plenty of trees, from which the leaves were falling in the chill November dawn. They drove up the broad avenue a part of the way, then stopped, evidently with as little noise as possible. The driver, a negro, jumped out, and held the mules; while the officer alighted, and helped out Catharine, who at first could scarcely stand.

"It is very early," said her attendant: "yet we are expected; and it is my friend's wish that our *entrée* should be as secret as possible. And it is best for you that it should be so. We will walk in as quietly as we can, and allow the negroes and dogs the pleasure of their morning nap."

There was no use in trying to resist the wishes or commands of her gentlemanly attendant; so she took his arm, and walked up to the mansion. At the door they were met by a fat, good-natured old negro woman, who welcomed them with a shrewd grin, and took them into a warm, handsomely-furnished, well-lighted parlor. Here the gentleman, after hoping she would experience no harm from her night journey, and be the happier for it in the future, bade her "Good-morning," and departed. Feeling as if there were no use in resisting the fate that brought her there, and completely worn out with fear, fatigue, excitement, and the effects of the deadly narcotic, she longed for rest. Signifying as much, she was piloted up stairs, and ushered into a handsome suite of rooms, where a cheerful fire was burning in the grate, and every thing looked neat and comfortable. She sat down before the fire in a luxurious easy-chair, completely tired out and chilled through. The old woman took off her bonnet and wraps, and then stood gazing at her admiringly.

"Looks drefful pale an' sick like," she muttered; "but 'deed she's a pretty critter. No wonder she set all dese men-folks crazy. Don't blame de ole feller a bit, or de young one eider. But Chloe t'ink it bad bizness, for all dat."

"Of whom are you speaking, good mother?" said Catharine wearily.

"Oh! no matter. Massa say Chloe keep still tongue in her head; an' she must."

"Who is your master, my good woman?"

"Missis know soon enuf, an' like him well nuff, I reckon. All de gals du dat, Chloe t'ink. He hansum as a picter. But won't de lady hab some breakfus?"

"No, no! But pray let me lie down: I feel sick as death." The woman led her to the bed, and attempted to undress her; but, fearing some sudden surprise, she refused her assistance, and lay down in the dark merino dress she happened to have on at the time of her abduction.

Her head ached intolerably. She was sick at the
stomach, with every wretched feeling engendered by
fright, an overdose of chloroform, and the cold she had
evidently taken in her long night-journey. The old
woman covered her up warmly, shut the blinds, and at
last she slept: but it was a fitful slumber, broken by
wild dreams of rapine and bloodshed. She awoke when
the sun was high in the heavens: but her head and bones
still ached with a dull, dreary pain, her flesh was hot
and sore, her tongue was parched, her cheeks burned;
and she knew that she had taken a heavy cold, and
was threatened with fever. She did not regret it much,
except for her unpleasant sensations; for she felt so
wretched mentally, that she hardly cared what became
of her. She did not forget that this was the day he was
coming, — her lord and master; and there was a feeling
of relief in the thought that she was far away, and
probably out of his reach.

Yet he was her husband; and, if they were ever to
meet, she did not like the idea of his thinking that she
had fled from Richmond to get out of his way, as she
was sure he must under the circumstances. That she
had been forcibly abducted for that reason, she could not
doubt. But who could have known the facts, or cared
to take advantage of them in that way, she could not
imagine. At last she thought of the letter, the loss of
which had given her a good deal of uneasiness; and
that partially solved the mystery. Some one who felt
an interest in her must have found it; and, guessing her
feelings, had contrived this plan to get her out of her
husband's way. She felt so ill that she kept her bed the
greater part of the day, and did not attempt to leave the
room. The old negro woman brought her every thing she

wanted, which was not much, but refused to enlighten
her as to her employers, or their motives, if she knew
them. The prospect from her windows was very
beautiful, overlooking, as it did, a fine extent of country; though the sear foliage of the deciduous trees,
and added brilliancy of the evergreens, testified to the
near approach of winter. She thought of escape; but,
too sick to entertain that thought long, she tacitly resigned herself to her destiny. That night passed in
much the same manner as the morning. Still she was
no better when it was over, though able to walk about
the room. She still thought of escape, but was too miserable to care much about it, so long as she was undisturbed by noise, or the arrival of troublesome visitors.
There were plenty of books in the room, and she tried
to read; but it made her head and eyes ache worse, and
she could fix her mind on nothing long. The morning
dragged slowly away. When her nice dinner was
brought in, it was hardly tasted.

At last she heard the clock strike one, and soon after
the roll of carriage-wheels up the avenue. Her pulses
now beat high with excitement as well as fever; but
her windows were so situated that she could see nothing
of the arrival. She heard the murmur of voices; the
tread of feet in the halls and alleys, and up and down
the stairs; the clatter of dishes, and moving of tables;
and at last grew so anxious, that she thought she would
step out into the hall to listen. For the first time she
attempted to open the door of her chamber, but found,
to her surprise, that it was bolted on the outside, and
she was a prisoner. Chloe had been coming and going
so often, that she had not mistrusted it before. The
shock to her feelings was so great that she could scarcely

stand. Weak, nervous, and terrified at the thought,
she sunk down upon the lounge, laid her face upon her
clasped hands, and burst into tears.

And thus it was that Philip Atherton found her when,
preceded by Chloe, a few minutes later, he entered the
room.

"What, in tears, Catharine!" he exclaimed, as he
came and sat down beside her, and attempted to take
her hand. "I am surprised. I had hoped to see you
rejoicing in any fate that took you out of Richmond
just at this time. Did I not guess your feelings truly?"

Catharine was astounded. She had not dreamed of
Philip being her real abductor, or that he, if he really
knew the truth, would have dared to thwart and circum-
vent his own father. Did he know that she was really
his father's wife? If not, dared she tell him, after
promising so solemnly not to divulge it until her husband's return?

He looked upon her pityingly and in silence for a few
moments, longing to hush her sobs upon his bosom;
but somehow he dared not try it.

"Catharine," he said at length, "I had hoped for a
different reception from this. I had flattered myself
that you would prefer the shelter of my fond, enduring
love to the fate I found awaited you in Richmond, — to
which I thought, from your every look and tone, you
looked forward with fear and dread."

"You took a fine way to coax me over to your views,
Philip Atherton," said Catharine, raising her head
proudly, — "one worthy the ingenuity of a first-class
pirate or brigand. But pray to what fate worse than
this do you allude, sir?"

"That of a marriage with a man old enough to be

your father, whom you may fear and respect, but can
never love. The means I took to save you from it were
the only ones I could think of, that would at once
preclude objections on your part, from some mistaken
sense of duty, and elude the vigilance of martial law,"
he said with his face flushing hotly at her scornful allusions to his brigandism.

Catharine sprang to her feet, and began to pace the
room rapidly, and in the greatest consternation, trying
to think of what it was best for her to do. That Philip
loved her quite as passionately, and more unscrupulously,
than his father, she could no longer doubt. And this
daring outrage, in sending her out of his father's way,
believing her evidently still free to choose, warned her
that he had come to bring the affair to a crisis in some
desperate way. She saw plainly that he was not to be
turned from his purpose, or trifled with. Back and
forth she paced the room for some time, with a flushed
and excited countenance; while he watched her furtively, trying to read his fate in her expressive face, and
wondering how she could hesitate in a choice between
the son, glowing with youth and health and beauty,
and the father stern and faded and old. He forgot the
fact, that, if she could have had a choice, she would have
selected neither the one nor the other as the companion
of her future life.

She decided at last that concealments and half-way
measures were unadvisable in the present crisis; so,
with a face pale with excitement, all excepting a bright
red spot on either cheek, she came tremblingly up to
Philip, took both his hands in hers, and said in a deeply-
agitated yet pitying tone, —

"Philip, you have done yourself a great wrong, as well

as me, in bringing me here as you have done, — exposing, not only my health, but my character to the
greatest misconstructions. Yet I forgive you, though
another may not, because you knew not what you were
doing. Like all the rest of the world, you seem ignorant
of the fact, that for more than three months I have
been your father's wife."

"My father's wife! Good heavens! is that the truth?"
he exclaimed, starting to his feet as suddenly as if a
cannon-ball had rolled under them, and looking into
Catharine's eyes with a wild, strange, agonized expression, that fairly startled her.

"It is the solemn truth, Philip," she said. "I am
his wife, at least in name. We were privately married
at Manassas the morning previous to his departure for
the South-west. How, or why, I dare not tell you. I
promised not to reveal the fact, or leave the country before his return. But to save *you, his son,* from further
errors, if not crimes, I feel that I must confess the truth.
Oh! pity, and leave me now, Philip, to a fate that is irrevocable, and forget that you have ever loved me."

"I wish I could, God knows! But it is impossible.
What, *you* my father's wife! — *my mother!* and forever beyond my reach! Oh, the thought will drive me
mad!" and it was his turn now to walk the floor, and
wring his hands in bitter agony of spirit; while she
sat down, leaned her aching head upon her hands, and
silently wept.

At last he came up, and bending over her, and putting
his arm around her, said in a husky voice, "O Catharine! even now, if you only loved me, we might fly
from" —

"Let me hear no such words as those from your lips!"

she exclaimed, rising in majesty. "You forget what is due to yourself and your father's wife. Bear your disappointment like a man, even as I have borne mine, and lived on to suffer still more. But I may not live long. I took a severe cold in coming here, and I am very ill at this moment. Don't you see the fever in my bloodshot eyes and flushed cheeks, and feel it in my burning hands?" and she laid her hot hand upon his cold and clammy ones.

He pressed the hand to his lips, and looked drearily into the flushed face, but to be convinced that she told him the truth.

"O Catharine!" he exclaimed in alarm. "You are really ill. If my bringing you here should cause your death, I should never forgive myself."

"I should not murmur, Philip. The sleep of death would seem sweet to me now, the life before me seems so dreary and joyless."

"Without love, or congeniality of soul, or suitability of age, or even the strong bond of political affinities, — O Catharine!"

"Say no more, Philip, but leave me now, I beg of you, — leave me to my fate."

"But what will you do? *He* is in Richmond making inquiries for you everywhere."

"Does he acknowledge me as his wife?"

"No, indeed; or I should not have come here to woo or insult my father's wife!" said he bitterly.

"Do not mention it again, but go, — go. I forgive and pity you. But my head is bursting with pain: I can hardly see. I cannot think what to say to you any longer," she exclaimed in an agonized tone.

18

"But you must have a doctor immediately," he said in a tone of alarm.

"No, no: that would reveal the secret. It must not be known that I am here. How it would disgrace me, and him too, if it were known that I had run away from him to stay here alone with his son! Chloe can doctor me, I'll warrant; and she won't tell him — I took poison, and went off to get rid of him. Ha, ha, ha! Funny, wasn't it, to hide from him in this way? To sell myself to save *his* life, and then cheat him out of the price. Was that right, do you think? I don't. But then I was so afraid I couldn't help it. He'll be jealous as an ogre, I'll warrant, if I look at Lloyd, or Philip, or anybody younger or handsomer. But who cares? One can't always keep her thoughts from roving, if she is tied with cords or matrimonial bands. I'm not one to break over them, though. Maybe I shall learn to love him as he said. I hope so. Oh! is that you, Philip? You came to see your father, did you? He is just returned, and you will find him in the library. He will be delighted to see you safe home after that bloody battle. Was Theodore there? or Harry? Wounded, did you say? Oh, I must go to him at once!" And she started up in wild alarm; while Philip, who had thus far listened in astonishment to her wild ravings, doubtful at first that they were so in reality, but convinced at last that they were the incoherent utterances of delirium, caught her by the arm to prevent her from dashing out of the room and down the stairs.

Her eyes grew wilder and wilder every moment, and were fixed on vacancy, or roving restlessly. Her face was hotly flushed, her pulse bounding; and there was every symptom of a raging fever. He led her back to a

seat, and then, completely at his wits' end, rang for
Chloe, who had retired. Besides Catharine, there was no
white woman on the plantation; and he knew, that, if a
doctor was sent for, it would excite a great deal of wonder
and speculation in the neighborhood, get to the ears of
his father, and lead to unpleasant consequences. Chloe
was quite a celebrated doctress among the negroes. She
thought she could manage the case skilfully; and Philip
finally concluded that it was better to risk it in her
hands, under a charge of secrecy, than to hazard Catharine's reputation by calling in medical aid. So she was
persuaded by Chloe to go to bed, opiates were adminis-
tered, and then she proceeded to give her a famous sweat.
But, in spite of all Chloe could do, Catharine was stupid
or raving by turns for several days. Philip had planned
to spend them with her in a very different manner. Now
he sat by her at times, when Chloe, worn out with watching, slept upon the lounge near by, listening to her incoherent ravings, and gathering up, first and last, the whole
story of her devoted self-sacrifice to save her brother's
life, as well as indubitable proofs of her innocence, purity,
and truth. He felt indignant at his father for taking
advantage of her as he had done; though conscience whispered that he would have done the like in the same circumstances, — or worse if he could. Yet he bitterly
cursed himself now for the ungenerous part he had acted
towards her first and last, and all he had made her suffer. If he could have won the love of such a woman, he
felt that he would have become a better man; and his
thoughts went back regretfully to his conduct regarding
Lloyd Hunter, and the pride and haughtiness that repelled her in the bright morning of their lives.

Catharine grew calmer at last; but she was then completely exhausted, and still dangerously sick, when Philip was compelled to tear himself away, and return to his regiment. But the time spent in that sick-room was not wholly lost upon him. His mad passion was cooled by the knowledge that her most secret earthly thoughts were all of another; while her perfect sincerity, truth, purity of soul, high sense of honor, and strong religious principle, and trust in God, awed, and inspired him for the time with such a respect for her as he had never felt for any other woman, — such a reverence for sacred things as he had never in his life experienced before. He left the place a sadder, wiser, but exceedingly anxious man.

Philip had a private conference with his overseer before leaving, and also left a letter with Chloe for Catharine, in case she recovered, but to be burned if she did not, with strict injunctions that she should have the best of care, and every thing that was necessary for her restoration.

It was late in November when Catharine was brought to the plantation : it was mid-winter before she could sit up a moment, and a much longer time before she was able to leave her sick-chamber. A physician at first might have broken up the fever; though that is doubtful, so strongly was it fastened upon her system. As it was, she had it the natural way; though Chloe took great credit to herself for her wonderful cure of the sick lady, who ran away from the guerillas, and came to her for protection one dark November morning. The life-giving spring breezes brought health and strength, and a more refined and delicate beauty, back to the poor invalid, but the greatest anxiety regarding her future destiny.

As soon as she thought her well enough, Aunt Chloe put Philip's letter into Catharine's hands, with money enough for all present exigencies. It began thus: —

"O Catharine! what can I say to you in this dreadful hour, that I see you lying there upon the confines of eternity, through my means, and yet must, by a strong necessity, leave you to your fate, and bid you perhaps an eternal farewell? Yet it may be better for you and for me that it is so; for I cannot endure the thought of your really becoming his bride, or ever forgive him for taking advantage of you as he has done. And oh! would it not be better for you to be rejoicing among the angels — as you would, if mortal ever did or can — than to live on, a life of fear, disgust, and loathing? For I know all, Catharine. The whole truth has been revealed to me in your wild ravings; though I should not have understood it but for my previous knowledge of that captivity and escape. As it is, family pride will forever seal my lips; and you must burn this epistle if you live to read it, lest in some way a clew should be afforded to his enemies. Reading your heart thus, as I have done, Catharine, I truly honor and exonerate you from all blame. Knowing your most secret thoughts, I believe you to be a pure, self-sacrificing angel, of whom neither of us was in the smallest degree worthy. Led on by a passionate, self-indulgent nature, I have wronged you in the past, dear Catharine, more than I dare to think of. And I had come to believe female purity and virtue a myth, and that there was none unpurchasable, until this hour that I read your pure and noble soul. Oh, if I could have a wife like you, it would be my salvation! But that is now impossible. The past cannot be re-

19*

called. In the present I am reaping its punishments
with a vengeance, in a blighted and unhappy life. For
the future I have only a mad, sleepless ambition, that
may lead me on to death. Forgive all I have made you
suffer. Think of me as kindly as you can. If possible,
I beg of you to conceal the part I have taken in your
abduction, and thus shield me from his anger. My own
private feelings would bid me counsel you to return to
your friends at the North as soon as possible; yet I
know that a sense of duty may lead you back to Richmond and to him. In either case, I shall not blame
you. I enclose the means to do either; and you must
act as you think best. To-morrow I go back to my
duty, with a weight like a mountain on my heart. Oh,
how deeply I realize in this dreadful hour that 'the
wages of sin is misery, if not death'! Farewell, dear
Catharine, farewell forever.''

Catharine could not read this epistle without tears,
and the strongest emotions of pity and regret for the
evident suffering of what she believed to have been a
noble nature run to waste and wickedness, through early
indulgence, and a mistaken mother's training. She forgave, and felt sorry for him; yet she could not forget
that he probably was the cause of the bitterest disappointment of her life, — one, too, that had led her on,
step by step, to her present unenviable position. Philip
had left her free to act, and advised her to go home.
But no passes were granted at that time; and it was
not so easy to do so as it had previously been. But, in
spite of her repugnance, there was her solemn promise;
and did she not owe her first duty to her husband? If
he, through doubt or jealousy, refused to believe the

strange tale she had to tell, she could then decide upon some other course. Therefore, as soon as she was able to sit up, she wrote, not only to him, but to Mrs. Hunter, detailing her painful experiences, excepting what related to Philip's visit, and asking what she had better do.

The slave, sent on horseback to the nearest office with the letters, ran away, as hundreds of others were doing at that time. The letters never reached their destination; and Catharine waited in vain for a reply. After days of suspense and anxious solicitude, she wrote again, but with no better success than before. She did not know, of course, that neither of her letters ever reached their destination. Thinking at last that they doubted her story, and wanted to cast her off, she made some inquiries about crossing the lines. Finding she could not do this in safety, she concluded to return to Richmond at a venture, though a little doubtful of her reception.

But, in all those weeks and months that Catharine had lain there, sick, homesick, and suffering, the bloody work of war had gone on. Though the splendid army of the Potomac, from one cause and another, chafed in their canvas tents, sickened with inaction and hope deferred, and rapidly filled up the hospitals and grave-yards, bloody battles had been fought at many other places, with varied fortunes, all along the extended lines. Thousands of precious lives had been sacrificed, and millions of treasure had been expended.

But Catharine knew very little of all this: she saw no papers or intelligent people, and heard only the wild, garbled stories circulating among the slave population, who, unable to read themselves, were kept in as great ignorance as possible by their owners, especially at this time, when they were in a general expectation of a jubilee of freedom.

Philip Atherton's plantation was one he had inherited from his mother. Though large and isolated, and its owner thoroughly loyal to the Confederate cause, it had not been exempt from the desolating scourge of war, any more than others in Northern Virginia at that time. The slaves ran away in scores; the crops were overrun and wasted; the fences burned; and every thing seemed going to rack and ruin. None could prevent the spoiling of their possessions by the roving bands of soldiery and desperadoes, who swept like a tornado over the hills and valleys of the Old Dominion, emboldened by their successes, and feared alike by friend and foe. They had paid the plantation two or three visits previous to Catharine's arrival; ransacking the house, corn-cribs, smoke-houses, pig-sties, and hen-roosts, taking whatever they liked. But several months had passed away since that time; and they had begun to feel quite secure again.

Catharine had been very shy of exposing herself to the gaze of the people on or around the plantation; yet, as she gained strength, she began to walk out at certain hours to view the beautiful scenery, and breathe the refreshing spring breezes: though generally careful to choose unfrequented paths.

CHAPTER XII.

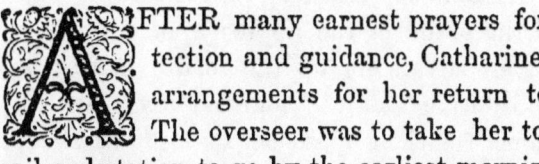FTER many earnest prayers for divine protection and guidance, Catharine finally made arrangements for her return to Richmond. The overseer was to take her to the nearest railroad station to go by the earliest morning train.

The afternoon previous to her expected departure, she thought she would walk down the avenue to the turnpike to view the scenery, and fix the location in her memory.

It was past the middle of April: the sky was blue and cloudless, and the air soft and balmy. The trees in this favored clime were putting forth fresh young leaves and opening buds. The early wild-flowers greeted her at every step, cheering her by their bright young faces. The birds were warbling their evening songs of thanksgiving to their great Creator, thus leading her own heart up in thankfulness to the kind Father who had scattered such life and beauty everywhere, and preserved her thus far in trouble and danger. She reached the little arched bridge that spanned a beautiful stream that crossed the grounds a few rods above the turnpike; and, tired with her unusual exertions, — for she was still far from strong, — she sat down upon the low railing to rest, and think over her plans for the future.

A little hill, covered with a fine growth of young timber, screened her from observation from the turnpike, and also deadened the sound of the approach of a party of soldiery, who were advancing up the road. It was not until an authoritative "Halt!" sounded upon her ear, that she dreamed of their approach, so lost was she in her meditations. Starting up in alarm, she looked towards the turnpike, and saw two men on horseback just rounding the curve of the hill, and turning their steeds up the avenue.

"Nice place to stop and recruit, by ginger! Plenty of bacon and nice fat fowls, and feed for the nags, I'll bet a fourpence," she heard one of them say to the other.

"So I reckon," echoed the other. "I wonder who lives here? But look there. Hallo! Stop, gal! Can't ye answer a civil question?"

"I'll be hanged if I didn't know that critter; and I'll be plaguy glad to see her tu," continued the first speaker.

Catharine did not wait for rejoinder or parley, but ran swiftly up the avenue, spreading consternation among the slaves by the news that the soldiery were coming; though not in so great a degree as she felt it herself: for, in the sharp, nasal twang, she had recognized the voice of Sweep, her old admirer and persecutor, though his face seemed somehow a good deal changed in appearance from what she remembered it. She feared from his words that he had recognized her; so, as soon as she got to the house, she ran up to her room, locked the door, and sunk down upon a seat breathless and terrified. She had supposed him dead, or at least out of the country; and she trembled to think of what new trouble might come of his machinations. There was no use in resisting the demands for entertainment of a party of twenty

armed soldiery; though the overseer tried to do it at first:
but the carabines of the troopers brought him to his
senses. They were guarding government property, they
said, and had a right to the best the country afforded.
So the big sutler's wagon they were guarding was drawn
under the shed, the beasts were fed and housed, and the
men were soon having a merry carouse over the nice
supper Aunt Chloe was obliged to have prepared for
them.

In spite of her hopes to the contrary, Sweep had
recognized Catharine; and, by questioning the negroes, he
found out that the lady had run away from the guerillas,
and come there sick ever so long ago, and was going
away again upon the morrow. He knew very well that
she would not want to see him; but for all that he determined to have an interview with "missy," as the negroes
called her.

As soon as supper was over, and it was quite dark, he
took Aunt Chloe aside, and told her privately that he
knew the young lady who was staying there well; that
he was, in fact, a particular friend of hers, and knew she ·
would be terrible glad to see him. He wanted her to go
and ask her if she wouldn't like to have an interview
with Mr. Kendall. Chloe did not like the looks of him,
but she was totally unsuspicious of his object: so,
taking a light, she waddled up the grand staircase to
Catharine's room. It was locked; but she opened it at
once at the sound of Aunt Chloe's welcome voice, letting
in, not only the old negress, but Sweep, who had followed
on tiptoe, and bolted in just behind her, before either
she or Catharine was aware of his presence. To avoid
suspicion, she had been sitting there in the darkness; and,
blinded by the sudden illumination, she did not perceive

the rascal until he had made good his entrance, locked the door after him, and put the key in his pocket.

"Dere's a great, tall, yaller-skinned, long-legged man down stairs, dat say he know ye, miss, an' want to see ye dreffully," said Chloe, who, being a little deaf, had not dreamed of his being so near.

"That's so, Miss Kate," echoed Sweep, coming forward at this moment, and grasping her hand as if he were the dearest friend she had in the world.

She drew back, too much surprised to speak for an instant, and then exclaimed in an indignant tone, "I would thank you to walk out of my room, sir! No gentleman would enter a lady's chamber in such an impudent way as this!"

"Oh! you're there, are you? I'm very much obleeged for the compliment!" he returned with a grin. "I'll let the old woman out, if you say so; but, as to myself, I'm very comfortable;" and he sat down composedly upon the side of the bed.

"Get 'long out yerself, you old villain! I'll not have my young mistis 'sulted in dis way!" screamed Chloe, as soon as she could catch her breath from astonishment at his audacity, and flourishing her black fist in his face. "If you don't go dis minit, I'll yell, an' rouse every nigger on de plantation."

"Do you see *that*, you old baboon?" he returned, drawing a glittering bowie from its sheath, flourishing it menacingly before her eyes, and then coolly returning it to its receptacle.

Poor Chloe subsided at once. She stood for a moment gazing in dumb terror into his glittering gray eyes, and then, turning with a faint shriek, she ran towards the door, followed by the equally frightened Catharine. He laughed sardonically, when he saw their consternation at finding the door locked upon them, and they prisoners, apparently at his mercy.

"Pray be seated, ladies, and make yourselves to home, jest as I du," he sneered. "I come to make a friendly call, and there's no need of makin' all this fuss about it."

"You see, I've bin wantin' to see ye, Miss Kate, ever sence that little affair at the major's, to tell ye how grateful I was for what you done for me."

"If you are so in reality, as I think you had reason to be, pray unlock this door, and walk out, sir!"

"Oh! that's another matter, my dear. I've got a great deal to tell ye before we part; though I'll let out the old woman if you say so;" and he grinned maliciously.

"No, no!" she eagerly exclaimed. "She shall stay if you do."

"As you will. I always love to please the ladies; though I'd a leetle ruther see you alone. You see, Miss Kate, I ain't done likin' on ye yet; and I wanted to tell ye how infarnal lucky I'd bin sence we parted. You know, I had a darned hard time on it then; but I weathered it somehow, and got off slick as grease at last, with my money tied round me in a leather belt under my shirt. You see, I got so crisped and singed, and looked so awful on the outside, and all the niggers and white folks was so mad, that they never thought to sarch me, and never spected that I'd got five thousand dollars under the rags and charcoal. So they let me slide; and slide I did. They wouldn't touch me arter you was gone, except to give me a kick, even when I yelled like murder for water. I suffered horribly, I can tell ye, and like to kicked the bucket. But I was determined I

19

wouldn't please 'em so well as to du that. So I crawled off at last to the cornfield by the spring, and lived there until I got well enough to quit that cussed plantation. I found an old tin dipper near the spring; so I could get water, and milk the cows, and eat green corn, and all the nice melons and fruit I wanted; so I didn't starve then, I'll bet a fourpence.

"Well, I skulked round a spell until I got better, and found some fellers going North who lent me a hoss, and went with me up to the Union lines by a kind of underground railroad management. You see, they was beginning to git kinder out of things down here, owin' to that tarnal blockade; and they wanted 'em dreadfully. So I went up home to see if I couldn't help 'em a little. When I got up to Washinton, who should I find there but my own brother, Jotham Sweep; and, as sure as you live, he had got to be one of the biggest government contractors in the Union, and, one way and another, was makin' money like smoke. He'd already made tew hundred thousand dollars, he told me; and all he wanted was jest sich a cute feller as me to make it a million in a few months. You see, the rebs were gittin' out of knives an' fish-hooks an' darnin'-needles an' guns an' swords an' pistols an' cloth an' shews, an' medsun most of all, 'cause old 'Stars an' Stripes' had blocked 'em in; and they was ready to pay 'most any price for 'em. Jotham was buyin' up all sich things for the government, an' shinnin' round the President an' secetaries an' generals, an' pickin' up all the news; for he was always a great hand to pry inter things. Then he'd let me inter all their secrets that he'd smelt out, an' fix me out slyly with a lot of the traps he'd bought for government, an' I'd start off for Old Dixie by the underground. I've kept it up ever

sence, an' no harm done to anybody. The rebs understand it, you see, an' furnish guards to bring me straight
through. When I've got news, or somethin' they want
bad, like that doctor stuff out there in the wagon, I go
clear to Richmond; but most of the time they take the
stuff right off my hands nearer home. I jest growed a
big beard, ye see, an' colored it black with dye-stuff, so
that my own mother wouldn't know me, Jotham says, —
if I only hold my tongue. Don't you see how it im-
proves my beauty? My new name, tu, is a plaguy
sight hansumer than the old one, agin which I always
had a spite. But the best of it is, I've made money
hand over fist ever sence I went inter the business. I've
already got tew hundred thousand safe and sound up
there in the banks to home; an', if you'll have me, we'll
go up to Washinton, build us a grand house, git us a
coach an' hosses, carry home a few niggers to du the
dirty work an' wait on us; an' then we'll cut as grand a
flourish as the best on 'em. Come now, what do you
say? . Will you du it?"

"No, indeed!" said Catharine indignantly. "I have
no desire to flourish on such ill-gotten gains."

"Ill-gotten, did you say? It's no sich thing. They
need the things dreadfully; and it's as fair a trade as can
be," said he spunkily.

"Don't you know that you are liable to dreadful penalties if you are caught on the Federal side of the
line?" said Catharine, who, with her anger and wonder at his audacity, had partially recovered her equanimity.

"Oh, that's all moonshine!" he replied. "Jotham
takes care of all that. They orter be thankful, tu; for I
carry 'em a sight of news every time I go to Washinton; an' Jotham knows how to make that pay."

"Ah! you play spy for both parties, then?"

"No spy about it. I jest tell 'em the news: that's all. An' they both want to hear it bad enough."

"Well, you had better go home and take up some more respectable calling than bringing aid and comfort to the enemies of your country, if you do not want your neck stretched."

"What are you duin' down here, ma'am?"

"I am staying because I cannot get home just now; and cannot very well help myself."

"Oh! if that's all, I can help ye jest as well as not. Go down to Richmond with me an' git spliced; an' the rebs won't say a word agin your goin' home with me. They'd help us along all the way. I know jest how to come round 'em; an' they think a sight of me. Why, the very biggest an' fattest on 'em, even to Jeff. Davis himself, — though he's poor enough, the Lord knows, — treat me jest as hansum as hansum can be. They some on 'em ask me to dine or take wine with 'em every time I come down here, and act as if they was darned glad to see me."

"Ay! and scorn you behind your back as a traitor to your country."

"Oh! not at all. They treat me like a prince, an' want me to come down as often as I can. But, arter all, it's jest a leetle mite dangerous; and I'm about tired of packing around from pillar to post. So, if you'll go home with me, Miss Kate, I'll quit the business, and we'll settle down comfortable together. I could then go inter the contractin' business with Jotham, if you think that's a little grander, and still make money enough to keep ye in gewgaws and fixin's. For, you see, I don't mean my wife shall be behind Jotham's one bit. If you could have seen her at the President's levy, as I did, you'd ha' thought it worth while to be a contractor's bride. She looked as grand as the best on 'em, I can tell ye, in her yaller silk gownd, with long red streamers on her head, and covered all over with flowers and diamonds and flounces and furbelows. I guess Mr. Lincoln and his wife thought so, tu, by the notice they took on her. But you're a great deal hansumer than Jotham's wife; and you'd show off the fixin's, I can tell ye, up there to Washinton : and you shall have all you want, if it costs ever so much. So jest. say you'll go now, an' it's all right."

"I shall say no such thing; so you may as well go about your business."

"Wall, I guess it's about time," he said with an evil smile. "But folks change their minds sometimes, and especially gals; so I guess I'll call agin. There was Jotham's wife, now, used to cut his head, and give him the mitten every time she got a chance, up there in old New England. But when he got to contractin', and begun to make a spread, she come round as sweet as molasses, and near about asked him to take her, I heard. And that's about the way with all the women. They want to be baited with a shiny hook. Maybe you won't be so different from the rest, after all. I'll jest call round in the. mornin', an' see. So good-night, an' pleasant dreams." He then unlocked the door, let himself out, and marched down stairs.

"What an unmitigated scoundrel!" Catharine exclaimed, as soon as anger would allow her to speak.

"Dat's sure nuff," returned Chloe, who sat all this time cowering in the corner, so much frightened by his threats as scarcely to understand a word he said.

19*

"Yes, indeed! and I was never more sorry for any thing I have done than for saving his life a few months ago."

"He mean you no good, miss. He eye show dat. Chloe glad when de house clare o' him."

"And I, too, Chloe. He's plausible enough, in his vulgar way; but he has not the least sense of honor or decency. Why, to think of his forcing himself in here as he did, is enough to make one's flesh creep. You must stay with me to-night, Chloe, or I shall not sleep a wink."

"Well, Chloe lock de door on de inside, put her bed across, an' keep de ole divle off."

They soon found, however, that, though Sweep had left their door unlocked, he had carried off the key. That decided Catharine to take another room that could be locked. Taking her money, and the old merino dress she had worn from Richmond in November, and intended wearing back again on the morrow, she went to the room immediately. During her stay at the plantation, she had been obliged to wear such garments as were brought to her, she knew not whose. These she intended to leave behind her, with the good seed she had endeavored to sow in the hearts of kind Aunt Chloe and some few other members of the family.

Chloe was obliged to go down to make preparations for the early breakfast, not only of Sweep and his guards, but also of Catharine and the overseer, who were expecting to start very early.

Too full of anxieties to think of sleeping, with the noise of a high carousal ringing in her ears, Catharine went to work and sewed her money and watch into her travelling-dress, put it on loosely, threw her shawl over her shoulders, and sat down upon the side of the bed to wait for Chloe. She was a long time in coming; and, tired at last and cold, she lay down in her clothes, neither expecting nor wishing to go to sleep until Chloe's return. But Chloe did not come, and Catharine did get to sleep; from which she was suddenly aroused towards morning by the light from a dark lantern flashing in her eyes. Starting up wildly, she found Sweep bending over her, and just in the act of tying a handkerchief over her mouth to stifle her screams.

"Not a word!" he hissed in her ear, as he dexterously tied the knot with his teeth, and caught her hands, so that she could neither help herself nor utter the cry for help that came to her lips. She tried to resist with all her might, and get the band off, but in vain. Sweep's companion, who was the driver of his wagon, put on her bonnet, that lay upon the dressing-table, and pinned up her shawl. Then, in spite of her feeble resistance, Sweep himself took her up as if she were a baby, and carried her down stairs, and out to the shed, the attendant carrying the light, and shutting the doors.

Almost wild with terror, she hardly knew what they were doing, until they lifted her up into the great covered sutler's wagon she had seen drive up the avenue the previous evening.

They seated her upon a pile of cushions they had stolen from the carriage-house, between piles of boxes, and bales of goods, put a blanket around her, and made every arrangement for her comfort and safety.

"There, Mistress Kate! You see you can't have it all your own way," said Sweep determinedly, after he had got her fixed to his liking. "If you hadn't bin so toppin', you might have rid with me on the outside, as

grand as Cuffee, an' Jake could gone on horseback
But here you'll be very comfortable, — as safe as a thief
in a mill, — an' can finish your nap at your leisure. I
felt kinder sorry to disturb it, you looked so plaguy
pretty sleepin'. I noticed, tu, that you didn't snore so
awful as them black wenches down stairs, arter they'd
got the lodnum in their stew. I thought they'd raise the
ruff, they made sich an infarnal noise. You see, my dear,
I wanted ye to git all the rest you could, before starting
on sich an excursion, an' not be bothered with that old
black monkey down stairs. I'm a sort of a feelin', tender-
hearted man, tu; an' it went agin my grain dreadfully to
tie ye up in this way. But you was so cantankerous, I see
it couldn't be helped. If you conclude to be quiet after
ridin' a spell, I'll take off the fixin's. I'll tell you one
thing, though, — that, if they were off, an' you roused
them rebel guards by yer howlin, 'twould be the worse for
ye. They're terrible bloodthirsty, hankerin' wretches
arter the gals ; an', if they knew I had one in the wagon,
the divle would be to pay. So·you'd better lie down
peaceable, my dear, an' finish your nap." And, with a
malicious grin, he shut the door, which resembled that of
a peddler's wagon, and locked it on the outside, leaving
Catharine in total darkness.

To describe or imagine her feelings would be impossible. She felt that she was completely in the power of
an artful villain, who would hesitate at no means, however vile, to accomplish his purposes, and who might sacrifice her to his whole band if he were well paid for it.
She trembled at the bare possibility this thought suggested. She presently heard the soldiers cursing and
swearing, as they were roused from their slumbers, ate
their hasty meal, and caparisoned their horses for the

day's ride. The wagon was then drawn out of the shed, the four mules attached to it, the driver clambered up to his seat, and the cavalcade moved on.

Day was just breaking in the east as they reached the turnpike, though all was yet dark to poor Catharine in her gloomy prison. Wedged in between boxes and bags and baskets, without the power of using her hands, and with the continued jar and jolt of the heavy wagon, her cramped limbs soon began to ache intolerably. The morning was clear but cool; and, confined and without the power of motion, she was soon chilled through. Desperate at last with mental and physical torture, she succeeded with her teeth in wrenching asunder the bonds that confined her hands; and with them it was easy enough to slip off the odious muffler, and shout, — if she had a mind to. She now succeeded in gaining a more comfortable position; and the relief was so great, that she was glad for a time to enjoy it. But there was still another trouble: the air within the wagon was very close and noxious, smelling strongly of opium and assafœtida, camphor and quinine, ether and sulphur; nor was it long before the powerfully-narcotic vapor began to have its influence upon her system. In spite of her determination to the contrary, she soon dropped off into a doze, which the regular, undulating motion of the wagon tended to perpetuate.

How long she slept she had no means of judging; but she was awakened at last by the rattling of the padlock upon the outside of the door of her prison-house. It swung open, and Sweep's disagreeable picture again presented itself to view.

"Well, raly, you seem to be enjoyin' yourself; but how in thunder did you get off your muzzler, and out of

the limboes?" he exclaimed in astonishment, and then
continued admiringly, "You always was a cute critter,
that's a fact; and that's the reason I like ye so well.
We'll make a pretty equal match, I reckon. Now, some
gals would have yelled like murder arter gettin' that
bandage off; but you'd sense enough to know better. I
guess you're pretty tired and hungry though, and would
like to come out, an' straiten, an' get some grub;
wouldn't ye?" and he held up his hand to assist her in
alighting from the wagon.

She could hardly believe it, yet the sun was high in
the heavens, and it was past noon. The mules were taken
off, and were eating at a rack near by; and the wagon
was standing in a long shed, — out of sight of the windows of the little wayside inn, from which the sound
of oaths and boisterous mirth was borne upon every
breeze. Catharine scorned to touch the mean wretch;
but her bones ached from long confinement, and she felt
such extreme nausea from the villanous smells, that she
was fain to accept any thing in the shape of relief: so
she suffered him to help her out of the wagon. She
could hardly stand at first, but soon regained the use of
her limbs, and began to look keenly about for some
chance to escape. He saw it at a glance.

"Now, Miss Kate," he began, "you needn't look in
that way: it's no sorter use. You can walk round here
a spell; but you can guess, as well as I, why you had
better keep out of the range of them winders, and get
back inter the wagon pretty soon. Jack's gone arter a
basket of grub an' a flask of water, to put in 'long side
on ye; so you can eat yer dinner at yer leisure. We
shall get to Richmond to-night; and you needn't worry
about it one bit. I'll take jest as good care on ye as if

we was spliced; and, when we get there, we can talk
that matter over at our leisure, and contrive what's best
to be done."

"Very well," said Catharine, who by this time had
considered the matter over, and become a little more
reconciled to her position. Sure now that Sweep intended to keep her for himself, in spite of his inordinate
love of gold, she thought she had no immediate cause
for terror. Believing there would be ten chances for
escape in Richmond, where there would be one in this
lonely spot, she concluded to make the best of it, and
use a little more policy in the treatment of her captor.
He sat down on a log, with his back towards her, but
the inn full in view, as if perfectly indifferent to her
movements; while she walked back and forth to get the
stiffness out of her limbs, and a little exercise. At last
she began to be uneasy herself, for fear the men would be
out; and, going up to him, she said, —

"I see your mules have eaten up their grain, Mr.
Sweep; and I am ready, if it's all the same to you."

"I'm tickled to death to hear you say so!" he returned with a grin that showed his long, broken yellow
teeth to advantage. "I always knew you was a sensible gal. I'm a great judge of wimin folks an' hosses.
I like them that's got the snap in 'em', tu; and that's the
reason I like you. But come, them fellers will be out;
and we must start, or they'll all be drunk as fury, and
full of the devil as they can be."

Catharine offered no objections; so he helped her up
into the wagon, folded the blanket around her, and fixed
the cushions as nice as possible, thinking all the time,
how pretty she looked, and how fast she was coming
around to meet him half-way.

Jack at this moment came out with the provisions, which were placed beside her, just as the boisterous troopers all came bolting out of the tavern.

Sweep instantly shut and locked the door, just as one of them sung out, —

"Hallo, there! Boss is at his toilet again. I'll bet a cool hundred that he's got his hair new dyed, his teeth pegged in, and the yaller scoured out of his complexion agin we git back among the pretty gals of Richmond."

The troopers all shouted and laughed at this sally, which Sweep pretended to take in good part, as he did not like to offend them.

They were soon ready, and started off at a brisk trot; the pretty girls of Richmond probably the subject of thought of more than one of them, who, had they known there was one so near, would, as Sweep knew very well, have been sorely tempted.

Considerably rested and refreshed, the narcotics did not this time completely overpower our heroine; though the stench from the noxious drugs, the warmth of the afternoon, and the want of fresh air, sometimes nearly took away her breath. But her mind was too keenly alive to a sense of the dangers that surrounded her to allow her to rest very comfortably. Sweep would, she thought, probably take her to some low haunt, where silence could be purchased, and there try to force her to his terms; and all sorts of plans she devised for escaping him, in the variety of circumstances in which she imagined she might be placed.

If she could do so, she decided to claim Mrs. Hunter's protection, let the consequences with regard to her husband, whom she almost equally dreaded with Sweep, be what they might. Whether they believed her story or

not, she knew that she had been guilty of no wrong.
The long afternoon was over at last; and long before
their arrival, she knew, by the varied sounds, that she was
nearing the city. She found, too, as Sweep had said,
that he had no difficulty in passing the guards, and
gaining admittance. He had only to show his papers,
and all was right. He had none of the difficulties of
slow coaches, red tape, or "mud up to the hub," the
Union army had to contend with at that time, in their
"On to Richmond;" so at Richmond they arrived just
after sunset.

20

CHAPTER XIII.

BUT what is the meaning of this unusual noise and confusion; this murmur of excited voices, and hurrying feet; this roll of carriage-wheels, and dashing of officers on fiery steeds through the streets; these shouts of eager newsboys with the evening papers; those ominous, troubled faces that Catharine could not see?

Alas for the rebel hopes and prospects! New Orleans had been captured by the Federal fleet, and Richmond was wild with excitement over the loss of their great stronghold of power in the South-west. The streets were full of eager and excited people, hurrying to and fro to gather the latest items of news, and to speculate upon its terrible and disastrous effect upon their cause and the hopes of the Southern people. Generals and colonels and cabinet officers on horseback were hurrying to confer with each other and President Davis, as to what had best to be done under the circumstances.

Battalions of troops and heavy baggage-trains were moving to their several destinations; and every thing and everybody seemed to be in commotion. In the midst of it all, Sweep and his gang came toiling through Main Street, riding close up to the curbstone here to avoid a

230

party of government officers on horseback; turning off there to clear two or three rapidly-driven carriages; stopping short yonder to escape collision with a squadron of cavalry. The rough guards, completely out of patience, were swearing like pirates at the multitude of obstacles that presented themselves, none of which Catharine, in her hiding-place clearly comprehended, although she thought they denoted some unusual occurrence. But they drew near their destination at last; and Sweep was congratulating himself upon his good luck in escaping so many dangers, when he gave the order for the teamster to turn into a narrow alley. This led to the low tavern where he usually lodged while he remained in the city, and where he knew that he could get such quarters, entertainment, and concealments as he liked. The patient driver turned the tired mules around the sharp corner, and the wheels made a revolution or two to follow, when a pair of runaway horses, attached to a carriage, came dashing down the street, followed by a breathless negro driver and a fast young gentleman, from whom they had in some way escaped.

Everybody who could cleared the track. But, unfortunately for Sweep, his big wagon was just in their wake at the instant. The wheels came together with a crash like thunder, smashing them into a hundred pieces, pitching the driver and the carriage-horses heels over head, detaching the mules from their fastenings, and upsetting both vehicles, in one mass of inextricable confusion. The carriage was badly injured by the concussion.

The frightened horses were caught and righted up by the bystanders without serious injury. The patient mules, free of their burden, ran with all speed towards their accustomed stable; while the wagon, with its precious freight, went over with a crash so sudden and heavy as nearly to burst it asunder.

The guards dismounted in a moment, cursing and swearing with a will; while men in scores came running from every direction to see what was the matter. So many delays had already occurred, that by this time it was dark; and the street-lamps, being lighted up just then, cast a lurid glare over the scene. Completely nonplussed at first, Sweep came to his senses at last, and was keenly alive to the fear of some untoward exposure.

"Pray stand off!" he exclaimed in a sharp, impatient tone to the crowd that grew denser every moment. "We can take care of our own business. There, my good fellows, take hold now, and give us a lift, while I slip under this old barrel for a prop, until we can get a wheel from somewhere to take us home."

A dozen or more of the guard took hold of the heavily-laden vehicle to lift it up, while the rest stood in the background behind the crowd holding the horses. Up, — up they raised it, until they had almost got it in the right position, when, from some unexplained cause, it slipped from their hands, and went down with a crash so sudden and violent as this time to burst it completely asunder. Out rolled poor Catharine into the mud, amid an almost interminable mass of boxes and bags, bottles and baskets, packages and demijohns, with a variety of odors that for a moment were quite as strong, if not as sweet, as those from the vales of Cashmere or Araby. Though terribly jarred and bruised by both concussions, Catharine was so keenly alive to the danger and the fear of exposure, that she suppressed the shrieks that rose to her lips; and it was only when Sweep rushed forward and attempted to raise her, that she uttered a groan. Her face was very pale;

her eyes were staring with fright; her bonnet was hanging by the strings; her short hair was dishevelled; her dress was torn, covered with mud, and in complete disorder; her shawl was torn from its fastenings, and trailing in the mud; and her whole appearance extremely woe-begone and pitiable. Exclamations of surprise and wonder greeted her on every hand, as was quite natural under the circumstances.

"So, old hoss, you kept your gal handy; did ye?" exclaimed one of his troopers ironically.

"I swear, if I'd known it, she'd had two strings to her bow," said another.

"Cussed mean to cheat us in this way!" growled a third.

At this moment a gentleman in the crowd pressed forward, stood for an instant regarding her earnestly, then exclaimed, —

"Good heavens, Catharine! Is this you?"

She looked up suddenly at the sound of that voice, then around upon the fierce, bold, passionate, and commiserating faces that surrounded her, until her gaze met one that was eager, startled, and terribly anxious; then, forgetting all else but her wild fear, her great peril, and their old friendship, she impulsively extended both hands to him for protection, and burst into tears.

"O Catharine! what is the meaning of this? How came you here?" he exclaimed, as he sprang forward, and eagerly grasped the offered hands.

But Sweep drew her back at once. Though nearly frantic at this exposure of his villany, he could not bear to lose the prize for which he had risked so much, at the last moment.

"It's none of your business how she come here," he

20*

said doggedly. "She's my wife, — or goin' to be; and she belongs to me, and nobody else. Here, Jake, — she's hurt somehow, — take hold here, and help me carry her to the doctor's."

"No, you don't!" echoed one of the troopers. "You've cheated us like fury all the way; and you don't get that gal out of sight agin till we know who she is, where she comes from, and who she belongs tu. Here, my pretty one," said he kindly, laying his hand upon her arm, "does that old chap tell the truth?"

"No, no!" said Catharine, suppressing her sobs. "He stole me from my room last night; forced me into his big wagon, and to-day brought me on to Richmond. O Lloyd! if there is any pity for me in your heart, protect and save me from this man!" she exclaimed in an imploring tone.

"Indeed I will!" he returned tremulously. "But are you seriously hurt, Catharine?"

"I don't know. My ankle pains me dreadfully; and I can scarcely stand."

"Will some of you please get a carriage?" he exclaimed.

"Ah, Dr. Huntley! Is that you? I was never more glad to see you in my life," he continued to a gentleman in a carriage, who halted near them at that moment to ascertain the cause of the uproar. "Will you be kind enough to take this lady to my mother's? She is a particular friend of hers, who has been seriously hurt by an accident."

"Oh, certainly, certainly!" said the complaisant doctor, instantly alighting, and, in spite of Sweep's threats and eager efforts to detain her, assisting Lloyd to lift her into the carriage, amid the joyful shouts of the guards.

They felt as if they had been disgraced and imposed upon by the whole proceeding, and now utterly refused to aid Sweep in guarding and gathering up his load, upon which precious lives, as well as his own gains, depended. Some government officers happening along just then, however, took the matter in hand, and helped him out of his difficulty. But a good many of his bottles were broken; and he lost, not only his intended bride, but a good deal of money, by the operation.

The surprise and joy of Mrs. Hunter and her family can be better imagined than described, when Lloyd came in, and in an agitated voice announced Catharine's unexpected arrival. They were truly astonished, as well as rejoiced; for, after an absence of five whole months, they had never hoped to see her more. They all ran out to meet and welcome her; and Catharine was so overcome with emotion, that she came near fainting in Mrs. Hunter's arms.

The circumstances of the accident were soon explained. She was still in great pain, and her ankle was found to be dislocated. After it was set by Dr. Huntley, she was comparatively comfortable, and able to render some account of herself.

She feared they would not believe the strange story she had to tell, when she found they had not received her letters, and was glad to see that not one of the family appeared to doubt it in the least: From the first moment of her return, they all testified their joy, and did every thing in their power to make her happy and at home once more.

But Lloyd's presence there was a great embarrassment to her. To remember the past; to believe, as she did, that he was her daughter's husband, and she his father-in-law's wife, aroused bitter memories of all the loves and hopes and fear and despair connected with their past intercourse. In the terror of their present meeting, she forgot every thing but the fact of their old friendship; but not long did the old memories sleep. When the pain, terror, and surprise were over, they awoke to a new life of bitterness and lasting regrets.

Did he still believe her the vile thing he had wooed and so nearly won, and then cast off in disgust and scorn? He must of course; for who would undeceive him? Perhaps he thought her whole story a deception, and an imposition upon the credulity of the family.

Catharine was so completely worn out by all she had undergone, that she was very glad for a few days to avail herself of an invalid's privileges. But for Lloyd's skilful medical suggestions, and Aunt Dinah's careful nursing, she would have had a dangerous relapse of fever.

As it was, though very lame, she soon began to recover in health, if not in spirits. She heard, casually, that Gen. Atherton had been transferred to the Army of the Potomac. As no allusions were made to their connection, she concluded that her mysterious departure, at the time of his return, had prevented his acknowledging her as his wife. She felt this to be a present relief; though it added greatly to her anxieties for the future. Owing to the severe sprain, as well as dislocation, it was some days before Catharine could bear her weight upon her lame ankle: so she reclined upon the lounge in the sitting-room; while the whole family vied with each other in paying her every attention.

"You are all too kind to me," she said to Mrs. Hunter one day. "I cannot bear to put you all to so much trouble."

"Not a word of that, Catharine," she returned. "Do you think we have forgotten the toilsome days, the sleep·less nights, the long hours of pain and terror and acute bodily and mental suffering you have endured for us all, that nothing we can do for you can ever repay? And, more than all the rest, we know that we owe the life of our dear Walter to your watchful care. Oh! do not be-lieve we are so ungrateful as to grudge the little we can do to make you comfortable, my dear Catharine. We have missed and mourned you so long, that we look upon you as one risen from the dead, — a recovered and pre-cious treasure; so you must submit to be petted a little while, instead of petting others."

"Well, you cannot be more rejoiced than I to be among kind friends once more. The past five months seem now like some dreadful and terrifying dream to me."

"They seemed real enough to us, Catharine. And oh! you cannot imagine how we felt when you did not return, and we could get no tidings, and feared some dreadful fate had befallen you! Brother Edward was here at the time; and I am sure I never saw a man more excited and anxious than he was on your account. He could not have been more so had you been his own daughter. He kept up the search for you until he became convinced, I believe, that you had gone.off on purpose, with some of your own Northern people. This had been Philip's opinion from the first; but I could hardly believe that one who had been so honest and truthful always could deceive us so at last. I told Edward so; but he would not believe it: yet I am sure he will be delighted to know that you have returned, and justified my good opinion. You see, after Philip had gone, and he had looked everywhere in vain, he grew angry at what he thought was the imposition you had practised, and could not bear to hear your name mentioned. How I shall delight in telling him in my letter to-day of your return, and that I was the nearest right, after all!"

"Oh! you need not hurry to spread the news," said Catharine eagerly, and with her cheek flushing, not only at the thought of Gen. Atherton's anger, but also because the eyes of Lloyd Hunter were eagerly reading her countenance, and she knew he was wondering at her too evident emotion.

"I am sorry he misjudged me, for I like to stand well with all my friends," she continued earnestly; "yet I have faith to believe that time — first or last, in life or death — will clear my fame from all misconstructions." She thought of Lloyd, but dared not look at him as she said it.

"Ah, it may do justice to all," he said, as if in answer to her thought, if not her words; "but sometimes that comes too late for our earthly happiness."

"If too late for earth, it is not for heaven," she returned reverently, "where richer rewards will crown all martyrs to the cause of truth and virtue."

"We earnestly hope so," he said, "yet cannot help longing for them sometimes this side of the dark river;" and the look he gave her was so earnest, pleading, deprecating, yet withal full of the old love-light, that it dwelt long in Catharine's memory.

Did he speak from experience? Did he indeed love her still? Had the truth in some way come to him after he was the husband of another, and she another man's wife? were the questions she asked herself,

that made her heart throb with a bitter pain, and her
eyes droop beneath his searching yet mournful gaze.
Knowing better the position of one, and guessing very
nearly the feelings of both, Mrs. Hunter turned away
with rare delicacy. In her heart she was deeply regretting the part she had taken in separating a pair
who were so well fitted to make each other's happiness,
and planning how she might bring them together once
more.

Catharine was very much surprised to hear of all the
battles, sieges, and other remarkable events that had
transpired during her seclusion. She had heard strange
accounts of some of them, it is true, from the slaves,
but so different from the reality, that it took her some
days to get a correct understanding of past events, or
the future prospects of the country.

The rebels had rejoiced over their victory at Ball's
Bluff, and mourned over the loss of several of their
strongholds along the eastern coast, previous to her
departure from Richmond. Since that time, they had
met with a fearful train of disasters, — at Port Royal,
and Mill Spring, Roanoke Island and Fort Donelson,
Pea Ridge and Newbern, Winchester and Pittsburg
Landing, besides the fight of the Merrimac with the
little Monitor. These and other reverses made the
South reel almost to fainting, and distrust the skill of
her leaders, and brought her almost to the brink of
ruin and despair. The loss of Roanoke Island especially, brought down maledictions upon the government,
as it was considered the granary, larder, and back door
to Norfolk, and the canals and railroads back of Richmond. This growing dissatisfaction with the secession
leaders was now so intensified by the loss of New

Orleans, that, but for the rigid conscription, recruits for the army could not have been obtained; and the fires of war would have ceased for the want of fuel.

During her seclusion, too, the Confederate Congress had been removed to Richmond, which was now the centre and head of both the civil and military power of the Southern people, and the place, of course, where all office-seekers and office-holders congregated.

She found Mrs. Hunter still engaged in the good work she had left in her hands; though not quite so earnestly perhaps as when she was there to assist, inspire, and encourage her in the performance of her arduous labors. Nor was this to be expected, with the care of her family, and reception of visitors, devolving so much more upon herself than formerly. Walter, too, was still in feeble health; and he had suffered so much and so acutely that his mind was in a very critical and morbid condition. It was quite evident that the doctor's fears of insanity or imbecility were not wholly groundless. By his orders he was taken out to ride every day, with his mother and sisters, and amused in every possible way. Catharine's return cheered and delighted him; and, when she ascertained the truth, she would not allow them to remit this daily exercise, as they had done for several days, on her account.

Lloyd generally went with them; but one day, after she supposed they were all gone, and she was alone, he came in from the street, and sat down near to her. "I thought you were out for a ride with the family," she said with a slight flush of surprise.

"No," he said: "Cæsar was their driver to-day. But wouldn't you like a ride, too, Miss Hale? I have a buggy at the door; and I believe it would do you good."

"No, thank you: I think I am better off here until I can do somebody some good by going out, and at least walk, and wait on myself."

"How that idea clings to you, Catharine, — that of waiting on yourself, and doing good to somebody!"

"You know, I was brought up where I was obliged to do the first: as to the last, I don't know that I do more good than other people."

"Yes, you do. And, here and now, let me thank you for all you have done for me and mine, and beg your forgiveness for all we have made you suffer. Will you grant it?" he said in a tremulous tone.

"What do you care for the forgiveness or good opinion of one you think so unworthy?" she could not help saying; though the look of pain and deprecation upon his pale, agitated face made her hesitate.

There was a pause. Suddenly he started up, caught her hand, and knelt down beside her, as he said, "O Catharine! more than aught else, I want your forgiveness for my cruel doubts and accusations, and the scorn and desertion, that must have wrung your heart, for which I have repented in dust and ashes."

"But you doubt — you wrong me still! and don't — pray don't kneel to me."

"No, Catharine. I was undeceived at last: I knew that I had thrown away a priceless gem for a worthless pebble, exchanged truth for falsehood, made your life wretched as well as my own, and perhaps brought down my father's gray hairs with sorrow to the grave."

"That is too true; and you did wrong me deeply and cruelly. But I believed you were deceived yourself, and not wholly to blame, or you would never have done it. So I forgave you when my heart was sorest, and pitied

21

your fate even more than my own. The consciousness
of my own innocence and integrity upheld me in that
dark and trying hour, as well as your father's earnest
sympathy, nerving me for the greater trials and sacri-
fices that were to come,"

"And now, Catharine" — He hesitated, and rose
with a flushed and eager look and tremulous tone.

"Now," she continued, "the feeling that we are but
blind instruments in the hands of a higher power, who
moulds us to his will, and shapes our destinies, has grown
upon me more and more, since passing through so many
troubles, and escaping so many frightful dangers. Is it
a wonder that I am weak, nervous, and hysterical, after
all I have been called to endure ? "

"No, Catharine; yet the history of your sufferings
seems like a bitter reproach to me. I, too, have suffered
deeply and bitterly, yet I confess justly, — you unjustly."

"I knew by your pale cheek· and mournful expression that you had suffered," she said pityingly. "But
where have you been, and what have you been doing,
since — since we parted."

"I have been in Charleston prison most of the time,
reviled, persecuted, accused, and for weeks lying at death's
door, without one friendly face near me, or hand out-
stretched to bestow needed comforts; and all for this
accursed rebellion, that is severing every friendly tie that
binds kindred or people together; that is desolating our
beautiful land with fire and sword, and watering it with
the best blood of the nation."

"Why, Lloyd, I am astonished! I thought you believed in the rebellion; upheld it by voice and vote and
influence; were fighting all this time to support and
make it successful ! "

" I did believe in it at first, — God forgive me ! — ere I knew all the madly-ambitious plans of our leaders. I believed in State rights, and that, when Virginia went into the Union, she reserved the right to secede ' whenever that Union should be perverted to the injury or oppression of her people.' Slavery had come down to us with our estates from past generations. I felt it to be an evil, and a wrong to the human race; but to us it seemed to be a necessary wrong. We could not fling it off like an old garment. It was our capital, our support, — the foundation of our prosperity, and yet our curse.

" To get rid of it without bloodshed would have involved one of the most difficult problems for human solution. To do it at the North, where there were but a few slaves, was easy enough ; but, where they composed more than a third of the whole population, it was another matter. We could not agree to abolish it among ourselves; that was impossible : yet we felt as if the North had no business to interfere with our peculiar institutions. We thought we had been defamed, wronged, and had terms dictated to us too much by your Northern people in Congress. Lincoln's election, so significant of our loss of power, and the triumph of principles utterly at variance with our prosperity as slaveholders, alarmed us for the safety of our rights. It awakened us as a people to the necessity of standing up stoutly in their defence, and, if possible, obtaining some better security for them than then existed in the future. I, with a good many others, believed, that, by a united and determined effort on the part of the whole South, we could gain this without bloodshed, and still remain in the Union ; but, if we could not get it, that it was better for both to separate, and form two republics, as, like oil and water, they could never peaceably mingle into one. I will own, that the bitter and disappointed state of feeling in which I came to Richmond at that time, the heated and eloquent oratory to which I listened, and the private influences to which I was exposed, had a good deal to do with the formation of these conclusions.

"After I was sent to Charleston, I began to be undeceived regarding the ambitious projects of our leaders, and bitterly regretted joining the secession party, in opposition to my dear father's wishes. I found it was not a free republic that they meditated, but an empire founded on slavery, of which they were to be the rulers. I disliked monarchical governments, and hated the Old-World tyrannies. I expressed my opinions too freely to those around me. When I refused to have any thing to do with the attack upon Sumter, I was arrested for contempt of my superiors, and imprisoned. Ill in body, unhappy in mind, and tortured by conscience for what I had done, I suffered unspeakably during the early days of my confinement. When the news came of my father's death, your consequent sufferings, and Walter's danger, it nearly killed me.

"Afterwards, as I grew better, and knew that the country was really convulsed by the horrors of civil war, I became more resigned; because I felt, that, if I was released, I could not conscientiously fight on either side. I would not fight to establish another monarchy, with slavery for its corner-stone. I could not fight against my beloved South, — my own people, my kindred, and all I held most dear on the earth. I could do nothing, then, to prevent the carnage, and scenes of horror, that were being enacted, if I were set at liberty. But as I grew better, I began to ask myself whether I might not do something to mitigate the pain, and assuage the anguish, I daily witnessed within the prison, and knew was rending the heart of the nation outside. I had previously attended a course of medical and surgical lectures in Europe, but not with the view of practising, except for the benefit of the people upon my own plantation. I had taken a deep interest in the subject at the time; but, in the multiplicity of new scenes and events that presented themselves afterwards, I had forgotten, or at least hidden away, my treasure of medical science in a napkin. Stimulated by the thought of mitigating some of the evils I had taken some small part in bringing upon the country, with returning health I dug up and unrolled my buried treasure. With plenty of leisure, and nothing else to do, I set myself resolutely to the work of mastering the science of healing. I made a friend of the prison surgeon, who, I think, entertained similar views with myself, approved my plans, lent me books, gave me all the assistance in his power, and was pleased at last to pronounce me a most ingenious adept in the profession. He afterwards interceded for me with the rebel authorities, rehearsing, I suppose, my merits and my plans. Finding I was willing to forget past injustice, and act for them in the capacity of a surgeon, — of whom there was a great scarcity in the army, —they set me at liberty. I came home a few days ago for a visit, but expect to return to the South, and commence my labors very soon. Have I acted wisely, Catharine, under all the circumstances?"

"I think so. And oh! if you are really a Union man at heart, Lloyd, let me entreat of you to use all the influence you acquire in discountenancing the frightful cruelties that are said to be practised upon Union sol-

21*

diers by some of your barbarous officials. I have heard
men in power deny the facts; yet I fear there is too
much truth in the reports that come to our ears, and
make one's blood run cold with horror. I love my own
people, as you love yours: but, so far as I have had experience, I have tried to be impartial in my treatment of
rebel and Union soldiers; for I know that many of the
former are but the helpless tools of ambitious but unprincipled leaders, and scarcely responsible for their
acts."

"That is too true; yet, if I know myself, I need no
urging to do a Christian's duty to the vilest, as well as
the noblest, of God's creatures. If I needed any incite-
ment to the work, your noble and unselfish example of
continually returning good for evil would furnish all
I require," he said with a fond, admiring glance into
the pale, spiritual face, and mournful, downcast eyes that
now seldom sought his own.

How pale and changed she was, he thought, from the
bright-eyed, rosy, active, gay young girl he had known
and loved in happier days; and yet how beautiful,
how bewitching still! She had loved him once, he did
not doubt. Could she do so still, after all the suffering
he had caused her?

Alas! he did not dream that the keenest pang of all
in her heart at that moment was the sure knowledge
that she did love him still, while bound irrevocably to
another, and the greatest wonder, why, bound in the
same way himself, he, in the history of his trials, should
never once mention his wife's name.

Where was she? Why did no one ever allude to
her when they could help it? Simply out of delicacy
to her feelings; and, for similar reasons, she had never

inquired after him or his supposed bride. The arrival of the family at this moment put an end to the conversation.

The next day, however, the same thing happened; and Catharine to her regret, for she knew it was a dear-bought pleasure, was again left *tête-à-tête* with her former lover.

The truth was, that Mrs. Hunter, now sincerely regretting the past, deeply impressed by Catharine's worth and nobleness, and believing they still loved each other, had resolved, if possible, to bring about the match. So, meeting him in the street this time, she sent him home to entertain and cheer her guest. Knowing nothing of her real position regarding her brother, she did not dream of the harm she was doing in leaving them together thus. Catharine did realize it, but dared say nothing to prevent it. As soon as they were alone, however, discarding politeness, she apparently became deeply interested in a book she was reading, half hoping he would be disgusted, and leave the room. He walked around it once or twice, looked out of the windows, trifled with his sister's fancy-work, and at last, out of patience with her persistent, and as he believed intentional, inattention, he came up to where she was sitting. Gently taking the book from her hands, he said in a slightly-tremulous tone, —

"Catharine, let us for once in our lives fully understand each other. Am I wrong in believing that we once loved each other, — tenderly and truly ? "

" I think not," she murmured, blushing deeply. "But, Lloyd, it is not for either of us now to turn back the leaves of the book of destiny."

"Why not! O Catharine! may we not tear out one

page blotted with tears, and begin a new and fairer record ? "

" It is impossible. The bitter consequences of the acts there recorded must make our happiness or misery while life endures."

" Oh, say not that you have ceased to love me; that my scorn and desertion have turned your love to loathing!"

" Better a thousand times if it had!" she exclaimed with deep emotion.

" No: love, with all its hopes and fears and penalties, is a precious treasure; though you may think mine for you, increased as it is a hundred-fold by absence and the consciousness of ill-desert, unworthy of your acceptance."

" O Lloyd, Lloyd! This to me! And you the husband of another!" she exclaimed excitedly; while burning blushes crimsoned her pale cheeks, and the light of injured delicacy flashed from her eyes.

" I the husband of another! O Catharine! what a mistake! You did not think I married Nell Atherton; did you ? "

" I supposed you did. You wrote that you were about to do so: I never knew but what you had."

" Strange, — how very strange, that, in all this time, they never told you!" he said with an evident feeling of relief. This, then, was the bar — the only one, he hoped — to their future union. This of course was the reason why she had been so distant and reserved. " Ah, Catharine!" he resumed in a gayer tone, " it seems next to impossible that you could remain in our family more than a year without learning the fact, that Nell Atherton, thanks to my good genius, deserted me at the last moment. She eloped, and was married privately to Count

Laroi, a Parisian adventurer, whom she first met in
Europe. As a last legacy, and indeed a precious one,
she left me a letter, in which she boasted of the meanness and lies and duplicity by which she had won me
from you, but to cast me off in the end, — out of revenge for some fancied slights during our past intercourse."

"This, then, was the way in which you found out the
truth; was it?"

"Yes; and oh! you cannot imagine what a comfort
and consolation the thought of your purity and truth
was to me in my gloomy prison-house, like a ray of
light shining into the deepest gloom. But that light
was suddenly quenched, when I came home upon the
wings of love and impatience to find that you had so
strangely disappeared, and that no one knew what had
become of you. When I found you so unexpectedly in
the street that night, and rescued you from such frightful danger, it again shone out, like a star of hope, cheering me by its benign radiance. And now, dear Catharine, that all these sad mistakes are cleared up, you must
not say that it is in vain for me to treasure such fond re-
membrances of you in my heart."

"Oh, it is! it is! I must not listen to such words
from your lips!" she exclaimed in a distressed tone.

"What! You do not forbid my loving you, Catharine?"

"Oh, I must! It is a sin, — God forgive me! I am
already bound by the most solemn vows to another;" and,
bowing her head upon her hands, she gave way to a
passionate burst of tears.

He did not comprehend it yet: he had no idea of
the magnitude of the trouble, as he laid his hand caress-

ingly upon her bowed head, and asked in a deeply-earnest tone, —

"What vows, Catharine? Surely, you have not promised to wed that scoundrel Sweep or some daring outlaw?"

"No, no! But oh, it is even worse than that!" she sobbed; "for I am already the wife of a general in the rebel army."

"My God! Is this true, Catharine?" he exclaimed fiercely, and starting up suddenly with a wild, questioning, yet unbelieving look.

"It is the truth, Lloyd; and you must know it now, whatever comes of it," she said, raising her bowed head, and trying to suppress her bitter sobs. "I have been a wife for months. When or why I became so, I dare not tell you. That is a profound secret, and for the present must remain so. I have never lived with my husband a day or an hour as his wife; though I have solemnly promised to do so when he claims me, and never to leave the South without his consent. My abduction last November was all that prevented me from becoming his acknowledged wife. When he hears of my return, he may doubt, disown, and cast me off, or come and claim me at any moment. And this it is that casts a shadow dark as midnight over my whole future life."

Lloyd stood for some time still as a statue, dumb with amazement, and looking at her drearily, as if he did not comprehend the truth: then, reeling as if struck by a heavy blow, he sunk upon a seat, and, with a bitter groan, buried his face in his clasped hands.

The sight of his wild, tearless agony wrung Catharine's heart more keenly than the sobs that burst from her own.

"O Lloyd, don't!" she exclaimed when she could bear it no longer. "You must bear it, even as I have done."

Her voice roused him. He raised his head, and looked at her gloomily, with a flushed face, and dry, bloodshot eyes, as he said, —

"You do not love this man, Catharine?"

"I only hope I shall, if he comes to claim me," she returned.

"Does my mother know this?"

"No, Lloyd; nor must she, or any one else, until he sees fit to announce the fact?"

"But who is this man, Catharine? — that I may know who has defrauded me of what I hold most dear in life!" said he fiercely.

"I must not tell you: you will know soon enough, if he comes to claim me. If he doubts and hesitates, — jealous of my seeming escape from him, and long seclusion, — it is best for you, and all others here, to be ignorant of his name."

"You were forced into this marriage, Catharine?"

"No: I did it to save — What did I say? Out of two great evils, I chose this as the less, when all brighter hopes were dead in my tortured heart."

"Does this man love you, Catharine?"

"Most ardently and passionately, I do believe; and with a magnetic fervor that might win a return from most disengaged female hearts."

"I have done," said he drearily. "Life is now robbed of every charm, and is no longer sweet to me. I am now ready to go to the front; and, should some stray bullet pierce my heart, it shall be welcome."

"You must not talk or think in this wild way. Is my fate preferable to yours, do you think?"

"No, no: it is a thousand times worse."

"Yet I shall try and make the best of it. It may put far greater power in my hands for good or evil than any I might have chosen. And if so, for the use I make of that power, I shall have to render a strict account in the judgment. But, Lloyd, what is all the good or evil one feeble woman can accomplish, in comparison with what it is in your power to do for poor, suffering humanity, if your life and health are spared to you? Oh, think of the hundreds and thousands of noble men from North and South, East and West, the stay and prop and most precious treasure of many a happy household, — bleeding, groaning, and dying on battle-fields, and in prisons and hospitals; rending the skies with agonized prayers for the help that never comes to them! Think of this, and then say whether, in the power and the skill to heal and to save, Heaven has not bestowed upon you an inestimable gift, not to be lightly cast away. In the path of duty, if anywhere on earth, peace will come to us both, if not the perfect happiness we sigh for. This life will soon be over; and, if we perform those duties faithfully, our reward is sure."

"Oh! I know: you are right in every thing. Yet, Catharine, I cannot now bear this great trial as I ought. I know you ought not to be blamed, however it may be with him; yet I must go away from you, or go mad. In other scenes, on bloody battle-fields and in prisons and hospitals, I may sometimes forget that another man's wife is dearer than my life to me. Oh! I must not forget my hope of heaven, or a Christian's life-work, in a sinful earthly love. If we never again meet on earth, I hope and pray that we may meet in heaven, that perfect world, where merely earthly ties and relationships are sundered and obliterated, and those who love truly love eternally."

He took her hand as he said this, pressed it to his lips, laid it gently in her lap, and then, with a pale, agonized face, and a look that spoke volumes of regret and tortured love, turned, and left the apartment.

When Catharine rose the next morning, Lloyd was gone. He had received a sudden, and, as she judged from his looks, unwelcome summons to the front, Mrs. Hunter said; and he had commissioned her to bid Catharine farewell.

Catharine knew that it was best for both to part under the circumstances; and she honored him for the resolution, and strength of moral principle, that sent him away from her at this time. Yet oh! the dreary, aching void, his presence alone could fill, that was left to torture and swell with vain regrets her tried yet faithful heart. The knowledge that he loved her still, that he had never been the husband of another, and that he had never, at heart, been unfaithful to her, made her own fate still harder to bear.

22

CHAPTER XIV.

MRS. HUNTER, as she had proposed to do, wrote immediately to her brother of Catharine's return to Richmond. The next mail brought a reply, not only to her, but to Catharine, overflowing with expressions of joy and gratitude for her deliverance from so many dangers. He wanted her to write him all the particulars of her captivities and escapes at once, he said: and she might be very sure of a close questioning when they did meet; which he hoped and trusted would be very soon.

Hardly had Catharine got over the excitement incident to Lloyd's departure, and the new train of fears and dread aroused by the reception of this letter, ere a new source of trouble presented itself. This was caused by the wild alarm created in Richmond by the near approach of the Union army. They were said to number at least two hundred thousand men. After many delays, they were known to be advancing up the peninsula, under the leadership of Gen. McClellan, knocking at the gates of Yorktown, and seriously threatening the rebel capital. In the midst of this new trouble, one afternoon when Catharine was alone, the family having gone out to ride, she was startled by the sudden entrance of a

254

party of soldiery, whom Dinah's vehement protestations could not prevent from forcing themselves into her presence. The leader of the band, a brutal fellow, with about as much delicacy or sense of propriety as a bull-dog, advanced, without waiting for compliments, and, laying his hand on her arm, demanded to know if her name was Catharine Hale.

"Yes," she faltered, so terrified at the thought of some new danger, that she forgot that she had any other.

"Then you are my prisoner," he returned doggedly.

"Prisoner, indeed!" screamed Aunt Dinah, who had followed them into the room, and advanced to Catharine's side to protect her from insult. "Prisoner in mistis's own house!" she continued. "Why, the poor dear lamb's jest got out o' de hands o' de Philistines, an' de jaws o' Daniel in de lion's den, an' now ye want to get her in agin, du ye? I'll send for mistis, an' have ye put in purgatory yerself, if ye don't clare out," said she vengefully.

"Hold yer jaw! or 'twill be the worse for you," he returned with his hand on his pistol, and with a fierce, steely gleam in his eyes, that quelled poor Aunt Dinah's belligerence at once.

"Get your things on at once, ma'am; for you must go with us," he continued to Catharine.

"Where, and for what?" she tremblingly demanded.

"To the Libby Prison, ma'am. Such are my orders; but for what, you know better than I."

"But I have done no wrong," she faltered. "I am innocent of all thought of crime."

"That's your lookout," he returned. "But hurry up. We've no time for trifling: our orders are imperative.

"Pray wait until the return of Mrs. Hunter?"

"Not another moment, ma'am. We've spent too much time already."

"But I am very lame: I can hardly walk or stand."

"We can carry you out to the hack, ma'am."

Catharine rose dizzily to her feet, stepped forward, and would have fallen, but for Dinah's watchful eye and protecting arm.

"Get my things, Dinah," she murmured huskily.

"'Tis my fate, and God's will be done. Tell Mrs. Hunter, that, of whatever they accuse, or falsely prove against me, I am innocent."

"It's some o' dat ole sneak's diveltry, Dinah no doubt. He want revenge, 'cause Miss Kate no want him. Missus git it all right when she come home."

"I hope so, Dinah, but fear the worst. Bid them all good-by for me, and especially poor little Walter. There, I am ready;" and, taking Dinah's arm, she hobbled out to the carriage, and was whirled away.

Dinah followed in hot haste to see if it was really a fact that Catharine was carried to the prison, or only a pretence to take her off somewhere else. But there was no deception about it this time. She saw the gloomy prison-doors close over her favorite, and returned to report the fact to Mrs. Hunter upon her arrival home. Mrs. Hunter could not rest until she had been to the authorities, and found out the truth. She was accused, upon the strongest proofs it was said, of being a spy in the Union service for months past, and of holding a secret correspondence with the enemy. Mrs. Hunter was deeply shocked. She could not believe in Catharine's guilt; and yet the story of her late mysterious adventures and long seclusion was strange enough to raise torturing ·doubts in the minds of her best friends. She went the next day, and had an affecting interview with her in the prison, and carried her a few things to make her more comfortable : but that was all she was allowed to do ; for the authorities just then were regarding with more than usually jealous eyes all who had the least intercourse or correspondence with their enemy, and, as prisoners, treated them with unusual rigor.

Put into a narrow, filthy cell, overflowing with vermin, Catharine had a chance to taste the sweets of prison-life, not at all qualified by the fact, that her jailer had, from some cause, been at variance with the families with whom he knew she had been associated. For this and other reasons, Mrs. Hunter and her family were refused further communication with her. Perhaps, too, that lady's increasing doubts of her innocence prevented her making any very strenuous exertions in her behalf.

But the decisions of childhood and ignorance, those keen judges of human character and motive, were wholly in Catharine's favor. Neither the children nor the slaves of the household could be made to believe a word against their favorite. If she had been well and strong, Catharine would not have felt the privation of coarse prison-fare, want of rest, and discomfort of every kind, as much as she did ; but she was weak and nervous, and could scarcely eat the repulsive yet scanty food set before her. She could not sleep on her hard straw bunk, because of the loathsome insects crawling over her. She knew not who were her accusers, or the extent of her implication ; and the future certainly looked very dark and cheerless. Yet she was saved the

22*

knowledge of the terror and excitement that swept over Richmond, as the miserable days and nights dragged their slow length along.

They brought battles and sieges, the capture of Norfolk, and destruction of millions of dollars' worth of rebel property to prevent its falling into Union hands. It also brought distraction into the councils, and vacillation and terror into the hearts of the rebel authorities, and the adjournment of the rebel Congress to assure its members of their own safety.

At last, after months of inexplicable delay, the Union army began to advance from Yorktown towards Richmond. The panic became fearful. The whole city was wild with terror and excitement; and the people were flying in every direction. Every rail-car, and vehicle of every description, was pressed into the service, and overloaded with passengers. The streets were full of people, — going, they hardly knew where themselves, — anywhere to get out of the way of the cruel, hated Yankees. Piles of furniture, boxes of goods, and baggage of every description, obstructed the streets, wharves, and dépôts; while children were crying, dogs barking, soldiers swearing, negroes running, and every thing and everybody seemed in the greatest commotion.

But there was still an element of firmness left in the minds of a few, says one historian, "who strove, by every argument in their power, to quiet the people, turn their terror into ridicule, and induce them to stay at home, and prepare for the worst."

Among those who led this general stampede of the citizens, was Mrs. Davis, the wife of the President, with Mrs. Hunter, and other ladies of distinction, accompanied by their families, who fled to Raleigh, N.C.

It is now a matter of history, that, while the Union army had been for three whole months journeying by apparently easy yet really painful stages from Washington to Richmond, the Confederates had spent every hour of that time in preparing for them a bloody reception. They enlarged their resources in every possible way; prepared elaborate defences, mercilessly enforced the conscription, gathered re-enforcements from Norfolk, Charleston, North Carolina, the Shenandoah Valley and every other available source, until they had concentrated the largest army they were ever able to put in the field, as they said themselves long afterwards. They also said, what was undoubtedly the truth, that "our army waited and waited, — uncertain which course to pursue, our authorities divided in opinion, — when a rapid advance on either route would have insured them a victory."

But they waited too long. The summer heats and miasma of the interminable swamps of the Chickahominy, were quite as sure death as the enemy's guns. That enemy was now fully prepared to meet them. Arrogant and boasting, exasperated by their late losses, and fully aroused to a sense of their danger, they were now ready to fight with the most courageous daring, and reckless disregard of human life, in defence of their sacredly-cherished capital. Around this, for more than a year, immense labor had been expended in constructing redoubts, rifle-pits, hornworks, and enfilading and casemated batteries; while every other imaginable sort of defence crowned every hillock, and swept every road and defile, for miles around the city. So, with very good reasons for hoping that their skilfully-constructed works were impregnable, they awaited the onset of the Union army.

Ten weary days Catharine had been in the loathsome prison, without seeing one friendly human face. Ten years of agony and discomfort they seemed to her, when she was startled one evening, at an unusual hour, by the sound of approaching footsteps and voices, and the rattling of a key in the lock of her door. One of those voices thrilled her like an electric shock, and brought her to her feet in an instant. The door opened; and a light that almost blinded her flashed in upon the midnight darkness, followed by the under-keeper, and beside him — she knew she could not mistake those deep, low tones — was Gen. Atherton.

She shrunk back to the wall, gazing at them with wild, blinded eyes, as the keeper set down the light, and left the room; and the general advanced to meet her.

"O Catharine! is it thus we meet after months of painful separation and vain longing?" he said, as he took her in his arms, and folded her to his bosom.

So utterly wretched and miserable was she feeling at the time, that there was really a sense of friendliness and protection in the clasp of those strong, loving arms for a moment; a powerful magnetism in his looks and tones, that enchained her senses; a feeling of relief and companionship in the light that once more illumined her dark prison-cell.

For several minutes he held her silently, overpowered himself by strong emotion: then he gently raised her head, and looked lovingly yet searchingly into her agitated countenance.

"How you have changed!" he said with a deep sigh. "It breaks my heart to see you in this gloomy prison-cell, with these sunken cheeks, hollow, tear-stained, glittering eyes, and troubled brow. How pale, shadowy, and unreal you look! Your hair, too, those beauteous auburn curls, all sacrificed! O Catharine! what am I to think of such a shocking change, — of all these strange adventures and frightful accusations ? "

"What you please," said she proudly, withdrawing herself from his clasp, and raising her downcast eyes to his face. "You said once, that no one who was a judge of the human countenance could look into mine, and doubt my innocence, purity, and truth. Has their loss effected all these changes, do you think ? "

"No, no. To me you are innocent and truthful still," he said, after a prolonged and searching glance, "whatever others may think. But, dear Catharine, you must be aware that circumstances have been and are terribly against you."

"Yes, I know. I ought to blame no one for doubting me. I wondered even that Mrs. Hunter and her family did not when I returned to Richmond in such a suspicious manner a few weeks ago."

"Catharine, did you write me *all* the particulars about that mysterious disappearance last autumn ? "

"I believe so, — at least, all I thought of consequence to you, or necessary to explain my position. But why ? "

"Because those explanations seemed imperfect, and left the painful impression upon my mind that there was something you wished to keep back and conceal from me."

A flush of surprise and shame, but not guilt, instantly suffused Catharine's face, revealing, as if by magic, the truth of his suspicions.

"I see I was right," he said with a keen glance and darkening frown. "You cannot hide your thoughts from me, Catharine, if you would."

"I did not and do not wish to, except for your own peace and happiness. I told you the facts just as they occurred, so far as the knowledge of them could do either of us any good. Yet I confess that there were some things connected with the affair, that reflect no blame on me, which, out of regard to your feelings, and pity for another, I did not think it best to reveal."

"Out of regard to me!" he exclaimed passionately. "Catharine, you can know nothing of a husband's feelings or rights, if you think one who loves as I do will bear such concealments."

"I think I do know what they ought to be; and won't you trust me to keep from you a knowledge that can only wound and pain, but do you no good?"

"No: I must know the truth, at whatever cost of feeling to myself."

"When it is only for your good, and the honor of your family alone, that I would be silent?"

"Yes: you know who were your abductors, and would shield them from my anger."

"No, I do not."

"Who employed them then?"

"Yes," said Catharine, after a pause. "But pray trust me in this, Gen. Atherton. If our marriage had been known, it would never have occurred. He who did this thing, knowing nothing of our secret marriage, had professed to love, and been rejected by me. Your last letter to me fell by accident into his hands, unfortunately. Mistaking its ambiguous language, thinking you were coming to *marry*, and not claim one already married, and maddened by disappointment, he procured my abduction to get me out of your way. I was carried to his plantation, miles away, where he followed,

a day or two afterwards, and presented himself before
me. We had a deeply-exciting interview, during which
I was obliged by the circumstances to reveal to him the
fact of our marriage, and beg of him to leave me. He
was terribly shocked, disappointed, and I believe penitent,
when he found out the truth. I had taken a severe cold
in my night journey. I was already very ill; my head
was bursting with pain; and this, joined to the excitement, made me alarmingly wild, and out of my head before the interview was over. I was, I suppose, very near
death for weeks after his departure. He left me a letter,
begging me to conceal his name, and thus shield him
from your anger; and that is the reason I have tried
to do so thus far, — not from any love of him, — for I
never loved him, — but out of pity for both him and
you. If you demand this name as your right, I yield it
at your bidding; yet I solemnly assure you that it will
be a thousand times better for you and him if the
words should never be spoken;" and she looked up
appealingly into the dark, passionate eyes, that were
sternly searching her agitated countenance.

A silence of several minutes fell between them: then
he said in a low, determined tone, —

"Catharine, I shall never rest easy without it: I would
know my despoiler's name."

Catharine paused in pity: she could not bear to inflict upon the proud father a blow so terrible, — the death-
blow of a father's faith in, and love of, an only and beloved son. He misconstrued her silence, and his brow
darkened, as he said, —

"Catharine, must I demand this knowledge as my
right? Tell me this man's name."

"It is Philip-Atherton, — your own son," she faltered in a low, tremulous, pitying tone.

The proud father's face grew pale as ashes; and he reeled, as if she had struck him a blow. He had suspected many others, but never once, strangely enough, thought of Philip in connection with this affair, as having dreamed of daring to rival him; though he might long before, had his own eyes and ears been disengaged.

Catharine pitied him from the bottom of her heart, much as both of them had made her suffer; and, with quick sympathy, she turned to him, and said, —

"God knows I would have saved you this pain if I could. You do not doubt me still, Gen. Atherton?"

"No, no: but oh, my son, my son! I cannot say as David did; but I can feel as David felt," he exclaimed in a tone of deep emotion.

"Absalom was blinded by one mad passion, Philip by another; but you must pity and forgive him, even as I have done, who am the greatest sufferer."

"To do it knowingly, in defiance of me and utter disregard of my feelings, — such a mean, dishonorable act too! Oh, I never, never can forgive him!" he groaned.

"You will think differently some day. Philip was blinded by passion: he could not endure the thought of my becoming his father's wife. The knowledge that I was so already made him almost wild. You know his ardent, impassioned nature: you know how he has been petted and indulged from childhood. Perhaps you have yourself helped to make him disregardful of the feelings of others. No doubt he deeply regrets the act now, and suffers all the horrors of disappointment and remorse. But let us talk of something else. If I am to die in this horrible prison, or on the gallows, I want" —

"O Catharine!" he exclaimed, "my only hope and

comfort now, you shall not do either, if I have to tear down the prison-walls with my own hands."

"But you know why I am here, and by whose agency ? "

" Yes : my sister wrote me the particulars. She did not know then, however, that Kendall, the sutler and spy, who operates between the lines, was your accuser."

" Then it is just as I suspected. I remember, now, that that was the name he told me he had assumed."

" You know him then ? "

" I think I have reason to."

" Well, I came home the first moment I could call my own ; have had an interview with the authorities, and been trying my best to sift out the truth."

" But you failed ? "

" Thus far, yes. Your accuser is gone, but is expected now every day. I fear I can do nothing towards getting you liberated until he comes, as the proofs, they say, are very strong, and almost incontrovertible."

" Then I shall die here," moaned Catharine; " for the wretch will never return. He told me as much when he tried to get me to go home with him."

" To go home with him ! Whom do you mean ? "

" Why, don't you know that Kendall and that scoundrel Sweep are one ? He told me so himself."

" That explains it all."

" Yes, indeed. It all comes from spite on his part, without doubt, to be revenged on me for disappointing him. Yet he is so capable of mischief, that the consequences may be very serious. But, whatever my fate may be, your Confederate authorities may assure themselves of one thing, — that he has been playing a double

23

game with them, and dares not return again to Richmond."

"I feared it, and told them so; but they would not
believe it. And he could do us a great deal of harm
just now, with the enemy so near us."

"How near?"

"Why, did you not know that the Federal army,
more than two hundred thousand strong, are within
twelve miles of Richmond? or that there has been a
great fright and panic in the city, and that everybody
that could get away has left it?"

"I only know that I have heard unusual noise and
confusion in the streets, and longed most earnestly to
get out, and fly away. And I warn you now, Gen.
Atherton, that, if in this great march of events, I should
have a chance to do so, you must consider yourself consulted, if I prefer escape to an ignominious death."

"You pain me deeply by such allusions. After such
bitter disappointment in both my children, I shall live
only in the hope of one day claiming and proclaiming
you as my wife."

"Then you have not done so yet?"

"No, I judged it to be inexpedient. As your husband, my hands and tongue would be tied, so far as
assisting you would be concerned. As a friend, I could
work for you, without embarrassment, and defend you
before any court of inquiry in the realm; yet I must tell
you honestly, my dear Catharine, that, if this man comes
back to substantiate his charges against you, and brings
all the proof to which he claimed to have access, the case
will look very dark, and will not be an easy one to defend. But for Philip's implication, the facts of your abduction and illness could be brought forward as rebut-

ting evidence. But as slaves cannot testify, and no one
else but Philip and his tools knew any thing about it,
they alone could save you by disgracing themselves, and
you, too, perhaps, by implication, if not in fact, — a thing
that must not be risked, except in the last extremity,
and hardly then. So you see, my dear, the difficulties
of your position; though you cannot feel, as I do, a deep
grief and regret for being, even remotely, the cause of
it. If it is in the power of man to save you, it shall be
done, you may rest assured; yet nothing can be done
while the city is in such fearful peril, beleaguered by a
hostile foe. I myself, with thousands of others, have
just been recalled from a distant station, and must go
to the front to-morrow, with a heart heavy, not only
with my own private griefs, but the woes of my country.
I cannot bear to leave you in this loathsome cell; but
I suppose it cannot be helped. The crime of which you
are accused precludes the idea of relief or amelioration,
as well as the fact that I do not stand well enough with
the authorities at the present time to gain many favors,
especially personal ones."

"Why so?"

"Catharine," and he spoke in a low, concentrated
tone, as if the walls had ears, "'our President has
disappointed the expectations of all his best friends.
He is a vain, wilful, obstinate, conceited fool, who will
listen to no sensible man's advice. He is notoriously
ruled by his wife, who sees in every prominent and
ambitious man a rival of her husband. So she endeavors to wield all the influence at her command in keeping such men in subordinate positions, where there will
be no chance for the display of brilliant talents, if they
possess them, or danger of their attracting the attention

of the people to the prejudice of her husband.' I have seen and felt this for months ; and so have Beauregard, Johnston, and Lee, in turn: and we fear, not without reason, that it will be the cause of the downfall of the Confederacy. But none of us can help ourselves so long as Jefferson Davis stands at the helm, with all the mighty power and patronage of the government in his hands. As my wife, I tell you this in confidence, knowing that you are too honorable to betray the trust, and that you may know with how many kinds of trouble I have to contend."

"I have felt from the first that you were trying a dangerous, a fearful experiment, that you will rue to the last day of your lives."

"It may be so. I confess, that thus far it has not answered our expectations. But we cannot, after accepting the gage of battle, retreat from it without dishonor."

"I believe you are mistaken. I know both parties are sick of this fratricidal warfare. Blood enough has been shed, and treasure wasted. All that is wanted are a few concessions to secure an honorable peace."

"Catharine, once for all, we will never, never consent to the only concession that would content your Northern people now, — the utter abolition and extinction of slavery. It may come to that at last: they may set our own slaves to cut our throats, and desolate our homes. But never, while we have blood to shed, or strength to fight, will we consent to be thus ground into the dust by the ironshod heel of Federal power."

At this moment footsteps were heard approaching along the gallery outside, a knock was heard at the door, and "Time's up," in a gruff voice, rang through the stilly air.

"Catharine, that summons is imperative," he said with a deep sigh. "I go to-morrow to defend my country against her invaders, subject to all the chances of defeat, death, or victory. But before I go I shall make such provision for you, as my wife, as shall not only insure you against want, but also reveal to the world your true position with regard to me. If I fall," he continued gloomily, "you will perhaps rejoice in the chance"—

"No, Gen. Atherton. Whatever comes to me of joy or woe, I would that not another life should be sacrificed in this unholy contest."

The rap came again, still more imperative; and, with a passionate caress and mournful "Farewell!" he turned and left the apartment.

By his influence a few needed comforts were added to her desolate cell; and then Catharine returned to her old round of darkness and silence by night, and sepulchral light by day; interrupted only by the gruff visits of the jailer, the voices and tramp of the sentinels, and the indistinct noises of the busy streets, yet with feelings a little more cheerful for Gen. Atherton's visit. She felt that she had one friend left to think of and care for her, if he was a selfish one : she was not forgotten by the whole world. If he lived, she would have an able defender. Yet the price she must pay for it made her sometimes doubt whether it would not be better to die than live to endure a loveless marriage. Several days passed away; and the feeling of nervousness and discontent was again getting the mastery, when the jailer one afternoon presented himself, bowing with a politeness altogether at variance with his previous brutal conduct.

' Madam," he said in a very plausible tone, "I am

23*

very happy to inform you that the charges against you have been withdrawn; and I have orders from the authorities for your release from prison. A carriage will be at the door in half an hour, that will take you to any part of the city you desire."

He left the room before Catharine had sufficiently recovered from her astonishment to reply or question. Then she impulsively knelt down, and offered heartfelt thanksgiving to a kind heavenly Father for this unexpected deliverance.

Poor girl! She thought her troubles were over, when, in fact, they had but just begun. She gathered up her few articles of apparel, put them into her satchel; and, when Major Turner appeared, she descended with him to the street. He helped her into the carriage; and, at her request, ordered the coachman to take her to Mrs. Hunter's. They arrived at last; and, driving up to the gate, the man helped Catharine out, satchel in hand; jumped up to his seat again, and was whirled away. Imagining her reception, and the joy of the family at her return, she walked up to the front entrance, and rung the bell. But she waited in vain for Cæsar to answer the summons. She rang again repeatedly, but with like results. Filled with gloomy forebodings, she next went around the house, and tried the side and rear entrances, but found them all locked against her. She remembered now, for the first time, what Gen. Atherton had told her in the prison, — that everybody had left Richmond who had anywhere to go to; and that she had forgotten in her surprise and excitement to inquire after Mrs. Hunter and her family. Here was a dilemma she had not dreamed of; and another still worse soon presented itself. She had not a cent of money in her possession to procure a hack, or hire a lodging. She had taken none with her to the prison, thinking it needless; and Gen. Atherton, never dreaming of her enlargement before his return, had not once thought of making such provision for her. Overcome now by the thought of her misery and friendlessness, she sat down on the steps, and burst into tears. "Where in the world should she go, or what could she do?" were the questions she asked herself.

There were near neighbors, it was true; but they were rich, proud, and aristocratic, and had some of them treated her so superciliously, that she could not bring herself to ask of them a favor.

At last she thought of Mrs. Gordon, who, she believed, was a true friend to her; and to her she resolved to go for a refuge. She raised her bowed head as she came to this conclusion, and there, standing but a few feet from her, was an old negro man she remembered to have seen in the neighborhood regarding her with eyes full of pity and compassion.

"Massa ober dere to de big house see miss get out o' de carriage, an' t'ink she dunno Missy Hunter an' all de folks here gone off to Nort' Carliny wid Missy Davis, an' lots o' ladies an' chillens from Shockoe Hill."

"I did not indeed. But is your mistress gone too?"

"Yes: de wimin folks all gone. King an' Pinky stay to keep house for ole massa. All de ladies in dose housen gone somewhere. All de young massas gone to fight."

"Indeed! Then there is no chance to get in here. But do you know Mrs. James Gordon of —— Street?"

"I guess King dunno him. But dat a long way off."

"I know it. But I don't know where else to go."

"Terrible times, miss. Eberybody gone crazy coz de Jubilee's comin'."

"Do you think so?"

"King no doubt on't. De spirit o' de Lord tell him. But he no sich fool as to run off inter de swamp, when he got good enuf massa to home. He stay till it come right along."

"You are right there, unless you want to go and help fight for your liberty and that of your race."

"Time 'nuff for dat when de big Linkum army come long. King t'ink dey come right away. De streets full o' sogers from eberywhere; an, dere's goin' to be terrible times rite off."

"Well," sighed Catharine, "I suppose it is so; and I must go and try to find a place to stay until Mrs. Hunter comes home."

The negro hesitated a moment, then said, —

"Does miss know dat de streets pretty dangerous for wimin folks jes' now? Pretty miss got no veil on, an' de men stare; an' some on 'em t'ink de Yankee spy got loose."

Catharine started. He knew her, then, — her accusation, and where she came from, — and so would others. So the tears came again to her eyes as she said, —

"I have indeed been accused, but wrongfully. I have been in prison, but have been honorably liberated by the authorities. My veil must have been left in the prison."

"King spects so, an' wish he dare help miss a good deal. But old massa up dere to de winder watchin'. He hate de Yankees, an' no let him. But if miss no find a place, an' come back here to-night, he t'ink he an' Pinky hide her somewhere for all massa."

"Thank you, my friend. I will do s), but hope I may find friends elsewhere."

"King hope so tu, an' wish miss good luck an' good-by," he returned, and then hobbled off to report to his master, who was keenly observing every movement from his chamber-window.

CHAPTER XV.

ITH a prayer for help in her heart, Catharine took up her satchel, and marched out into the crowded streets in the direction of Mrs. Gordon's. They were indeed crowded with soldiery and citizens; and long trains of ambulances and army-wagons, full of stragglers and camp-followers of every description, were rolling on towards the battle-fields outside of Richmond. But there was scarcely a white female to be seen in the streets; and, terrified at the thought of her unprotected situation, she glided along with hasty but silent footfalls, trying to attract as little attention as possible.

But with such a face and figure as hers, in its nice-fitting brown suit and jaunty hat, it was impossible to escape observation; and many were the admiring glances that followed her retreating footsteps. When, after a long and tiresome walk, she arrived at Gordon house, it was but to ring repeatedly, but in vain, for admittance. The house was closed; and the family, she was told, had left the city. She turned away in tears, uncertain where to go next. At last she thought of two families on the same street, who had always been very intimate at Hunter House, and always treated her politely, upon whom she resolved to call and ask for a shelter.

274

Upon application to the first, she was ushered into the parlor, but received with freezing coldness by the mistress; and, when she told her story in tremulous tones, and asked for refuge and protection, the lady told her she would harbor no one who was under suspicion as a Yankee spy. When she attempted to expostulate and plead her cause, she was, without ceremony, turned into the street. Anger dried the tears upon her cheek; for this lady, who was a widow, in a dangerous illness a few months previous, had been under great obligation to her for watching and kindly care, as well as to Mrs. Hunter; and she had also been a candidate for the favor of Gen. Atherton.

At the next place, though she saw the lady plainly through the window, she was peremptorily denied admittance by the well-instructed servant in waiting. Probably the fear of being themselves suspected in some measure influenced the decisions of these ladies regarding her. Overwhelmed now by despair, she wandered on, applying in vain at every house where she knew the owners for shelter and protection.

The sun had set; and, as it grew dusk, she was jostled by the rude throng that filled the street, some of whom impudently peered in her face, and spoke to her in a way that increased her fears, and made her tremble for her safety.

She thought at last of an old colored woman, who, being free, owned a little house in the suburbs, and took in washing, who, she felt sure, would receive her if she could only find the place. She was one of Aunt Dinah's particular friends, who often came to visit her; and she knew her to be a respectable woman. She had been there with Dinah and the children once or twice, but always in the carriage with a driver. So, not being quite sure of the way, she soon got bewildered in the growing darkness, and, in the labyrinth of streets that were new and strange to her, was completely lost. She made several inquiries, but no one she asked knew such a woman as Mrs. Milly Conly.

At last she was overtaken by a tall, gaunt, unhappy-looking woman in tawdry apparel, who professed to know Mrs. Conly well. She said that if she would go home with her and spend the night, she would be perfectly welcome. If she preferred going to Mrs. Conly's, she would show her the way, after getting her supper, and making a few home arrangements, as they lived in the same neighborhood. The manners and appearance of the woman were such as to excite poor Catharine's suspicions; but what could she do in her desperate circumstances but accept the offered hospitality and kindness? They soon turned off from the travelled street into a long lane, that led to an old, dilapidated mansion, where the woman said she resided. It was quite dark when they entered the house; but the woman struck a light, kindled a fire, and soon had a comfortable meal to set before her suspicious and watchful guest.

Just as they were rising from the table, the rolling of wheels was heard without; and the woman exclaimed in evident alarm, —

"There, he is coming! I thought he would be away to-night. I cannot go with you; but go somewhere, — if you would be safe; for he is a " —

"Where, oh! where can I go?" said Catharine in tremulous tones, as she seized her hat, and ran towards the door.

"Not there! you are too late: I hear his step on

the gravel," the woman exclaimed in a frightened tone. "Here, take this light, and run up stairs to the little room at the end of the hall ;" and she lit and gave her an extra candle. "Blow out the light as soon as you find the room, and keep still as death."

Not knowing what else to do, Catharine obeyed; for she felt sure, that, whatever the character of the woman might be, she was trying to shield her from some great danger.

She cast her eyes hastily around the desolate room, saw that it was impossible to fasten it from within, extinguished the light, and sat down upon the humble bed, trembling in every limb. Immediately afterwards she heard the heavy tramp of feet entering the house, the slamming of doors, and then the sound of angry, high-pitched voices in eager and excited conversation.

There was something in the gruff tones of one of them that made her shiver with renewed terror ; for, as she listened intently, she grew surer every moment that it was the voice of the murderous Blondel. The voices lowered at last to a calmer tone, and then there was the rattle and clink of dishes and· domestic utensils, as if supper was prepared, and devoured by the new comer, or comers.

And, while it was being partaken of evidently, Catharine's heart stood still, as she heard stealthy footsteps ascending the stairs, and approaching the door of her room — in the darkness.

There was a fumbling for the latch, — the entrance, turning, and click of a key in the lock, — the retreating of the stealthy footsteps down the stairs; and she knew that she was a prisoner, — probably in a den of infamy.

To describe her feelings would be impossible. She was

24

sure it was the woman's step she had heard. It might be that she had locked her in to save her from great danger. This thought was her only consolation. After a while, there was again loud talking, and tramping in and around the house, the sound of a wagon going down the lane towards the city; and then all was still.

That night a terrific thunder-storm swept over the city and country, fitly symbolizing the era of horror the morrow was to usher in. The rain fell in torrents; the wind whistled around the tall chimneys; the lightning darted and blazed, until the heavens seemed lit up by a grand and terrible illumination; the thunder rolled overhead, as if all the artillery of heaven were beginning the murderous roar that was to be echoed and repeated during the succeeding memorable days. To Catharine, locked in that desolate room, it was a night of unmingled horrors.

But we must pause here to explain how, under the weight of such fearful accusations, Catharine came to be released by the authorities from the Libby Prison. For several days they had been looking anxiously for the return of Kendall, with some special news he had promised to bring them from Washington, regarding the peace views of the Federal Government, and the movements of the Union armies. They felt as if a great deal depended upon this news, which they could obtain in no other way.

It must be remembered, that, for several months, they had had nothing but a continued succession of reverses, losses, and defeats; and the imminence of the impending danger made them all the more anxious to obtain this news before fighting seriously commenced with McClellan's dreaded army.

They were talking of this one day in a cabinet council, when a letter was brought in, addressed to *"President Davis and the Authorities of the Confederate States."* It was known to have come from a perfectly reliable source; and, having been ordered to be read by one of the secretaries, was found to be as follows : —

WASHINGTON, May 27, 1862.

MY DERE FRENDS, — Having conclooded that it wouldn't be for my helth to cum back to Richmond jest now, I thort I'd rite, and let you no how matters stand. I got back to Washintun safe an' sound, an' found 'em all tickled to deth to see me; especially Jotham an' his wife, who is fat an' flourishin', an' dresses as fine as a peacock. He's makin' a sight of money contractin'; which, up here, means, in perlite circles, patriotically and gratooitusly, furnishin' things for the grand army of the Union, but, in common langwidge, cheatin' Uncle Sam. I think of goin' into it myself, it's so mity fashinable; and then I can have a grand house, a gilt carridge, a hansum wife, an' fat hosses, like the rest on 'em.

To-day I called on the Secretary of War an' President Lincon; an' they was both mity glad to see me. Miss Lincon smiled on me as sweet as molasses, and little Tad cum an' set on my nee to get the candy an' jacknife I carried him. But that was on'y a little by-play, you onderstand : tho' I du think little Tad a dreadful interestin' child; an' I told his father so. He laffed, an' axed me if Miss Jeff. Davis had any ekal tu him. I said yes, her young ones was jest as keen and cute as if they was Yankees. But we talked most of the time about war an' pollyticks. He's expectin', I see, to hear every day, that Maclellan has whipped the South within

an' inch of her life, laid Richmond in ashes, and hung
you leaders all up to the lamp-posts. At that, I told
him I gessed he'd got a leetle tu fast in his kalculations;
for you'd got surcumvolutions an' parryhellograms an'
ridouts, and all sorts of fortyfycations, piled sky-high
around Richmond, full ekal to the walls of Babylon.

I told him, tu, that you'd got an army there, that I
should judge, by the looks on't, would count nigh upon
a million, with several generals quite ekal to the great
Napoleon; and that you'd (in my private opinion) be
quite as likely tu send Jackson to whip 'round Banks
and Shields, and take Washintun, as Maclellan was tu
take the Confederate capitul.

He kinder looked scairt at that, you may depend, an'
immegiately sent out orders for the guards to keep a
sharp lookout, and be ready for ye.

By the best I can find out, I reckon Maclellan ain't
got more'n five hundred thousand men before Richmond;
so I gess you'll get along well enuf if I don't cum back.

But I like ter forgot the main thing I wanted to tell
ye; an' that's about the gal I got ye to put in the Libby
for me, jest afore I cum away from Richmond. The fact
is, the critter was as innercent as a lam on all them charges
I brought agin her; and I don't mind tellin' ye on't,
now I've got away, safe an' sound. You see, she'd riled
me up like fury, an' I got so tarnal mad and spiteful,
that I thort I'd cum up with her somehow. To tell ye
the exact truth about it, we both used to live out to old
Major Hunter's at Hunter Hills, — she as governess an'
I as overseer; an' I got plagily streaked with her.
Wall, she was mity toppin' an' top-lofty at first, an'
would hardly speak tu a feller, till arter Master Loyd
courted an' left her; an' I couldn't get acquainted nohow.

But when she cum back from Richmond to take care of the old major ('cause his wife wouldn't), you see, she was kinder alone, an' we all eat together, and she was kinder plausible. But jest as quick as I offered tu have her, she turned up her nose an' cut my head over an' over. Now, you know that don't feel good; but I didn't pretend to mind it. I wa'n't goin' tu kick over my stew in that way; so I held on as perlite as could be. At last I happened to think that I'd forgot to tell her about the twenty thousand dollars I'd got banked up at the North; and then I thort I'd got her sure. But—would you bleve it? —jest as quick as I told her that, an' said we could go up North an' cut a big swell with our money, the sassy critter up an' told me that "no amount of gold would indooce her to wed a Yankee slave-driver." That, I tell ye, raised my dander. "You were ready enough to wed a slave-owner," says I, "and where's the difference?" "All the difference in the world," says Miss Imperdence. "For a man who inherits slaves from past generations, to many of whom he is strongly attatched, I can have some sympethy; but for one, with a Northern edication an' decent abilities, to 'cum down here to be a slave-driver, I have none at all." Now wa'n't that aggravatin'? and there was considerable more of the same sort of thing tu.

Wall, that onfortynite affair at the major's pervented my persuin' the business; and I lost her that time; tho' I may as well confess, while I'm about it, that she had me dragged away from the fire, and saved my life when everybody else turned agin me, an' was reddy to give me a kick. Wall, I jest got out of that affair by the skin of my teeth; an' that was about all the skin I had left, I was so singed. But, like a singed cat, I cum out pretty

24*

slick arter all. I saved all my money. I'd allers hated my name, an' my red an' yaller head-fixins; so, now that my hair was all singed off, I had a chance to change to a much more desirable color for both. I was mity tickled at that; an' it gin me a much better chance in this agency bisness, in which I've had the honor to sarve your lordships of the Confederate States, as I think, with immense satisfaction to both parties. Wall, you see, on this last little excursion to Richmond, I cum across this gal agin, as cute, imperdent, and sassy as ever; an', finding her as top-lofty, I thort I'd cum up with her nicely: so I got a feller to help me for a dollar, and we gin the nigs lodnum, an' nabbed her in her sleep, an' brought her on to Richmond in my big wagon, without the guards noin' any thing about it. But the devil was in it, tu purvent my gittin' her, arter all. My wagon got smashed up, an' the gal spilt out, an' Loyd Hunter, her old spark, cum along, as Satan would have it, and carted her off, in spite of me, to his mother's. I never was so mad an' disappinted in my life. An' when I read a letter I found in her room when we nabbed her, I fairly biled over with righteous indignation. I found out then, that I'd got awfully cheated and took in; for, as sure as you live, the critter had been an' got slyly married to one of your darned old rebel generals, and was really another man's wife. Another feller, it seemed, had carted her off, she s'posed, to get her out of his way; and this was a letter she'd rit to her husban', and never sent. I put it in my pocket, but forgot to read it till arter it was all over. Wall, I felt terribly imposed upon; an', thinkin' I'd cum up with her, I went tu work pretty soon to try an' copy her ritin', an' finally manyfacturd them dockyments I had the honor tu present tu you. You'll find copys of 'em, in the N. E. corner of the cupboard of my room, at the tavern where I staid, that I forgot to burn when I cum away, if nobody hasn't moved 'em.

I felt dreadful tickled when I got her shet up in that nasty prison, an' cum away mity triumphant. But it didn't last long; for I'm naterally dreadful soft-shelled and tender-hearted towards the femenine sect: an' I begun tu think pretty soon, that 'twas tu bad to treat the gal so arter she'd saved my life, even if she was sassy; an' that she'd jest as good a rite tu git rich by matrimony as I had in this agency business. Then I was alwus a dreadful consiencious man, an' Orthodox as fury when I'm to home; an' I thort if I should want tu set up for deacon or squire, or tu go tu Congress, when the war's over, an' this story should git round, it might hurt my popularity. Wall, my conshence kept prickin' like nettles an' pins all the way tu Washintun, until I gin in, and conclooded tu du the hansum thing by lettin' you no the truth, and havin' the gal let out of jail. An', thinkin' you mite be jest a leetle stuffy, I thort I wouldn't cum back to Richmond jest now, tho' I mean to cum and see you all when the war's over.

Good-by.

Yours truly an' affectionately,

KENDALL.

It would be impossible to describe the feelings of the august Cabinet at the reading of this precious epistle, which was received with mingled expressions of rage, contempt, and laughter. Thus far they had all had a good deal of confidence, — not of course in Kendall's principles, but in his serving them in good faith for the sake of his idol, gold, — a faith that Gen. Atherton had tried in vain to shake. But they saw clear enough now that they had been, not only bought, but sold. In extreme disgust with the whole affair, the President ordered the man's lodgings searched, and, if the proofs he named were found, the enlargement of the prisoner.

"We probably see now why Atherton was so deeply interested in this lady's case," said one of the secretaries.

"Yes," said another: "but I think, if it had been my case, I would have been manly enough to have owned the truth regarding so fair and talented a lady as Miss Hale, if she was a Yankee governess. Her reply to this accursed scoundrel, regarding the slave-owner, sets her up wonderfully in my estimation."

The proofs were found where Sweep had indicated; and the intimation that she was allied to some one in authority procured her respectful treatment at the time of her release. Most likely, if she had applied in the proper quarter, a refuge would have been provided for her until she could have communicated with her friends; but this was not so to be.

Morning dawned upon her at last, bright and beautiful; though the deep mud everywhere testified to the force of the storm, and made locomotion difficult. For the fact that she had been undisturbed by any thing through the night but the rats, the storm, and her own fears, she thanked God, and took courage.

After a while, the woman came in with some bread and coffee on a tray, but kept the door in her hand as she set them down, and would scarcely answer Catharine's questions or salutations.

She looked darker, fiercer, and even more repulsive by the light of day than she had done the evening previous; and Catharine saw at once that she either would not or

dared not set her at liberty. She went out soon, locking
the door behind her. Sure, from her gruff replies, that
Blondel might be expected at any moment, Catharine
soon began to look around keenly, seeking vainly for some
mode of escape. Her room was comfortless and dilapidated, as indeed appeared to be the whole establishment.
The plastering had fallen from the walls in unsightly
patches; the floor was covered with dirt, piles of rags, old
clothes, and worn-out boots and shoes, as if it had been
the general reservoir of coarse, cast-off wearing apparel.
Some of it had lain there until it was nearly devoured
by moths and rats, with which the building seemed over-
stocked. The only window looked out upon a cheerless
back yard, overgrown with weeds, beyond which lay the
open country outside of Richmond. The floor was un-
carpeted of course; the bed, a sack of straw upon an
ancient cot bedstead, which, with a broken chair, composed the furniture. She examined the door, the window, — nailed down with a rusty spike, — the cupboard,
the closet, and in fact every thing that could be supposed to afford an avenue of escape, like some wild animal pursued by the hunter and the hounds.

But to whom and to what should she escape, when she
knew no one in Richmond who would receive her? Must
she go on foot and alone, through mud and mire, and
throw herself upon the protection of Gen. Atherton, who
had never yet announced their marriage to the world,
and, for aught she knew, might have insuperable objections against doing so at all? Every instinct of pride,
propriety, and female delicacy forbade such a thought;
though even that were preferable to falling into the
hands of the odious Blondel. She felt as if every hour in
that place was fraught with terrible danger, and that there

could scarce be more anywhere else. She must and would get out of that house, she thought, before the day was over; for the night would bring the odious wretch, she was very sure. The hours passed slowly away. She began to grow sleepy, for she had not slept a wink the previous night. She would not give way to the feeling; but walked the room, looked out of the window, and tried its fastening with all her wit and strength, but in vain, for the want of some instrument to unloosen the spike. Almost desperate, she began to turn over the piles of dust-covered rubbish to see what she could find. At last, hung up behind the closet-door, she found an old blouse, and a pair of pants to match, that had evidently belonged to some slender youth, which put new ideas into her head, and suggested a plan for escape. An old palm-leaf hat with a torn brim, and a pair of old boots, the best and smallest she could find, completed the disguise; without which she felt sure no woman could traverse town or country at that time without subjecting herself to insult.

Placing the things in the closet all together, she thought she would lie down for a moment to rest and arrange her plan for escape. She did not mean to go to sleep; but her heavy eyes unconsciously closed, and she was in the land of dreams.

From this state of blissful unconsciousness she was aroused at last by a deep, prolonged, and thunderous roar, that rattled the glass in the old window, shook the earth, and brought her to her feet, strongly excited by terror and apprehension. She knew, however, as soon as she had time to think, that it was the awful roar of battle, — the thunder of the great conflict Gen. Atherton had assured her was so near at hand. There had been a good deal of firing for several days, but nothing to be compared with this. So near and distinct seemed the fearful utterances, that for some minutes she really thought the city was besieged by the Union army.

But Catharine was not the only one who had been suddenly awakened and alarmed by the terrible sounds; for hardly had she come to her senses before the old stairs began to creak from rapidly-ascending footsteps, the door was unlocked, and her female jailer rushed in. She was half dressed, her eyes were wild with terror, and her gray hair was streaming behind her like the snaky locks of Medusa. Without stopping to close the door, she ran up to Catharine, exclaiming, —

"We're lost! — we're lost! The Yankees are coming! We'll all be murdered in a trice!" and wrung her hands in agony of spirit; while the tears streamed down her sallow cheeks like rain.

This restored Catharine to her senses, and she realized at once the ludicrousness of the fears of both. The door stood open, and the idea of instant flight presented itself; but, being unprepared, it was discarded.

"You are mistaken, my good woman," she returned in answer to her wild appeal. "The Yankees are miles away from Richmond; but the two armies are no doubt cannonading each other. They may come here in a few days: but, if they do, I am not afraid; for I have friends in the Union army, who will protect me, and you, too, if you will let me stay with you. I've no friends in Richmond now; and I am sure I do not know where else to go."

Assured by Catharine's manner and tones, the poor woman became calmer, but still looked at her suspiciously, as she said, —

"Well, I dunno what the boss will say. He ordered me to keep ye locked up: and there's the door wide open;" and she sprang towards it in evident fear of Catharine's escape. "But I wonder he don't come," she added: "he said, if he didn't come back last night, he would to-day, sure. If there's a big fight, though, he'll want to stay to clear up the ground."

"What do you mean by that?"

"Oh! no matter. I guess he knows where he gets the biggest harvest with the fewest hard knocks."

"Where is that?"

"Don't you know that a battle-field's ekal to a bank or a jeweller's shop for money, watches, an' sich fixins'?"

"Ah, I understand," said Catharine in disgust; "and there is a big fight, I should think by the noise: so I guess he'll stay, and we will try and make ourselves comfortable; won't we?"

"Well, I dunno: I'm 'fraid he'll come and swear at me or beat me, as he allus does."

"Why do you care for him? Are you his wife?"

"His wife!" and a bitter sneer crossed her dark visage. "I ought to be; but he wants no wife. I have been his victim, and he is as merciless as the grave. Not even you, with all your youth and beauty, will escape him, or be more to him in a week than I am to-day;" and she glanced at Catharine with a look of ill-concealed jealousy and hatred.

"I will not be your rival if I can help it," she returned; "and you certainly can prevent it by letting me go."

"I dare not do it: if he knew I did, he would kill me."

"Well, if I must stay, do go and get a cup of tea, and we will eat together, and be friends."

"I want some myself, for I've had no dinner; and he's like enough to come hungry as a bear. But there's sich a horrible din, I'm 'most 'fraid to go down alone. But I must: for I dare not take ye with me, for fear he'd come and find us."

So, with fear and trembling, she did leave the room to prepare a meal for him, as well as herself and Catharine, locking the door behind her.

Now was Catharine's time; and there was not a moment to lose, if he was expected every moment.

With nervous eagerness, she pulled out the strange garments from the closet, and hastily exchanged them for most of her own, which she put in their places.

They felt stiff and awkward at first, but were a tolerably decent fit of gray Kentucky jean. The old boots went on very well over her cloth gaiters, — otherwise they would have been too large. She could not help smiling at the figure she cut, but missed the big hoops more than any thing else.

Luckily for her now, though she thought it unlucky enough at the time, Catharine had lost her long, shining hair by the fever, and her head now covered by a short crop of fine, silky auburn curls. This made her look very much like a pretty, fair-skinned, delicate boy of sixteen; and, when she put on the old hat, the metamorphosis was complete.

She next looked out of the window to see if any thing could be seen of Blondel, — the act strongly reminding her of Fatima in the old nursery tale of Bluebeard. And behold, an equal to Bluebeard was there!

As to what she was to do with herself, if she did get away, she could not tell. Any way, it would be better to starve in the streets than fall into the hands of

25

the grizzly jayhawker. In boy's clothes, she could surely find something to do, and be comparatively safe from insult.

The continued and tremendous concussions of the cannon that were still reverberating in her ears strongly suggested the thought of flight to the Union army.

Having completed her arrangements, she knelt down, and fervently commended herself to God for protection and guidance.

The door of her room and that of the closet opened outwards side by side. So, as soon as she heard the woman's footstep on the stairs, she slipped into the closet, leaving the door ajar. When she came up, unlocked the door, and came in with a waiter in her hands, and moved along to set it down on the bed, Catharine slipped out just behind her, and was out of the room, and had the door locked upon her former jailer, before that lady was hardly aware of what was going on.

She had indeed been struck with astonishment at the glimpse of a strange boy coming out of the closet; and in her surprise nearly let her waiter fall before she missed her charge, or at all comprehended the truth.

Leaving her screaming "Murder! Fire! Thieves!" and all other sorts of imprecations, Catharine ran like lightning down the stairs to the front entrance. Finding that bolted, she started to go through a front room to the rear, thinking she might there find an easier mode of egress. Hearing the sound of wheels, she looked out of the window, and there, to her horror, beheld the odious Blondel driving around the house to the rear in his old rickety mule-wagon.

For an instant she was paralyzed: but he was looking up to the chamber-windows, listening to the woman's

horrid imprecations; so she recovered her wits, and ran
back to the front door. By her utmost exertions she
at last succeeded in removing the heavy bolt, and opening it. The street, or rather lane, that led to the city,
was in sight all the way from the front of the house,
and of course out of sight from the rear; so it was just
possible for her to secure her retreat before he discovered her escape. Her heart stood still for a moment,
as she realized her position, then gave a quick bound
as she sprang from the threshold, and ran swiftly down
the lane.

We may be sure that she did not let the grass grow
under her feet as she ran back to Richmond, and very
sure that the old roof was nearly raised with curses,
when Blondel came in, found the woman locked up, and
Catharine gone: he had come back almost wholly on her
account; for he had seen her through the window the
evening previous, and compelled the woman to confess
the truth. Before she got to the city, her lameness had
partially returned, and her fictitious strength was fast
deserting her. When she reached the main street, she
looked back, and, seeing no one in pursuit, stopped a moment to take breath. She then timidly mingled with the
great crowd of people on foot, on horseback, and in
carriages, wagons, and ambulances, all seemingly moving in one unbroken stream, in the direction of the ominous sounds that still continued to stun the ear, and rend
the smoky, sulphurous atmosphere. She thought, at
first, that everybody must notice her awkwardness in
her strange garments; but, as no one seemed to think or
care, she became more assured, and paused a moment
before a handsome house to consider what she had better do.

At this moment a gentleman in the uniform of a Confederate colonel, whose face seemed somehow familiar, rode up to the curbstone, and, seeing no one else more available, said, —

"Boy, will you hold my horse a few moments? I have business here."

"Certainly," said Catharine, promptly taking the reins, yet sorry for it the next moment, when she thought of Blondel.

The gentleman went into the mansion, was gone some time, and came out looking very sorrowful. He mounted his fine horse, tossed her a few small coins for her trouble, and then said, as he looked her over keenly, —

"What is your name, my son? It seems as if I ought to know you."

"My name is — is Ellery Hale, sir," she returned, as the hot color flashed over her face. She had not once thought of assuming a name; so, upon the impulse of the moment, she gave a part of her own maiden name, which was Catharine Ellery Hale.

"Do you belong here in Richmond?" he questioned.

"No, sir," she replied, "I am from the country."

"What are you doing here?"

"Nothing; but I want something to do. My friends were all gone when I arrived: their house is shut, and I am homeless."

"Would you like to enlist? My regiment will be along very soon. We want men, boys, — any thing, to fill up the ranks, that can handle a musket."

"No," she instantly replied, "I could never consent to kill men, — made in God's own image."

"Well, you do look rather young for the business.

But what can you do? That fair, blushing face, and those white, slender hands never saw many hardships, I fancy."

"The hand is a feeble one, it is true; for I have been ill: yet it can take care of the sick and wounded, and has done it, not only here, but at Manassas."

"Indeed! Well, if that is the case, you can have plenty of business by going with us, if that tremendous roar signifies any thing. But will you go?"

Catharine hesitated a moment: then, with a sudden impulse, she said, "I will go, sir."

It was her first chance; and she was ready to do almost any thing, to get out of the way of the odious Blondel, who, she felt sure, would be seeking for her everywhere.

She had remembered, at that moment, seeing Col. Elliot at Mrs. Hunter's. She knew him to be an honorable man, too; and that decided her to accept his proposal in her desperate circumstances. She never once thought of making herself known to him, and claiming his protection, as she might have done: and, if she had, the thought of her repulses the day before from those of her own sex, upon whom she felt that she had some claim, would have made her hesitate. She knew enough other distinguished people in Richmond; but if those ladies, knowing her and her desperate circumstances so much better, would suspect and scorn her, she felt as if all the rest would do the same.

But she had little time for reflection. The troops soon came along: a place was found for her in one of the ambulances; and, before she hardly realized what she was about, she was on her way to the battle-field. Was it destiny?

25*

CHAPTER XVI.

ESCAPING. — THE FIELD OF BATTLE.

N her way to the Chickahominy, Catharine had plenty of time for reflection; and her heart became oppressed with new alarms, as she thought of the chances of battle, the constant exposure to detection, the fear of insult, and all the horrors connected with army life.

Her travelling companions proved to be a surgeon and his assistant, with a half-invalid officer, who, she found from the conversation, had just come from a distant post to the support of the army before Richmond. They seemed to have greatly exaggerated ideas of the strength and immensity of McClellan's army; and rather doubtful of the success of their cause generally.

She drew her old hat down over her eyes, so as to escape observation; and for a while they scarcely noticed her. At last the surgeon turned to her, and said, —

"So you, too, are going out to the camp, my boy; are you?"

"That is my intention, sir," she replied.

"You have no arms I see. What are you going there for?"

"To help take care of the wounded, sir."

"Your hands don't look like bloody work, or indeed work of any kind : they are as white as a lady's."

"They can work for all that; though I have been sick, and for a long time idle," she said with a heightened color.

"You are unfit for the camp then, as well as myself," said the young officer. "Why do you go there?"

"Because I have neither friends nor money now, and have nowhere else to go."

"Well, it's a pity you were not a lady, with that fair face, those beautiful hands, and clear, silvery tones. If you were, I expect I should fall in love with you," said the surgeon's assistant with a merry laugh.

"And then what would become of the charming widow?" said his companion laughingly.

"Her reign no doubt would be over, and, like all past dynasties, make but a line on the pages of the history of one human heart."

"You are so philosophical about it, that I guess the impression was not very deep. For myself, I would rather have this young chap remain a boy: for I need another assistant; and a green hand is better than none. If I am not mistaken," he continued aside to his companion, "there is a world of grit and resolution in those mournful eyes, — a look, too, that one trusts and puts confidence in."

The torrent of rain the night before, and the constant stream of travel, made the roads horribly muddy; yet, as it was within seven miles of Richmond that the armies were contending, the journey was soon over; and the sublime horrors of the battle-field burst upon their view.

The corps-commander to whom Col. Elliot had orders to report did not happen to be engaged that day; so they soon found their place in the line, and made their arrangements for whatever exigencies might befall them.

Long before they reached their position, Catharine had begun to realize — in the murderous and deafening roar, the whistling of shot, the shrieking of shell, the sulphurous smoke, and difficulty of breathing the stifling air — some of the horrors of the battle-field; but it was not until the battle for the day was over, and she, with others, was ordered to assist in bringing in the wounded, — following the track of carnage red with human gore, and thickly strewn with dead horses, torn limbs, and dead and dying wrecks of mortality, — that she felt, in all its horrors, the woe and anguish the mad passions of men had brought upon her suffering country.

The attack that day had been a surprise to the Union army; some divisions of which had been driven from their positions with terrible slaughter, leaving in their retreat a track red with carnage, and piled with heaps of the slain. The brave Union generals did every thing in their power to check the retreat, and turn the fortunes of the day, but all in vain.

By some strange oversight or mismanagement, Gens. Casey and Keyes had been stationed so far in advance of the main army, with the former five, and the latter but eight thousand men, that, though they fought with the most heroic valor, they could not be expected to conquer the sixty-four thousand valiant soldiers that the keen-sighted rebels, who well understood their weakness, brought against them.

Nothing but disaster could have been expected; so the Confederates claimed a great victory at Fair Oaks, and Seven Pines.

But, if victory it was, it was terribly dear-bought, as the thousands of their own dead and dying too surely testified. The next day, which was Sunday, the rebels again attacked the Union army with determined bravery, but were driven back with great slaughter, leaving their dead and wounded behind them.

For some days Catharine shared the fortunes of Col. Elliot's regiment, — sleeping at night, when sleep was possible, among the piles of baggage, and employed by day, as a waiter and assistant, in the work of the field-hospitals.

The Union army at this time was stretched for twenty miles along the banks of the Chickahominy; and the line of battle was ten miles long.

Though she saw nothing of Gen. Atherton, Catharine heard that he was posted some three or four miles away from her. In her present state of mind, she preferred that that space should divide them. She preferred the toil, hardship, and danger of her position to the idea of going to him humbly and unsolicited, and throwing herself upon his protection. Yet there was an uncomfortable feeling in the thought of his displeasure, if they ever did meet, and he found out the truth. This, with the constant temptation to escape to the Union lines, was torturing, to say the least of it.

But the lines were so closely watched and guarded, and deserters were so severely punished, that she dared not make the experiment.

For days, there was constant skirmishing and several serious engagements, but as yet none as tremendous and bloody as that of Seven Pines, where the rebels confessed to a loss of four thousand, which Catharine had every reason for supposing was three or four times that number.

She had taken the place Dr. Garnett assigned her; and he found, as the days went by, that he had no reason to doubt his first impressions regarding the courage and resolution of the pale, slight youth who had from the first taken his fancy, and won his protection and friendship.

Silent, shy, and reserved, she yet won the respect, esteem, and confidence of those around her by her constant and devoted attention to the wants of the wounded, and by her eagerness to seek out and to save all, both friends and foes, who were lying on the field of battle. Buoyed up by the most heroic courage, and repelled by no scene of horror, no hand was firmer or as tender as hers in binding up broken limbs, or washing ghastly wounds, or cleansing the mud and gore from the most brutal and repulsive of the swearing. godless wretches who came sometimes under her care. No skill was found greater than hers in restoring the fluttering pulses of the sorely-wounded, or in re-animating and cheering their fainting spirits. And, when all earthly hope was over, she could point them to that better land, where a Saviour was waiting to receive all true penitents. It was noticed, too, by some that she was especially kind to the wounded Union prisoners who had fallen into rebel hands; whose claims others around her were inclined to ignore, and who, but for her intercession, would sometimes be treated with positive unkindness and inhumanity.

If she afforded " aid and comfort to the enemy" by caring for them, it was certainly offset by the lives she saved, the agony she mitigated, and the loving care she bestowed upon her loyal friends.

The wounded were transferred to Richmond as fast as the means of transportation would admit, until every

hospital, warehouse, public building, and almost every
private residence, was full ; and still the continued fighting kept the field-hospitals crowded, and the surgeons
and their assistants fully occupied.

Nearly a month had elapsed since Catharine had
come to the camp ; during which time she had made
several trips on the cars to Richmond, in care of wounded
soldiers. In spite of her life of toil, exposure, and excitement, she had been growing physically better every day.
By using Dr. Garnett's prescriptions, her lameness had
vanished. The bright color of health, as well as the
brownness of exposure, tinged both cheek and brow;
though at heart she was sorely troubled and discon-
tented : for, in spite of her position and connections,
we must remember that she was still loyal to the Union
cause, still exultant at their successes, still overwhelmed
with grief at their defeats.

It is true, that, if it had depended upon her, the war
would never have been. But, in spite of her opinions, it
was a fixed fact; and, being so, it was the most natural
thing in the world that she should side with her Northern people.

And now that Richmond was threatened by them as
by a moving pillar of fire, and she knew their success
would at once crush the rebellion. or their defeat fearfully prolong the struggle, she could not but hope and
pray for the success of their arms, and the overthrow
of the immense hosts gathered to oppose them. Yet
she could not blame the Confederates, under the circumstances, for defending their capital, — the ark, as
they considered it, of their public safety.

But as the days went by, and Catharine learned, from
Union prisoners, the real fact, she trembled for the safety

of the Union army. She knew that they had lingered so long on the way, and been exposed to such deleterious influences, that, notwithstanding their large numbers, they were now no fit match for the formidable, exultant, and acclimated hosts, secure in their own defence, fighting on their own ground, and in defence of their own homes, brought to oppose them. This being so, it was in vain for the brave Union leaders to go up, as they did, in Prof. Lowe's balloon, a thousand feet or more in the air, to survey the battle-fields or Richmond, — that Mecca of their hopes they were never destined to reach. They had indeed a splendid view unfolded to their gaze, but not one calculated to inflame them with enthusiasm, or inspire them with undoubting assurances of success.

"There indeed lay Richmond, across the western horizon, — a confused medley of red and brown and black, — with its white spires glittering in the sunshine; but before and around it, in all directions, were great, heavy brown fortifications, with thick, solid walls, plentifully sprinkled with frowning cannon, that looked any thing but inviting to an assaulting foe."

Away to the South, the James River rolled its glittering waves through a deep, crooked valley; bearing many white sails upon its bosom, that looked, in the distance, like swans breasting the angry current.

Beneath their feet, from beyond the line of vision, ran the now famous but dreaded Chickahominy, — like a thread of silver, bordered by its dark-green, miasmatic swamps, — beautiful to the upper, if not the lower view, but full of disease and lingering death. "Between this and the fortifications before Richmond, as far as the eye could reach, lay the rebel camps, and all the paraphernalia of war that surrounded them. Opposite to them, and partly on the other side of the river, lay their own magnificent but depleted army, waiting eagerly for the signal of onset their leaders, now that they realized the truth, dared not give." "Between the two armies lay a broad, dark-green and yellow curved belt; upon which neither men nor teams nor wagons, nor any other military signs were visible; but over which cannon-balls were thrown, and scouts and pickets hid from each other. Broad, quiet, apparently deserted, solemn and sombre, Jupiter's rings or Saturn's belts never presented a grander sight to mortal eye."

It was easy enough in those days to blame generals and statesmen for the failure of that peninsular campaign; but we know now that the hand of God was in it, leading us in deep humiliation, by a way we knew not, to do tardy justice to the down-trodden and afflicted millions who had groaned so long beneath the yoke of bondage.

Until that dark hour of humiliation and disappointment, our rulers, and the nation generally, had not looked the thing steadily in the face. They had hoped to gain peace by a shorter and far less objectionable route. The South must be coaxed back; so they sent the poor fugitives off from our lines, thus consigning them to the lash and the torture and a still more unendurable bondage. Our generals refused, at their hands, that knowledge of the country and its armies that would have insured them victories where they suffered defeats. Now, however, both rulers and people were made to see that they must choose between the dissolution of the Union and the dethronement of slavery; and that the latter alone was the price of victory. An

26

earlier recognition of this fact would have saved rivers of blood and millions of treasure; but the nation was not then prepared for this, and had to pay a bitter penalty for its blindness.

The beautiful June days nearly all passed away; and still the Union army were no nearer Richmond than they were a month before. And while the whole North were wondering at the delay, and looking eagerly forward to the hour that was to give the coveted prize into their hands, the whole South was boiling over with rage, hatred, and plans of vengeance against the invaders, who dared to dream of conquering them, and capturing the stronghold of Confederate power.

Gen. Lee had taken the place of Johnston, the leader of the army of the Potomac, who was seriously wounded at Seven Pines; and they waited only for the arrival of the brave Jackson to commence the demolition of the Union army.

He had just met with brilliant successes in the Shenandoah Valley. He had captured an immense amount of army and medical stores from another division of the Union army, and immediately transferred them to the relief of the Confederates before Richmond; to whom they were a godsend just at that time. As he retreated immediately after his exploit, the Union generals felt as if they had driven him out of the valley, when in fact he was only hastening, by special orders, to the relief of the beleaguered capital.

Catharine knew all this; and when, upon the afternoon of the 26th of June, Jackson's advance began to arrive upon the field, and the joyful news was echoed from lip to lip, she began to tremble for the fate of the Union army.

All that long, weary afternoon a fierce battle raged along the lines, but without any definite results, except the destruction of human life, and the rapid filling up of the field-hospitals. The next morning at daybreak the bloody work commenced anew.

Having passed a sleepless night caring for the poor sufferers, she felt wretched, weary, and nervous, and realized more acutely than ever before the momentous issues that might be decided by the conflict of an hour or a day. She knew that Jackson was hourly expected upon the field, and that the prestige of his already famous name would go nearly as far towards inspiring the brave Southern heart as that of Napoleon did with his indomitable French legions.

An inward prescience she had felt once before, and did not presume to question, assured her that some one she loved, and with whom she held invisible chords of communion, would be in that day's fight, and in great danger. She thought of her brothers, of Lloyd Hunter, and even Gen. Atherton, in the wordless prayer sent up for the safety of all who were dear to her.

That day was fought the battle of Gaines Mills, conceded by all to be one of the bloodiest and most hotly contested of the campaign.

From the first, the Confederates had determined that this should be a decisive day to them. For a month, the people and the soldiery had borne the infliction of a Union army before their gates with ill-concealed impatience; but their leaders knew that they lost nothing by delay. The miasma of the swamps of the Chickahominy was reaping for them a far richer but quieter death-harvest than any common series of battles could bestow.

But every thing was now prepared for the final issue.

The South demanded it, and it must come.   With Richmond at their backs, — their national existence, as well as all their slave property, at stake, — with skilful generals, and superabounding in regiments fierce and resolute as tigers, they had every advantage that position, skill, and numbers could give.

So it was in vain for McClellan to plan ; or for Porter to thunder with his terrific cannon ; or for Smith and Sumner, Hooker and Kearney, to reap them with a frightful death-harvest ; for still they rolled upon the Union lines in successive and thunderous waves, until, after long hours of bloody and useless resistance, the Union forces were obliged to give way or be annihilated.

Catharine saw the advancing columns as they went to their bloody work.   Through blinding dust, and stifling smoke, she eagerly watched the evolutions of large bodies of cavalry, infantry, and artillery without pretending to understand them.   But she did understand the meaning of the shouts that rent the air when Jackson came upon the field with his war-worn legions ; and she felt as if there was a glorious inspiration in the presence of that stern warrior, that would go far towards insuring to the South a victory.   Nor was she mistaken. He had arrived at the most critical moment, — when the shattered Southern columns, pressed back with terrible slaughter, wavered, and were about to fly ; and by the prestige of his renown, and the valor of his veteran troops, turned the fortunes of the day.

He took his appointed place in the line, and "with fierce grandeur the charge swept on, unchecked by the terrible fire of the triple lines of infantry on the hills, or the cannon on both sides of the river, that reverberated, and mingled in one grand roar, like the noise

of a great cataract," or the sweep of a tornado over a
forest of giant trees, bearing them down like a bed of
reeds beneath its terrible stroke, and with a terrific
power that seemed to shake the earth. Through the
thick, blinding, sulphurous smoke, the sun looked down,
like a red fiery eye, upon a scene over which Humanity shuddered, Pity veiled her terrified gaze, and Mercy
wept tears of blood. The red sun sank at last beneath
the western horizon; and night put an end to a conflict in which the Union army was forced to retreat,
and the Confederates claimed a great victory.

Long after that conflict ceased, the air was filled with
dust and smoke and sulphurous vapor. The earth shook
no more with the deafening roar of cannon and musketry,
with the tramp of mighty armies or the continued roll
of heavy wagons; yet Death continued to reap a rich
harvest of human souls, and the widespread fields and
woods for miles were dabbled with human gore.

Friends and foes, by thousands, lay side by side, or
in piles, where the battle raged fiercest, — peaceful now,
in the last long sleep of death.

Men of noble intellect and lofty ambition, who fought
for glory and renown, were there, — men of pure lives
and generous impulses, who fought, as they believed,
for the cause of truth, justice, and human liberty. Men
of shining talents, cultivated intellect, and holy aspira-
tions, who believed they were God's instruments in the
establishment of the Redeemer's kingdom on earth, were
mingled in frightful confusion with some of the greatest
villains who ever cursed it by their presence. Some of
these were still sending up shrieks and groans and oaths
and curses, mingled with prayers, to pitying Heaven
for forgiveness, help, and mercy. The banners under

which they had fought lay torn and bloody, and trampled in the dust; while arms and trappings, caissons and broken wagons, and dead and dying horses, cumbered the ground, and completed the horror and desolation of the scene.

As the night came on, patrolling and fatigue parties of soldiers, with lanterns, ambulances, and stretchers, traversed field and meadow, swamp and woodland, — wherever the battle raged fiercest, — gathering up the wounded, and administering temporary relief to those who were evidently bound upon that last sad journey to the land where wars and fightings are over, and all is peace.

Among the fatigue-parties ranging over the battle-field, was one from the regiment to which Catharine was attached, accompanied by herself and Dr. Garnett. They were making a special search for the body of Col. Elliot, who was known to have fallen in the fight, but who, thus far, had not been distinguished from the slain thousands around him. They had found plenty of others, however, to whose appeals for help they could not turn a deaf ear, until their ambulance was full, and it was necessary to return to the camp.

"It is strange we do not find him," said the sergeant. "I know that it was somewhere near this big tree that he fell from his horse in the heat of the battle; but the exact spot I do not remember."

"Well," said Dr. Garnett, "we will return to the hospital with these poor men, and then come back and renew the search for our noble colonel."

"I am afraid we could not again find the spot in the darkness and gloom of night, sir."

"We might leave some one with a lantern to signalize us by and by," said the doctor.

"But who'll want to stay, — alone with the dead? I don't."

"Nor I!" said his companion.

"I'll bet you an X that this little fellow has got more pluck than either of you," said the doctor, laughing in spite of their sad surroundings. "How is it, my son? Are you afraid to stay?"

A feeling of awe crept over Catharine, as she looked around upon the ghastly faces, and glazed and glazing eyes; yet she said, almost in spite of herself, —

"I am not afraid of the dead: I can still care for the living. I will stay."

"Well, then, my brave boy, we will leave you a lantern, a flask of brandy, and a canteen of water; and I want you to continue the search all around here for Col. Elliot. If he is still living, you may, by staying here, save his life; and you know how dear that is to us all." She needed no urging to do this; for he had been very kind to her from the first, and she was deeply grateful. So, as soon as they were gone, she commenced the search among the dead and dying, who had fallen thickly around that particular tree. She had begun, and made the circuit of the tree, and was bending over a poor ragged and wounded rebel soldier, and pouring water between his parched lips, when she heard a deep groan just behind her. She turned, and, flashing the light in that direction, saw that it did indeed come from her friend, Col. Elliot. He had raised himself upon one elbow, and, with a dull, dreary look and pallid face, was looking around him. He was but just aroused from a deathlike stupor, caused by the loss of life-blood. She was joyfully surprised to find him alive, but shocked by his ghastly appearance. She ran to him at once, pronouncing his name. He feebly held out his hand to her, and smiled gratefully as he said, in a faint, spasmodic tone, —

"How glad I am to see you, my son! You see, I am sorely wounded. I am very weak. I guess I must — have fainted. Did we gain the victory?"

"Yes, sir: the Union army has retreated," she said with a keen pang of disappointment.

"Thank God! Our cause is just, and must prosper in the end. Please give me some water. Oh, how horribly that limb pains me! — and my side! I fear, Ellery, — that I am mortally wounded. If I die here, carry my best love — to my friends. God, in whom I trust, knows — I would gladly die — to save my country — from defeat and shame."

"Oh, I think you will live!" said she earnestly. "Your voice grows stronger every moment. Let me bind up your wounds as well as I can, and stop the flow of life-blood; and I think you will survive."

"I hope so, — if only — to help — drive these invaders — from our soil."

She did not reply, but busied herself in tearing strips from a torn and blood-stained banner, with which she bound up his wounds to the best of her ability. Soothed and comforted by her kind ministrations, he soon began to look around the gory field, which was mostly shrouded in darkness.

"What is that?" he suddenly exclaimed, — "those lights moving yonder?"

"I think it must be some of the patrols, or perhaps Dr. Garnett and some of your men, who were coming back to look for you. I must wave the signal;" and she swung the lantern back and forth to attract their attention. " There ! They see it now, and are coming this way. How glad I am that I have found you alive ! "

" And I, too, thank God ! I always felt — as if you were somehow — akin to me, and would do me good. Perhaps it was because —you so strongly resemble — a lady I saw last year — in Richmond. She was from the North, — and I would give a great deal — to know what became of her. She was said to have been carried off — by bandits last autumn. I have watched you — a great deal, — tracing the semblance ; and sometimes — I have thought — But look ! Those are not — the patrols. They have none of their equipments ! Good heavens ! They are the robbers — of the dead, — the accursed jayhawkers."

They were indeed the jayhawkers; and Catharine, with her heart beating with a wild and terrible fear, instinctively lowered the slides of her dark lantern, as, with strained gaze, she watched them at their hellish work

On, on they came, nearer and nearer, apparently some fifteen or twenty in the gang. They rifled the pockets of the dead of money, rings, watches, miniatures, knives, and small arms, — every thing in fact that was valuable, or pleased their fancy. They robbed the wounded too; and if they resisted, or attempted to expostulate, plunged their knives into their bosoms, while shrieks of fear, and wails of agony, followed in their train. The battle had been the most fiercely contested, and Death's richest harvest had been reaped, in that portion of the field where Col. Elliot had fallen. Many officers, in both Union and rebel uniform, lay there, cold and still. It was from such as these they hoped for the most abundant spoil ; and they pursued their nefarious work with the greatest celerity and despatch.

"See! They are coming!" exclaimed the wounded officer in a hoarse whisper. "Fly to the woods, my dear boy, and save yourself if you can."

"Oh, I cannot go, and leave you here to die in that horrible way!" she murmured tremblingly. "Here, take some of this brandy; and then let me see if I cannot help you to fly too."

He took the brandy; and then Catharine got hold of his hands and, tried to raise him, or at least drag him towards the woods, that were near at hand."

"It is in vain!" said he mournfully, as, after repeated but unsuccessful efforts to rise, he fell back upon the sod. "My strength has all vanished with my life-blood, and yours is unequal to the task of dragging me to a place of safety. I must stay, and meet my fate as best I may! Here, take my pistols: they are loaded! Go, and may God bless, protect, and guide you!"

"I, too, have arms, and know how to use them. Hark! what's that?" and she sunk down upon her knees beside him.

"It is the patrols," he whispered with deep feeling.

"Thank God! we shall be saved."

Instantly, upon the sound of their approach, the lights of the blood-and-gold seekers vanished; and, cowering behind rocks, bushes, and heaps of slain, no one, upon a casual inspection, would have dreamed of the living power of evil lurking upon that terrible field of death.

But Catharine and the poor colonel were doomed to disappointment. The robbers, though still at a little distance, were much nearer than the patrols, who soon turned off in another direction, and were lost to their view behind the woods.

The fiendish wretches then rose to their feet, and resumed their satanic work.

"God's will be done!" moaned the wretched colonel.
"It is my destiny! Stoop down here, Ellery, and take
my watch and purse, and one kiss in memory of her
you so strongly resemble, and then go, — go, and God
bless you!"

She took the precious keepsakes, even to the brotherly
kiss, yet with blinding tears of grief and regret, and
was still hesitating whether to go, or stay and defend
her friend with her life, when her eye fell upon the fore-
most villain of the gang.

After finishing the struggles of a wounded Union
officer, who attempted evidently to resist his brutality,
and fruitlessly searching his pockets, he raised himself
to look around, and scent some richer prey. As he did
so, the light he carried gleamed over his swarthy visage;
and, with chilling blood and paralyzed limbs, Catharine
beheld the malignant face of Blondel.

"God help us! it is he!" she murmured, — "the
wretch who murdered Major Hunter, and captured " —

"Go, — go, then, in God's name! He will be here in
a few minutes. But the strength is coming back to this
right arm. I shall not die unavenged. Farewell, dear
boy. Don't wait another instant," he whispered.

She needed no more urging; but, pressing the friendly
hand that held hers, then relinquishing it with a wordless prayer for their mutual safety, she glided noiselessly
towards the woods. The colonel, who was leaning on his
elbow, sank down upon the sod to escape, if possible, the
notice of this lynx-eyed old buzzard of the battle-field.
As he did so, the glitter of his military trappings caught
a gleam of the robber's lantern, that betrayed to the
wretch the vicinity of life and promising plunder. He
stopped a few moments to arrange the sack that con-

tained his booty, looked back towards his comrades, who were a few rods in the rear, and then advanced to examine and make sure of his prey.

Catharine, meantime, having gained the covert of the woods, was withheld as by a spell from going farther. She sunk down upon her knees, and, with hushed breath and glittering eyes, looked out fearfully upon the appalling scene. Instinctively, and almost without conscious thought, she set down her dark lantern, and grasped the pistol she had found upon the battle-field of Seven Pines. Assuring herself that the caps were all right, she waited in breathless eagerness for what was to come. She had not long to wait, and was near enough to hear every footfall, and witness every diabolical act.

Blondel advanced cautiously, flashing his light around to select the most promising victim, and at last stood beside Col. Elliot.

"Aha!" he exclaimed in evident surprise, as the light gleamed over his pallid features; while a flash of recognition and malignant satisfaction passed over his own bloated visage. "So you are here at last, my fine popinjay! You won't swear an honest feller's life away agin in a hurry, I take it;" and with vengeful spite, he kicked and turned the colonel over with his foot. It was too much for a brave man's endurance. The colonel, who had lain still in the faint hope of escaping the eye of this human vulture, instantly raised himself up on his left elbow, and, with the pistol grasped in his right hand, attempted to fire.

But the old robber was too quick for him. Before he could pull the trigger with his weak and trembling fingers, the piece was knocked from his nerveless grasp, and exploded in the air.

"Villain!" exclaimed the colonel fiercely, "I would give millions to be able to put a bullet through your murderous heart, and rid the world of such a monster!"

"Aha! Don't you wish the Devil would give you the power?" he returned with a sardonic laugh. "Neither heaven nor hell shall prevent the execution of Blondel's vengeance upon one who attempted - to thwart, and expose him to the government. No amount of prayers or ransom could purchase your life of me, Col. Elliot, at this moment," said he fiercely, as he raised his glittering bowie in the air to plunge to the heart of his helpless victim.

At this instant a sharp report rang out upon the stilly night: an unseen messenger was sent upon its way. Blondel's arm fell paralyzed at his side; and, with a horrid oath, he rolled over at Col. Elliot's feet, — not dead, but sorely wounded.

Catharine, who had sped the deadly missile, cowered tremblingly to the earth, with a heart filled by a strange terror at the thought that she had sent a human soul unprepared into eternity.

But this fear vanished when she heard the robber's oaths and curses, and saw his ineffectual attempts to reach Col. Elliot with the knife he still held in his left hand, but which his inability to move a little nearer would not enable him to do.

The noise of the two reports of pistols aroused Blondel's comrades, who at once came running towards the spot. Some of them were gesticulating violently, and pointing to the woods, towards which two of them cautiously ventured; while the others went towards the place where Blondel and the colonel lay.

27

As the two brave villains came near the woods, they discharged their pieces at a venture, the ball from one of them just grazing Catharine's ear.

Terrified now almost out of her senses, she mechanically caught up her lantern and pistol, and ran with all speed into the thick woods.

She did not know until afterwards, that, at that very moment, Dr. Garnett and his party made their appearance, — just in time to capture Blondel, and save Col. Elliot's life. The rest of the robbers made their escape.

CHAPTER XVII.

THEODORE. — THE MEMORABLE SEVEN DAYS.

CATHARINE dared not open her lantern; so by the light of the stars she pressed on through the tangled underbrush, until she began to see the faint light of a clearing on the other side. There she ventured to halt, look back, and listen. But all was darkness, and, so far as human sounds were concerned, profound silence. Her pursuers had vanished. Probably they had not followed her far. Here, then, she was probably as safe as anywhere, until the morning. If she emerged upon the open plain, she thought she might meet other parties of a similar character; yet she resolved to venture to the edge of the wood to see if there were any living or moving objects in view.

The forest here was almost destitute of undergrowth; so she went swiftly forward, cheered by the faint light that every moment grew stronger. All at once she stumbled, and fell over some obstacle that lay across her pathway. She thought that it was a rock or fallen tree, until a faint moan saluted her ears. Then she knew that it was a human form. A strange, shuddering thrill shot through her, as she rose to her feet; and she listened eagerly for farther signs of life in the dark

315

form before her. There was none. Not a sigh or motion, or a single sound of pursuers.

Summoning courage at last, she opened her lantern,
and flashed the light upon the prostrate body. She
saw at once that it bore the uniform of a Federal
officer. The regimental hat was drawn down over a
handsome, manly face, darkened by southern suns ; and
for several minutes she gazed curiously upon it, wondering who it could be.

All at once she started eagerly forward, sunk down
upon her knees beside him, and, with trembling hand,
raised the hat from the rigid brow, and looked for a
moment upon the pallid face.

"O my God ! it is — it must be — my brother ! My
dear Theodore !" she exclaimed with quivering lips and
sinking heart. A sudden faintness came over her ;
but she conquered it by a strong effort of the will. He
seemed perfectly insensible, though still warm in the
region of the heart ; and she felt that there was not a
moment to lose : so, pressing a kiss upon the pale brow,
she began, with eager hands and blinding tears, the work
of trying to restore the feeble pulses, that she imagined
still beat faintly in the stiffening form. She found that
he was grievously, yet she hoped not mortally, wounded
through the right side ; and loss of blood, she judged,
was the cause of his inanimate condition. She had
still the flask of brandy and the canteen of water strung
to her belt ; and, by the judicious application of these
remedies, the life-currents were soon restored to their
natural channels, and he began slowly to revive.

He opened his eyes at last, and fixed them wonderingly, and for some time dreamily, upon her face. Her
old hat had fallen off ; and, with the short auburn ring-

lets curling around her sunburned face, it so strongly
resembled a sunny one he remembered in the long ago,
that he murmured feebly, "Strange! I ought to know
— that face! Who are you?"

Catharine hesitated: she had not thought he would
recognize her. Should she tell him, that in those dark
Virginia woods, at dead of night, in such a garb,
and surrounded by such fearful scenes, he had found his
dear lost sister? She longed to do so, and weep out her
joy and fear and despair upon his friendly bosom. But
reason whispered, "Forbear, rash girl! The shock
would kill him. His life is but a feeble, glimmering
taper: a breath would blow it out." So she did forbear; and when, as he grew stronger, and repeated the
question, she said, "I am a poor, forlorn waif from the
Confederate camp, lost in the darkness, seeking friends."

"Then you will betray me," he murmured mournfully.

"No, I will not. I would be glad to get to the Union
lines myself; for I have dearer friends there than here."

"Indeed! I wish you could, then. But how strangely
— familiar your voice sounds. It carries me back — to
the home of my youth — and the mother — and sisters
— I may never live to see more," said he feebly.

"Oh! you will live, I am sure," she returned, controlling her emotion by a strong effort. "I have seen
many wounds; and yours, I hope, is not mortal."

"It grows painful enough, any way. But what is
that?"

Catharine turned quickly in the direction of the
sound. The twigs and branches were parted carefully
from the fringe of shrubbery that skirted the woods, a
dark face appeared at the opening; and she could hardly

27*

suppress a cry of joy that rose to her lips, as Uncle Nick's honest visage was presented to her view. He gazed at her for a moment in astonishment; while she, remembering her disguise, put on her old hat, and drew it down over her eyes, to prevent the half-formed recognition. Her looks assured him of her friendliness; so he came at once to Theodore's side.

"Ay, young massa captin!" he exclaimed. "Nick drefful glad he find ye. He bin lookin' dis long time. But for dis lantern he tink he neber du it. De rebs all round de plain; an' he dodged about till he forgit de spot. Drefful ticklish bisiness to get away, massa."

"Then you must go without me, Nick. I am a great deal weaker than I was when you dragged me into the bushes. I doubt if I could walk a rod to save my life. I think I have been in a swoon; from which I should never have awakened but for this generous little rebel. You'll have to leave me to my fate, my kind friend."

"Ah! but Nick tink ob all dat; an' he done cotch a big, grand hoss dat was runnin' round so frisky; an' he got him all fixed, an' de ole banner an' tings to put round him, an' tie up de shot-hole; an' he tink he put young massa on his back, an' lead him troo de danger like an ole weazel."

"It is impossible! I find I cannot sit up a moment. O Uncle Nick, there is no help for it! I must die here," said he mournfully.

"Not a bit on't, Massa Tedo. Nick no leave massa behind, if he die for't. He put him on de hoss, git up behind him, hold on, an' ride like de debble. He die here: he no more'n die on de hoss's back, or in Massa Linkum's army."

"That is true enough. But, Nick, without me, you

could escape; burdened with me, you would be sure —
to lose your life or liberty. This youth wants to escape
too. He is light as a feather compared — to me. Take
him behind you, and fly."

"No, no!" said Catharine eagerly. "I will not take
your place. Your wounds want immediate attention,
which they would never get here, if you were found, till
it would be too late to save you : for the thousands of
their own wounded will be cared for first; and then you
would be doomed to suffer untold agonies in some cruel,
bungling experimenter's hands, if cared for at all. We
will dress your wound first as well as we can to stop the
flow of blood; and then I, who know all about it, say
that you had better go, if you die on the way, to the
Union lines, than to remain where I shall be safe
enough to stay."

"Then I will try," he said in an exhausted tone.
"Get your horse, Uncle Nick; and we will see what can
be done."

"But the wound first," said Catharine.

She gave him first some of the brandy and water:
then Uncle Nick held Theodore up, while Catharine put
a thick compress of rags and dead leaves upon the
wound, and bound it there with strips torn from the old
banner: the remainder she wound around him to protect him from the chilliness and damp that already,
though it was a summer night, made him shiver, lying
as he did upon the cold, bare ground.

Nick then went for the horse; and, while he was
gone, Theodore, whose strength was restored a little by
the stimulant, again turned his attention to Catharine.

"How much you do look like — and your voice —
Where do you live, my boy, — when at home?"

" In Richmond."

" Indeed! Well, did you ever see a lady there by the name of Catharine Hale ? "

" Yes, sir: I knew her well."

" Is it possible ! " and he started up eagerly, but fell back from extreme weakness, as he murmured, " Is she there still ? "

" No, sir. She lived with Major Hunter, who was killed, and his house burned by the guerillas. The family have now all gone off to North Carolina."

" That accounts for it, then. She is my sister, and very dear to me. We have been greatly concerned because she did not come home, and we have not heard from her lately."

" Well, sir, I know she wanted to go home, but was prevented after the battle of Bull Run by some unforeseen circumstances; and now travelling is so dangerous, and passes so hard to obtain, she may have to stay until the war is over. But, if I see her again, shall I tell her that " —

" Her friends are all well but — Theodore ; and that she is still dear to every one, and remembered in their prayers."

By this time Nick had arrived with the horse, — a fine, spirited but well-trained animal, whose master, most likely, was among the slain. Tying him to a sapling, he, by Catharine's help, succeeded in placing Theodore upon his back, with a couple of blankets he had found under and over him, and he then mounted behind him. But still he lingered ; and at last, stooping down, said, —

" If little massa on'y strong nuff to hold up de captin, Nick go afoot."

"I could not do it; and it would only add to the danger."

"Nick tink he know dat voice," he whispered, "an' he want dreffully to take him along."

"You are right," she returned in a low tone; "but be silent. He is so weak he cannot bear the shock. I may come hereafter. There, the patrols are coming this way. Go, and may God help us — all" —

"Good-by, den, till next time," said Nick; and "Farewell, with a thousand thanks for your kindness," murmured the young officer faintly, as they, slowly at first, and as noiselessly as possible, moved out of the woods, and away towards the Union army.

As they did so, a sudden impulse seized her to follow them on foot, and, if possible, reach the Union lines, that she might extend to Theodore that loving care which she felt could alone save his life.

She acted upon it instantly, by starting in as close pursuit of them as possible, keeping stealthily for a time in the shadow of the woods to avoid the notice of the patrolling parties, who were scouring the plain in various directions, looking after their own wounded.

As soon as Nick thought he had avoided the danger from the patrols, he struck out boldly for the Union lines; which, though he knew it not, were fast melting away. Knowing, of course, nothing of her pursuit, and warned of the value of time by the fainting condition of his charge, he now gave his horse the rein, and dashed on as fast as possible. Unavoidably falling in the rear, Catharine soon lost sight of them in the darkness, and lost herself in the interminable intricacies of a seemingly pathless swamp.

For a while she wandered on, hoping she was in the

right track, but getting deeper and deeper into the mire; and, completely worn out at last by toil, excitement, and anxiety, she sunk down upon a little hillock at the roots of a giant tree, and, in despair gave up her hopeless pursuit. Having eaten nothing since the early morning, she was completely famished and exhausted for the want of food, as well as rest. So, in spite of all the dangers that surrounded her, and the croaking of multitudes of frogs and tree-toads, and the bite of myriads of mosquitoes, she laid her aching head up against the body of the tree, and with a wordless prayer upon her lips, dropped off into a doze. Just as day was breaking in the east, she awoke in a fright, and started to her feet, having been aroused by a dream of attacking rebels and Indians.

The hiss of a serpent that was startled by her sudden motion warned her, as he moved noiselessly away, that the dangers to which she had been exposed had not all been imaginary. Nor was her feeling of security increased a moment later by the challenge of a rebel sentinel, who was himself alarmed by her exclamation of terror, and within a few yards of whom she had spent a part of that terrible night.

Stiff and sore, and sick from cold, exhaustion, and exposure; disappointed in her hope of getting away with Theodore, and with a heart racked with anxiety regarding him and the fear of meeting her husband, she now gave way to a feeling of despair, and resigned herself passively to the direction of the soldier, who presently took her to the encampment.

When questioned, she told them of her escape from the robbers, but not of her meeting with her brother, or attempted escape to the Union lines.

The facts of Col. Elliot's rescue were known in camp; so her story was credited, her courage praised, and his keepsakes sent back to him just as they were removing him to Richmond.

As a reward, perhaps, she was ordered to join another division that was to follow in the pursuit of the Union army, which was now in full retreat.

Through all that terrible Saturday, Sunday, and Monday, she followed with the pursuing rebel hosts; hoping that in some way she might fall into Union hands. Worn out in body, yet so excited in mind as hardly to realize her true condition, she strove through it all to do what she could towards assuaging the pain, mitigating the horror, and healing the wounds of the hundreds and thousands who were sick, suffering, and dying all around her.

All through those memorable seven days there was continued fighting with the sorely-pressed and retreating Union army, culminating at last in the awful battle of Malvern Hill.

This was the last and bloodiest in the list of those tragic scenes that wound up the second great attempt to take the rebel capital.

The rebel army was here repulsed with terrible slaughter; and that of the Union gained a secure position, where they were protected by their gunboats, but at the cost of thousands of precious lives, and millions of dollars' worth of ordnance and army stores, that were burnt, or fell into the hands of the enemy.

They had indeed, though exhibiting the most heroic courage and endurance, met with a sad succession of disasters. But none among them all seems sadder or more humiliating than this, — that, by the stern neces-

sities of their forced and hasty retreat, they were obliged
to leave thousands of their sick and wounded men in
the hands of those whose tenderest mercies to them
proved to be only refined cruelty.

Following in the track of this wide-spread wreck,
ruin, and anguish for miles and miles, Catharine's heart
bled so much for the woes of her country and her kindred, that her own troubles seemed as nothing in the comparison : yet it was with a heavy heart that she turned
back, footsore and weary, sick and disheartened, with
the rebel hosts who were returning to Richmond.
Her hope of in some way falling into Union hands had
vanished; and there had been no opportunity for escape.
So again she seemed obliged to yield to her destiny.

But she was now completely worn out by the mental
anguish, as well as the physical hardships, she had endured. No hope of meeting and caring for her brother
cheered her on. Her strength was all gone. Her spirit
was paralyzed by the chill hand of despair. She was
continually reprimanded for lagging behind the troops,
but was refused a ride in the wagons; and at last, completely exhausted, she sunk down fainting by the roadside.

It was no uncommon thing for men and boys to drop
out of the ranks in this way; yet they were generally
looked after, and cared for : but the regiment to which
she was now attached had taken no such deep interest
in her as had that of Col. Elliot; and now, in their
eagerness to get back to Richmond, they passed on without noticing or caring for her, as did all the others belonging to the same division.

Dead men, dying men, and wounded men and boys,
were too common a sight on that march to attract much

Dismounting in haste, he threw his bridle to his black servant, and went up to where she was lying.

Page 325.

attention; yet the slender, graceful form, perfect, marble-like features, and bright auburn curls of poor Catharine did attract the attention of the next party who came along, — a general officer on horseback, who had left his staff behind him. He halted suddenly, looked at her a moment, evidently in great surprise; then, dismounting in haste, threw his bridle to his black servant, and went up to where she was lying. He bent over the inanimate form with his dark face growing paler every moment; smoothed back the bright curly hair from which the old hat had fallen, and then took off his glove, and felt the pulse that was still faintly throbbing.

His color came back when he found that life was not extinct; and, kneeling down, he put some strong stimulus to her nose, that was the means of her revival. Opening her eyes at last, she fixed them, dreamily at first, then consciously, upon the deeply-anxious face of Gen. Atherton. He raised her up partially. For a minute they looked in each other's eyes: and then, when she saw that she was recognized, and remembered their respective positions, the faint color stole back to her cheek; and, turning her face away, she burst into tears.

"O Catharine!" he exclaimed, "is it thus we meet, among these bloody, heart-rending scenes, — in this miserable garb, dying by the roadside? Pray tell me what it all means."

"Oh! not here, — not now; for I am so weary — so wretched — so miserable! Pray go — go away, and let me die in peace. It is better so — oh! so much better — for us both," she murmured; and again she went off into a dead faint.

CHAPTER XVIII.

THE REBEL GENERAL. — HOME AT LAST.

WHEN Catharine again opened her eyes consciously, it was to find herself in a darkened yet elegantly-furnished apartment, in a bed hung with gorgeous crimson draperies, and with every refinement of wealth, taste, and luxury around her.

It was some time before she could persuade herself that this change from the horrors of the camp, the hospital, and the battle-fields, which began to come back to her, were not all the wild phantasmagoria of a dream. For some time she gazed around with a listless, dreamy, languor, hardly conscious that she was awake, yet wondering where she was. It was only when she attempted to rise that she became conscious of her extreme weakness, and inability to help herself. The motion at once brought a sable attendant to her side; in whom, to her extreme surprise, she recognized dear old Aunt Dinah.

"O aunty!" she exclaimed in a feeble tone, "how glad I am to see you!" and, with tears of joy filling her eyes, she drew the kind black face down to her, and kissed it, as she received a compassionate motherly kiss in return.

"If missis glad, Dinah be bery much gladder," she returned ; "for she bin terrible 'fraid de poor leetle dear neber come out on't."

"Out of what, Dinah ? "

"Don't missis know she bin in a kinder faint like, dis tu tree days ? "

"No ; I don't know any thing about it. I was so tired and worn out, and my head swam, and every thing grew dark ; and I dreamed — I saw" — and here the thought of Gen. Atherton came like a dark cloud over her memory ; and she covered her face with her hands and wept silently. It must be so, she thought. It was not all a dream : she had seen Gen. Atherton some-where.

"Dinah, where am I ? " she suddenly exclaimed, uncovering her face, and looking around the room. "This is not Mrs. Hunter's ; but you are here. Where are she and the children ? "

"Dey no come home yet. Dinah keep house well nuff. She no 'fraid ob de Yankees."

"But this is none of Mrs. Hunter's rooms, Dinah !"

"Laws, chile ! don't worry 'bout dat. Dinah tink missis got grand house o' her own dis time. Take a leetle o' dis doctor stuff, darlin', an' go to sleep now."

"If you knew how miserable I was, Dinah, you would not plague me so," she sobbed with fretful weakness, as the truth began to dawn upon her clouded mind.

"Dere, dere, don't cry ! *He* feel terrible, tu, an' walk de room, an' cry, Dinah tink, when nobody see 'im ; an' Dinah no onderstand it one bit."

"*He* is here, then ? " said Catharine eagerly.

"Laws yes, chile ! He back an' forth, here an' to Richmond, 'most ebery day. But missis needn't see him 'thout she wants tu."

"But I do want to see him now. Raise me up, Dinah, and put that shawl around me," she exclaimed with a desperate sort of courage. "There, that is right; thank you. Now, please go and tell him I would like to see him."

We may be sure that the general waited for no second summons; for Catharine had lain, like a pale, storm-beaten lily, in a kind of stupor ever since she had been brought to Atherton; and for a time there had been faint hope of her recovery. There was a complete prostration of the vital energies, the doctor said; from which it would take her some time to recover, if she did at all.

So it was with eager, trembling joy that she had come out of that critical state, as well as fear of a relapse, that Gen. Atherton presented himself at her bidding. He looked pale and careworn; and his face presented traces of strong emotion as he came up to the side of the bed, took the offered hand, and pressed a kiss upon the fair, pale brow.

"Did you really want to see me, dear Catharine?" he said.

"Yes," she replied in a faint yet excited tone; "but first tell me where I am."

"You are *at home*, darling, — on Atherton Plantation."

"And Dinah" —

"I brought her from Richmond, that you might have some one you knew, and who also knew our relations, around you when you revived, to make you feel more at home here. But you are very pale and weak. I fear you are exhausting yourself. And, much as I long for your confidence, I can wait until you are better able to give it."

"No, no: I want you to know all now. And, first, do you believe what I told you in the Libby Prison?"

"Yes, Catharine. In anticipation of your trial, I sent a trusty messenger to Philip's plantation, and ascertained all the facts. And besides, you may not know that it was because of that villain Sweep's confessions that you were set at liberty."

"Indeed! Then you will believe me when I tell you why I am here?"

"Of course I shall. In all our acquaintance I have never found cause to doubt your word: yet I must tell you that the knowledge that you had left the prison, and again disappeared, has given me the deepest anxiety; and that this exhibition of your want of trust and confidence, in neglecting to come or send to me for assistance, has deeply pained me."

"I could not help it, general, — indeed I could not, — at first; and afterwards a feeling of — of — I can't explain it to you, — prevented my doing so;" and the faint, fitful color flashed over her face, as she said it.

"I can understand it, Catharine, without an explanation," he returned with a sigh; "and some day, when you are stronger and less afraid of me, you shall tell me all about it."

She would have gone on; but he would not allow it: so, kissing her tenderly, he went out, and sent in Dinah.

His forbearance, seeming trust, and regard for her feelings, were not lost upon the poor, weary invalid: so, with a little less dread of him and her future, she soon forgot self, and dropped off into a refreshing slumber, that seemed to do her a world of good.

He came back the next morning, delighted to find her

28*

so much better, and then listened with eager interest
to her story of her coming out of prison; her vain
search for a refuge; her meeting the woman, and escape from the odious Blondel; her joining Col. Elliot's
party, and adventures in the camp and upon the various fields of battle.

"You seem doomed to suffer, and meet with many
strange adventures," he said. "But, my dear, you should
have applied to the authorities for help; and, at the
worst, gone back to the prison for shelter."

"I had no money to pay for a ride: the streets were
full of rude soldiery; and I knew not what to do."

"I tremble even now to think of what might have
been your fate. But, when you met Col. Elliot, he
would have protected you, had you told him all, until
you could have come or sent to me."

"I did not even think of it then; and I don't know
as I should if I had, I was so frightened and disheartened by my repeated repulses from those upon whom I
thought I had a better claim. He was hurrying, too,
to the field of battle; and want of time and my questionable garb and strange story would most likely have
made even him doubt, and cast me off at once. I believe now, however, that there was a hand of Providence
in my going as I did upon the battle-fields. It was the
means, under God, of saving Col. Elliot's life, and perhaps that of my brother Theodore and others."

"It may be so; but, Catharine, after you had come
to the army, why were you willing to expose your life to
a thousand dangers, your character to the greatest misconstructions, and even face death itself, rather than
come to the heart that beats for you alone, the arms
that would so gladly and lovingly infold you as my
bride?" said he reproachfully.

"If I was your bride, it was an unacknowledged one. And how should I know that you would acknowledge my right to your protection before that army and the world?" said she blushingly.

"You could not doubt it, Catharine."

"But I did doubt it, — coming, too, as I did in so humble and questionable a guise. Delicacy forbade my coming to you, and urging such a claim; and that, with many other feelings you cannot understand, impelled me into the current that took me to the hospital and the field of battle. If, when there, and agonized by thoughts of my brother's danger, an inexpressible longing for home and friends made me forget for a time my promise to you, in a vain effort to escape to the Union lines, I trust I shall be forgiven."

"Are, then, the home and friends you have left at the North still so much dearer than every thing the South has to offer, my dear Catharine?"

"Oh! I cannot tell you how very dear they have seemed ever since that awful night, when I found and parted from my brother; how I think of them, and dream of them, and long for them, day-and night, as I never in all my life have done before. And sometimes I feel as if I should die of this longing and homesickness if I cannot see them. O Gen. Atherton! let me ask, — let me beg of you to release me from that fearful promise, and allow me to go home. I have been nothing but a trouble and a burden to you, from the first: you would be a thousand times better off without me. If I stay, I cannot fulfil that solemn promise to love you as a wife should. If I could go, I should respect and honor you, if nothing more. Oh, I implore you to release, and let me go! even though I come back again," she said in a deeply-agitated voice.

He, too, was strongly moved. He gazed upon her flushed, imploring countenance for a moment with a pitiful, yearning tenderness, then turned away, and began to walk the room. At last he came back to her, and said in a tremulous tone, as he smoothed her short, silky hair, —

"Catharine, did you realize, even imperfectly, how very dear you are to me, — how far above all my earthly possessions I prize you, or the extent of the sacrifice you require at my hands, you would never have made this request; yet, as you have done so, I will give it due consideration. At present, you are in no condition to go home, or anywhere else; and I want you to consider *this* as your home, — at least, until you can leave it in safety. In consideration of your present feelings, and also because my conscience hardly acquits me for the way in which it was obtained, I shall never, you may feel assured, enforce, against your wishes, a husband's claim upon you. For the present, I ask only the privileges of a friend or elder brother, which, I trust, you will accord to me. As yet we are almost strangers to each other. I hope your feelings towards me will change upon a better acquaintance. After the toils and dangers of the past few months, I am having a short furlough; and I think I cannot employ it to better advantage than in looking after the affairs of my plantation, and at the same time cultivating more friendly relations with one who has the power to make or mar the happiness of my whole future life. Allow me the privileges of friendship, dear Catharine, to converse and associate with you freely, to nurse you back to health, to familiarize you with my people and my surroundings. And if, after all, you prefer your own

people to mine; if you feel that you still love another
too well truthfully to perform your vows to me, I solemnly promise to let you go home, and hereafter take
measures to break the tie that binds us together, if it
also break my heart. Shall it be so, dear Catharine?"
he continued in a tone of deep emotion.

"Yes," she replied, affected to tears by the unexpected
generosity that promised a present reprieve, if not a
future emancipation, from what she had previously regarded as an intolerable bondage.

She knew very well that he was a man whose word
was as good as his bond, even though he was sometimes
ruled almost wholly by ambition and its political necessities. She could not help seeing in every word, look,
and tone how very dear she was to him, and, of course,
how great to him would be the sacrifice if compelled
hereafter to resign her forever. So, woman like, she began to pity him. If ever a man set himself resolutely to
the task of winning a woman's heart, it was Gen. Atherton now. The promise had been drawn from him by her
tears, and too evident dread of him; but, once given, he
felt that he must abide by it. He felt, too, that this
promise had brought him down to the level of an humble
suppliant for her favor. But, while regretting this, he
did not know that he made himself much more lovable
in Catharine's eyes, than when his display of a domineering and determined feeling of ownership, suggest-
ing thoughts of slavery, had aroused a spirit of resistance
in her proud, rebellious heart. Having no special disease, she improved rapidly under Dinah's careful nursing and the general's special attentions. The color
came back to her pale cheek, and the light to her eyes;
though the longing for home and mother, and espe-

cially to know Theodore's fate, devoured her continually. Dinah, who, it may be remembered, was a witness of their marriage, having been charged to be silent regarding it then, had sense enough not to bother Catharine with questions now; though she no doubt wondered over many things. To her it was a labor of love to wait on Catharine, who had completely won her affection; and, when not thus engaged, it was her greatest delight to talk over her miraculous adventures, virtues, and perfections, and sound her praises to a select audience in the kitchen, who were her old acquaintances, and to whom she could enlarge upon the facts in the most glowing terms, without the fear of contradiction. Dinah had, it seemed, been left in charge of Mrs. Hunter's establishment in Richmond; and it was by accident alone that she and Cæsar happened to be away at the time Catharine knocked in vain for admittance.

When not obliged to go to Richmond, the general spent his mornings in writing, and overlooking his estate, — taking Catharine out to ride with him as soon as she was well enough, that he might show her the most beautiful views, and the improvements he had planned, and make her acquainted with his surroundings. His afternoons and evenings, too, when not otherwise engaged, were always spent in her society; and it was very evident that he meant to make the most of his time.

His plantation was situated upon the James River, upon the magnificent scenery of which she was never tired of gazing. The mansion vied with Hunter House in its bygone splendor, as well as its antiquity; but there had been additions, improvements, and furnishings of a later date, that made it much more acceptable to

modern tastes, and left no reasonable wish or necessity
unprovided for. It had a large and choice library, a
splendid collection of rare pictures, with many other
choice specimens of art and taste to please the eye and
entertain and improve the mind and heart. Yes,
Atherton Place was beautiful; in fact, just the spot
where one could contentedly dream away a lifetime, if —
and there Catharine generally wound up her reflections,
leaving the sentence unfinished, and sighing over a lost
hope.

We have said before that Gen. Atherton, for a man of
his age, was strongly attractive; that his voice was
deep-toned and melodious; that his eye had a peculiarly
magnetic power over Catharine, from which she felt impelled to fly. And now she was wholly surrendered to
this influence, without the power to fly.

Hard and stern as he sometimes appeared, there was
really a great deal of poetry and romance in his composition, and genuine feeling, earnestness, and eloquence
in his conversation. And now, as he explained to her
the beautiful paintings, and specimens of art, he had gathered in his own, as well as foreign lands; or read to her
from his favorite authors; or talked with her of his own
hopes and plans, of the beautiful scenery, or the great
issues at stake in the past, present, and future of the country; or joined his deep-toned voice with hers in the ren-
dering of some grand harmony, — she could not help yielding to him the tribute of admiration, and appreciation of
his fine talents, if not that of the love he so earnestly
hoped to inspire. As a father, brother, or friend, with no
special claim upon her, she felt as if she could have given
him the tribute of an affectionate regard; and, even as a
lover or husband, he would not have been as objection-

able as some who had sought her favor, but for his devotion to the cause of the rebellion.

Upon this subject they seldom argued now, as she felt as if it were of no earthly use. She believed that he now at heart as bitterly regretted the steps the South had taken as she could do. That he, and in fact the whole South, were deeply disappointed, — not only in the failure of the Democracy of the North to support their cause, but also in the powerful resistance they had met from the Federal Government. She knew that he was sick of bloodshed and such fearful sacrifice of human life, and, in spite of present dear-bought successes, doubtful of the final issue of the contest. She knew, too, that his great misleading passion — a towering ambition — had thus far been deeply disappointed; for he had found other men, plenty of them, equally ambitious with himself. With more tact and subtlety, or ability to please the multitude, and propitiate favor in influential quarters, they had supplanted, cast him into the shade, and more than rivalled him in the regard of the administration, and thus attained to greater preferment and power.

The supreme ruler of the Southern people saw in him a talented and dangerous rival, eager to distinguish himself, and, if possible, get the reins of government into his own guiding hands; so that chief ruler felt it to be a matter of vital interest to himself to prevent Gen. Atherton, in one way and another, from attaining to any prominent distinction.

Catharine knew that he felt this keenly, but, from the power of surrounding circumstances, was unable to help it. And from this cause, if there were no other, he inwardly hated the administration, and the way in which they had conducted the affairs of the Confederacy. She might have taunted him about the splendid eminence to which he had promised to raise her : but she cared nothing for the eminence ; and she was really too kind-hearted, and too much of a Christian in spirit, to wish to add bitterness to the discontent that she knew was gnawing at his heart.   Perhaps, too, in their present re-lations, she thought it would be unadvisable to recrimi-nate and anger him.

He had, besides these, other serious causes of discon-tent.   His slaves, thrilled by the tocsin of war, and the hope of freedom, were escaping in scores; and this, to a born slaveholder, was a constant source of trouble and irritation, in which he knew she could not sympathize. From all appearances, she judged that he was kinder and more just and generous than most slave-owners were with, their slaves ; that he furnished them with better fare, and neater cabins, demanded fewer hours of labor, and allowed them many more privileges ; reasoning truly that he was better served in return than those who treated them more unkindly.   But however indulgent he or others might be, these people felt as if it were slavery still.   Their dreams of liberty included an easy, happy life, free from toil and care and bondage.   They were wild and unreal, and they were sure to find it so in the end ; but still they preferred to dare the risk of pain, privation, recapture, and death itself, to remaining longer in the galling shackles of bondage.

As Catharine mingled among those who were left, — held mostly by weakness, cowardice, or the strong and endearing bonds of love, — she could not help feeling how much better it would be for both master and slave, if they were all free men and women ; allowed to live on the estate, serving him more faithfully and gratefully,

29

from the knowledge that their posterity would not wear the yoke of slavery. She told their owner so one morning, when they were out for a ride around the plantation, and used her best arguments to support her position.

"I don't know but you are right," he said after a long pause, and with a keen, searching glance; "and that you might make a practical abolitionist of me if you tried. There are some things we cannot understand until we feel them; and this is one. I never knew what it was to be in bonds, fettered even by a rash promise, until the past few weeks. And I assure you, that, although they are invisible to the outward eye, I find them inexpressibly galling. I cannot blame the slaves much, if they feel as I do, for snapping their bonds, as Samson did his, and setting law, gospel, and conscience at defiance. Seriously, Catharine, I cannot much longer endure this thraldom. Every strong impulse of my soul cries out against it every hour; and every hour is a torture until I know what the future has in store for me. I could not bear the thought of separation; and yet every hour spent in your society has only made you dearer to my heart, and the thought of a future parting harder to bear. Oh! tell me now honestly, my darling, whether I have made myself sufficiently tolerable in your eyes for you to endure the thought of being presented to the world as my wife!" he said in a pleading tone.

Catharine had been expecting this ordeal; but it came upon her unexpectedly now. The warm blood flashed over her face in an instant, and then rushed back to her heart, leaving it pale as ashes; and the hand he had clasped trembled like a leaf in his own.

"Does the thought distress you still?" he asked tenderly, yet in a disappointed tone, when he found she did

not reply. "I had hoped that by this time you had become accustomed to it — and me. I am going down the
river to-day," he continued, "to reconnoitre, and meet
Gen. Lee; and to-morrow or next day I shall return, on my
way to Richmond. I entreat you then, dear Catharine, to
be ready to decide whether you will go there with me to
be presented to the world as my bride, or break my heart
by asking to be transmitted through the lines. In either
case you shall have a safe conduct and a free choice; by
which I feel bound to abide. Will you be ready then?"

"I will try to be," she faltered, as he helped her from
the carriage, and bade her an affectionate "Good-by!"

He left the mansion on horseback soon afterwards, attended by his black servant; and Catharine was left to
her own reflections. We can very well imagine that they
were not pleasant ones, and that the questions she had
to ask herself were hard to decide. They were questions
of duty, not inclination, as that would have led her at
once through the lines. She did not for an instant doubt
his regard for her; for his every word, look, and tone de-
clared it. But he was an enemy to her country. He had
gone now to hatch treason against the government. To be
his wife, was affording aid and comfort to the enemy, — was
it not? — the greatest he could receive, he had given her
to understand; and would she not be justified in refusing
it? Ay: but was not the solemn marriage-vow she had
pronounced a higher law than that, — one of God's own
institution, and more binding than any she owed her
country? In his pity and forbearance, as well as the
strong hope of winning her love, he had promised to give
her leave to break or evade it. But did that abrogate her
own solemn promise to love, honor, and obey this man
till death? Yet she felt that she had promised what

she could not perform. She liked him well enough, but
knew that she did not love him; and she felt then as if
she never could. And would it not be a greater sin to
live with him, acting a lie, than any she would commit
in leaving him?

These were some of the questions conscience pro-
pounded, which she pondered sleeplessly, but was far
from deciding. Dinah had gone back to Richmond to
prepare for Mrs. Hunter's expected return: the other
servants were comparative strangers; so she had none but
God and her own conscience to consult in this trying
emergency. She laid her case before that dread tribunal,
but could get no clear indications from the inward monitor
regarding the true path of duty. Her mind veered from
one side of the question to the other, like a vane in a
gale of wind; and the eager longing for home and friends,
and rest and freedom, each hour grew stronger in her
heart.

The first day passed slowly away, and the second still
more wearily and anxiously; but still he did not come.
The third at last dawned upon the weary watcher, and
dragged its slow length along. She tried to beguile the
time by books and music and art; but their illusions
were but momentary. They could not distract her attention from the decision she was hourly expecting to be
called upon to make.

It was about the last of July; and the weather was
very warm and sultry. Feeling weary, languid, and oppressed, not only by the heat, but her own foreboding
fancies, she wandered away from the mansion some time
in the afternoon with her sketch-book to beguile the
hours of their tediousness. The place she sought was a
rocky ledge near the main road, overhung by giant trees,

the growth of centuries. This ledge overlooked a high, arched stone bridge, that spanned a beautiful and rapid stream, and commanded many other bright glimpses of bold and beautiful scenery. This stream often overflowed its banks, and had a deep and dangerous current that made its way over the rocks to the dam and mills and mightier stream below. She had been there twice before with Gen. Atherton, never ceasing to admire the bold scenery, which she had resolved to sketch that day. So, after reaching the place, and cooling off in the shade of the splendid trees, she gained the most desirable position, and began her work. She drew the outlines of her sketch with a masterly hand. Then she began to fill in with the bold rocks, the giant trees, the high, arched bridge, half in sunlight, half in shadow, the steep bluff, covered with clumps of laurel, wild roses, and other shrubbery. Then she endeavored to portray the deeply-shadowed stream, with a few bright glimpses of sunshine playing upon the bright ripples of foam, in sparkling diamond points of light, and the soft summer haze that lay like a thin, fleecy cloud over the distant landscape, that no pencil of artist, however skilful, could ever truthfully portray.

As she paused at last to compare, not admire, what she felt to be but a faint and feeble imitation of the grandeur of the original, though another might have pronounced it faultless, the sound of merry voices and shouts of musical laughter rang out upon the sultry air.

A few minutes afterwards a small party of negro children came out from the shadow of the pines upon the opposite bank, that she had just been sketching. Completely tired out with their berry-picking, and ramble over the hills, they set down their baskets, and threw

29*

themselves upon the mossy carpet to rest. The roar of
the stream between her and them prevented her hearing
much of their conversation; yet they were near enough
for her to recognize them as children she had often seen
playing around the slave-cabins, — one of whom, a thin-
faced girl of ten, was hopelessly deformed.

It immediately occurred to her that these were the
very objects needed to give animation to her picture, besides representing a striking phase of Southern life and
character; so, while the children lay there at rest, or
were tumbling over the green carpet of moss, she rubbed
out a portion of her foreground, and rapidly and skilfully
sketched the little group; startled a little at the last
through fear that the little hunchback was in too dangerous proximity to the edge of the cliff of rock that
bordered the river. Over this she seemed to be peering
in search of wild-flowers that grew in great profusion
among the crevices of the rocks, and a large bunch of
which she held in her hand. Eager in the pursuit, she
grew so venturesome, that Catharine, who was watching
her, trembled at her danger, and opened her lips to shout
a warning.

But it was too late. There was a wild shriek, — little
dark hands were flung out, clutching at nothing, — a dull
splash, and the little waif was struggling in the deep
water. For an instant Catharine was paralyzed: then
she threw down her sketch, and ran down the steep bank,
forgetting, in her eagerness, that it was necessary to
cross the bridge some rods below to get anywhere near
the little sufferer. She saw her error in a moment, and
hastened to retrieve it by running towards the bridge.
She realized, almost intuitively, that it was only below
it, where the swift current would be sure to carry the

child through the arches, that she could hope to render her the least assistance. As she neared the bridge with an old fishing-rod she had caught up on the way in her hand, a new actor suddenly appeared upon the scene.

A man on horseback, who came down the road that crossed the bridge at the most critical moment, heard the shriek, and saw the child fall over the cliff. With ready sympathy, and disregard of danger, he sprang from his horse, threw off his coat and hat, and, without noticing Catharine in the deep shadow of the opposite bank, slid down the steep rocks into the water. By the time she had reached the bridge, he had caught the little drowning girl by the arm, just as she was sinking for the last time.

CHAPTER XIX.

BUT the danger was not over yet; for the banks were so very steep, that it was necessary for the man to breast the strong current to find a secure landing, or else glide down beneath the arches of the bridge, at the risk of being carried over the dam to the mill-wheel below, which would be certain death. Unburdened, he could easily reach the place he sought: as it was, he found it impossible, and was soon, almost in spite of himself, gliding down towards the bridge. He raised his head, and cast a despairing glance around.

Was it wise to risk his own life for this puny creature, who, if she lived, must ever be a burden to herself and him?

This was his thought; and Catharine read it as she looked down into the dark, despairing eyes of Gen. Atherton. She had not seen clearly before who it was; nor had he as yet seen her at all. Yet her agitation and surprise did not prevent her from comprehending all the circumstances. She saw that her rod would not begin to reach the water; and then another expedient occurred to her: so, as soon as they neared the arch, she bent over the railing of the bridge, and shouted in a voice heard above the roar of the stream, —

344

"Hold on as long as you can! There is a tree below the arches. I believe I can bend down one of the branches within your reach."

The tree grew out gnarled and knotted between the rocks, with long lateral branches extending over the stream. With little thought of the danger, Catharine sprung from the bridge upon the craggy wall of steep rocks that formed the bank of the stream, and slid down these until she alighted upon the crooked body of the tree. Then she walked out cautiously upon the longest limb, steadying herself by the one above her, until it bent beneath her weight so as to dip in the rapid current. By this time the general had floated through the arch with the child, and, by a little exertion, he reached and caught the branch with one hand, while he held on to her with the other.

"Thank you!" he said, looking up to her gratefully. "But now I shall be more obliged, if you will tell me what to do next. I used to breast this current easily; but I am very weary, and it seems cannot do it now. You know what is below us; and the banks are very steep all the way. The water is very deep here; and I cannot hold on long. Alone I should be safe enough; but" — and he looked down significantly upon his helpless burden.

"I have it!" she exclaimed joyfully, after a moment's thought. "There is your horse just where you left him. If I can get off his bridle, and you could slip it under her arms with your teeth, or somehow, I believe I could draw her to the shore, and lift her upon the rocks."

No sooner said than done. She walked back to the body of the tree, clambered up the steep wall of rock as quickly as possible, by a little petting and coaxing got off

Selim's bridle; and, while he ran home with all speed, she descended again to the tree. This time her head swam as she walked out over the water; but she held on a moment, and the weakness passed away. The general saw her sudden pallor; and his heart almost ceased to beat as he realized her danger: but it was over very soon. She held on bravely; and by dint of courage, perseverance, and the blessing she had silently implored, she succeeded in saving little Effie, and helping the exhausted general, too, to reach the land. The child was nearly senseless, but soon revived, and was able to walk home with her hand in that of her preserver.

Their arrival gave unbounded joy, not only to the mother, but others in the little community, whom the story of the children, of the loss of the pet of the flock, had withdrawn from their labors, and whom they met rushing, too late, to the rescue.

They received the child with tears and kisses, as one risen from the dead; and their gratitude to her rescuers was unbounded.

The general seemed so silent and depressed on his way home, that Catharine suspected some ill news from the army weighed upon his spirits, as well as the natural seriousness caused by so recent an escape from death, to say nothing of his anxiety regarding his relations with her.

This unexpected rencounter, however, subtracted something from the embarrassment she would otherwise have felt at meeting him. His self-sacrificing conduct regarding the child really raised him higher in her esteem than he had ever been before. If he had known she was a witness of the act, she might have believed he did it to win her admiration; but she knew he could

not have seen her, with so many intervening obstacles.
And, if the child had been a perfect and healthy one,
she might have suspected the self-interest of the master.
As it was, nothing but an impulse of humanity could
have tempted him to risk his life for one who might
always be an expense and a burden.

At tea she met him again as usual, and he talked a
little of the fine condition of Gen. Lee's army, and of
the disappearance of the favorite slave who accompanied
him, who, upon his favorite charger, had undoubtedly
escaped to the Union lines. He had supposed him perfectly contented, trusty, and more strongly attached to
him than any other slave upon the plantation.

The general said he was very tired, and far from well.
He ate scarcely any thing; did not once allude to the
subject that probably occupied the minds of both, and
retired early.

Towards morning Catharine was aroused by an unusual noise and bustle in the house, and, upon inquiry
in the morning, was told that the general was ill. They
had sent to Richmond for a doctor, and Aunt Phillis
was afraid he was going to have a fever. She could not
help reproaching herself for the feeling of relief — reprieve — this reply gave to her. She breakfasted alone ;
and, as soon as it was over, she was informed that the
general was very anxious to see her. Her heart beat like
a trip-hammer, as she followed Aunt Phillis, who was
the old family nurse, into his chamber. But her fear
turned to pity when she saw what a change one night
had made in his appearance. He was propped up in
bed, evidently in great pain ; breathing with difficulty,
and showing every symptom of pleurisy or lung-fever.
She went up to him ; and he took her hand in his hot,

burning ones, as he said in a labored tone, " You see, dear Catharine, that I am very ill ; do you not ? I have always been a healthy man, and never in all my life suffered so much from pain as during the past night. I have been longing to see you for hours."

" I am very sorry," she replied. " I fear your impromptu bath had something to do with it."

" It was not wholly that. I had been excited by the loss of my favorite man and horse, as well as by other causes which I cannot explain to you now ; and I was quite unwell before I left the camp. The weather was very warm ; and I was hot, dusty, and perspiring freely when I came upon that scene we have such cause to remember. This is the result of all these causes combined."

" You performed a noble, self-sacrificing deed; for which I hope you will not suffer seriously, general."

" You risked your life as well as I mine ; and I had more interest at stake than you, Catharine ; but we will not talk of that now. This throbbing brain, oppression of the breast, and difficulty of breathing, makes it very hard for me to converse at all."

" Pray do not do it then. I will retire."

" No, no ! It is growing worse every hour. I must talk while I can. I have sent for Dr. Huntley, and for Mrs. Hunter, if she has arrived in town ; but at the best they cannot get here for hours. In the mean time, I want to make my peace with you, dear Catharine. I feel now as if I had wronged you deeply, and indirectly been the cause of much suffering to you. Oh ! can you, in your unbounded compassion, forgive me ? "

" Yes," she faltered, affected to tears by his evident distress and penitence.

"Catharine, I do not ask this with a view of enfor-
cing my claims upon you hereafter: they were un-
blessed, because unjustly obtained; and I yield them all
up, here and now, upon the altar of truth and right.
Hereafter, if I live, I will tell you why; but oh, I cannot do it now! If I die, you will find, that in the
thought of death you were not forgotten. You are now
free to go where you please, — to the Union lines if you
desire it; yet, for all that, I still love you as my life.
In parting from you, I resign every hope of earthly happiness, if not life itself. And just now I need you so
much, — oh! so very much; though I know I ought not to
ask you to stay. Yet I feel as if my punishment would
be greater than I can bear if you leave me; " and the
look of intense agony that passed over his face gave the
most convincing testimony to the depth of his feelings,
and strongly appealed to her kind and generous heart.

"What is it you wish?" she faltered in answer to
that mute appeal.

"Dear Catharine, I feel that I am alone in the world,
and in great danger. My ungrateful children are far
away from me in spirit and in fact. It is very doubtful
whether Mrs. Hunter has returned, or can leave Walter to come to me if she has. Slavery, upon which
I leaned, and of which, in my supreme ignorance, I
boasted, like a reed has broken, and pierced my hand.
Almost every slave upon this plantation, both male and
female, whom I considered intelligent and worthy of
trust, has left me since the occupation of the country by
the Union army. My staff have all gone to their homes
on a furlough. My overseer is a jack-at-a-pinch, a
blundering blockhead. Old Phillis is kind in her way,
but could not read a prescription, or hardly count the

30

hours. So you see there is not one among them all fit to nurse a sick donkey, to say nothing of a man."

There was a long silence. Catharine saw what he wanted: but she could not speak with such a fierce struggle between duty and inclination going on in her heart. She wanted to go and find, or at least hear from, Theodore. She longed inexpressibly to go home; yet she had promised before God to love, honor, and obey this man; to care for him in sickness and in health, through life, till death. And, though from pity or some other reason he had given her leave to forsake him in his greatest need, was not her duty before God as plain as the open day?"

"Ay," whispered conscience: "your path is plain enough now. Why do you hesitate?"

And when at last Gen. Atherton, eagerly scanning her changing countenance, said in a tremulous tone, "Catharine, you were ever kind and pitiful; you nursed poor Major Hunter and little Walter; you took care of the sick and dying soldiers: is it too much for me to ask of you to stay?" she said, without a moment's hesitation, "I *will* stay, Gen. Atherton, and by God's help do all I can for you."

How little we know, in these great and solemn crises of our lives, what weighty events hang upon the decisions of a moment! Those words decided Catharine's destiny.

"Oh, how can I ever be grateful enough for that decision!" he said in a tone of deep emotion. "If I live or die, you shall not repent of it. Yet, dear Catharine, separate yourself, if you can, from the thought of being bound to me by solemn ties; for you are so no longer. I have not the strength or courage now to tell you why. Every thing and everybody left upon this plantation is at your service; and I trust myself unreservedly to your care. The thought that you will stay with me takes a great burden from my mind, and will go far towards my recovery. But here you have been standing all this time. Please ring for Tull, and then go and rest yourself. I must spare you all I can, and myself too; for I am very weary: it is such an effort to talk so much."

Before leaving, Catharine recommended such treatment as she had seen practised in similar cases in the hospitals. The doctors, she said, were all fully occupied in caring for the thousands of sick and wounded in Richmond, and might not come for many hours; and in a case like this delay might be fatal.

So he gratefully submitted to any thing promising relief that she and Aunt Phillis thought best to administer or apply. And well was it for him that he did so, as no doctor could be procured until the afternoon of the following day, and Mrs. Hunter had not returned to Richmond.

When one did arrive at last, Catharine was rejoiced to find that it was Dr. Huntley, with whom she was well acquainted. He approved of every thing they had been doing, and said, that, but for their timely antiphlogistic treatment, the patient would have been a great deal worse; as it was, he said, he would probably have a pretty severe course of pleurisy and fever.

The doctor was obliged to go back that night to Richmond; but he staid to tea: so Catharine had a chance to hear a great deal about how matters and things were progressing in the Confederate capital.

He said Mrs. Hunter had been delayed on her way from Raleigh to Richmond by the illness of some of her family, and could not be expected at Atherton at present. The doctor had known something of Catharine's previous history; and she had to tell him more to account for her presence there, which he might or might not regard with suspicion.

"You can't think how sorry I am that Mrs. Hunter cannot be here," said Catharine, as the doctor was about to leave. "It is so unpleasant, so trying for me to be here in such circumstances, — the only white woman on this plantation, or indeed in this neighborhood. You know, my nursing old Major Hunter would be regarded by the world as a very different thing;" and the color flushed her cheek as she said it.

"Yes, I know," he returned. "But Gen. Atherton is dangerously ill. You owe him something for picking you up, bringing you home with him, and probably saving your life. There is no one else, he tells me, anywhere about here, who can be at all depended upon; so I see no way for you but to stay here, make the best of it, and save his life if you can. I know you are a skilful nurse, if your strength will only hold out; and Mrs. Hunter may be able to come soon."

"Oh, I hope so! But which of them is it who is sick?"

"I do not know; probably little Walter, who, I fear, may not live long. He was a very sensitive child; and, to say nothing of his wound, he has never got over the shock of his father's death. It was a sad affair every way: the whole family seem to be very unfortunate. Sad news awaits them now, too, as soon as they reach home."

"What is that?" she questioned with paling cheek, faltering tongue, and foreboding heart.

"Well, perhaps you had better not tell the general;

but a despatch was received by the government a day or two ago from the south-western army, announcing, among others, the death of Lloyd, Major Hunter's eldest son. He was killed in one of the late engagements with the Union army. He was a fine, noble-spirited young man; and I was sorry to hear — But how white you are, Miss Hale! You are fainting;" and he sprung forward, and supported her with his arm.

"No, no!" she gasped with white lips; "but I am deeply shocked! He was once my — friend, and — and — it will be terrible news to them — all."

"I am very, very sorry," continued the kind-hearted doctor, pressing a glass of water to her lips, and beginning, as he thought, to understand the case; remembering that she had been some time in the family. "This dreadful war makes shocking work in these proud old families, — shocking indeed! Are you better now, Miss Hale?"

"Yes," she faltered: "I shall be over it in a moment. I have been ill: I am still far from strong, — and it was the surprise — the suddenness — Pray don't let me detain you, doctor."

"But are you sure of yourself? Hadn't I better give you something? Your life and health are precious here just now."

"Oh, no! I am better. But, if Mrs. Hunter comes, tell her we need her here very, very much."

"Well, then, if I can do nothing for you, I must go. But pray take care of yourself if you can. I will be sure to tell Mrs. Hunter if she comes. Good-night."

He looked back lingeringly upon the pale but lovely face, and saw the hopeless, agonized expression that swept over it, which no effort at self-control could,

wholly conceal from him. Only a love thrown back
upon itself, only a heart almost breaking with its burden of repressed and stifled agony, could send such a
look as that upon a human countenance, he thought;
and all the way to Richmond he could not get it out of
his mind.

And it was a terrible blow to Catharine; for in spite
of legal bonds, or earnest endeavors to forget, she loved
Lloyd Hunter still. His sudden death snapped some
of the sweetest and tenderest chords of life, and made
the light of hope, dim enough before, go out in darkness. "Yet what was the life or death of Lloyd Hunter
to her?" whispered conscience in that hour of bitter
sorrow. "Was she not another man's wife? Was she
not bound by irrevocable ties to one who was suffering
at that very moment for the kind ministrations she had
promised before God to perform for him?"

In an agony of contending emotions she ran up to
her room, knelt down, and implored her heavenly Father
for help to conquer all wrong or unholy emotions, for grace
to support her through the stern trials that beset her
path on every side, for spiritual and temporal strength
to support and assist her in the performance of the solemn and responsible duties that were about to devolve
upon her; and that he would shape all the events of her
life in such a way as would be for his honor and glory,
her own best good, and that of all others around her.

Perhaps it was well for Catharine in that trying hour
that she had unavoidable duties to perform, that tasked
her thought and strength to the uttermost, to keep her
from dwelling too much upon a bereavement which no
inner sense of right and wrong could make her feel was
any thing else than the sundering of the deepest and

tenderest ties of earthly affection. But she was no
stranger to the spirit of self-sacrifice, that vicarious
"enthusiasm of humanity," that a late author says
"our Saviour came into the world to inaugurate." It
was, in fact, one of the strongest impulses of her true
and noble heart. One, too, that would forever prevent
her from giving up wholly to a sorrow that would have
crushed a gentler and more yielding soul to the earth.
So, with a pallid face, quivering lip, and sinking heart,
yet with tearless eyes, and a firm resolve to do the
duty God seemed to have assigned to her, she entered
upon her work. With her there was no looking back
regretfully from that time. Whether friend or enemy,
husband or not, the man's life, under God, depended
almost wholly upon her; and night and day she did her
duty nobly, watching over him with the most patient
and tender care, taking the whole charge of the medi-
cines, and administering them herself; resting only
when it was absolutely necessary in the adjoining
room, and ready at any moment to attend to a summons from the ignorant attendants, who, for a short
time, took her place. She found Tull and Aunt Phillis
able coadjutors; but they could not read: so the real
care came almost wholly upon herself. Little Effie, who
had recovered from the effects of her immersion, was
now her chosen attendant, and made herself extremely
useful by her peculiar tact in adapting herself to surrounding circumstances. She would sit by the patient's
bedside for hours of her own free choice, to fan him, and
keep off the flies, while Catharine, completely worn out,
was trying to rest; and she would watch the hands of
the clock with eager interest to see when they had got
to the time when she must call Catharine to give the

medicine. The poor thing was little and lame, ignorant
and humpbacked; but she was deeply grateful for the
life they had saved: and Catharine found in her a mine
of affection and trust that was well worth the working,
though she was black as midnight.

The general had a very severe illness; and for two or
three days his life was despaired of. But she made the
best of all the attending circumstances, and acquitted
herself in such a way that Dr. Huntley said she had
undoubtedly been the means of saving the patient's life.

The case had been all the more critical, from the fact
that no doctor could be obtained oftener than once in
two or three days; so she had to abide by written in-
structions, and the medical books she found in the general's library.

There were women enough in the country at that
time who would have felt it to be no crime to let an
enemy of the cause they espoused die for the want of
the care they might have extended; and some, too, who
would have helped his onward journey to the realms
of glory or of woe.

But Catharine had not so learned the Saviour's pre-
cept, "If thine enemy hunger, feed him; if he thirst,
give him drink: for in so doing thou shalt heap coals
of fire on his head." Some may think her very foolish;
but she herself felt that her mission was not one of
vengeance, but rather that of philanthropy and love to
the human race.

Her patient was better at last, — able to sit up, then
to walk about the room, and at last ride out on pleasant
days. He had been much more patient and forbearing
throughout his illness than she would have believed
possible; for brought up, as all slaveholders think they

are, to command, it was but natural to expect some displays of irritability and imperiousness. He was very much changed, she thought, from the haughty, domineering man she had thought him at first, to one of a much more meek and quiet spirit. Yet, as he grew better, a deep and settled gloom seemed to come over him, which no effort of hers could dissipate. At his desire, she read and sung and played to him, or tried to beguile the tediousness of convalescence by cheerful conversation; but ever and always with the result of deepening the gloom upon his countenance.

One day he was more restless and irritable than usual, and spoke rather sharply to little Effie before Catharine. Ashamed of it afterwards, he turned to her and said, —

"Catharine, you must be shocked by my ill-temper and ugliness. Let what will happen, I observe that you never display any yourself. Where do you get such admirable forbearance? and what is it that supports you through all the stern trials that have beset your path for months?"

Catharine looked up reverently, but did not reply.

"Ah! I see, — among the angels, to whom I have often thought you must be akin, if there are any angels."

"From One higher than the angels, I hope, — One who would guide and support you, too, if you would only ask it."

"No, Catharine: I have not faith enough in that far-off sphere, or any such omnipotent Being who inhabits it, as to wing any prayer I could make so that it would soar above the earth and what is earthly; while yours would reach the highest heaven, if there be any."

"If there be any? Can you doubt it, or that there is a God who rules in the affairs of the universe?"

said she eagerly, shocked by this admission of doubts she had often suspected, but never really knew he entertained before.

"I have doubted it for long years," said he gloomily; "believed in no other God than that of Nature, and that man was but another name for universal selfishness. And believing thus, and seeing it acted out daily during my whole past life, you don't know how your noble, self-sacrificing example has affected me since I have lain there trembling on the brink of the grave. It has almost convinced me that there is a spirit in man — or at least one woman — nobler, purer, and holier than any I had ever dreamed of; and that such a spirit must be connected with some power that is invisible to mortal eyes, intangible to human senses, and altogether incomprehensible to my human understanding."

"My example is nothing, general, only in that I strive to make it a Christian one. I am but an humble imitator of Him who came into the world to give the noblest example of self-sacrifice and love and forbearance to enemies; and who, to prove that love, at last laid down his life for their redemption. Of myself I am of small account in God's economy of the universe; yet even my poor example, in his hands, may serve as an illustration to you of the eternal principles of his love and good-will to man. But rest assured that it is his Spirit, and not what I have done, that has been striving powerfully with you during this distressing illness. I have seen it before to-day, and earnestly beg of you to attend to its warnings, and make your peace with him, before you are brought to some other crisis in your destiny that may have a fatal termination."

"Catharine, if I could have you for a guide and helper

always, there might be some hope of my attaining to a better faith than infidelity teaches. Without you, Nature will and must be to me the supreme power in the universe."

"Oh! there is, there must be, a great first cause for every thing. Your idea of nature is but another name for God, the Author, Ruler, and Supreme Disposer of every thing in the universe. In your heart, I believe you feel this to be true, though you may not like to confess it with your lips."

"I will confess that you are an earnest and eloquent preacher, and deserve a better and larger audience," he returned with a ghastly smile.

"It is of consequence to us sometimes to turn one from the error of his ways, that he may do the same by others. And I am earnest because I have felt it all, and believe it to be a solemn truth."

"But, Catharine, I have never felt; so I cannot believe these things."

"I am sure you will, and, in fact, are beginning to do so now; for 'I believe in the intimate presence of God in the soul of every man, though sin and worldliness may blind him to that sacred presence. His handwriting is on our innermost shrines of thought; his voice thrills through the deepest recesses of our being. None can shut out the thought that he sends; but unsought, unsuggested by the ordinary laws of association, — nay, often unwelcomed, — they remain, return, haunt the soul, knock at the heart's door, as they are doing at yours to-day, and often forsake it not until they are cherished and obeyed. Not we ourselves can hold so close communion with our own souls as God can and does.'"

"And you have felt all this?"

"If I know myself, I have."

"Then perhaps you could teach me the way to the truth and the light. I am sure no one else ever could. Preaching and Bible-reading, I am sure, never sounded so sweet to me from any other lips."

"That is because you never before felt the need of a better and more satisfying faith. Having been a healthy man, you never before stood upon the confines of two worlds, shrinking from that dark and dreadful plunge into the vast unknown beyond the grave, that only a Christian hope can gild and brighten·to the true believer, or make otherwise tolerable to human thought. The hope of meeting in a future life those from whom death has severed us in this is dear to almost every human heart;" and she dropped a tear to the memory of one, who, in spite of her multiplied cares and efforts to forget, was very often present to her thoughts.

"There is truth in what you say. We who have the courage to face the cannon's mouth tremble sometimes at the thought of death and its unsolved mysteries; though, in the heat of the bloodiest battle, it never seemed so near to me as it has within the past few weeks. The thought, too, of annihilation, of death without a future resurrection, sometimes brings to me a horror that no words can express;" and he bowed his head upon his hand, and seemed lost in troubled thought. Catharine pitied him from the bottom of her heart.

That he had many causes for disquiet of a temporal and earthly nature, she knew very well. But, above and beyond all this, she felt sure that conscience, startled by its late outlook into the eternal world, was torturing him with a conviction of those great truths of revelation, that he had hitherto denied or ignored. But for once she felt that she had said enough. It was better now to leave him with God and his own conscience. And, rising quietly, she was leaving the room, when he raised his head, with dry, bloodshot eyes, flushed cheek, and a look of earnest entreaty, as he said, —

"Catharine, don't go yet. There is something I must say to you; and the sooner it is said now the better;" and he took her hand, and drew her down beside him, a good deal agitated by the thought of what it was to be.

"Do you know," he continued, "that I am wickedly ungrateful for the life you have been the means of saving? That your staying here, and wearing your life out in nursing me back to health, was all a mistake, unless" —

"Why? Why, then, did you entreat me to stay?" she exclaimed almost indignantly.

"I scarcely know myself, unless it was to make myself in the end a thousand times more miserable. Promising what I had, and knowing what I did, I should have sent you off at once with blessings; and then, if I had died, it would have been the end of it. If I loved you then, what is it now — that you have saved my life, endeared yourself in a hundred ways, intwined yourself around every chord of my heart, and become all the world to me — but a wild worship? And now, when life and energy are coming back to me, every day, every hour, makes the thought of a separation still harder to bear."

"Why, then — then — the sooner I go, the better," she said, rising in a good deal of agitation.

"Pray sit down. We have been talking of heavenly things, now let us speak of the earthly. I want to ask you a few serious questions."

31

" Well, then " —

" Catharine, if I had never entangled you by those fatal bonds, if you really believed yourself free to choose, and not my wife, and I should ask you now to marry me, what would be your reply ? "

" I — I really do not know," she said, as the bright color flashed over her face, and the tears gathered in her eyes.

He turned and looked at her eagerly.

" O Catharine ! tell me truly," he exclaimed, " whether you really like me better than you did a year ago."

" Yes," she faltered : "I think I do."

" But, dear Catharine, do you — can you — love me well enough to be willing to spend your life with me ? " and his face grew pale, and his voice trembled, with the intensity of his emotions.

Had those words the power to rend the veil, and reveal the inner soul to the outer vision, or was she powerfully magnetized by the pleading tones and beseeching glances of this eloquent and talented man ? She could not tell. Yet she became conscious at that moment, for the first time, of the fact that she did care more for him now than any other living man, and that the thought of leaving him forever was a painful one. She realized, too, that there had been a great change in her feeling towards him, and that the thought of her friends, her duty to her country, and even Lloyd Hunter's cherished image, had faded into indistinctness in her heart.

Did ever a woman nurse a sick child through a dangerous illness, without in the end getting strongly attached to it ? — much more, watch over a man of strong powers of attraction, brought down to the feebleness of

an infant, looking up to her with patient trust day
after day, grateful for every trifling service, strong only
in the power of an undying affection, that the eyes, those
" windows of the soul," following her everywhere, reveal, even when no word is spoken ? Can she fervently
hope he will not die while under her care; pray that
he may be spared to repent of his misdeeds; watch
for hours the feeble, fluttering pulse, the glazing eye,
and fleeting breath, and thank God for the miraculous
restoration, — even when death for her own sake seemed
most desirable, — without some change in her sentiments regarding him ?

Could any disengaged female heart, in fact, of tender
sensibilities, go through with all this, as Catharine had
done, without acquiring a far deeper interest in her patient
than she had ever felt before, and without forgetting, in
part at least, all previous prepossessions, in her absorb-
ing interest in her charge ?

We think not, most decidedly. And such at least
had been her experience, though she did not realize it
till now. She had known indeed that her extreme
longing for home and friends had given place to the
pressure of care and anxiety that weighed upon her so
heavily; that Atherton grew more like home to her
every day; that the thought of returning to the North
did not give her the joy it had done a few weeks before;
and even the memory of Theodore's danger, and her
country's peril, and Lloyd's sudden death, were often
forgotten in the danger and suffering of one, who, in one
way and another, contrived to occupy most of her
thoughts. She believed he was her husband, it is true,
and perhaps that it was her duty to forget all other attachments, devote her life to him, and no longer try to

evade her destiny. So now, when he repeated the question in faltering tones, "Do you indeed love me well enough to spend your life with me?" she murmured with tremulous lips, "Perhaps I do."

"Thanks, thanks for that precious admission, my Catharine! But oh, you do not know what a terrible temptation you are placing in my path at this moment?"

"What is that?"

"I hardly dare tell you, through fear that you will retract those welcome words; yet I must be honest and truthful with you now, dear Catharine, if by it I lose you forever. *You are not my wife*, as both you and I have believed so long. The chaplain who united us at Manassas Junction was a scoundrel, silenced by his order, and therefore unqualified to perform the rite of marriage. I heard it all from Major Mulford while in camp; and that, more than aught else, was the cause of my illness. If it was the hand of Him you acknowledge as a Father that has kept us separated until now, I also may be brought to acknowledge it with gratitude, if, with you, it also bestow upon me at last what I have not deserved, — the priceless gift of your affection. You are not my wife, dear Catharine, by any human tie; but it remains with you to decide whether you will become so. My presence is imperatively demanded in Richmond. I think I shall be well enough to go there in a day or two; and then and there, if you will forgive the past, and reward my patience and constancy by the gift of your hand, I shall be everlastingly grateful."

The next morning, feeling better than usual, the general decided to make the journey to Richmond. He had made every arrangement for their departure, the carriage was ordered, and Catharine, with a trembling hand and faltering heart, dressed for the journey, was just descending the stairs, when a party of soldiery halted in front of the mansion.

One of them, an officer, singled off from the troops, and, dashing up to the door, inquired for Gen. Atherton. The general stepped to the door at once.

"Why, Atherton! how do you do? I heard you were sick; and I am sure your looks do not belie the story."

"Yes," said the general: "it has been the most serious illness I ever had in my life. I am better, however, and am going to Richmond to-day. But how goes it with the army, Mulford?"

"Well, my friend. But I have no time for particulars: I'm in an awful hurry, but thought I must stop a moment to correct a little mistake I made while you were in camp, that I thought might affect you seriously and personally. It is regarding the story about that chaplain you remember who married you to Miss Hale at Bull Run. It seems, after all, that I was misinformed. I have it now upon the most indisputable evidence of those high in position in the army, who had a personal knowledge of the affair. They say the man was unjustly accused, came off victorious from the slander of his enemies, and was never silenced by his order. So you see, your marriage is valid after all; and please give my best regards to your wife when you see her. Good-morning, general." With a polite bow and smile at the general's surprised and joyous countenance, Major, or rather Col. Mulford turned, and rode on after his troops.

Catharine meantime, through the open door, had

heard every word of this colloquy, and, overcome with emotion, sunk down upon the stairs, dizzy and as strengthless as a child.

For that very morning, after a fervent petition for help and guidance, she had come to the conclusion that it would be wrong for her now, whatever her present feelings towards him, to marry Gen. Atherton, and help him, as she indirectly must, to foster the rebellion. He had fully absolved her from her promise on Harry's account; and to marry him now would be treason to her country and her God. If she had really been married, as she supposed, why, then, it would have been her duty to abide by those solemn vows, that she considered the most sacred of all human obligations.

The conclusion was inevitable. She was already the wife of Edward Atherton; she realized now that her solemn promise to become so was witnessed by men and angels, and recorded on high: so she must abide by her own decisions.

The carriage rolled up to the door at that moment; and, turning to look after Catharine, the general saw her sitting there pale and agitated. He understood it at once; and going up to her, and taking her hand tenderly in his, he said, —

"You heard it all?"

"Yes;" and the color flashed over her cheek as she rose to her feet.

"Dear Catharine, it is our destiny. Henceforth we will be one in heart and life and fortune," he said in tones of deep emotion.

He led her down the stairs, bade "Good-by" to the faithful servants, and helped her into the carriage that was to convey them to Richmond.

As we are not writing a history of the rebellion other-wise than as it affects the lives and fortunes of the prin-cipal characters in our story, we leave it for abler pens than ours to describe the mortification and disappoint-ment of the North at the sad results of that peninsular campaign, and the triumphant joy of the South in view of the same unfortunate occurrences.

The South had, it is true, lost tens of thousands of men ; and the people were disappointed because they had not captured the whole Union army: but the leaders made the best and the most of their successes, and offered a solemn thanksgiving to God for their great victories.

But, in spite of all human calculations, these reverses of the Northern army were being overruled by an al-mighty arm at that very time to the overthrow of the slave power and downfall of the rebellion; for this great disaster was the first thing that opened the eyes of the nation to the folly of trying to coax back the re-bellious States by returning the poor fugitive slaves, and refusing at their hands that knowledge of the country and the enemy's plans that could alone insure success.

Fremont, Phelps, and others had already tried in vain to inaugurate opposite measures : they had been defeated in their humane plans by those higher in power, who had different views; and the nation had to pay the penalty.

The demand of that nation for a change of policy was now so plainly indicated that the government could not mistake its duty. The emancipation proclamation was the response to that momentous call. This, more than aught else, gave the death-blow to slavery; though in its dying agonies it made still more frantic struggles to pro-long its life and extend its power. This, and the large amount of ordnance and army stores the South had captured, gave a new impetus to the car of war, that, like a mighty Juggernaut, was rolling over the land; crushing out the lives of hundreds of thousands of noble men beneath its ponderous wheels; leaving a broad track, red with the blood of the best and the bravest, and drenching it at the North and South, East and West, with the tears of the widow and the orphan.

On hundreds of blood-stained fields, men fought and bled and died in opposing ranks for what each considered the cause of God, humanity, and the best good of their country; while the nations of the Old World and the New looked on in astonishment and wonder. The republic seemed trembling in the balance; and monarchies and free governments feared or rejoiced, as the scales seemed inclining one way or the other.

Monarchies hastily and rejoicingly proclaimed the republic a failure, as they had prophesied ever since it was established; and all who loved freedom throughout the world feared for our national life.

The North at that time seemed exhausted by her mighty, but thus far seemingly-fruitless efforts; and never did her night look darker than just after that unsuccessful peninsular campaign. But humiliation and defeat brought wiser councils, and perhaps a firmer reliance upon the God of battles: it also led to a more energetic prosecution of the war, and to future victories.

CHAPTER XX.

E must now pass on to some of the closing scenes in the rebellion.

Scores of bloody battles had been fought on land and sea, in which Victory sometimes perched upon one banner, and then the other: but, for all that, the anaconda policy of the government was all the time slowly tightening such giant folds around the twin monsters, Slavery and Secession, as must ere long result in their destruction; for the united voice of the nation now demanded, not only the death of Slavery, but also the release of her imprisoned thousands, who were suffering untold horrors in Southern prisons.

They were dying by thousands of hunger and thirst, cold and nakedness; shelterless beneath burning suns of summer and the frosts of winter, and exposed to every indignity and outrage that could kill them off without the sin of actual murder.

Yet it was just as much actual murder as if they had cut the throats of sixty thousand unarmed men, — a crime for which the Southern leaders will have to answer in the judgment.

Our government may have been blameworthy regarding the difficulty about the exchange of prisoners; but, if so, that did not justify the Confederacy in planning and executing this wholesale slaughter.

The nation had now learned that a continual changing of military leaders was not the wisest policy, even in a republican government; and, with a new-found faith in him who was now at the head of the armies of the Union, they concluded that it was best to march on, through reverses, to victory.

While events of the greatest military importance were transpiring all over the country, the armies of the James and the Potomac sat down before Petersburg and Richmond, bombarding the former, and harassing the rebels in every way, by cutting their railroads, and stopping their supplies in every direction. Being in an enemy's country, and subject to the greatest disadvantages, the Northern armies lost large numbers of men; while the rebels, suffering little for a while behind their fortifications, laughed to scorn the assaults of the invaders: yet, though their progress was slow, it was sure, and certain in the end to lead to victory.

It was in one of the assaults upon the rebel works at this time, that Theodore Hale, who had recovered from his wound, and was now a lieutenant-colonel in the Union army, exhibited the greatest heroism, and won, by his courage, bravery, and the skilful handling of his troops, the commendatory notice of the commanding general. It was, too, in this terrible battle, when the Union troops were being pressed back by overpowering numbers, that Theodore, all at once, found himself face to face and hand to hand with Col. Philip Atherton.

They knew each other at once, and, for a few moments, fought, sword in hand, with equal skill and bravery. Theodore, however, devoutly wished his foe was some one else than his old schoolmate and rival; while Philip, with the old rivalries in love and scholarship and his humiliating capture at Tremont House all rushing back to his memory, was rejoicing in the prospect of a bloody revenge.

All at once Theodore saw that his men were retreating, and the rebels surrounding him. He turned, quick as thought, and tried to cut his way back to his troops, but found it impossible: he was hemmed in on every side. He saw at once that there were but two alternatives, — surrender or death. He chose the former, for life was still dear to him; and, turning back towards Philip, who was evidently in command, he, with a heavy heart, lowered the point of his sword in token of surrender.

But Philip's blood was all aflame: his eyes were blazing. Nothing at that moment could appease his vengeance for all the disappointments of his own life and the humiliation of his country but the blood of him whom he had once considered his rival. Deliberately drawing his pistol, he aimed at Theodore's heart, and fired.

But God's care was over Theodore. The ball cut his clothing, and grazed the skin, but passed between his arm and his heart.

The hot, angry blood swept over Theodore's face at the thought of such murderous treatment. His keen eye swept the field with eagle gaze. It saw a slight gap in the rebel lines. Raising his sword once more, he gave the dastardly Philip a sweeping blow: then, dashing his spurs into his horse's sides, he swept through the gap like a whirlwind. Before the rebels had recovered from their astonishment at his audacity, he had joined his troop, halted, and turned them back to their duty, and was the means of changing the fortunes of the day.

But many brave men had fallen, and especially officers whose places were to be filled; and for this, as well as many another brave deed, Theodore was afterwards created a brigadier-general.

Philip, however, was not slain by Theodore's sweeping blow, though it gave him a severe cut across the cheek; but, just as he was turning to follow his flying troop, he received a still more serious wound from a Minie-ball, in the knee. Agonized with pain and mad with passion, he still tried vainly to rally his panic-stricken troops. When he found he could not do so, he turned, and was glad to seek safety in flight. His wounds were considered very serious; and as soon as possible he was sent back to Richmond.

The surgeons tried to save his limb, but, after a few days, found that it was impossible. His horror may be imagined when told that amputation alone could save his life. He could not die. Life was every thing to Philip Atherton; so he submitted to the dreadful operation. Yet it was a terrible thing for one who had been so proud of his strength, and his manly beauty of face and form, to be thus mutilated by those he hated; and no expletives were too horrible for him to launch against Theodore and the universal Yankee nation. But what availed all his rebellion against the inevitable? Philip Atherton was doomed.

From the memorable night of Gen. Atherton's visit to Catharine in the Libby Prison, and knowledge of his son's abduction to get her out of his way, he and Philip had mutually avoided each other.

He wrote to him at that time, charging him with his villany, and threatening him with disinheritance, if, in the future, he in any way molested her who was now his honored wife.

Over that letter Philip gnashed his teeth in impotent rage; yet he dared not accuse his father of the crime, the treason, by which he had won her; and that was the last of their correspondence. He hated his father then as much as he had ever loved him; and he could not respect him either, because he had unfairly won the only woman he had ever really loved. They seldom met, and never spoke to each other through those terrible years of war and blood. The alienation was indeed complete.

Generous, public-spirited, and devoted to the cause of the rebellion, Gen. Atherton had offered his elegantly-furnished mansion in Richmond for the use of the government; and at that time it was occupied as a hospital for officers of distinction, who were sick or wounded.

And it was here that Philip was brought after the battle, — to the home of his youth, the house where he was born, and where the sister, who still loved him, had preceded him, and taken up her abode.

A few days after his arrival, strangely enough, Gen. Atherton, too, came from the army near Petersburg on a hurried visit to Richmond. He came to consult with the authorities, and find for them a paper of great value, that was stored in a cabinet in a locked apartment of this mansion, of which he alone had the key.

He knew nothing of the fate that had befallen Philip, supposing him to be still with his division, when he entered the mansion, and went up to his room. And it was only by accident, as he stood upon the platform, about

32

to descend the stairs, that he heard the agonized tones of his voice. Thoroughly aroused and startled by those well, and, even now, lovingly remembered tones, he stepped quickly to the door of the room from whence they proceeded, opened it, and looked in. But oh, what a sight met the wretched father's gaze! Upon the bed in the middle of the room, propped up by pillows, and surrounded by surgeons, chaplain, and attendants, lay all that was left of his once proud, handsome, and talented son, — the pride and hope of long years of his early life.

He was as pale as marble; while the black patch on his left cheek made his sunken features look all the more ghastly and horrible. His great black eyes wore a terribly brilliant yet frightened expression, and were roving restlessly about the room, eagerly scanning every face, as if seeking for some help or hope, where none was to be found; while great drops of agony, the damp of death, bedewed his pallid brow. And these were the words that poured in a wild torrent from his lips, as the general stood appalled upon the threshold.

"Chaplain, you are deceiving me! I am not dying! I will not die yet! I shall live to whip Theodore Hale, and those infernal Yankees who shot me. Samson slew his enemies with the jaw-bone of an ass; and I swear I will mine with a wooden leg. I will not be cheated of my revenge: it is all I have to live for. If they take the city, we'll murder every slave we can lay our hands on! — yes, every devil of 'em, and then burn it over their heads. You needn't stare at me so, all of you! I'm not going to die yet, chaplain!"

"But you must die, my dear young friend," said the chaplain tearfully. "You are, in fact, dying now. Oh! let me beseech of you to cast away earthly thoughts,

and endeavor to make your peace with Him who is plen-
teous in mercy, and ready to forgive all who come to
him in sincerity and truth. Oh! come to that atoning
Saviour" —

"Away with such fictions!" exclaimed Philip impatiently. "If I am dying, as you say, and there is such
a God, it is too late for me to cringe and fawn for his
favor. If there is a hell, I shall go to it. But I had
rather 'reign in hell than serve in heaven,' if it's full of
Yankees. Don't sob so, Nell, — dear Nell!" and he
turned to a female form that was bending over him,
with the face buried in the pillows, and whom the general had not before observed. "Alas!" he continued,
"both of us ruined, scarred, mutilated, deceived, betrayed!
What have we to live for but each other? Yes, dear
Nell, you shall live with me. We have no one else to
love: we will love each other. And he who has cast
us off for a fair young bride" —

At this moment his roving eyes fell upon his father,
who was standing in the doorway; and, starting up with
the wild, nervous energy of the dying, he reached out
his hand, and, pointing at him with his long, bony finger,
he continued, —

"Yes: you who have cast us off, and threatened disinheritance, may gloat over your hoarded treasures, and
cherish the bride you have wrested from the arms of
your only son, — the bride who must hate and despise
you for the treason by which you won her. If you want
to see your work, the result of your false training, here
it is in these poor mutilated bodies and ruined souls,"
and he pointed to Nell and himself. "You instilled the
pride that made us scorn to wed what we were doomed
to love, and then falsified all your teachings by wedding

the poor governess yourself. You planted the ambition for titles and honors, that led poor Nell to sacrifice herself to a false shadow of titled greatness, that has led her on to ruin and shame. You helped to plan and foster the spirit of rebellion in my heart, and those of all others around you, that has plunged the country into a bloody war, and will lead us only to ruin, shame, and death! You — you " — He tried to proceed, but fell back fainting, and completely exhausted by the intensity of his emotions; while a spasm of terrible agony swept over his pallid face.

Stimulants were applied, and he again revived; but the spell that bound the wretched father was broken. He stepped forward to the bedside, motioned the attendants away, and, bending over his dying son, exclaimed in a broken, agonized tone, —

"O Philip, Philip! If I have done all this, it was ignorantly, blindly, — at least that part that relates to you. I knew not that you loved her until it was too late to change her destiny. I never dreamed of training you falsely, or of leading you or my country to crime and ruin! Oh! can you not forgive the father who has loved you always, and whose heart has been wrung by this unhappy alienation? "

Philip looked up eagerly in his father's convulsed countenance, and his expression softened. They had loved each other truly once: and, as he looked upon him now, the old tide of affection rushed back to his heart; and the hardness and bitterness he had treasured so long vanished.

"Yes, father: I do forgive!" he murmured, as he feebly put up his arms, and drew his father's face down to his, and kissed it; "and oh! you must forgive me now, as

Catharine did, for all I made her suffer. I loved her always, but was too proud to marry her if I could: so it is just to me; but oh! not to her, — not to Lloyd, who was worthy of her, and whom Nell and I both deceived and wronged. We are both sorry, but cannot help it now, or the retributions it has brought upon us both. And, O father! you must forgive poor heart-broken Nell, who, through terrible scenes of suffering, has come back to us, bereft of beauty, health, wealth, — every thing but life, which must be a burden."

Gen. Atherton raised his head, and turned with streaming eyes towards her, in whose tear-stained, fire-marked, haggard face, he could hardly recognize the lineaments of his once beautiful and idolized daughter. For a minute he gazed upon her in astonishment: then, becoming convinced that it was indeed his child, he opened his arms, and she threw herself sobbing upon his bosom, beseeching in tones of anguish for his forgiveness. He could not refuse it then and there; but his proud heart was wrung with the deepest grief at the sight and thought of the ruin that had blighted these once brilliant and promising blossoms of his household tree. And he could not help looking back with the keenest regret to the sceptical and thoroughly-worldly training and example that had helped to make them what they were, and led them on to ruin and death. But Gen. Atherton's views had changed from what they once were. He believed now in an eternity of joy and woe. He saw that Philip was dying; and, bending over him with tear-dimmed eyes, he told him so, and besought him to prepare for that last great change, that was evidently very near. The terrified look came back at once to Philip's eyes. He asked for the chaplain, who was recalled, and at once

32*

offered prayers for the dying, and tried to lead his erring soul, through penitence and faith in a Redeemer, up to the Father in heaven.

But poor Philip had lived a sceptical, godless life; and, trembling upon the brink of eternity, oh, how vainly he longed for that bridge of faith that spans two worlds to the Christian believer! With his dying breath he besought Nell and his father, and all around him, to seek for that better way, it was too late for him to find, before they came to the dark river of death. These were his last distinct words. From that time he sank into a stupor; but, before the light of another morning, his soul had passed over the dark river to fathom the mysteries of eternity. We will not dwell upon the deep grief of the bereaved father and sister, or the pageantry of the grand military funeral; but only say, that, after it was over, Nell had a confidential interview with her father, and, by his advice and consent, retired to Atherton Plantation; for she could not bear to see Catharine or Mrs. Hunter, or face the people of Richmond, who had seen her only in the bloom of her beauty. For just that reason, too, none of Philip's friends had been notified of his dangerous condition; and she did not appear at the funeral.

Poor Nell had indeed met with a dreadful retribution for all her pride and folly and sin. For a time she had queened it right royally in New-Orleans society. She dressed splendidly: they lived luxuriously, spent money lavishly; and both she and Laroi rode upon the topmost wave of popular favor. She had given him her money; and after the city was captured by the Union army, and it was nearly spent, he pretended that he had been robbed by the Union troops. Being among those who insulted the Union soldiers, they were obliged to leave the city to avoid arrest and imprisonment. They went to Vicksburg, and from thence to Atlanta, where, for two years, they lived a wretched, quarrelsome life, supported mostly by his success as a gambler. On the eve of arrest for past crime, and when poor Nell was near confinement, he deserted her, as he had long intended to do, taking with him Jett, her pretty quadroon waiting-maid, with the best of her wardrobe and jewelry.

The shock of his desertion, and knowledge of his villany, nearly killed her. Just as soon as she could walk, however, after the birth of her child, she was turned into the street by a cruel landlord, to whom they were deeply indebted for board and lodgings. And it was there, sitting on the curbstone, weeping over her beautiful babe, that Lloyd Hunter found, succored, and sent her on her way to Richmond.

She stopped in Columbia, where she had relations, but found a cold welcome from those who had met with great reverses, as well as herself, and who had also been shamed by her past conduct.

When the city was captured by the Union army, and the rebels set it on fire, by burning the cotton in the streets, to prevent its falling into Union hands, she, like hundreds of others, rushed out of a burning house, with her babe in her arms, and fled before the advancing conflagration. Her clothes caught fire from the flaming brands and tufts of burning cotton that were whirling through the air. Her babe was smothered; and her own life would have been sacrificed, but for the timely help of James Hooker and Harry Hale, friends and admirers of her youthful days, and then officers in the Union army.

As it was, she escaped only with such terrible scars, that few would now recognize in her the belle and beauty of other days, whose machinations had been so · fatal to the peace of Catharine Hale and Lloyd Hunter.

It came out afterwards that Laroi was a bigamist, a murderer, and a villain of the deepest dye, who had no rightful claim to either title or estate.

He was a West Indian by birth, of a French father and slave mother, and, having murdered his uncle for the sake of his gold, had been obliged to fly from his country. But, after he left poor Nell, he was captured, carried home, condemned, and executed. And for a villain like that the proud and beautiful Nell had sacrificed friends, home, beauty, wealth, and every thing that was dear to her in life.

So, humbled in spirit, and with a heart full of bitter regrets, she went back to the home of her childhood to mourn and dream over Philip's early death and her own blighted earthly prospects, and prepare, if she would, for those that were more enduring and heavenly.

We must now return once more to Catharine, who, since her return to Richmond, had been presented to the world as the Bride of the Rebel General. He would have installed her at once in his elegant town mansion, with a troop of servants, but for the entreaties of Mrs. Hunter, who was delighted to welcome her as a sister now, and very unwilling to part with her.

Her brother would be gone most of the time, she said ; and they would all be so lonely in these troublous times, that it would be far better to form one house-. hold. As Catharine also favored this plan, it was so arranged, to the great joy of Mrs. Hunter and her whole family.

Catharine knew that the report of Lloyd's death had proved premature almost as soon as she arrived in Richmond. But regrets were idle. She was now another man's wife, and felt it to be a crime to cherish the old affection.

All her doubts and fears, and scruples of conscience, were now laid aside. She saw her duty clearly, and firmly resolved that she would be true to her marriage-vows, so far as they were consistent with her duty to God and her country. Nor was she wholly unhappy in their performance.

The general had said that no one could love as really and ardently as he did her, without in some sort compelling a return ; and she soon began to realize this as a truth. She already regarded him with respect, affection, and a high appreciation of his fine though misdi- rected talents ; and she learned at last to regard him with a fonder love. With her warm, generous, and affection-ate heart, her isolation from all other near friends, and his constant endeavor to please and win, it could not long be otherwise. She thought of Lloyd Hunter, sometimes, it is true, with pity and regret ; yet, for all that, she had a higher regard for Gen. Atherton than many women have for the husbands of their choice ; and she influenced him too, though not to the extent of giving up the cause of the rebellion, which, as one of its leaders, he felt himself bound by honor to support. It was a cause that her strong influence at an earlier day might have prevented him from espous-ing, and of the success of which he was now more than doubtful. He had, it is true, overcome some of the obstacles that barred his own promotion, and won some distinction in the army; yet he was still regarded with jealous eyes by those highest in power.

His efforts to obtain some amelioration for the unhappy condition of the poor, suffering prisoners, and the slaves at work upon the fortifications, were sneered at by some, who attributed them to the influence of his disloyal Northern bride. A few were still inclined to look upon her with suspicion, and, but for Mrs. Hunter, might have treated her with scorn; yet, for all that, Catharine did exert an influence that was the means of saving many human lives. Even those who felt inclined to look down upon the plebeian Yankee governess were obliged in the end to own, honor, and admire her self-denying philanthropy, and that true nobility of soul she exhibited upon every occasion.

Earlier in the war, some of these same ladies had exhibited the spirit of fiends in their treatment of dead and dying Union soldiers. Now, sobered by repeated bereavements, loss of wealth, and troubles of every kind, some of them were wonderfully subdued in spirit, and were ready to join Catharine and Mrs. Hunter in their noble work of charity and mercy.

Soon after her return to Richmond, she succeeded in establishing a correspondence with her friends, which, though under government supervision, was a great comfort to her. It assured her of Theodore's escape and recovery, and of their general welfare. She frequently accompanied the general in his campaigns; and furnished always with abundant means, as he had promised, and every possible help, she found unnumbered opportunities for performing good service, not only to the cause of humanity, but also that of liberty and loyalty.

On the battle-fields of Kentucky and Tennessee, where she was known only as the wife of a rebel general, she met no such jealousy and suspicion as she had sometimes encountered in Richmond, where she was better known, and was of course enabled to do a far greater amount of good. Her tact, courage, and great organizing and executive ability, had only to be seen to be appreciated by officers and surgeons, who gave her the highest award of praise. With the ability to fill the highest social positions as well as any Southern lady of them all, joined to that which few of them possessed, — the power and the will to make herself useful, — she was enabled to exert a controlling influence wherever she found herself in the Master's vineyard.

Able to bring order out of confusion; to oversee the cooking of large quantities of palatable food and delicacies for the sick and starving; to dress grievous wounds; and to comfort the sick, wounded, and dying in numberless ways, — she never found time hang heavy on her hands, or lack of useful employment. The very impartiality of her kindness to friends and foes had the effect of shaming those who were inclined to cruelty and intolerance, and won for her a respect and consideration she would not otherwise have acquired. It was the very thing that gave her the power to help and benefit the poor sick and wounded Union soldiers; and many a time she thanked God for the precious opportunities afforded her, that she never would have had but for her marriage with the "Rebel General." She came at last to feel as if it was for this that her hopes had been crossed, her plans disarranged, her will subdued, and her escape from the Confederacy cut off; and that her late trials and adventures had been ordained to fit her for just this work, that no one else could do as well. Perhaps in this she was right. But, whether she was or not, good influences surrounded her like a halo; and no one could be near her long without feeling their spirit and their power, or believing there was a divine principle that governed all her motives, influenced her actions, and formed the basis of her character.

And especially was this the case with her husband, who had previously despised women, from the fact of seeing the exhibitions of vanity, frivolity, and the spirit of coquetry and intrigue, that had characterized all with whom he had previously come into close communion. For this very reason he was all the more impressed by the strict moral and religious principle, the honesty, truthfulness, and generosity Catharine exhibited in all the relations of life. And, however lax and faulty himself, he could not help appreciating such purity of purpose and sterling integrity of character as it deserved. Yet her moral greatness made him feel his own selfish littleness and short-comings in the comparison, until the strongest desire of his heart was, that he might become worthy of so noble a wife. His scepticism, too, was constantly rebuked by her undoubting faith and perfect trust in God. And God's love to man, and the way of salvation through his Son, was made so plain to him at last by her eloquent lips, that he could not help believing what had all his life before been a scorned as well as a sealed book to him. He had been a nominal Christian before, had been baptized in infancy, and always read prayers in church : now he became truly penitent and believing, and seemed to be a Christian in reality.

CHAPTER XXI.

ND thus it was that Catharine had fulfilled her mission to the "Rebel General."

She had made two years of his life as happy as they could be, alienated from his children, and in the midst of such scenes of excitement and suffering. She had convinced him at heart of the sin and folly and madness of his disloyalty to the government, and the utter hopelessness of the cause of the rebellion, though too late for his own interest, or that of his suffering country. She had, by her noble example, led him to believe in the possibility of virtue, purity, and truth in the heart of woman. And above all, and what was of more consequence to him now than all the rest, she had led him from a state of doubt, darkness, and infidelity, up to light and faith and trust in God in this life, and a faint and trembling hope in his forgiveness and mercy in the world to come. She was the good angel, it may be, sent by the Father of mercies to reclaim and prepare a man of great capabilities but misdirected talents for the last great change that was awaiting him on earth, and a happier home beyond the grave. We may say that he was unworthy of so noble a wife, and that he deserved severe punishment

33   385

as one of the contrivers of the rebellion; but who but He who reads all hearts shall say who is worthy, and who is not, or set bounds to his goodness, mercy, and love?

Gen. Atherton, who at that time had been summoned to Virginia, and was stationed near Petersburg, had returned from the camp very much disheartened by the dubious prospects of the Confederacy, and with his mind overshadowed by the cloud of coming defeat, — which he saw in the distant horizon a great deal larger than a man's hand.

He had for some time been subject to serious bilious diseases; and, ill in body and troubled in mind, Philip's sudden and shocking death was all that was needed to prostrate him completely.

Dr. Huntley was sent for immediately after the funeral; but he could do him no good. He called in counsel; but they could do nothing to arrest the progress of the painful disease that soon sapped the foundations of life. He knew very soon that he was doomed, and held interviews with government officers, and did all he could to bring peace to the country, and prepare for that better land, where it is to be hoped all wars and fightings and rebellions are over.

Catharine, though ill herself, and wholly unfitted for such a scene, with Mrs. Hunter, watched over him with the tenderest solicitude, and, when they knew that he must die, were overwhelmed with the keenest anguish. Once she would have been perfectly resigned to such a dispensation. Now she could not bear the thought of a bereavement that was to leave her desolate at a time, when, more than ever before, she needed a consoler and comforter.

He realized her trouble and his own danger full well;

and between the paroxysms of pain, towards the last, tried to fortify and prepare her mind for what was to come. At intervals, when the pain was beyond human endurance, his mind wandered; and he would talk incoherently: then again it would come back to a keener perception of the realities that surrounded him.

"Catharine," he exclaimed in one of these lucid intervals, "do you indeed regret this bitter, bitter parting? Alas! how little reason have I given you to do so first and last! And oh, how much to rejoice in the freedom it will give you to contract other and happier ties!"

"God knows I want no such freedom," said Catharine with a bitter sob; "though it is true that I did before I learned to love you. Now I want you to live, — to be with me through this great trial, — to be my guide and protector through all my future life."

"O my darling! it breaks my heart to know that this cannot be; yet your love is the only strong tie that binds me to earth. I have proved the vanity of all other earthly things. Ambition, fame, wealth, parental love and pride, have each in turn lured, blinded, and then eluded my grasp, and pierced my heart with the keenest anguish, until I lived only in my love for you, and the unborn hope you were bringing to my longing heart. But I shall not live to see its fruition: I have sinned too deeply in the past to be permitted to do that. Alas for poor Philip and Nell, ruined by my towering pride, my fond parental indulgence, and godless example! Will they rise up to testify against me in the judgment? God grant their souls may not be lost through my means! And yet how I loved, how I worshipped them! How proud I was of their beauty and talents! I made them my idols; so they were cast down into the

dust. I have made you another; so I must leave you
It is only through God's mercy and a Saviour's love that
I can hope to escape future retribution for all that I have
done. And for this trembling hope, dear Catharine,
which I should not have had in this dread hour but for
you, I owe you more than words can express. Oh! forgive and be kind to poor penitent, suffering Nell, and
try and teach her, too, the way to heaven, to immortal
life, and true glory. Nothing else will support us in the
trying hour of death."

Nell, who had been sent for as soon as it was known
that her father was in danger, arrived, and came into the
room just in time to hear those words referring to herself. With her dormant fraternal and filial love pre-
ternaturally excited by Philip's death and her father's
danger, she rushed forward, threw her arms around her
dying father, and burst into a passion of tears.

He did not weep, but kissed and tenderly caressed
her, murmuring, "Poor, poor Nell! scarred, bereaved,
ruined, and deserted by a villain! And oh! it was partly
my work, — my own false training; for which I hope
God will forgive me, even as we have forgiven each
other. And will not you forgive her, too, my Catharine,
— you whom we have all so deeply wronged?" and he
looked up at her beseechingly.

Nell, too, looked up with streaming eyes into Catharine's agonized face; and she held out her arms, and received the trembling penitent in a loving embrace, —
her who for long years had been her bitterest enemy.

And thus, by the dying-bed of the husband and father,
that enmity was laid forever at rest.

From this time the general sunk into a perturbed
slumber that lasted several hours, during which Cath-

arine was persuaded to try to get a little rest. Towards
midnight he awoke, and called for her. She was recalled; and he knew her at once, though he seemed to
recognize no one else. He put up his feeble arms, drew
her down to him, and kissed her tenderly, as he said
in a low, broken tone, "I know: it is hard to meet
it — alone — surrounded by the burning — city — by
the roar of artillery, and the shrieks and groans of the
dying, — beset with pain and grief, — sorrow and danger! Yes: it is very hard and bitter! But courage,
darling: your mission is a noble one. God is with
you: the Saviour bears you in his arms; and there
is light and glory at the end. They despised you
once. You were found worthier than them all! And
through you, daughter of our foes, a noble name — two
noble names — will alone be transmitted to future generations! — a long and glorious line, — sons of God,
benefactors of the race, rulers of nations! A desolated land lies before you, overwhelmed with ignorance, darkness, and woe! You leave a shining
track behind you, full of light and knowledge and
happiness, with glory immortal at the end of life's
journey! Isn't that something worth living for, my
darling, — immortal life, glory everlasting? "

Then, turning away from her, with his wild eyes fixed
on vacancy, he continued in a louder and stronger tone,
"We shall scarcely find it, general! If we do, it is by
God's mercy only; for we fought only for ambition
and earthly glory. Jackson gets both! He thought
our cause just: we did not; so he gets both, — earthly
fame, immortal glory! Don't you remember how we
used to laugh at his awkwardness? Now how he towers
above us all! We get curses here, if we don't there;

and no wonder. For just look at them, — hundreds, thousands, tens of thousands, writhing in agony, bleeding, groaning, dying, in horrible tortures ! A whole land desolated ! Cities in flames ! The air filled with shrieks and groans of anguish. Heavens ! what a fearful spectacle !" and he looked off with wild, distended eyes into that space his disordered fancy peopled with the wretched victims of that fatal ambition and lust of power that had led to all the horrors of civil war.

For a while he lay still, gazing breathlessly upon the awful vision. Then he started up suddenly ; and it was as much as they could do to hold him, through the excitement of a bloody battle.

The advance of large bodies of the enemy, the charging of squadrons, the roar of artillery, the order of battle, the words of command to his officers, the shouts of onset, the wild excitement of a terrible conflict, — repulse, retreat, and rout, — were all enacted over again, and described in such vivid coloring as to excite the wonder and astonishment of all around him.

When this was over, he again lay still for a while : then roused up, and began an eager conference with some of the most distinguished rebel generals ; and questioned and replied to Johnson and Lee, Hill and Pickett, Longstreet and Early, in such a way as to reveal the late tenor of his own thoughts, as well as that of their prvate conferences.

" I tell you," he exclaimed at last, " that our cause is hopeless, our rebellion is played out ! Our chief magistrate has proved himself wholly insufficient for so lofty a station. By his miserable favoritism, ignorance of details, general mismanagement, and jealousy of nobler men than himself, he is causing the downfall

of what might have been one of the grandest empires
on the globe. If you or I had been at the head of
affairs, it would have been different: then victory would
have perched upon our banners. Now we shall have
the shame of defeat. You cannot see it! Where are
your eyes, general? Have you forgotten that Sherman is sweeping through the South like a tornado;
that Grant surrounds us with his brave veteran troops
on every side; that our network of railroads and
sources of supply are cut off in every direction; that
our army and the whole people are in rags, and many
of them starving; and, worse than all, that slavery,
for the right to secure and spread which we have so
madly contended, has proved the broken reed which has
pierced our hearts, and sapped the life of the Confederacy? Can it be that it is God's hand that has done
it, as a retribution for the wrongs we have inflicted
upon that accursed race?" he continued in a low, fearful voice.

He had previously spoken in a loud, vehement tone,
and with great rapidity of utterance; and now seemed
wholly exhausted by the terrible mental conflict.

He never rallied again, except to utter disconnected
words: yet his thoughts seemed to have gone back to
happier scenes; and Catharine's name, in low, thrilling
tones, was the last word that fell from his stiffening lips.
His end was so peaceful at last, that they scarcely
knew when the darkened spirit left its clay tenement,
and the long agony was over.

We will not dwell upon the grief of the survivors or
the pageantry of the funeral, which was too frequent a
thing in those days to make more than a ripple upon
the current of the common affairs of life.

For Richmond was at that time environed by contending armies; and events of greater importance were of daily occurrence. Communications were being cut off in every direction; and the danger was growing more imminent every day.

Though seeming to make little progress to Northern eyes at that time, the loyal leaders were striking fearful blows at the heart and life of the Confederacy; and the rebel leaders knew well enough by this time, that some providential interference alone could save them from utter defeat and ruin.

But Divine Providence did not see fit to interpose in the cause of the oppressor, but rather in that of the oppressed; so in the early April days fell the hardest blow of all, — the capture of the South-side Railroad. This, their last hope, line of communication, and source of supply, made retreat, capture, or starvation inevitable. This sealed the doom of Petersburg and Richmond, and made their capture inevitable.

Seeing that all was lost, for which they had so long contended, the rebel leaders ordered both cities evacuated, and attempted to escape, hoping to make a more successful stand in the South-west.

All this, with the fact that they were pursued, overtaken, and, after a brave, most heroic, but useless resistance, captured, and that the lives their leaders had forfeited by their treason were magnanimously spared by our government, is now a matter of history

But it is not a matter of history, so we will here record it for the benefit of future generations, that, in the midst of all the panic and turmoil consequent upon the evacuation of Richmond, Catharine, our poor sorrowing heroine, gave birth to the son of whom his father in his delirium predicted so noble a line. The shock of her husband's death but a few weeks before had been a severe blow to her at such a time; and this, superadded to other causes, had nearly cost her her life.

Scarcely was the first danger over, however, before it was known that the city was in flames. With a madness similar to that which possessed the rebel leaders in Columbia, the authorities here set fire to the city to prevent the tobacco and other stores from falling into the hands of the Union army.

When that loyal army did enter the city, they were received by the dark race whom their blood and toil had redeemed from chains and stripes and all the horrors of slavery, with the most enthusiastic demonstrations of joy. But their kind and considerate treatment of the whites who remained was regarded with wonder and astonishment. Their leaders had led them to expect the most shocking barbarities; and they looked for nothing better from the hated Yankees than murder, rapine, and plunder. The real thieves and murderers who did pursue their fiendish work, committing outrages upon those unable to escape their rapacity, were the stragglers from their own disorganized rebel army. As in Columbia, so now in Richmond, the victors were obliged to go to work at once to extinguish the flames the maddened rebel leaders had set in the homes of their own people; but for their almost superhuman exertions the whole city would have been reduced to ashes.

And while the billowy flames were roaring, and the walls crumbling, and the chimneys tottering, and the people shouting, screaming, and rushing wildly through the streets, poor Catharine lay faint, weak, and trembling with excitement, in her darkened chamber, half suffocated by the smoky air; though the house was at some distance from the real scene of the wide-spread conflagration.

Listening nervously, as she had been for hours, to the explosions of gunboats and magazines, set on fire by rebel authority; to the measured tramp of many feet, the shrill tones of numerous high-pitched voices, and the distant roar of the flames, — it was no wonder if she was nearly distracted, and at last begged Mrs. Hunter to go out and see what it all meant. To her astonishment, when she descended the stairs, Mrs. Hunter found that children, servants, even to Aunt Dinah, — everybody in the house in fact but little Effie, — had gone out to join in the general jubilee of terror as well as rejoicing. Alarmed at once for the safety of her children, she took the child up to stay with poor Catharine and the wee baby, and hurried down stairs, and out upon the street, to look in considerable alarm for her scattered family.

After wondering over and kissing the baby, which she now delightedly saw for the first time, Effie placed herself, at Catharine's request, at a front window to report the progress of affairs in the street.

She did this for some time without thinking much of the fire in the distance. All at once she was startled by a torrent of smoke that came drifting around the corner from the sheds and stables in the rear, which, unfortunately, were all connected with the mansion.

Child as she was, she suspected the truth, and, with a rare instinct, felt that a knowledge of it would alarm and harm her sick mistress, whom she almost worshipped.

So, rising, and saying she must go down a minute, she ran out, and through the upper hall to a back window.

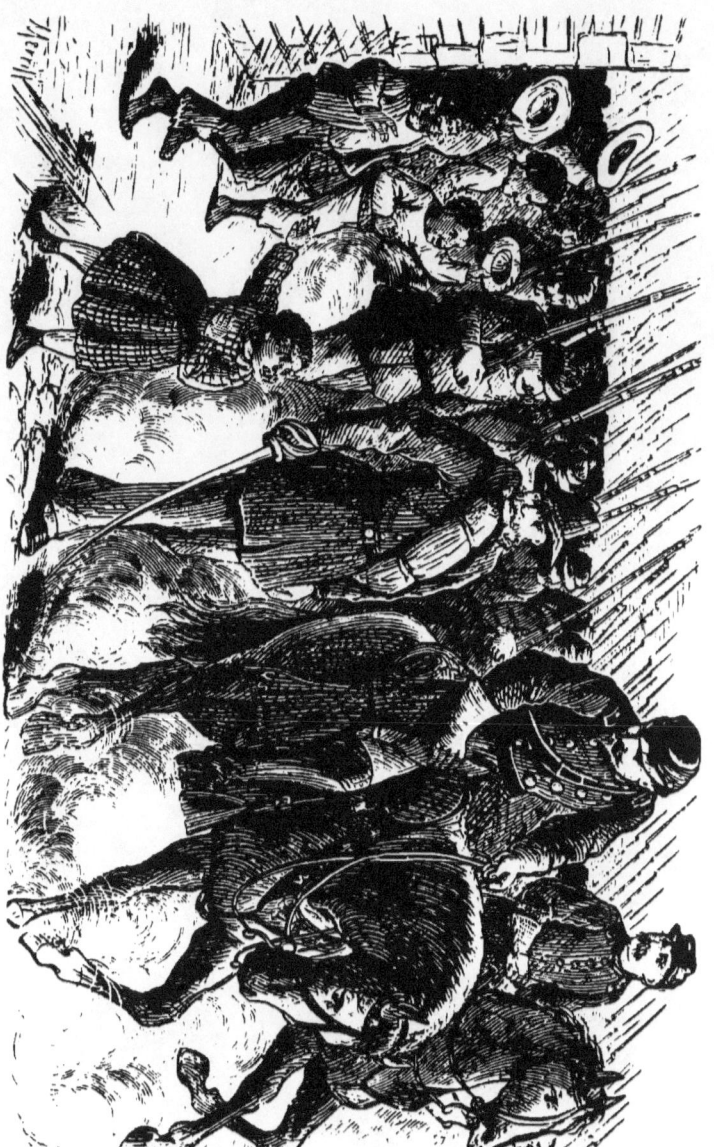

The child ran shouting at the top of her voice, "Oh, come! come! come 'quick: de shed all burn to blazes and de house go next," &c.

Page 395.

Sure enough, there were the flames just rising from
the roof of the shed, where they had caught from some
of the sparks or flaming brands that were beginning to
fill the air in every direction. She knew that Mrs.
Hunter had locked or bolted all the doors; but, frightened half out of her senses, she ran down the stairs,
unfastened one of the low front windows, opened it,
jumped out, and ran into the street. A party of Union
soldiery, it so happened, had just halted from some cause
in front of the mansion; and to these the child ran,
shouting at the top of her voice, —

"Oh, come! come quick! de shed all burn to blazes;
an' de house go next, wid de dear sick missis an' de leetle
mite of a baby. Oh, come, quick, quick!"

And Catharine, wondering at the child's conduct, and
listening intently, heard that startling cry. The Union
officers meantime, ever ready to attend to the calls of
humanity, instantly dismounted, threw their bridles to
their attendants, and entered the yard, where they
found there was really serious cause for alarm; and also
that it was a matter of great importance to arrest the
progress of the conflagration in this new locality, which
was one of the finest portions of the city.

So the most suitable men were summoned, and went
to work with a will; and though for some little time it
seemed impossible to save the dwelling, it was done at
last by tearing down the connecting buildings. When
the danger seemed most imminent, the little humpbacked
girl, who was watching them, ran to him who seemed to
be the leader of the party, exclaiming with uplifted
hands and streaming eyes, —

"Oh! oh! it'll all burn up, with poor sick missus, an'
de leetle baby, an' de pretty dresses, an' ebery ting."

"Are they here, — in this house?" he asked, with his interest strongly excited.

"Oh, yes! up de stair. I'll show massa de way."

So she took him around through the open window, parlor, and hall, and up the front staircase. On the landing, at the top of the stairs, the young officer was met by an apparition that startled and surprised him. It was Catharine in her white night-dress, with her babe in her arms, who, supposing herself alone in the burning dwelling, had forgotten her weakness in her extreme terror, and, crawling from the bed, was feebly trying to make her escape. She stopped short at the sight of a man in loyal uniform ascending the stairs, looked eagerly in his face for a moment, murmured Theodore's name, and fell forward fainting in his arms. The precious babe dropped from her nerveless grasp, but was caught by little watchful Effie before it struck the floor. Theodore himself came near losing his balance, and falling down the stairs, he was so shocked and overcome by this strange and unexpected meeting: but he recovered in a moment; and, following the child into Catharine's chamber, he laid her upon the bed, where she soon regained her consciousness. The arrival of Mrs. Hunter just then was warmly welcomed. She had found Aunt Dinah and the children, and brought them home, only to find, that, but for the Union soldiers, they would have found no home to receive them. Catharine was soon restored, without in the end sustaining serious injury. The meeting with Theodore, and the news he brought from home, was like a cordial to her fainting spirit.

Mrs. Hunter was obliged to confess her past injustice to those who treated the people of Richmond so forbearingly. When the great and good President visited it a few days afterwards, she was glad to welcome him whom she had once bitterly denounced, and to mourn for him, too, with a whole restored nation, when, a few days later still, he was cruelly murdered. This seemed a strange consummation of the horrors of a bloody civil war, to come as it did in the hour of victory, like a black cloud that overshadows the brightness of a glorious day.

He alone who knows the end from the beginning could tell why this great affliction was sent upon our distracted country then, — perhaps that the glorious martyr's death should be the means of healing some of its sectional and party bitterness. The rebellion was now virtually over; and, after a few more struggles, peace was restored to our bereaved and desolated country.

34

CHAPTER XXII.

UST as soon as Catharine was able to travel, and Theodore could obtain a furlough, they made the journey home, where they were welcomed by the dear mother and sister with open arms and warm, loving hearts, that found abundant room for the beautiful little black-eyed stranger, who bore the name of Edward Atherton.

Harry, pale, emaciated, and just recovering from sickness and a severe wound, had arrived a few days before them; so the joy of the meeting was as complete as it could be, after all their strange and terrible experiences.

Yet they had all grown much more than four years older in feeling since they parted; and the dear, patient mother's head had visibly whitened by her long and sometimes agonizing suspense regarding the children of her love. Dr. Morven, who was now a physician of large practice, beloved and respected by the whole community, had gone to live with Mrs. Hale; and little Jessie, as they used to call her, with her head, heart, and hands full of her husband, two beautiful children, and domestic matters generally, seemed perfectly happy and contented with her surroundings.

"You have not told me yet how you came by the

398

wound that occasions your lameness," said Catharine to
Harry a few days after their return. "It must be a
great affliction to an active young fellow like you."

"Yes: it is so;" and Harry's smiling face sobered in an
instant. "Yet I have so much reason to thank God
that it is no worse, that I scarcely mind it most of the
time. You see, after I escaped from Manassas, where I
met with you, I was sent West and South, and finally,
with Sherman's loyal army, made that famous march to
the sea. First and last, I passed through a score of
battles and sieges unscathed, until we got to that miserable little village of Bentonville last March. There,
in a hotly-contested battle with Joe Johnston's army, I
was shot through, — just below the knee. Our regiment
just then met with a sharp repulse, and were obliged to
turn and retreat before the rebel squadrons. In their
hot haste, they could not stop to pick me up; so I was left
to the mercy of the enemy. After lying for hours in the
hot sunshine and night-dew, I was picked up and taken
to a rebel field-hospital; and there, but for Lloyd Hunter,
I should no doubt have lost, not only my limb, but my life."

"Lloyd Hunter!" echoed Catharine in surprise.

"Yes: Lloyd Hunter, who, though he recognized me
only as a suffering human being, kindly interposed to
save me from the barbarity of an ignorant and savage
rebel surgeon, who, in spite of my piteous pleading, was,
it seemed, almost in sport, about to apply the knife and
saw to my quivering limb. Though not a regular surgeon, Lloyd, it seemed, had attained to wondrous skill
and great reputation in the rebel army, — so much indeed
as to make his word a law; and his humanity and piety
were quite as proverbial as his skill. He decided, that
in my case amputation was unnecessary, dressed my

wound himself, and afterwards, when he found me out, treated me in the kindest manner. And for that I owe him unspeakable obligations, as I think do hundreds of other Union soldiers, who came within the sphere of his influence. His heart, I am sure, was not in the rebellion; and he worked day and night to ameliorate as far as possible the suffering caused by it."

"But how did you escape at last?" said Catharine, with a mental backward glance and her eyes filling with tears, as she remembered their last parting in Richmond, and the earnestness of her appeal to Lloyd to do this very work that had undoubtedly been the means of saving her brother's life. Was not that, too, one of the rewards of her self-sacrifice? How many streams of beneficence sometimes flow from one unselfish act, word, .or thought!

"I remained with the rebels until the surrender of Johnston's army," said Harry in reply to her question, "when, I assure you, I was very glad to be surrendered myself, and sent home."

Harry had always liked Lloyd Hunter, and knew well enough how Catharine had regarded him in the past; and he was not sorry to see that his name had still the power to awaken some of the old emotion in her heart; for not only Harry, but the whole family, in their active loyalty, had felt indignant at Catharine for marrying the "old Rebel General," as he called him, — supposing, of course, that she had done it from motives of ambition, and the desire for wealth and power.

She would not undeceive them in his lifetime for a good many reasons; but now, when she heard the feeling plainly expressed, she felt as if it were due to herself, once for all, to explain the facts to her own family. Yet for the honor of the name she bore, — her child's, — and the memory of him, who, for love of her, had committed such treason, they were not to reveal it to others. So, in saddened tones, and with many tender memories, she told them the story of her wedded life. And then indeed they were all deeply affected by the knowledge of the price she had paid for Harry's life, and all she had suffered on account of it, — and Harry more than all the rest, who begged her forgiveness for his harsh judgment.

And when they heard of all Gen. Atherton's after kindness, — his sincere penitence and deep sorrow for his part in bringing about the rebellion, his late efforts to bring peace to his distracted country, and of all his really noble qualities of head and heart, — they were ready to forgive him. And they felt, too, as Catharine did, as if God's hand were really guiding her through it all, that she might become a blessing to hundreds.

Her visit to the old home was eminently satisfactory to the whole family, who enjoyed every moment of that precious re-union; for each one had a separate history, that would have filled volumes, in all those bloody years, that must be rehearsed for the benefit of the others. And each heart became more endeared to the others by this close communion and mutual sympathy. But every thing in life must have an end; and so did this memorable visit: for it was necessary for Catharine to return to Richmond to settle up her husband's affairs, and look after the poor dependants upon his estates, who now, though free, in their ignorance and darkness, needed some one to instruct and guide them, until they had learned the art of taking care of themselves. So, taking Theodore with her to look after her affairs, Catharine bade her friends adieu, and set out for Richmond.

34*

They stopped a few days in Washington, where Theodore had business connected with the army; and while there they also visited Grace and Helen Tremont, who, since the death of their father in a rebel prison, had made that city their home. But they were now anxious to return to Richmond, and look after the relics of their once large fortune; so they accepted Catharine's invitation to join her party.

One evening, while they were in Washington, they went, for a diversion, to one of President Johnson's levees. For some time they wandered through the gorgeous rooms, considerably amused by watching the indiscriminate crowd of people who on such occasions throng the executive mansion, sunning themselves for a moment in the beams that ever like a halo surround the heads of those in power, — at least to some admiring eyes. They had shaken hands with the presidential party, and were on the retreat, — Theodore and Grace in the advance, and Catharine and Helen in the rear, — when all at once Catharine felt a hand firmly laid upon her shoulder.

She turned back angrily to see who had taken such an unwarrantable liberty, and was confronted by a face close up to her own, which, though it made her start, she did not at first recognize. But there was no mistaking the voice that exclaimed a moment later, —

"Why, how d'ye du, Miss Kate? I'm darned glad to see ye. Where in the world did ye come from, any way? Come, let me introduce ye to my wife;" and, with his long, yellow finger, he pointed admiringly to a prematurely-faded yet still fine-looking woman, elegantly dressed, and blazing with jewels, whose casual yet scornful glance at him at that moment plainly announced the degree of estimation in which she held him. Her extravagant style of dress, too, clearly indicated the reason why she, a deserted and disappointed belle, had married him, — for the sake of his ill-gotten millions.

But millions could not hide his innate vulgarity, or teach him the decencies of life, or the manners of respectable society. Catharine tried to rebuke, and get rid of him, by turning silently away, — as if she did not recognize him; but it was of no use.

"Ah, I see!" he continued with a wicked leer of those little malignant gray eyes she remembered so well, — "top-lofty as ever! I always liked it, though: it made you look so handsome and queenly. I always had a fancy for queens. It was jest the reason I married that gal yonder, — 'cause she looked so much like ye. But she's proud as Lucifer and ugly as sin," he whispered confidentially, as he kept close to Catharine's side as she moved along. "You see," he continued, "that I know all about ye still, Mistress Catharine. I know you've got rid of that darned old rebel general; and, if I was only a widower now — by golly, I'd be steppin' up tu ye!"

"Do you mean to insult me, sir?" exclaimed Catharine with a withering look of contempt. "I have no desire now or ever, Mr. Sweep, for your further acquaintance; and she swept by him like a queen indeed, caught Theodore's arm, and was soon out of the reach of his impudence and importunity.

Sweep had indeed gathered his millions; but he had also caught a Tartar, who despised him, would spend his money in careless extravagance, and harass and torment his whole future life.

Catharine re-opened the old Atherton mansion soon

after her return to Richmond; and Nell, who since her father's death had remained on the old plantation, was invited to make it her home once more. She seemed grateful for the invitation, accepted it at once; and all her old stiffness and acrimony were soon swept away by Catharine's kindness and forgiving love. They met, not as mother and daughter, however, but more like long-estranged sisters; united by the tie of that beautiful child, the first sight of whom brought back the bitter memory of her own to Nell's bereaved heart, as well as that of the lost father and brother it so strongly resembled.

That memory was indeed a blessed one to poor storm-tossed, life-wrecked Nell Atherton; and it bore blessed fruits in a fervent love for the child that had come to fill the places of the dead in more than one bereaved and mourning heart, and to bear the name of a proud race to future generations.

The change in Nell was indeed as wonderful as it was unlooked for. Her old proud, intriguing spirit had been bowed to the dust in shame and humiliation. And in her wretchedness, misery, and deep regret for all the sins of her past life, she had sought, and felt as if she had found, forgiveness through a Saviour's love, and obtained that glorious hope for the future, that can alone make the thought of a blasted and disappointed life endurable.

And not only had the deformities of the soul been healed, but also those of the countenance; from which the scars had mostly been erased by the healing hand of Time. So, with little of the old pride and arrogance left, she retained much of the old beauty, that ever and always commands attention and admiration.

Soon after their return to Richmond, Catharine and
Theodore had a call from Col. James Hooker, one of
their friends and near neighbors in early life: and
Nell, who happened to be present, proved her power by
renewing the passion with which she had inspired him
while at school at the North in youth's bright and
glorious morning.

She had fascinated, bewitched, and flirted with him
then, though considering him her inferior; but now,
when she herself felt as if he was her superior, he succeeded in inspiring her with a nobler and truer affection.

Catharine at first felt some anxiety regarding his
attentions, because he had helped to save her from the
fire in Columbia, and knew her past history.   Knowing
it, and a good many of her faults besides, she thought he
would be unwilling to marry her.   But she was mistaken.   He had loved her always, and was for that reason willing to overlook the past, and make her his wife.
There were Southern men too, old admirers of hers,
who would have been glad to retrieve their fallen fortunes by marrying her; but, in spite of her former
treasonable proclivities, she now preferred an energetic,
intelligent, Northern business-man to a dilapidated
Southern gentleman.   All who knew the man considered her fortunate indeed, and felt as if he were far too
good and worthy for the lady of his choice.

Theodore and Grace Tremont, who had also treasured
a fond regard for each other since their early school-
days, and who had met several times during the war,
were to be married at Christmas.   Mrs. Hunter, with
her old hospitable spirit, had insisted on making the
wedding: so now she contrived at the same time to

marry off two nieces instead of one; though the melancholy state of the country made a great display unadvisable.

So, when the time arrived, the double wedding came off privately; only the particular friends and relatives of the families being present. Uncle Nick, who was home once more, and Aunt Dinah, were particularly resplendent upon the great occasion; and Nick especially, who had loved little Grace always, and who, after saving Theodore's life, had become strongly attached to him, shed real tears of joy as he pronounced his blessing upon the union. Lloyd, too, was there, and met Catharine for the first time since their sad and hopeless parting. Both had dreaded yet perhaps desired this meeting; yet, knowing nothing of each other's present feelings, had felt some anxiety regarding the manner of their future intercourse.

There was some embarrassment at first; but, before the evening was over, they found themselves talking quietly together regarding the events of the war, and finally of some of their plans for the future.

He had, it seemed, since peace was declared, been trying to gather the people upon the old plantation at Hunter Hills, and his own near Richmond, to instruct them in their duties to God, each other, and their late masters; to establish schools among them, and teach them how to live so as to be self-dependent in this life, and prepared for that which was to come. His whole heart seemed to be in the work; which was one in which he had her entire sympathy, and one too, which, by Harry's help, she was already planning to put in operation upon Atherton Plantation.

The meeting between Nell and Lloyd was very em-

barrassing, as well it might be: but she was used to disagreeable *contretemps ;* and he was so glad, through all
his troubles, that she had not chosen to marry him, that
both soon recovered their equanimity.

Upon the whole, the wedding was a very pleasant
affair, and, as is often the case, the means of bringing
about another a few months later between Harry Hale and
Helen Tremont. As she and Grace had inherited considerable wealth, some of her Southern friends tried to
interfere to prevent, as they said, her sacrificing herself
to a poor limping Yankee lover. But neither their per-
suasions, Harry's poverty, nor the surgeon's fiat of "lame
for life" could in the least destroy the affection she had
conceived for him, or her faith in his inherent nobleness.
So in the early springtime she married him; and poor
Harry did not seem at all displeased about it. And
afterwards, when Theodore and Grace, and Mrs. Hale
and Jessie, had gone back to the North, she and Harry
settled down upon the old Tremont plantation.

Catharine had calculated so much upon having Harry
to manage her estate, that she was a good deal disappointed by this new arrangement, even though she
rejoiced in their happiness. Yet she found, after her
return to Atherton plantation, that she had some capacity for farming, as well as several other avocations.

The work was performed as well indeed as it could
be done by the wretched remainder of the people, who
once belonged to the estate, with all she was able to
gather from the surrounding country. They had, it is
true, run wild with their vague, unreal ideas of freedom;
and it took some time to initiate them into the true idea
of earning their living by paid labor. But she understood the case much better than they; was very patient

with their shortcomings, and very soon they began to see the wisdom of the plan, that so easily procured subsistence for their starving families. Nor was it long before they almost worshipped her who had led them so wisely, knowing it was for their own best good.

She established a school and sabbath school, in which grateful little Effie, whom she had taught to read, and a young lady of the neighborhood who had been left homeless and destitute by the war, proved valuable assistants. She also cultivated the acquaintance of her neighbors, and especially of the poor whites, who were very destitute, whom she assisted physically, mentally, and morally, to the extent of her power. So you see, the old idea of trying to do good had not left our heroine yet, nor will it probably to the end of her useful life.

So busy had she been, and so much had she found to do, that Catharine hardly realized that summer was over, until one fine September morning, when she received an unexpected call from Lloyd Hunter. When the slightly-embarrassed greetings were over, he said he had called to announce the fact that his mother, with her family, had returned from the Springs, where they had spent most of the summer, and Walter had grown better every day; and that they might be expected upon the morrow at Atherton Plantation.

"Well, I shall be delighted to see them all," said Catharine with a glad look; "and will not you also remain with us, and add to the pleasure of the visit?"

"I should be most happy to do so, but cannot spare the time. You know, that, like yourself, I am trying my hand at farming; and that, with a little unavoidable surgery, gives me plenty of occupation."

They talked of his plans a while, and then turned to other subjects, — the weather, the crops, the political aspects of the country, her school, her improvements, and at last her baby, who, just beginning to walk, at that moment, followed by Effie, came toddling into the room. He looked shyly at Lloyd at first, and ran to his mother; but, before a half-hour was over, he had sidled up to him, climbed upon his knee, and seemed very much inclined to make his acquaintance by laughing, crowing, and pulling his hair and whiskers.

"He is getting too rude. Pray put him down, Mr. Hunter: I never saw him so familiar with a stranger," said his mother, coloring with vexation at the child's conduct. "Here, Effie, take him out for a walk."

"He seems to have uncommon sense and penetration," said Lloyd, smiling, as he surrendered the child to his little nurse. "He has discovered that I am not a stranger, but a friend, — or at least ought to be. He seems willing to accept me as one; will not you?"

"Certainly. I hope we shall never be any thing else."

"But I hope for something else, dear Catharine, — a tie that is nearer and dearer. Is it in vain for me to think of it?" said he earnestly.

"You cannot really wish it, after all I have gone through," said Catharine in surprise.

"But I do wish for it, hope for it, pray for it. Oh! you do not know how I long for your presence, your help, your sympathy. I live on, it is true, and do the best I can. But life is cheerless, joyless, and incomplete without that sweet communion of soul you alone can bring to me, — you, who of all the women in the world I still love."

35

Catharine was deeply affected by this avowal, which touched a responsive chord in her soul; yet after a few moments' silence, during which she was trying to command her feelings, she said in a tremulous tone, —

"Lloyd, I owe it to your truth and love and constancy to own that you are still dear to me. Yet I have little faith, as a general thing, in the happiness of second marriages, and especially those of widows with children, and young men, who, like you, have wealth, talents, and every advantage that could win for them a choice of the youngest and fairest. The world, too, always sneers at such marriages, and talks of the artful, scheming widow, who has entrapped that fine young man by her intrigues."

"But, Catharine, though a widow, you are not a scheming one; and certainly you have never sought to entrap, but rather repelled me."

"They would believe it none the less."

"I care not what they believe, if you will only become my wife, dear Catharine, — the sharer of my destiny."

"It is not wholly the world's opinion that I care for," said Catharine with a troubled look. "I also care for your happiness, which I do not believe would be increased by such a union. The memory of our early love may be very sweet to us both: yet I have known other loves since then; so we are no longer equals. I have lived much faster than you: I am older than you in thought and feeling, physically and mentally. You are still young, having had none of my sad experiences; and, if you wish to marry, you can have a choice of youth, beauty, and fortune."

"I do not wish it if I could. I am four years your senior; so I am older than you in years, if not in experience. But, whether young or old, it is you alone I love, and no one else in this world can, or ever will, fill your place to me. I could wish indeed that you had never been another man's wife; but, knowing my own past delinquencies, I can never blame you for that."

"Nor can I regret it," said Catharine thoughtfully. "When I think of that marriage now, it is with the feeling that it was ordained of God to bring about certain events; and that I was but a feeble instrument in his hands to accomplish his plans of mercy and love."

"Why, then, may you not believe that another with me may be ordained by him to work out other plans quite as important to the welfare of a great people?"

"If I thought so, I might not hesitate. But thus far since my husband's death my path of duty has seemed plain to me. My child, and these poor people around me, literally starving, not only for the bread of earth, but that of heaven, have demanded all my time and care."

"The same demands are made upon me. But, Catharine," he continued eagerly, "could I not be a help, and not a hinderance, in your path of duty? Could I not be a father to your beautiful boy, and help you to bring him up 'in the nurture and admonition of the Lord'? Could I not assist you in devising plans for the benefit of the people, not only upon your plantation, and mine ten miles away, but also through the whole Southern country? United, could we not do much, —very much more than either of us could do alone; come nearer to the hearts and homes of our suffering people; more abundantly and efficiently influence their lives?"

"I don't know," she began doubtingly.

"But I know, dear Catharine, if you do not, that it would be so. I know, too, that you must often feel the need of a strong arm and a loving heart on which to lean. You expected to have found it in Harry; but you were disappointed in that hope. Then, why not accept one upon which you would have a claim for life."

"I will own that I have often felt this need since I came here, and especially at first; yet there are a great many considerations that forbid the thought of a second marriage for me."

"Well, I want you to think of it," said he earnestly: "I will not take your decision now. I know you can sympathize in all my views for the future. I know that your heart is full of that enthusiasm of humanity that would lead you to a life of toil and self-sacrifice for the benefit of the human race. You have the true missionary spirit, as you have abundantly proved during the war. And I know that you are more capable of inspiring other souls with the same feelings — even as you once did mine — than any other woman of my acquaintance."

"I think you overrate my powers."

"No: I do not. And if you were to go through the whole South, as I have done during and since the war, you would feel, as I do, the imperative need of using them; for the mental and moral darkness, destitution, and ignorance are everywhere. The late masters, most of them ruined, bereaved, and terribly imbittered against the redeemed race, who are ignorant, helpless, and starving, oppress and tyrannize over them to the extent of their power. They are imbittered, too, against all Northern men and women, and will scarcely listen to their suggestions; but Southern men of just, generous, and philanthropic spirit, and able to support themselves, might just now do them an immense amount of good."

"I have no doubt of that, or that you are just the man for such a place; for you have a strong, sympathetic, and personal influence that would convince where others would fail."

"Well, if I have, I hope you will feel it," said he, smiling. "I think myself that I can do some good by personal effort: at any rate, I shall try. But, if I had a faithful female coadjutor, — one whose heart was in the work, and who could mingle freely with the women of the South, who now fearfully preponderate, — I could do a hundred times more, — work that would benefit the present, and the results of which might endure to future generations. And will not you, dear Catharine, who have the requisite talents, the thoroughly-practical education, the energetic will, and the generous enthusiasm needed in such a position, join me in this noble work, before which all other selfish and thoroughly personal considerations should at the present time sink into insignificance?

"Oh! I do think it a work that is needed, — in fact, to fully restore peace and prosperity to the country, imperatively demanded. But I know you over-estimate my capabilities; and, above all, forget that I am a Northern woman, a hated Yankee."

"You have identified yourself so fully with the South during the war, that you are now regarded as a Southern woman by all. Your praises are on many grateful Southern lips, your memory a green oasis in the desert soil of many Southern hearts. What you have done and suffered for friends and foes during the past five years will never, never be forgotten."

35*

"Well, I believe my own conscience bears me witness that I have done what I could."

"And do not heart and conscience both respond to this 'call from Macedonia, — "Come over and help us "' ? "

"Yes: I cannot deny it, or that it is just what I have been dreaming about and longing to do for months. And, had not my home duties seemed to demand all my care, I might have done something more than dream," said Catharine frankly.

"Those home duties can be easily arranged, now that we have made so fair a beginning. And there are plenty of active business men and women, ruined by the war, who would be glad to take care of our estates, and manage them as we directed. Your child we should prefer to take with us wherever we went. The necessity for this work, now so urgently demanded, will, I hope, soon cease; and then we can return to our home, with the consciousness that we have done what we could, in the vineyard of the Master, and not misimproved whatever talents God has given us. I believe no thoughtful man could see hundreds and thousands of men falling like autumn leaves around him, as I have done during the war, many of them going to their death with oaths and curses or agonizing prayers for mercy upon their lips, without feeling as if it were the noblest work in the universe to fit men to live as they ought while they are here upon the earth, and to induce them to prepare for the life to come. But this work, to which I have previously referred, seems to be what is demanded of us to-day. I feel as if God demanded it of those whom he has fitted for it; of whom you, Catharine, are one. And I want you to think of it prayerfully before coming to a final decision."

When Mrs. Hunter arrived, and heard of Lloyd's proposal, she gave it her unqualified approval, and urged Catharine to accept of it.

They had been wronged by everybody, she said, in their past separation; and this would make it all right again. It was just what she had been planning in her own mind for some time.

A woman had just as much right to make a second marriage as a man, she said; though it was not always quite as advisable. Yet the wives of Washington, Franklin, Jackson, and Bonaparte had done it, with multitudes of other noble women, whom the world delighted to honor. It would surely be no discredit to the noble name she bore to exchange it for another quite as distinguished; and she was sure it would be the best thing that could happen to all concerned.

Once Mrs. Hunter would hardly have given Catharine such counsel as this; but now she loved her as a sister, and had such a high regard for her worth and talents, that she felt as if Lloyd could not find a nobler woman in the universe to share his destiny.

Catharine finally consulted her friends at the North; and, as they were all of Mrs. Hunter's opinion, she concluded to follow the bent of her own inclinations, and become Lloyd Hunter's bride.

So they were quietly married upon the ensuing Christmas, and, after a brief visit to her Northern home, returned to the South, and began their noble work. From their past connection with army life, both had many acquaintances among all classes of the Southern people, many of whom were deeply indebted to them for past favors, and very grateful. So they were enabled to go with safety into the darkest and most benighted regions, where light from the Freedman's Bureau could not penetrate, and where Northern men and women would at that time have been repulsed with indignation and scorn.

Their own wealth, fine talents, and high Southern connections enabled them to go among the highest as well as the lowest; to plead with and persuade the people, in public and in private, in churches, school-houses, or log-cabins, that it was not only for their best earthly interest, but also their solemn duty, to extend the hand of friendship and encouragement to the ignorant, oppressed, and long down-trodden slaves. They also endeavored, so far as it was in their power, to inspire both the late masters and the new-born freemen with a spirit of forbearance and conciliation, of mutual forgiveness and forgetfulness of past injuries, which was the only thing that could conduce to the welfare and happiness of both, and save them and their country from ruin.

Both could plead earnestly, eloquently, and convincingly; and the good they have been enabled to do in the years that have passed since the war is incalculable. They have succeeded in opening the eyes of hundreds of the former masters and mistresses to the injustice, oppression, inhumanity, and unworthiness of their conduct towards their former slaves, and led them to forbearance and amendment. They have inspired in many other hearts that spirit of the Master that will lead them to try to imitate his noble example. They have been the means of establishing schools, and houses of worship, in many dark and desolate places; from which streams of knowledge and light from on high will eventually flow to civilize, enlighten, and redeem all the surrounding country. They have mingled among the people, and taught those who were ignorant and shiftless how to make the best use of their slender means, which they increased upon many fitting occasions.

Thousands of the former masters and mistresses who have lived in affluence, and boasted of their aristocracy, were now poor, spiritless, and dejected, and needed some such reviving influence to lead them to a better and more useful life and a higher destiny. Catharine's eminently practical education fitted her admirably to be a domestic adviser to such as these, as she had been brought up in a home of thrift and economy, where small means had been made to work out the great ends of education, improvement, and respectability.

Wherever they went, they endeavored, so far as was in their power, to abate old and sinful prejudices, to initiate needed reforms, to persuade the discouraged to cast off their indolence, and begin a thorough reformation of heart, life, and character; and, above all, to lead souls out of darkness, ignorance, and discouragement, up to light and hope here, and a better prospect of glory in that beyond the grave. They are now resting at home; and happy in their mutual affection, and rich in the gratitude of multitudes, they are on earth laying up treasure in heaven.